THE
TEMPLARS'
LAST
SECRET

Also by Martin Walker

Death in the Dordogne
(originally published as *Bruno, Chief of Police*)
The Dark Vineyard
Black Diamond
The Crowded Grave
The Devil's Cave
The Resistance Man
Death Undercover
(originally published as *Children of War*)
The Dying Season
Fatal Pursuit

THE
TEMPLARS'
LAST
SECRET

A Bruno,
Chief *of* Police
Novel

MARTIN WALKER

Quercus

First published in Great Britain in 2017 by

Quercus Editions Ltd
Carmelite House
50 Victoria Embankment
London EC4Y 0DZ

An Hachette UK company

A CIP catalogue record for this book is available
from the British Library

HB ISBN 978 1 78429 465 6
TPB ISBN 978 1 78429 466 3

10 9 8 7 6 5 4 3 2 1

Typeset by CC Book Production

Printed and bound in Great Britain by Clays Ltd, St Ives plc

For Adele

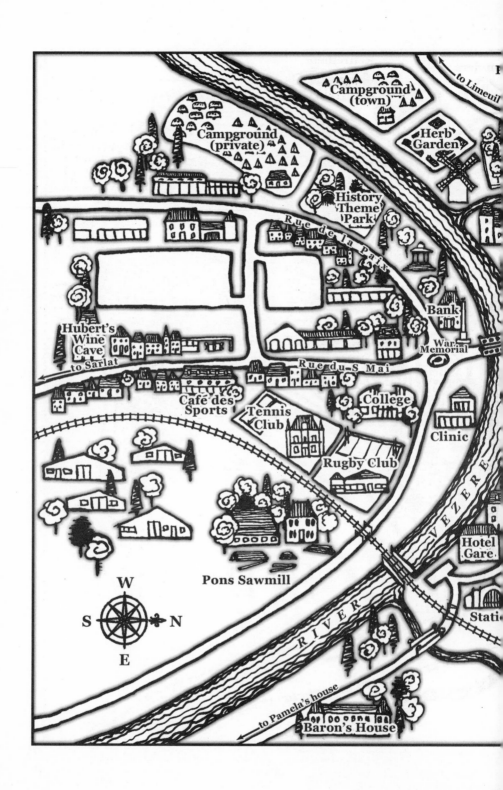

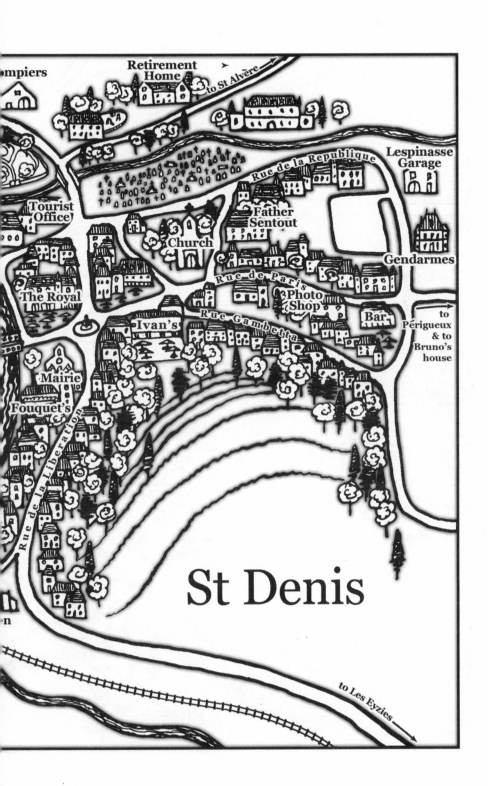

1

Bruno Courrèges, chief of police of the small French town of St Denis, awoke a few seconds before six, just as the dawn was breaking. His cockerel, Blanco, named for a French rugby hero, greeted the new day as Bruno donned his tracksuit and running shoes. The morning jog through the springtime woods around his home in the Périgord countryside was a delight; the sun would soon cast long beams through the pale green of the new buds and leaves on the trees. The temperature was exactly as he liked it, not cold enough for gloves but crisp and fresh enough for him to enjoy warming up as he ran, his basset hound, Balzac, bounding along at his side.

Back at his home, its old stone walls glowing in the early light, Bruno fed his geese and chickens, watered his vegetable garden and took a look at the seedlings in the new greenhouse he had built from a kit. He placed his kettle on the stove for coffee and put one of his fresh eggs into a saucepan to boil while he checked his emails, then turned on the radio, tuned to *France Bleu Périgord*. He grilled the last half of yesterday's baguette, shared it with Balzac, and sliced his toast thin so he could dip it into the still runny yolk. The headline news ended and he shifted to the local news. At the third item, Bruno pricked up his ears.

'Périgueux psychologist Marie-France Duteiller has filed a complaint with the *Procureur* on the slow progress of the investigation into allegations of paedophilia at a Church-run children's home near Mussidan some thirty years ago. She claims that the inquiry led by chief detective Jean-Jacques Jalipeau had been "insensitive and dilatory" and had denied justice to the victims who accused several local notables of abuse when they were orphans at the home. Commissaire Jalipeau said last night that inquiries continued, although the investigation was highly complex and controversial, since the allegations depended on memories that had been recovered during hypnosis by psychologist Duteiller.'

His good mood of the morning evaporated as Bruno sighed in sympathy with his friend Jean-Jacques, known throughout the police as J-J. The case had been running for months and evidently was not getting very far. This was unusual. Bruno might agree that at times J-J could be insensitive, but dilatory was one of the last words he'd use to describe the big, untidy man whom he'd come to admire on the occasions they had worked together. Such cases usually ended with a celebratory dinner, at which J-J played generous host, in recognition of the many times during the inquiry when he had lunched and dined at Bruno's hospitable table. J-J's cheerful personality matched his bulk and he shared Bruno's fondness for good food and wine. Their warm relations had even survived a waspish newspaper cartoon after one recent terrorist case when Bruno had been portrayed as Astérix the Gaul and J-J as his gigantic and overfed friend Obélix. The cartoonist had come closer to reality when he portrayed each of them with a bottle of Bergerac wine, suggesting it was their equivalent of the magic potion Astérix swigged before battling the Roman legions.

Above all, and unlike many in the Police Nationale, J-J did not treat a municipal policeman like Bruno as a lower form of life. He'd come to value Bruno's profound knowledge of the people of the commune of St Denis, developed through years spent as an active member of the local tennis, rugby and hunting clubs. He accepted Bruno's idiosyncratic way of doing his job and recognized his role in ensuring that St Denis had the lowest rate of reported crimes in the *département* of the Dordogne. Bruno in return respected J-J as a relentless detective with a deceptively subtle way of navigating the politics of policing in France. Whatever the radio might be reporting, J-J was old enough and experienced enough to take care of himself. And if he needed Bruno's help, he knew he would only have to ask.

Bruno planned this morning to go first to the riding school of his British friend Pamela to exercise Hector, his horse, before heading for his office in the *mairie*. Perhaps on horseback he'd get some inspiration for the speech he had to give at the end of the week. And perhaps I should think about getting some new clothes, Bruno thought as he scanned his wardrobe with the forthcoming wedding in mind.

Two-thirds of the hanging space was occupied by his official dress. There were police uniforms for summer and for winter, plus a full-dress parade uniform and a greatcoat. At the back of the cupboard was a separate plastic bag holding his French army reserve uniform with its sergeant's chevrons, in which he was required to report if summoned back to duty. Hanging in the utility room where he kept his washing machine and the

3

secure cabinet with his guns was a set of military camouflage that he used for hunting, along with the old army tracksuit he had just taken off to air after his morning jog.

Bruno's civilian clothes were few. There was a dark-blue wool suit. He'd bought it when invalided out of the French army after taking a sniper's bullet in his hip during a tour of duty in Bosnia. He'd long since lost the extra kilos he'd gained during the months in hospital and while convalescing, so it hung loosely on him these days. A dark-blue blazer and a pair of grey slacks shared a wooden coat hanger. Khaki chinos hung with the dark red windcheater that he wore over his uniform shirt and trousers when he wanted to look plausibly civilian. Its equivalent in black was kept in his official van. A pair of jeans was folded on the top shelf with his polo shirts and sweaters, his police képis and a blue UN Peacekeeper's helmet that he kept for sentimental reasons, despite its dent and scrapes.

Anyone could take one glance at my wardrobe, he mused, and tell the story of my life: the army and then the police, all the signs of a man more at home in uniform than in civilian dress. His modest collection of clothes suggested a man who was careful with his money, seeing no need to splash out on new garments when the French services took care of most of his needs. And the dark suit was timeless, of a classic cut, paying no regard to the whims of fashion that dictated that this year trousers should be tight and ties and lapels narrow. It seemed only yesterday that trousers had been loose and ties and lapels bizarrely wide.

Even for a country policeman, he knew this was a sparse wardrobe. I am a man, he thought, of little imagination and less style; or perhaps I simply have other priorities. Bruno disliked shopping for clothes, although he could spend many hours happily perusing hunting magazines for a new shotgun that he could not afford or a new rod for when he went fishing with the Baron.

The good thing about weddings, he thought, was that people usually had eyes only for the bride. Nobody would care what he was wearing and the dark-blue suit would do fine. The ceremony was to take place in the *mairie*, followed by a reception and dinner for close friends at the national museum of prehistory in Les Eyzies. The gallery of flints, with its life-size models of early humans holding spears, knapping flints and wearing skins, might be considered an unusual place to choose. Bruno thought it very suitable, since bride and groom were professional archaeologists of renown. Clothilde was the museum's senior curator and Horst, after retiring from his university post in Germany, had joined the museum as an adjunct professor responsible for archaeological digs. Most of the guests were in the same profession.

Idly, Bruno wondered if they might offer the fashionable palaeolithic diet of nuts and berries, fruit and charred meats, instead of the more traditional wedding feast. No, he concluded. Horst might be amused by such a meal, but Clothilde was a sensible Frenchwoman. She would understand that when guests came to the culinary heartland of France, they expected the classic food of the Périgord.

As Horst's best man, Bruno was a little nervous about the speech he'd have to give. He would obviously be expected to make some reference to his friend's distinguished career in archaeology, before an audience that would include some of Europe's top experts in the field. On Bruno's bedside table lay the latest issue of *Archéologie*, a popular magazine that contained Professor Horst Vogelstern's latest article, comparing the various small statues of women that had been found at prehistoric sites across Europe.

Long before he had become Horst's friend, Bruno had subscribed to the journal, fascinated by the wealth of cave art and prehistory that surrounded him in the valley of the River Vézère. The cover of the magazine was arresting: a photograph of a woman fashioned from clay with gigantic hips, a prominent vulva and pendulous breasts. The caption was 'Miss Europa, 25,000 BC'. This Venus of Dolni Vestonice, the place where she had been found in the modern-day Czech Republic, was the oldest ceramic known. It was just one of several illustrations accompanying Horst's fascinating article.

Bruno had been intrigued to learn that just over a hundred of these statues, known as the Venus figurines, had been found. They had mostly been made between 28,000 and 20,000 BC, in the early Paleolithic or Stone Age, and had been rediscovered in caves and graves scattered across Europe. If there was one outstanding element that could be said to have connected our direct ancestors among early Stone Age peoples, Horst had argued, it was their fascination with generously proportioned women. Usually between five and twenty centimetres in height, the figurines were the first known depictions of any human form and they were highly stylized. The women – for they were all female – had, with only rare exceptions, enormous breasts, buttocks and thighs, a swollen stomach and a prominent pudenda.

Some had complex and carefully carved hairstyles, or perhaps headdresses made of small shells, rather like the one that was on display in the Les Eyzies museum.

Inevitably they had been seen as fertility symbols, since they focused so much on the female breasts and reproductive organs. Whole bookshelves had been written on these figurines and their role in prehistoric culture. There was speculation on whether they signified an early matriarchal society, in which female fertility had been viewed as the greatest mystery and an object of worship.

All this, Bruno told himself, provided excellent material for a light-hearted and slightly teasing speech to be made at the wedding. He could talk of Horst's lifelong fascination with the Venus figurines and the female form. And that gave Bruno the closing theme in a way that would flatter both bride and groom and refer to their common passion for prehistory. He would suggest that Horst had finally found his perfect woman in Clothilde and conclude that this marriage of the Frenchwoman Doctor Clothilde Daumier and Germany's Professor Horst Vogelstern of the University of Cologne symbolized all that was best of the new Europe.

Jotting down these notes, Bruno felt a weight lift from his shoulders. He dreaded having to give speeches and as a result put untold effort into preparing them, with the unforeseen consequence that his friends now kept pestering him to speak. At least this one was now sketched out. But he knew a few hours of careful drafting still awaited him, and he faced a busy day ahead. He was due to give evidence before a tribunal in Sarlat at ten, so Bruno checked his appearance in the bedroom mirror, summoned Balzac from his morning patrol of the garden and was about to set off to the riding school when his phone vibrated. It was Ahmed, one of the professional firemen who led the team of mostly volunteer *pompiers* in St Denis. As well as fighting fires, they also acted as the region's emergency medical service.

'We've got an urgent call to Commarque, that ruined chateau off the road to Sarlat,' Ahmed began. 'A woman, possibly dead, fallen from the cliff or the castle wall. The guy who phoned it in runs the entrance kiosk, said his name was Jean-Philippe Fumel and he'll be expecting you. Fabiola's on call today and she's meeting us at the spot. Shall we see you there?'

Bruno confirmed that he would join them at the chateau and then phoned the riding school to say that duty called; he could not exercise Hector this morning. Pamela replied that she'd just heard the same news from Fabiola and they'd expect him for the evening ride instead.

'*Bisous*,' she said as she hung up. It always slightly confused Bruno when Pamela used this affectionate French term, which meant 'kisses'. Their affair had been over for some months but the mutual attraction that remained reminded him that there was more than friendship between them. He had no time to think of that now. He phoned the *mairie* to leave a message explaining why he'd been called away. Then he thumbed through his phone's address book to find a number for the Count of Commarque, a genial giant of a man who had for the past thirty years mounted an ambitious project of research, restoration and public education at the grandiose ruin his ancestors had built. The Count, whom Bruno knew from the rugby club, deserved to know of the accident and might have some useful background to contribute. It was not long after seven in the morning, so Bruno was not surprised when there was no reply and he left a message.

Before he left, Bruno checked his mailbox at the end of the drive, on which he had painted '*Pas de pub*' to tell the postman not to deliver the endless supermarket and other advertising brochures that would otherwise clog the box. There was a bank statement and a postcard from London showing an unimpressive modern building captioned as the police headquarters at New Scotland Yard. The message was simple: '*Wish you were here instead of me. Give Balzac a big hug and a kiss from me, and a little hug for you.*'

It was signed with the single initial I, which meant Isabelle, the woman who got away. No, Bruno thought, that wasn't right. When she left the Périgord for a high-powered job on the staff of the Minister of the Interior in Paris, she had wanted him to join her. But Bruno could never see himself in some cramped apartment in Paris with no garden, where it would not be fair to keep a dog, let alone his chickens. He knew he'd lose touch with all his friends and the hunting and tennis and rugby clubs and the training sessions for the schoolkids that made up so much of his life. And now she had an even bigger job coordinating French and European anti-terrorist efforts. Balzac had been her gift to him when his previous dog had been killed, and these occasional postcards from foreign capitals always seemed more about Balzac than about him. Or perhaps it was just Isabelle's way of reminding him of what he was missing; not that he needed reminding. He sniffed the card, wondering if it were his imagination or if he really detected just a hint of her perfume. He offered the card to Balzac who sniffed and gave a discreet but plaintive howl. Balzac missed her, too.

2

Installing Balzac in his preferred place on the passenger seat, Bruno set off for Les Eyzies. He gave his usual wave of salute to the statue of prehistoric man on the rocky ledge above the town's main street. The statue symbolized the town's role as the centre of prehistoric studies. After finding the first prehistoric remains during the construction of a railway, skeletons of people with much more modern skulls than those of the first Neanderthals were then unearthed in 1868. Called Cro-Magnon people after a local place name, the skeletons emerged just as the arguments over Charles Darwin's new theory of evolution were raging across Europe. So many visitors began to descend on the region that a new hotel, inevitably called the Cro-Magnon, was built to receive them. A flurry of archaeological investigations nearby soon established that the valley of the River Vézère was an extraordinary repository of human and pre-human remains.

Close to the first Cro-Magnon find was the Abri Pataud, a hundred-metre-long balcony in a great cliff where modern archaeologists had found traces of forty separate camps of nomadic reindeer hunters. These early humans had used local stone to build a rough wall on the rim of the balcony to form a sheltered room, and the evidence of animal bones suggested it had been used for a prolonged period. The skeletons of a young woman and a baby were found there, some twenty thousand years old. These bones were used as a model to construct a life-sized statue of the woman, on display in the attached museum. Bruno had a great affection for this young woman, and it had been enhanced when he learned from Horst's article that another figurine, the Venus of Abri Pataud, had also been found nearby. She represented so much of what Bruno loved about this valley, the sense of history being so close, that across two hundred centuries there had lived a girl he might have loved. So he blew her a kiss as he drove past towards another of his favourite sites, the medieval fortress of Commarque.

Perched on a rocky outcrop in the hills between the Rivers Dordogne and Vézère, the half-ruined chateau was for Bruno one of the most impressive in the region. Unlike the famous medieval fortresses of Beynac and Castelnaud which glowered at each other across the Dordogne as they had during the Hundred Years War between the English and French, Commarque was not on the standard tourist route. Its remoteness added to its grandeur. The outer walls enclosed a large village which contained the remains of six grand houses, each inhabited in the Middle Ages by a different noble dynasty, while the Commarque family held the main keep with its high tower. Bruno had heard the ensemble described as a kind of holiday camp for the feudal elite, a place where they would gather for celebrations and feast days to scheme and plot and arrange marriages, while enjoying the magnificent view over the valley of the River Beune.

Standing atop the tower one day, the Count had told Bruno that its height had enabled his ancestors to see and signal to the town of Sarlat, twenty kilometres up the valley. In the Middle Ages, the trees that later would cover much of the region once more had been cut down to produce charcoal to feed the hungry furnaces of dozens of smithies and ironworks. The hills of the Périgord during that period had been covered with sheep rather than timber.

Bruno navigated the rough track down to the chateau entrance and parked. He let Balzac jump down from the police van, where the dog started sniffing his way around the area, as if recalling his previous visits and checking for any changes. The young man in the kiosk looked startled to see a policeman arrive with a basset hound. He shook hands, introduced himself as Jean-Philippe and asked, 'Sniffer dog?'

'The best,' said Bruno, before following him to the base of a forbidding cliff, where his friend, the doctor Fabiola, was waiting beside the corpse. Her examination seemed to be complete for she was gazing upwards, as though admiring the high walls and tower. At her feet lay the body of a middle-aged woman wearing a blue nylon tracksuit, one leg of which was almost torn away to reveal a leg bent in three places. Through one of the rips in the fabric Bruno could see that a broken bone poked through the skin, although there was little blood. Her heart must have stopped pumping when she hit the ground, Bruno thought.

He felt a wave of sadness, the sudden fall of silence and solemnity that always came upon him in the presence of death. Despite his years in the military and the nature of his work as a policeman, his duty to attend traffic accidents and the natural deaths to which he was called, he never became accustomed to it. If he ever did, Bruno suspected that he would feel compelled to resign.

Standing there beside Fabiola, Bruno recalled that she'd once told him that at medical school she'd attended a compulsory lecture on death and its impact on doctors. Doctors in hospitals would attend hundreds, probably thousands of deaths, but most of them would be strangers. Doctors in general practice would attend far fewer deaths, but the majority of them would be familiar, patients of many years perhaps. Either way, the lecturer had said, the emotional toll would grow and weigh more heavily over time. Bruno closed his eyes briefly and then forced himself to look at the corpse.

The dead woman had dark hair cut short, a plump face that was markedly suntanned although it was early in the year, and a livid scrape along one cheek. She was lying on her back, her head bent so badly to the right that her neck must have been broken. Her right arm was upraised and bent at the elbow, an old cow's horn close to her hand. Her other hand was resting on her stomach, which seemed an oddly peaceful pose for someone who had presumably fallen to her death. The foot attached to the broken leg was bare while the other foot wore a cheap running shoe rather than the specialized footwear used by rock climbers. Bruno looked around, but couldn't see the missing shoe.

'She's certainly dead, so I sent the *pompiers* away. There was nothing for them to do,' said Fabiola, after greeting him and then bending to caress Balzac, whose tail wagged furiously to express his pleasure at seeing her. The dog took one cautious sniff at the dead woman's bare foot and then backed away and sat, looking at Bruno and waiting for instructions.

'She has a broken neck and broken leg, so it looks like a fall,' Fabiola went on, her voice without emotion. 'She has no identification that I could see and you'll have trouble getting good fingerprints. Her fingers are scraped raw from the climb, but there's no obvious sign of foul play. I'd say she's around forty years old and considerably overweight so I'm surprised that she was climbing a cliff like that.'

'Would you have climbed it?' he asked, knowing that in her days as a student Fabiola had been a keen mountaineer.

'Not in the dark, I wouldn't,' she replied, shaking her head firmly. 'Even in daylight I'd want ropes and pitons before I tackled a climb like that. From her footwear, it looks like she didn't know what she was doing.'

Bruno looked up at the sheer wall of rock face above the overhang. It soared some twenty metres before giving way to the stone wall and tower, which rose another twenty metres further. The lower stretch of cliff contained a number of openings that Bruno remembered were troglodyte chambers. One of them had been a kitchen and the others were storerooms and places where the families of chateau servants had lived. After the place was ruined and abandoned during the religious wars of the seventeenth century, people had still lived in the caves, and the Resistance had used them for shelter during the war. The caves were dry, and there was water nearby.

The Count had told him that the entire rock on which the chateau had been built was honeycombed with caves and fissures, some of them containing evidence of human habitation dating back for millennia. A famous stone engraving of a horse's head had been found in one of them, reckoned to be fifteen thousand years old. But what made Bruno step back in surprise was the sight of freshly scrawled letters high on the tower, in luminous paint of a reddish-orange colour.

'I-F-T-I,' he said, spelling out the letters. 'Does that mean anything to you?'

'I've been puzzling over it,' said Fabiola. 'See where the paint fades away just after the final I, as though she was starting a new letter and that was when she fell. It could be an L or a K, a Y or even an R. I've no idea what she was trying to write. I was never much good at crossword puzzles.'

'I can't think of any words in French that begin with I-F but I suppose it could be English,' said Bruno. 'And that looks like the same colour paint on her hand. It's very distinctive.'

'Yes, mixed with blood from her fingers. That cow horn beside her right hand is odd. Quite a coincidence for her to have fallen and landed right beside it so the horn may have fallen from her pocket or it could have been placed there later. If so, someone else must have been involved. I had a quick look around but I saw no sign of the spray paint she seems to have used. If you can't find the can, somebody must have taken it away.'

'How long has she been dead?' Bruno asked.

'Not long, around three to four hours at a guess. Certainly not more than eight, which means she was climbing at night. No sign of a torch. In fact, there's nothing in her pockets.'

'Maybe she was climbing by moonlight. It's close to full moon.' Bruno kept a careful watch on the lunar calendar for his gardening. 'I'll have to find out if it was cloudy. Anything from her dentistry?'

'Not that I could see; just a few standard fillings that could have been done anywhere in Europe, but you might want to ask a dentist. I'm almost done. Just one or two final checks and then I'd better get back to the clinic.'

'Anything about this that strikes you as odd, apart from the cow horn?' Bruno asked. He trusted Fabiola's expertise and her instincts.

'There are a couple of marks on her wrist and neck that aren't clear to me. They could be rope burns if she was climbing with one. But there's no sign of any rope or harness so they could be marks from her fall. I know the police will take a good look at them, but I won't forgive myself if I miss something.'

'Could I use your magnifying glass?' Bruno took it and bent to peer closely at the mark on the woman's neck and the ones on her wrist and forearm. He saw something glinting, two or three shreds of greenish-blue material.

'Could those be strands of nylon, perhaps from a rope?' he asked, passing her the glass.

She squinted. 'Looks like that to me.'

'That means she was almost certainly climbing with a partner who's disappeared along with the rope and the paint. Your death certificate had better say that she died in a fall, in possibly suspicious circumstances.'

Fabiola nodded. 'Other than confirming the nylon threads, I don't see the point of going to the expense of an autopsy.'

'That will be up to J-J,' said Bruno. 'It's his budget.'

As the region's chief detective for the Police Nationale, J-J automatically took over any suspicious death inquiry. Not that they were frequent. The number of homicides each year in the

17

département was usually in single figures and J-J almost always solved them, sometimes with Bruno's help.

'Good luck with identifying her,' said Fabiola, closing her medical bag. 'Maybe you'll be finished in time for us to go riding together this evening. I'll leave the death certificate at the clinic for you to pick up and I'll put it down as death by a fall, probably suspicious. What I ought to write is suicide by stupidity.' She blew him a kiss by way of goodbye.

Bruno waved back as he pulled out his phone to call J-J, and sent Balzac off to search. By the time he had briefed J-J, Balzac's bark signalled that he had found something. Bruno strolled a few metres along the base of the cliff to see his dog standing beside the dead woman's missing shoe. Stroking Balzac in appreciation, Bruno sent him off to search for any traces of the woman's scent. Then he went back to his van for binoculars and began to scan the cliff. About twenty metres above the fallen shoe and slightly to its right, he saw something glinting in the morning sun. It could be a piton, one of the metal supports that climbers hammered into cracks in the rock to support a rope. He'd leave that for J-J's people to examine.

Balzac barked again, this time from about a hundred metres away across the valley. His tail was stretched out flat, one paw raised, his neck lifted, the pose he adopted when pointing at game. Bruno walked across the turf to join him, feeling the ground start to become boggy beneath his feet as he neared the bank of the small River Beune, which here spread out into several sluggish streams. His dog waited with the dutiful patience of a well-trained hunting hound, his whole body pointing to the slope across the valley. It seemed that the dead woman must

18

have come that way, across the watery meadow. Odd, therefore, that there had been no sign of mud on her legs or shoes.

Bruno returned to the body. Although J-J's team would doubtless take their own photos, he began taking pictures with his phone, just so he had a record and could begin the process of identification. He started with a general shot of the location, then used his zoom to capture the letters scrawled on the wall of the chateau and finally moved in for some close-ups of the face before examining the hands more closely. Good forensic work might get some partial prints but mostly the fingertips had been scraped bloody.

Other questions nagged at him, beyond the obvious one: did she fall or was she pushed? Why would anyone have wanted to climb the cliff? If she wanted to get inside the outer wall of the chateau, it would have been easier to climb where it was lower. Easier still, he thought, to come from the opposite direction, along the ridge where the only obstruction was a crumbling wall. Had she been trying to get into the tower itself? Or was she simply daubing some unfinished slogan? Perhaps the Count would know.

3

The Count appeared not long after Fabiola had left, and found Bruno poking through the grass at the base of the cliff where Balzac had found the missing shoe. Balzac darted across to greet the newcomer, who bent to fondle the basset's long ears. He rose as Bruno said hello and began to explain what little he knew as he led the Count to the body.

'I've never seen her before and I have no idea who she is, God rest her soul.' The Count's usually cheerful face was solemn as he stared down at the body, shaking his head. Then he raised his hand to his brow and crossed himself. Only then did he look up at the cliff looming above and step back in surprise as he spotted the large letters painted on the castle wall.

'What on earth . . . ?' He looked back and forth from the corpse to the vivid scrawl on the castle wall that seemed to glow an angry red as the sun's rays caught it. 'Is this supposed to be some kind of graffiti art? Was she painting these letters? It doesn't mean anything, not in any language I know.'

'I was hoping you might help identify her or whatever slogan she was daubing. She's not carrying any papers and you can see from the state of her hands we'll have trouble getting fingerprints.'

'I was assuming she'd be one of the Templar enthusiasts. We've had trouble with them before, trying to break in and dig around the place. I invited some of them in to watch at the last archaeological dig here, so they could be satisfied there's none of that legendary Templar treasure here. I thought we'd seen the end of them after that. I think I've got an email address somewhere for the secretary of their association. Perhaps he might be able to identify this poor woman.'

'At first this looked like an accidental fall, but some aspects are troubling,' Bruno said, explaining why he'd called in J-J and the detectives. 'It's not even clear how she got here.'

'Maybe she parked up the hill,' the Count said. 'I came here a different way.'

'There was nothing in the car park when I came and no car key in her pocket.'

'You'd better check the car park at Cap Blanc as well. It's just across the valley, an easy stroll, although a lot longer by road.' He pointed and Bruno turned to look. It was the same direction that Balzac had taken.

'I had no idea it was so close,' he said. Bruno knew Cap Blanc, a cave in which prehistoric people had carved bas-relief sculptures of horses so lifelike they seemed to be walking out of the wall.

'It's not the only one,' the Count replied, pointing. 'Just over there is the *gisement*, the rock shelter where they found the Venus of Laussel, and you know about the carving of the horse's head in the cave beneath the cliff. There have been more important prehistoric finds in this little spot that almost anywhere else on earth, quite apart from the chateau. Listen, Bruno, I'd rather not have this body here long. We have a group of schoolkids

21

coming from Bergerac later this morning. What are you planning on doing with her?'

'Detectives from the Police Nationale in Périgueux are on their way, so it will be up to them. I imagine we'll have to put her in the morgue in Bergerac until we can identify her, and then it will be up to the next of kin. We'll check the missing persons list, distribute a photo through the media, all the usual procedures.'

The Count nodded, looking down again at the dead woman. Suddenly he seemed to notice something. 'That horn beside her hand,' he said sharply. 'Who put it there?'

'It was here when I arrived. I was going to ask your young man in the kiosk if he'd seen it, too. Why?'

The Count was already striding back to the small hut, where Jean-Philippe was laying brochures, guidebooks and souvenirs on the counter. There was a smell of coffee in the air and Bruno saw a machine steaming away at the back of the hut.

'No, of course I didn't put it there. Where would I have found it? The horn was lying by her hand when I first saw her,' Jean-Philippe was saying as the Count looked fiercely at him.

'Whoever did it, it's not funny,' said the Count. He pulled a guidebook from the stack, opened it to a page and handed it to Bruno. 'Here, look at this. The Venus of Laussel, found just across the way.'

It was a photo that Bruno remembered seeing in the magazine that carried Horst's article, of a plump stone woman standing with an arm raised, holding the horn close to her ear. It might almost have been a telephone. The woman had no face; the stone above her chest had been eroded. But there was a suggestion of long hair on the opposite side of her head from the horn.

'It's the same pose,' the Count said. 'That couldn't have happened by chance. Somebody who knows about the Venus of Laussel put that horn by her hand deliberately.'

And she wasn't climbing alone, Bruno thought. He looked again at the photo. This Venus was not a statue, but an engraving carved into the rock. There was no sense of scale and Bruno asked what size it was.

'About half a metre tall. It was found here with several other engravings, all from the same period, about twenty-five thousand years old,' the Count said. There had been another Venus, less well preserved, also holding what could have been a horn. It was called the Venus of Berlin because it had been sold to a German museum back in 1912, where it was destroyed during the last war. But there was also an engraving of a much slimmer young woman, seen from the side, and another of two women joined at the hip, one sitting upright, the other upside down.

'It's a real treasure trove,' the Count went on. 'Alongside the two women was another engraving, the *Femme à la Tête Quadrillée*, or the Venus with the Net, since her head is covered in something that looks like one. If they'd left it all in place, it would be one of the most important sites in France, but the collection was broken up and the main engravings are now in the Bordeaux museum.'

'Are they sure it was a horn?' Bruno asked, squinting at the guidebook photo. 'It could be a big seashell.'

'It could also be a crescent moon,' the Count replied. 'There are thirteen vertical stripes on it, which could refer to the lunar calendar, and if these Venus figures are fertility symbols, those stripes could be linked to the female menstrual cycle. We don't know. Some scholars suggest it might be one of the first known musical instruments, perhaps a hunting horn.'

'So do you still think the Templar enthusiasts are involved in this?'

The Count shrugged. 'Your guess is as good as mine but the Templar people have been here several times, bringing metal detectors and spades to dig around. They're a menace, but any serious archaeologist is always welcome, they just have to go through the usual application procedures with the Ministry of Culture and the museum at Les Eyzies. We've got two or three who have been approved and are coming this summer, working under Horst's supervision. We've also got a seismic and radio-sounding team starting work looking for caves we haven't found yet. Clothilde at the museum arranged that.'

'Tell me about these Templar enthusiasts and what they thought they were looking for,' Bruno said, nodding his thanks as Jean-Philippe handed him a paper cup of coffee. 'I know they were Crusaders, some kind of religious order in the Holy Land, but that's about all I do know.'

The Count grinned, looking almost boyish. 'Have you ever crossed the Pont Neuf in Paris?'

Bruno nodded. 'Both ways. Left bank to right bank and back again.'

'Then when you reached the island in the middle of the Seine, you went past the entrance to Place Dauphine. Right at that spot was where Jacques de Molay, the last Master of the Templars, was burned at the stake in 1314. It's also where he pronounced his famous curse on Philip IV and the Pope and on the royal line of the Capetians. Before the year was out, King and Pope were both dead and the throne of France had passed to the House of Valois. The Templar curse had come true.'

The King's excuse for their suppression, the Count went on to explain, was the allegation that the Templars had become corrupted, indulging in witchcraft, sodomy and every other sin he and the Pope could think of. The King's real motives were less high-minded: he feared that they were becoming a state within the state and he wanted their lands and their money. Not long before, he'd embarked on a pogrom against the Jews in France, confiscating their wealth. Having spent that, the Templars offered the next available fortune.

'There's even a story,' the Count added, 'that when Louis XVI was guillotined in the Revolution, nearly five centuries later, somebody dipped a handkerchief in the royal blood and called out, "Jacques de Molay, you are avenged." Of course, that was in the Place de la Concorde.'

'So the Templars weren't wiped out?'

The Count shrugged. 'A lot of the Freemason groups of the eighteenth century claimed descent from the Templars. Freemasons were for reform, a constitution, reducing the power of the Church, all those Enlightenment causes. That's why several of the leaders of the American Revolution were Freemasons. Did you ever see an American dollar bill? It carries the eye in the pyramid, one of the symbols of the Illuminati, a Freemason sect. Curious, no?'

Bruno had over the years heard various conspiracy theories about the Freemasons, but this was a new one. He asked, 'But why are people still so interested in the Templars?'

'It's the legend of lost treasure. The Templars were supposed to be very rich, which is why the King of France suppressed them and took all their property after the Crusaders had been driven out of the Holy Land. I'm no expert but there's a very clever medieval scholar called Dumesnil who lives in Sarlat and has written a couple of books about them. I think he teaches at the lycée in Brive.'

'And what have the Templars to do with your chateau?'

'It's a Templar site. When my ancestor, Gérard de Commarque, went off to the Crusades in the early twelfth century, he entrusted the place to the Templars.'

'When did your family get it back?'

'Good question. Ownership became somewhat confused. But there's no doubt it belonged to us, although the Counts of Beynac kept trying to take it over. Charlemagne gave the land around here to my earliest known ancestor, Bovon de Commarque, for brave deeds in fighting off the Viking raids. You know they sacked Bordeaux and Bergerac and even the Abbey of Paunat, just downstream from St Denis?'

Bruno nodded. 'Looking for loot, just like King Philip and the Templars.'

The Count laughed. 'You don't call it looting when the King does it.' He looked down at the body. 'Sometimes I wonder if we don't have too much history here in France.'

'Your family made a lot of it,' said Bruno, trying to keep his voice neutral. As an orphan who had never known his parents, he'd always assumed that his own family had played humble roles in France's past. At best they had been poor peasants, dying young of disease or famine; at worst, they had been victims, foot soldiers or cannon-fodder for the dreams and ambitions of the nobles. Bruno was a good Republican, reckoning that despite the horrors of the Terror, the Revolution of 1789 had on the whole been good for France. The Count had probably lost some of his forebears to the guillotine and may have felt differently.

The Count looked at him sharply. 'Your ancestors also helped make our history, one way or another. And mine at least had the good sense to look for wives elsewhere than their fellow aristocrats. That's probably why our line didn't die out. And I didn't inherit this place, you know. I had to buy it back.'

'And you're doing well by it,' Bruno said, and meant it. He admired the research and restoration work the Count had maintained for three decades. 'Where could I find this secretary of the Templar enthusiasts?'

The Count pulled out a mobile phone and read out the name and number. 'He's a pleasant enough chap, if somewhat dull, a retired civil servant who worked for the Finance Ministry. I imagine the Templars added some interest to his life. And here is that Templar scholar I mentioned, Auguste Dumesnil. I don't have a phone number, but for his email put a dot between his names and just add *orange.fr*.'

Bruno thanked him, scribbling down the details in his notebook. 'Can you think of any reason other than treasure-hunting for this woman's presence here?'

'If she was climbing the cliff to the donjon wall, I doubt she was looking for treasure,' the Count replied. 'There are easier ways to get into the various courtyards, where the treasure-hunters usually go with their metal detectors. And those who don't look in the courtyard concentrate on the caves beneath.'

'So what might she have been looking for in the donjon?'

'I have no idea,' the Count replied, shaking his head. 'Since we stabilized the ruins and began the restoration, the donjon has been very thoroughly examined as part of the rebuilding. There's nothing in the place, apart from the exhibition of photographs of various archaeological finds, and anybody can pay the admission and see those. Over the centuries since the wars of religion, it was thoroughly looted. Even some of the stones were taken for building. Maybe the graffiti was her only purpose and, if so, perhaps she wasn't climbing up but climbing down from the tower. Let's go up and take a look.'

He unlocked the entrance gate to the chateau and they climbed up the winding path to the donjon, the fortified keep where the defenders could hold out even if the courtyard had fallen to the attackers. The Count's guided tour revealed nothing of interest, no furniture except for some display cases in an upper room showing the process of restoration. As they came down, Bruno saw J-J's car crawling carefully down the rutted track, followed by the crime scene truck.

Looking at his watch and saying he was expected in court, Bruno introduced J-J to the Count, led the way to the body and pointed out the graffiti.

'When I get back from court, I'll distribute the photos I've taken to the local media,' Bruno said. 'Anything else I can do, just let me know.'

'We'll stay in touch,' said J-J, looking up at the graffiti and scratching his head. 'Any idea what the hell that daub could mean?'

'It could be English or some other language,' said Bruno,

shrugging. 'I'm pretty sure it isn't French.'

'I'll call you this afternoon, after what I imagine will be a difficult meeting with the Prefect about this paedophile business,' J-J said.

'Why is he involved?' Bruno asked. 'It's a police matter.'

Prefects were appointed by the President of France to be the representative of the French state in each of the country's 101 *départements*. Mainly concerned with ensuring the local governments operated in accord with national policy, Prefects also took charge during national disasters and had a special role in coordinating the various arms of the police. Operational matters, however, were usually left to the police officials.

'He says it's a question of public confidence in the police.'

'Are you getting anywhere with it?'

'Not really. It's a devil of a case, all happening thirty years ago. The three complainants have histories of mental illness and their accusations come from what the psychologist treating them calls "recovered memories". In other words, they never mentioned being abused until this woman began working with them. We've tracked down and interviewed every one of the other kids at the home at the time and not one admits to being mistreated.' He looked up at Bruno. 'You were in one of those Church orphanages, weren't you?'

'Yes, but I was at the one in Bergerac. And I was only there for a few years before my aunt was able to take me in to live with her family. I was caned on the backside and had my knuckles rapped with a ruler a few times. But I was never abused sexually and didn't hear of anything like that while I was at the home. The worse thing that ever happened to me was when the priest said animals didn't have souls and so would never go to heaven. That broke my little heart. I'd have been about five at the time and I've never felt the same about religion since.'

J-J nodded. 'It's a hellish business and I'm in the middle, with all my detectives almost ready to go on strike if they have to do any more work on a case they think is a bunch of fantasies. But the magistrate in charge seems ready to believe anything this psychologist says and insists we keep up the inquiry. And the Prefect's wife is just the same.'

'What does Prunier say?' Bruno asked, referring to J-J's boss, the police commissioner for the region.

'He's tried to get the file closed but the Prefect won't hear of it, even though most of the other inmates at Mussidan don't believe it ever happened. It's just these three and one of the ex-nuns, who says there was a discreet policy not to leave a couple of the priests alone with any of the children. She's not the most reliable witness since she became an alcoholic after she left the Church.' J-J rolled his eyes. 'She's another one being treated by this same psychologist.'

'It all sounds a bit thin.'

'Not to the investigating magistrate it doesn't. She's out to make a name for herself and thinks everything this psychologist says is gospel truth. Anyway, that's my problem. I'll call you after I see the Prefect.'

4

Bruno reached the courthouse in Sarlat with a few minutes to spare, but had to push his way through two small groups of demonstrators confronting one another on the steps. One was waving banners proclaiming their membership of the CGT trade union, long linked to the communists, while others of the group held placards declaring 'No Slave Labour' and were chanting, 'Keep Sundays Free'. The other lot, dressed in bakery white with flour smeared on their faces, chanted, 'We Want to Work'. The scene did not look angry to Bruno, and one of the trade union demonstrators, a man with whom he'd played rugby, greeted him and shook his hand. But Bruno reminded himself that you never knew where trouble might start.

Two of the town policemen kept a path clear for people to enter the courthouse but made no other attempt to interfere. Hugues and his lawyer greeted him with smiles of relief, although Bruno was only there to be a character witness for one of the hardest-working men he knew. Hugues had been born and raised in St Denis but ran his thriving bakery business in a new development for light industry outside Sarlat. Bruno had known him as a teenager, learning the bakery trade as an apprentice at Fauquet's. When his grandmother died, leaving her house to the family, Hugues had persuaded his father to sell it and invest the money in Hugues' plan for a bakery of his own. It had been the peak of the property market, just before the crash, and he took over the lease of a small, sleepy bakery on the outskirts of Sarlat.

From the beginning, Hugues had big ambitions. He had enough money to install modern equipment and then pursued his belief that the baking industry was poised for a revolution. The tradition of small artisan bakers serving a static neighbourhood clientele was already under threat from the supermarkets selling bread and cakes more cheaply. But Hugues reckoned there was another market to attack. He visited every hotel, restaurant and campsite in the area, and offered to deliver them fresh breads and croissants every morning in time for breakfast. The goods would be free for the first week, and if they liked the products, they could sign a contract.

Supplying the hotels and campsites meant that he had to deliver his goods seven days a week, and that was where Hugues ran into trouble. Under French employment law, a bakery was supposed to close at least one day a week, to ensure that the employees had a day off. Hugues was proud of his employees, and by now had opened a second bakery in Périgueux and was employing sixteen people, all of them earning above minimum wage with a profit-sharing bonus on top. The thirty-five-hour working week was in force so he organized them on a shift system, which meant that every employee worked only five days each week although the baking ovens were working flat out each day. In Hugues' view, he was in full compliance with the labour laws.

But that was not the view of the Clic-P movement, an alliance of labour unions in the retail and service industries that had launched a nationwide campaign against Sunday working and late hours. Bruno understood the principle of their campaign but could not understand why they had picked on Hugues and suspected that the local union leaders simply saw him as an easy target.

'I can't believe I'm facing a criminal record for delivering bread on Sundays,' Hugues said. 'Nor can the staff.' He pointed to the group of employees outside who had rallied to support him, some still in the white aprons and hairnets they wore in the bakery.

'Will you really have to close down?' Bruno asked.

'No, not now we have the second bakery. With each one working six days a week I can juggle things so we make bread every day,' he replied. 'But delivering to the Sarlat area from Périgueux and then from Périgueux to Sarlat just for one day each week means I'll have to hire more delivery people. That drives up costs and I've already got to pay off a new bank loan for the second bakery. Not to mention the legal fees. What really annoys me is that the whole thing has become political. The unions are trying to get the left-wing mayors and councils to boycott my products, and the conservatives want to turn me into some kind of martyr. That's the last thing I want.'

The case was called. A police tribunal was a relatively informal court meant to try minor offences before a single judge supported by a legal clerk. Bruno's role was brief. He was called as a character witness who had known Hugues for ten years, and praised him as a generous and kindly man always prepared to support local causes. At the end of each day, the last delivery of his drivers was to hand over that day's unsold bread to the Restos du Coeur, which fed the needy, and to other local charities. Hugues' lawyer then called three of Hugues' employees, each of them a union member and one of them a socialist councillor, who praised their employer and his working practices. The problem, the lawyer suggested, was the careless phrasing of the law.

'It's clear that we are dealing with an exemplary employer who does not seek to flout the law,' the judge finally declared. 'I sympathize with him and wonder whether some members of the union, especially those currently out of work, might want to ask their leaders whether their campaign against this particular bakery makes any sense. However, given the law as it stands, I sincerely regret that I have little choice in the matter but to impose the minimum fine of five hundred euros and order each bakery to close one day each week.'

A bunch of media people were waiting outside the court talking to the two sets of demonstrators when Vaugier, the union representative, pushed brusquely past Bruno and Hugues to ensure he was the first to get to the microphones and proclaim the union's victory.

'This is just the beginning, and I warn other bosses who try to exploit our workers by making them work every day of the week that we'll be coming after them as well,' Vaugier announced proudly. A thin-faced man with close-cut grey hair, he was wearing a dark-blue shirt and red tie and sported a Parti de Gauche badge in his lapel.

The local police had disappeared and already a brief scuffle had broken out as two of Hugues' bakers advanced angrily on Vaugier to denounce him as a liar. Bruno took Hugues' arm in a tight grip to hold him back from the fray.

'Stay out of this and let your lawyer do the talking,' Bruno told him. 'Anything you say will make this worse.'

Bruno tried to push Hugues out to the side but found the way blocked by a big man who was carrying a sign that said 'Make the Rich Pay' and chanting some slogan Bruno could not make out. He put out a beefy hand to grab Hugues' arm but Bruno pushed it aside and tried to move on. The man began to bring his sign down on Bruno's head as someone else tried to grab his arms from the rear.

Bruno had learned about street brawls in the army and knew he needed some space, free arms and one decisive blow. He slammed one elbow back hard into the belly of the man behind him, raised his other arm to block the descending sign and then moved forward, lifted his leg and slammed the side of his boot down hard, scraping it along the shin of the man before him. It did no permanent damage but the pain was intense and the man's face collapsed as he screeched in pain and sank down to clutch his leg.

Bruno turned and pushed Hugues to get him clear, seeing two of the bakery employees suddenly surrounding them in support. Bruno looked back and heard the union leader, Vaugier, shouting about police brutality.

'Stop this now or you're next,' Bruno shouted to him, feeling his blood rising. Then the trade unionist who'd greeted him stepped between Bruno and Vaugier, his arms outstretched and calling for calm, and the moment was over. Bruno thanked him and followed Hugues as the bakery workers dispersed. Then Philippe Delaron of *Sud Ouest*, the regional daily, came up to tell Bruno he had a good photo of the sign being aimed at Bruno's head, just in case he might need it.

'I've got a better photo than that for your paper,' Bruno said, and told him of the dead woman and the graffiti that now desecrated the chateau of Commarque. In return, Bruno added, he'd expect a prominent placement for the dead woman's photo to help identify her.

'Thanks, Bruno. I'd heard about the dead woman from the *pompiers*, but the graffiti makes it a better story. Fluorescent red paint, you say? And what is it, some kind of political slogan?'

'More than that, it's a mystery. Go to Commarque and take a look and see for yourself. Maybe your readers can work out what it means. And there's another mystery. The unknown woman wasn't alone. Somebody took away the spray can of paint and the climbing rope she was using. Your headline writes itself – mystery woman's secret slogan defaces national monument. Did she fall or was she pushed?'

Back in his office, Bruno emailed a description of the dead woman to other newspapers and radio stations, along with an appeal for anyone who might have known or met her to call him. He looked at the photo of her face that he taken on his phone. She looked peaceful and French law recognized no privacy in death. The priority now was to identify her so he emailed the photo he had taken of her face to the message network of *mairies*, tourist information offices and hotels in the communes up and down the valley. The kids in the computer club at the local *collège* had developed the system at Bruno's request. He then posted the woman's few details onto the missing persons register, in the hope that some family member wondering where she might be would contact the police. Finally he called the number the Count had given him for the secretary to the Templars' club, left a message asking for a call back and emailed him the photo, asking if he would share it with other club members. He was about to turn to the day's mail when the Mayor rang on the internal line and asked Bruno to step into his office.

Assuming the Mayor wanted to hear about the unknown woman, Bruno left Balzac in his office, closing the door to stop the dog wandering into the kitchen in the hope that someone would give him a biscuit. He took his notes and a printout of her face, but instead the Mayor introduced him to a young black woman whose perfume already filled the room with a powerful blend of musk and gardenias. She rose from the visitor's chair to shake Bruno's hand.

'Amélie Plessis,' she said. '*Enchantée.*'

She had a strong grip, wide shoulders, her hair had been cut very short and her black patent leather shoes boasted perilously high heels. She had lively eyes with maybe a hint of mischief in them. Bright red lipstick and even brighter blue eyeshadow combined with very white teeth to make Bruno think of the French Tricolore. Amused by the thought and impressed by the self-confidence of the young woman, he smiled at her as they exchanged business cards.

'From the Ministry of Justice,' she added, superfluously, since her card already explained her provenance. And so did her bureaucrat's uniform: black suit, knee-length skirt and white blouse. 'I'm looking forward to our working together and learning about your philosophy of policing.'

What on earth did that mean? He tried not to show his surprise. And why was the Justice Ministry sending someone like this down to St Denis, rather than the usual pasty-faced clerk from Paris? And to work with him? What were her origins? Her accent was not entirely French; the vowels were a little too generous, the rhythm of speech bubbling rather than tinkling in the approved Parisian style. It was not quite Caribbean, not quite the accent of Quebec, not quite from Marseilles, but had hints of all three. Her smile was perfunctory rather than genuine, not reaching her eyes. Bruno detected a touch of suspicion, or perhaps apprehension, in her gaze, as if she'd learned to be wary of policemen.

'Mademoiselle Plessis was telling me that the new Minister is a great supporter of the municipal police as being much closer to the public than the gendarmes and with a more friendly image,' the Mayor said, one eyelid drooping in what might have been the ghost of a wink at Bruno. 'But the Minister needs some evidence that would allow her to act upon her belief and we think you might provide it. Mademoiselle Plessis would like to accompany you for the next two weeks for a time and motion study, recording your work minute by minute throughout the day.'

Bruno was speechless. A Paris bureaucrat at his side every moment of the day, recording everything he said or did? He felt his jaw dropping as he gazed helplessly at the Mayor, wondering what on earth could have induced him to commit this act of betrayal to his faithful chief of police.

'I knew you'd like the idea,' said the Mayor. 'And there'll probably be a security aspect to her work, given the opening of the new Lascaux museum later this year. Mademoiselle Plessis tells me that the President of the Republic is planning to attend. You've always been a great supporter of the village police and their local knowledge against the gendarmes who seldom stay long enough in one place to be useful. Now's your chance to prove it.'

'Understood, *Monsieur le Maire*,' said Bruno, thinking fast what excuse might extract him from this chore. 'But now that we have such excellent relations with the new head of the gendarmerie here, those concerns have largely disappeared. As you told the local newspaper only last week, relations between us and Commandante Yveline are now exemplary.'

'Yes, yes, but our guest has no time to lose. Perhaps you could escort her to the hotel where she'll be staying, and then come back here while she unpacks before taking her with you for the rest of the day.'

5

Bruno did as he was told, picking up the suitcase and leading the way across the square to the hotel, his mind reeling as he tried to pay attention to the young woman who insisted that he call her Amélie. She announced briskly that she'd recently graduated from magistrates' school and had been recruited by the Ministry. Her family, she went on, came originally from Haiti but she had been born on French soil, the island of Guadeloupe, after her parents had fled the corrupt rule of the Duvaliers. She had grown up in Marseilles and won a scholarship to university in Montreal, sang in nightclubs to earn extra money, returned to France, joined the socialist party and decided on a career in politics via the law. She relayed all this in a walk of less than a hundred metres, leaving Bruno breathless by her sheer energy.

'How did you get the job in the Ministry?' he asked when they reached the hotel and Amélie paused for breath. He was more interested in her singing but thought he'd better show polite interest in her career.

'I got to know the Minister through politics. We're in the same branch of the party. I suppose you're on the right, given your mayor's politics. But I'll try hard not to let that shape my conclusions.'

'I don't think party politics has anything to do with policing,' Bruno said, wishing he'd asked about the nightclubs.

'Really?' she said, raising an eyebrow. 'In my view everything is to do with politics.'

He waited while she checked in, then walked back to the Mayor's office, trying to think of some way to squeeze out of this absurd imposition. As if any policeman could ever act normally when his every moment was under the scrutiny of someone from the Ministry!

He'd no longer be able to throw away after a quick glance the reams of paperwork that came from the Ministry, but would have to pretend to read the stuff, which would leave little time for any sensible work. Nobody would tell him anything with this young woman constantly at his side, scribbling notes on a clipboard. Fauquet at the café would shrink from passing on any choice item of gossip if he suspected for a moment that it was being recorded. Bruno's habit of stopping at various houses in the tiny hamlets that surrounded St Denis for a small glass of something would be entirely misunderstood by the bureaucrats at the Ministry.

Worst of all, it was just approaching that moment in late spring when the fish were rising and Bruno's garden needed maximum attention. People living in Paris would never understand that no country policeman would command respect if his vegetable garden were less than exemplary, or if he failed to demonstrate his skills at hunting and fishing and other rural pastimes. He'd have to think of a good excuse to give the Mayor, and he rehearsed a couple as he climbed the stairs to the Mayor's office.

'Much as I'd like to cooperate with the Ministry, I honestly don't think I'm the right police officer—'

'Forget it, Bruno. It's settled and you can't back out. And if you can't charm that nice young woman who's still wet behind the ears, you're not the Bruno I know. Now go and take your medicine like a man.'

Dismissed and admonished, Bruno turned to go, thinking at least that time spent with Amélie promised to be interesting, if exhausting. As he opened the door, the Mayor said, in a kinder tone, 'Look on the bright side, Bruno. When she logs all those drives you have to do, perhaps those idiots in the capital will finally realize that this commune alone is larger than Paris. And she's a protegée of the new Minister. So she has *piston*, political influence.

'She's already on the executive committee of the socialist party youth wing and I know she's having dinner with my esteemed colleague, the pharmacist, this evening. So bear that in mind. A bright young black woman with a law degree and political ambitions is just what his party is hoping to publicize and promote. This young woman is going places.'

The pharmacist was the socialist party chairman in the valley, who would doubtless be aware of just how much *piston* Amélie commanded. And since both Amélie and the Mayor had now confirmed that the President of the Republic, a socialist, would attend the opening of the new Lascaux museum, half the local socialist party would be angling for invitations.

Bruno himself was interested to see the new project, which went by the name of Lascaux IV. Lascaux I was the original cave, discovered in 1940 and closed to the public in 1963

42

when their respiration and the bacteria they brought into the cave had combined to produce a white fungus that was damaging the seventeen-thousand-year-old paintings. Lascaux II, an exact and impressive copy of the two most impressive chambers of the cave, had been opened to tourists after it was completed in 1983. Lascaux III, a travelling exhibition of partial copies, films, fossils and audio-visual explanations, had been on display at successive museums around the world for the past five years.

The new Lascaux IV, at a cost of some sixty million euros, was designed to be a showroom for French high-technology to display a Lascaux for the twenty-first century, with a new copy of the entire cave as precise as modern computers could achieve. It was planned to include 3D presentations, interactive demonstrations of how the images had originally been painted, comparisons with cave art from other cultures, prehistoric and more recent. Above all it was to allow more tourists to experience the cave than the thirty at most that Lascaux II could accommodate.

Promoted and pushed by a veteran socialist politician of the region, with financial backing from socialist governments, the project had become a political football with opponents grumbling that the money could have been better spent elsewhere. Bruno disagreed. He had been so awed by his first sight of Lascaux, so struck by the realization that he would never again think of the people who had produced this masterpiece as primitive, that he wanted the whole of the human race to see the cave and be similarly moved. He had already attended meetings to plan the security measures for the grand opening.

Bruno collected Balzac and was about to cross the square to meet Mademoiselle Plessis when he was hailed by Father Sentout, the priest of St Denis who followed the fortunes of the town's rugby team with the same devotion he gave to his dwindling band of worshippers.

'My dear Bruno, is there any progress on the dreadful paedophile business they were discussing on the radio this morning?'

'None at all, I gather. It's a difficult case, involving memories recovered many years after the events. Why are you interested?'

'The priest who has been accused of this, Father Francis. I knew him before his death when he was a colleague, another teacher at my seminary. This was after he'd been at Mussidan and I find it impossible to believe he could have done such wicked things.'

'He wouldn't have been the first priest to have gone astray like that.'

'No, indeed, and that is a tragedy for the Church. But I knew Francis to have been a truly good man. Since he can't stand up for himself surely his friends and those who knew him should try to defend his memory. Is there some way I and some other priests could give some kind of character reference to the police or the investigating magistrate?'

Bruno gave the priest J-J's name and address at the police headquarters in Périgueux and suggested he write a letter but then excused himself, since he saw Amélie emerge from the hotel. The priest laid a hand on Bruno's arm.

'Francis may be dead, Bruno, but for this unjust accusation to continue to sully his name would be an offence against God and man. You believe in justice on earth just as I believe in the ultimate justice of heaven. I know that you must understand that.'

Father Sentout released his grip, but Bruno could feel the priest's curious gaze follow him as Bruno crossed the square to greet the young woman on the hotel steps. She had changed from her suit into tight jeans over the same black shoes and now wore a black leather jacket over her white blouse.

He introduced her to Balzac, who was already charmed by the woman and she seemed equally enchanted with the basset hound. She bent down despite the tight jeans and caressed the dog's ears. Balzac responded by leaping up to give her face a friendly lick. She laughed and gave him a kiss in return, on his head. Even though he usually warmed to anyone who liked his dog, Bruno grimaced. Balzac was now her slave for life, although heaven knows what her powerful perfume would do to his sense of smell.

'Do you have any other shoes, suitable for walking in the countryside?' he asked. 'Not a lot of my time is spent on paved streets.'

She darted back up to her room to change and descended in a pair of suede boots, with heels that were chunky and lower than the stilettos. He sighed, thinking it would be quite a challenge to persuade her into the spare rubber boots he kept in his van.

He escorted her back across the square to Fauquet's for a coffee and an attempt to lay down some ground rules. He'd decided he would try to get her to stay in the car more often than not, noting down simply that he was making inquiries, seeing confidential sources, following up reports of suspicious activity. He introduced her to Fauquet and the regulars as a colleague from Paris. Not quite sure what to make of this, and

45

clearly startled by Bruno's guest, they greeted her with reserved formality and quickly left the bar. Bruno was surprised they hadn't stayed long enough to ask about the dead woman. By now they must have heard the news from the *pompiers*. Fauquet turned his back in silence to make the coffees.

'This the best place in the region for croissants,' Bruno told Amélie. 'You'll soon be a regular customer, just like all the rest of us.' He spoke too loudly for Fauquet to ignore him.

Suitably mollified, Fauquet put a complimentary chocolate biscuit onto each saucer and gave her a croissant from the basket on the counter. 'On the house,' he said. 'Just so you know Bruno is right about my baking. You going to be here long?'

The interviewing technique of the veteran café owner would put most policemen to shame. Before the croissant was finished, Fauquet had learned Amélie's name, her origins, her education, her current job and that her father was a teacher in Lyon. She had two older brothers, one an engineer working at Air France and the other in the Ministry of Pensions, which established her in Fauquet's eyes as a respectable young woman from the professional classes, and thus a suitable, if somewhat unusual, adornment to his establishment. There was only one black family in St Denis: that of Léopold from Senegal, whose market stall did a good trade in African cloths and belts, carvings and bead necklaces. Bruno was particularly fond of Léopold's two sons, stalwarts of the *collège* rugby team and a formidable doubles partnership at tennis.

Bruno steered Amélie out to the terrace where they could enjoy the spring sunshine and Bruno could set his ground rules away from Fauquet's ears.

'I started at seven this morning, with a call-out to an unknown woman who died falling from climbing a chateau wall. I'd just got back when the Mayor called me in to meet you,' he began.

'Why was she doing that?' Amélie asked.

Bruno shrugged. 'It was the middle of the night. She might have been drunk. My first job is to identify her, which could take some time.'

'Was it an accident?'

'Possibly, but it's certainly suspicious. Someone else was at the scene but disappeared before we got there. I'll take you there now, if you like. It's on the way to colleagues I need to see in Les Eyzies and Montignac. We may have to go door-to-door to show photos of her. First, I'll call on the gendarmes to brief them. I can introduce you at the same time.'

He passed over to her one of the printouts from his phone and a copy of Fabiola's death certificate, and then went into the café to leave another printout with Fauquet. One of his customers might know the woman.

'The gendarmes are giving us trouble on this Ministry project I'm on,' Amélie said on his return. 'They don't want our team monitoring them at all. They say we have no jurisdiction and even if they wanted to cooperate, it would make their work more difficult.'

'Have you tried seeing it from their point of view?' Bruno asked. 'I have to say that it will be difficult doing some of my usual work with you alongside me, starting with seeing my confidential informants. And then there are people who are friendly and who offer me coffee and cakes or a glass of wine and who talk frankly about things they know but who would hate to be considered as informants in any sense. If I took you along, I could lose those contacts, and they make up the heart of my police work here where it's all about knowing everybody.'

'I don't want to make things tough, but I do have to do this job properly,' Amélie replied, with a hesitant smile. 'I suppose I don't need to put down names and addresses of confidential informants, or even to get close enough to listen.'

'If I were to ask you from time to time, and told you what I was doing, could you stay in the van, out of sight?'

She looked unhappy at the thought of this, so he asked, 'Do you have your brief, or some form of letter saying exactly what is expected of you?'

She pulled from her bag a transparent folder. The papers inside had the familiar red, white and blue diagonal stripes of the Justice Ministry across the top corner. The relevant letter of instruction told her: 'to accompany the officer throughout the working period and keep a detailed and timed record of the officer's work and movements, while staying as close as reasonable or possible without obstructing the policeman in the course of his duty.'

Noting that phrase 'throughout the working period', Bruno realized that he could operate in his usual way without Amélie outside the formal thirty-five-hour week he was supposed to work. But he pointed to the last phrase about 'obstructing the policeman'.

'As I read it, that means I can reasonably ask you to stay in the van. I'll try not to do that too often. And now, let's go and say hello to the gendarmes, but I'll stop on the way at a company that rents out *gîtes* to tourists and give them a photo to show their staff. They may recognize the dead woman.'

'I put her photo on Instagram and on Facebook while you were in the café, asking if anyone knew her,' Amélie said casually. 'That may help. I hardly ever use it these days but I've got over fifteen hundred Facebook friends and I asked all of them to share the photo so that will be thousands of eyeballs for you. Even more on Instagram.'

'You did what?' Bruno sat up in surprise. 'I appreciate that you were trying to help, but you should have asked me first. I'm not sure it's a good idea to put a dead woman's face all over social media. What if a family member finds out that way? It would be quite a shock.'

She shrugged. 'Too late now, it's done. And I presume the priority is to identify her as soon as we can.' She paused, looking at him coolly. 'Or are you just covering your resentment at not thinking of it yourself?'

'I'd hope I'm more professional than that,' he retorted, his tone crisp. He realized he was glaring at her. He forced himself to soften his expression, aware that this was a professional relationship and he'd better make it work or the next two weeks would be miserable.

'The fact is I'm not very familiar with social media,' he said. 'We're not exactly at the forefront of the information age here in the Périgord. Emails and searching the web are about my limit. Let's hope your idea works.'

She surprised him with a quick grin that didn't reach her eyes. 'And let's hope her nearest and dearest don't see it first. I can see that you might be right about that.'

'And maybe it will work and we'll save a lot of time,' he replied, hoping some kind of truce had been established.

'I couldn't find you on Twitter,' she went on, not even looking at him, her face bent down over the screen of her phone as she tapped in some note or message. 'And while the *mairie* has a Facebook page the only reference it has to you is your phone number.'

She put her phone into her bag and looked up at him. 'That's not good enough, Bruno. I hope you understand the importance of social media in the future of policing. It's the way most young people communicate these days. I think my report had better recommend that we set up courses for you rural policemen on how to use it.'

Bruno nodded politely, his heart sinking at the prospect. 'Let's see how your Facebook inquiry works out.'

6

Traditionally the gendarmes of France had lived in military-style barracks. Founded after the French Revolution, the gendarmes were deployed almost as an army of occupation in rural areas, where the Church and the old ways remained strong and distrust of the Revolution was fierce and sometimes violent. Gendarmes came under the orders of the Ministry of Defence and were a paramilitary force. They were never assigned to their home areas and retained a distinct separation from the communities they policed. Although a modest building, the St Denis gendarmerie looked as if it had been designed to withstand a siege and, as with most such police posts, the yard and parking area behind it had long been sealed off from the public.

So Amélie expressed surprise to see the gates to the inside yard open and some young civilians playing a game of basketball with shirt-sleeved gendarmes. She was even more surprised that the front door was wide open and the hallway decorated with colourful kids' paintings from the local junior school. Balzac trotted in behind them as if he owned the place.

'Not your usual gendarmerie,' she said, sounding as though she approved.

'And not your usual commander,' Bruno replied. 'Her name is

Yveline and I think you'll like her. She was on the last Olympics squad for hockey and she's well liked, even by the old guard among the gendarmes who were horrified at the thought of being led by a woman. Firm but fair, they say.'

Sergeant Jules was on the desk, the very image of the old guard gendarme, big and burly with a craggy face that seemed to say he had seen it all twice before and wasn't much enjoying seeing it again. This grim exterior concealed a kindly nature and an affection for St Denis that almost matched his devotion to the town's hunting club. Under some of the more rigid commanders of the past, Bruno had only been able to retain relations with the gendarmes by going through Sergeant Jules. But now the old sergeant was Yveline's greatest fan, and in return she had turned a blind eye to his skill at evading the regional headquarter's attempts to reassign him to another district.

He greeted Bruno and Balzac cheerily, but Jules's eyes widened when Bruno introduced her as a colleague from the Justice Ministry in Paris, here to pay a courtesy call on the commandant. Jules glanced with dismay at the paintings, which would doubtless strike any Parisian bureaucrat as too messy and informal for the authority of the gendarmerie of *la République*!

'We got permission from the general in Périgueux, a special exhibition,' he stammered as Amélie stretched out a hand to him.

'I like it,' she said. 'It makes a nice change from those boring public service posters you usually see in these places. And it's good to see your guys playing basketball outside.'

Yveline came out with a welcoming smile and led them into her office where a pot of coffee awaited them, more of the kids' paintings on her wall. Balzac greeted her as an old friend.

'The Mayor called to let me know you were on the way, and I'd like to add my own welcome to St Denis,' Yveline said. 'As you know, our leaders in Paris have decided not to cooperate formally with your project, but that won't stop us helping as far as we can. I think it's a great idea and Bruno is a very suitable subject for your work. We work closely with him and depend heavily on his local knowledge and friendships, something that we haven't always been good at.'

'Perhaps at some point I could have a very informal and off-the-record chat with you about how you see the future of police–gendarme relations. You seem to have a rather refreshing approach,' said Amélie.

'Maybe we could do it over dinner one evening at my place,' said Bruno, remembering what the Mayor had said about the need to win over Amélie and knowing that a good meal always helped cement relations.

'That's a good idea,' said Yveline. 'Bruno's a great cook, so we'll be in for a treat.'

Amélie's face broke into a smile. 'And if I'm with you, Yveline, perhaps we may be able to drink a little more wine than the regulations usually recommend.'

'Maybe not if Yveline is driving,' said Bruno, grinning. 'I could pick you up at the hotel and then get the pair of you a taxi for the run back to town. We'd better not start this project with any embarrassments. Shall we say tomorrow night at seven?'

In the hallway Philippe Delaron was photographing the display of paintings under Sergeant Jules's beady eye. Still focusing his camera, the *Sud Ouest* reporter spoke without taking his eye from his viewfinder. 'Hi again, Bruno. Jules told me you were here. I sent in the photo from the chateau and the picture desk likes the idea of asking the readers to solve the puzzle. Can you give me anything more on this dead woman, Bruno? Any idea yet who she is?'

He turned, and looked almost as surprised as Sergeant Jules had been to see Amélie.

'Well, hello,' he said, sticking out his hand and giving her a smile of practised charm that had secured him girlfriends in most of the villages up and down the valley. 'And who might you be, mademoiselle?' Automatically, he raised his camera to take a snapshot, a trick that Philippe had found usually worked with girls before.

Bruno put his hand in front of the lens. 'None of your business, Philippe,' he said genially. A photo in *Sud Ouest* of Amélie visiting the gendarmerie might prove uncomfortable for Yveline. Philippe took it in good heart; he and Bruno went back a long way. 'And we have nothing new on the dead woman, which is why we're asking you to run the photo in tomorrow's edition.'

'It's already up on our website,' said Philippe.

'But the only people who read that are you and your competitors, and very occasionally me.'

'So you're not Bruno's new girlfriend and you're obviously not under arrest, which means that you must be something official.' Philippe was smiling at Amélie in his engaging way. 'I'm Philippe, photographer and news reporter for *Sud Ouest*, a newspaper with a bigger circulation than *Le Monde*. And we're much more readable. Are you going to be in town long?'

'Stop it, Philippe,' said Bruno. Amélie remained silent, her face expressionless. She seemed thoroughly unimpressed by

54

Philippe's chatty attempts at charm, however well they might work on the maidens of the Vézère valley. Good for her, thought Bruno. 'This is police business. I'm taking her to the place where the dead woman was found.'

'No point, nothing to see. I've just been there and J-J's boys had already taken her off to the morgue and the Count was closeted with J-J. I got a quote from the guy selling tickets. So, the usual routine, Bruno, let me know what you can, when you can.' He turned to Amélie and gave her a rather more sincere smile. 'Don't let Bruno frighten you. He's got a heart of gold, really. He even kept me out of jail.' He waved and disappeared.

'You seem to have a special relationship with the local press even though he does overplay the role of the eager young news-hound,' she said as Bruno led the way up the rue de Paris, Balzac at their heels. He'd intended to show her the old streets of St Denis, the medieval houses and fountain. But Amélie had some-thing else in mind.

'What was it that Philippe said about your keeping him out of jail?'

'I'd rather not arrest people if there's a better solution.'

'Tell me the story, just for my own interest,' she said.

'It was nearly ten years ago, not too long after I arrived in St Denis,' Bruno explained. 'Philippe was in his last year at school and along with three friends he'd stolen the car of an elderly British resident to go joy-riding. They were going too fast, crashed it on a corner, abandoned the car and fled, wiping their fingerprints from the steering wheel, gear lever and door handles. They thought they were being very clever.

'I'd kept an eye on Philippe as a young tearaway, and managed to get some prints from the lever that adjusted the seat. I went to see the Englishman, then to see Lespinasse at the local garage, and finally I called on Pascal the insurance agent. All this was before I went to the Delaron house to inform Philippe and his parents that he was in deep trouble and that I was taking him to the gendarmerie to be fingerprinted.'

'I thought you said you didn't like to arrest people,' Amélie interrupted.

'The story doesn't end there,' he replied. 'The fingerprints matched, and Philippe was led down to the cells and left to stew while I had a beer in the nearby café with Sergeant Jules. Then I went down to Philippe's cell and asked who the other boys were. Philippe said nothing. So I named two of the lads who were Philippe's usual cronies, one now a sous-chef at an up-and-coming restaurant in Bordeaux and the other who works for a balloon ride business that's very popular with the tourists. The third name I kept in reserve. Philippe refused to confirm their names, which pleased me although I pretended to be angry.'

'So he had not been formally arrested at this point,' Amélie said. 'That means you didn't have the right to take his fingerprints.'

'Right, and that's why I said that I'd offer him a choice,' Bruno went on. 'I could call the *Procureur* and let the law take its course. But I gave him an alternative. The Englishman liked his wood stoves, but with the current price of firewood he was prepared to forgive Philippe if he and his chums came in person to apologize, supplied and chopped him a winter's supply of firewood, and undertook to wash and polish his car regularly for the foreseeable future. The insurance agent was prepared to forego damages if the three youngsters reimbursed over the coming year the cost of the insurance payout. At the garage, Lespinasse was prepared to charge very much less than his usual rate for the repair, since he and I both suspected that Lespinasse's nephew Maurice had been the fourth youngster in the car.

'So four fundamentally decent if mischievous youngsters had learned their lesson and been kept out of the criminal justice system. The Englishman was spared the cost of buying firewood and his car was repaired and washed regularly. Philippe and his friends found odd jobs and repaid the insurance agent the minimal sum that Lespinasse had charged for repairs.

'It was a solution that not only gave me pleasure,' Bruno continued. 'It also made me a number of friends, including Lespinasse, Pascal the insurer and the kindly English maths teacher who had retired to St Denis.'

'But that's exactly what a sensible cop ought to do,' said Amélie. 'Young boys are always full of devilment, but detention just makes them worse. Unfortunately such a solution isn't available for most of the young kids picked up these days for smoking weed or shoplifting. Can I use that in my report as an example of local police solutions? I won't use your name.'

'I suppose so. Philippe talks of it often enough,' Bruno said. 'You realize that it's almost impossible for a gendarme to do something like that. They just don't have the flexibility.'

'How do you mean?'

'The gendarmes have been given targets for so many arrests, so many fines and traffic tickets issued. It's crazy. You don't judge a cop by how many people he puts in jail. I'd rather judge them by the ones they keep out.'

'I agree,' Amélie said, 'But for that to work you need cops who know the local people. Now you know why I picked St Denis to do my research project.'

He stopped in his tracks. 'No, I don't know why you picked us. You didn't know that story.'

'No, it was another one, about fraud in the truffle market that led to a big case on illegal immigration.'

'Where on earth did you hear about that?'

'In magistrates' school. We had a visiting lecturer from Eurojust telling us about European arrest warrants and different styles of policing. She told us about the importance of our municipal police here in France and mentioned St Denis as an example.'

Bruno felt a lump forming in his chest. There could only be one Eurojust official who knew about St Denis and the truffle business.

'Would that have been Commissaire Perrault?' he asked.

'Isabelle Perrault, that's right. You must know her. She said she used to be based down here. She's great, a real star.'

He nodded, the sadness that thoughts of Isabelle summoned mixing with pride that she had chosen to cite him as an example of local policing that she admired. The summer of their love affair was still the happiest time of his life, just as the weeks after her decision to move to Paris and pursue her career had been the saddest. A star indeed but not a lucky one for Bruno.

And with that, they reached the door to Ivan's bistro. The clock on the *mairie* was striking noon, which every good French citizen knew to be the signal for lunch.

7

The price of Ivan's daily lunch menu had risen to fourteen euros, which was still excellent value for the soup, home-made pâté, main course, salad with cheese and dessert, with a quarter litre of house wine included. The bistro was full, and not only because word had raced around town about Bruno's new colleague from Paris. Ivan's place was a local institution and thanks to his love life, Ivan's restaurant had steered the tastes of St Denis in new directions. There had been all the variants of mussels – à la Normande, à la crème, au curry – as well as the usual marinière thanks to a Belgian girl he'd met on a beach in Ibiza and persuaded to return with him. When she stalked out and began walking with her suitcase to the station, the whole town had mourned with Ivan.

After a springtime break in Turkey, Ivan had returned with a Spanish girl for a memorable summer menu of paella, tapas and gazpacho. Bruno could still almost taste her dessert of *leche frita*, a rich creamy centre encased in flour and beaten egg, fried and then dusted with sugar and cinnamon. A German girl had turned the entire valley into admirers of her Wiener Schnitzel, which she served with a rich and slightly tart potato salad. Ivan's last holiday in Thailand and Malaysia had excited great expectations of curries cooked with coconut milk and lemongrass, which was what arrived, except that the girl had been Australian rather than Thai.

Ivan was currently living and cooking alone. Mandy, the Australian, had gone to her wine course in Bordeaux and Ivan was back serving his traditional cuisine of the Périgord, which he did very well. But even as they devoured with pleasure his soups and his roast meat and fowl, the diners would sometimes fall silent, a distant look appearing on their faces. Like hunting dogs on a scent, they would cock their heads as if hearing the crash of surf on some tropical beach and the unfamiliar cries of foreign fishermen bringing the promise of new sensation for the increasingly cosmoplitan taste buds of St Denis.

And so when Ivan asked whether Amélie had enjoyed her meal and questioned her about her native cuisine, all other conversation ceased. When she said 'Guadeloupe', the chorus of wistful sighs was like a tropical breeze wafting through the room. Dreams of fresh fish steaming over the embers of a fire on the beach as the Caribbean sunset blazed in the west convened Ivan's customers into the kind of spiritual union that Father Sentout's Sunday sermons seldom achieved.

'And what do you miss most about it?' Ivan asked.

'*Épice*,' she said. 'It's the classic sauce, made of stewed peppers and garlic, parsley, thyme and green onions. We use it in everything, but I like it best on rice and red beans along with my mother's chicken and cashew nuts.'

Even though he had eaten well, Bruno felt his taste buds start to stir again, and around the room he saw others licking their lips. Ivan asked, 'Could you teach me how to make that?'

'You're a bad man, stealing my mother's secrets,' Amélie said with a laugh, and the whole bistro chuckled with her.

One by one, they came up to be introduced: Rollo, the headmaster of the local *collège*; Dougal, the Scotsman who ran the agency for holiday lettings, along with Hubert who ran the town's famous wine *cave*. It was Joe, Bruno's predecessor as town policeman, who lingered longest. He took Amélie's hand in his own gnarled paws and asked what wine the locals drank with Caribbean food.

'People drink rum, sometimes with cola, sometimes with a squeeze of lemon juice. Here in France, my parents usually drink rosé in summer and red wine in winter.'

Joe looked at the carafe of Bergerac sec white wine that Ivan had served. He bought ten-litre boxes of cuvée Roxanne from Hubert's *cave*, the same wine that Bruno usually bought in summer for everyday drinking.

'And do you think our local Bergerac would go well with your Caribbean food?'

'Very well,' Amélie replied, smiling at the courteous old man.

'We'll have to start her education in our wines, Bruno,' Joe said, and raised her hand to his lips before departing.

'That was quick. Your first day and you've won over half the town,' Bruno said as they left, after an amiable dispute over the bill. Amélie insisted on buying the lunch, saying she was being given a daily allowance for this mission, and it was only fair since she was dining as his guest the following evening.

'Now we'll head up the valley since I have to see my two colleagues,' Bruno went on. He put Balzac into the back of his van and they set off. 'You said you'd sung in nightclubs. What do you sing?'

'Anything at all,' she replied. 'I started in a church choir and had childish dreams of being an opera singer, but then I discovered Broadway musicals and jazz. Then my mum bought me an album of Ella Fitzgerald and I fell in love with scat, improvised vocals that use the human voice like an instrument.'

'You mean like *Wop-bop-a-doo-bop*?'

She laughed, a rich, treacly sound that warmed the heart and was so infectious that Bruno laughed in turn.

'Not really, more like this.'

And off she soared, with an extraordinary cascade of sounds, not a single word to be recognized, only the pure, clear notes and syllables that seemed to mark the rhythm, almost as if they replaced the drums of a jazz combo. She went on with infinite variations until she sang the title of the song that Bruno had groped to recognize. It was 'How High the Moon'. He noticed that his fingers were beating along on the steering wheel, his head nodding in time with her music.

'That's wonderful,' he said. 'I used to wonder if it just meant the singer had forgotten the words.'

'Not at all, it's about the creation of new sounds, new words if you like. And it comes in different styles. Listen to Ella Fitzgerald sing scat and you can hear that she's catching the sound of the Big Band era in which she began her career. But listen to Sarah Vaughan and it sounds like one of the bebop jazz combos where she started out. Two women, two styles, but all scat, jazz for the human voice. People in the Caribbean have sung that way for generations, and some claim it began with slaves singing African dialects when they were brought across the sea. Who knows? But it needn't be only jazz. Listen.'

She launched into a classic operatic aria, slow and evidently tragic, that Bruno half recognized. As she sang her invented sounds, he realized that it was not greatly different from hearing it sung in the original Italian, a language he did not know.

'That's from *Tosca*,' she said. 'An aria called "Vissi d'Arte" and if you ever heard it performed by Leontyne Price, it sounds like scat to me. Or listen to Maria Callas sing "Casta Diva" from *Norma* and it's the same. But that's not all I sing. Do you like Cole Porter and Irving Berlin?'

Without waiting for an answer, she launched into 'Cheek to Cheek', a song Bruno knew in a French version by Daniel Roure. Although she was a far better singer, he began singing along, he in French, Amélie in English, until they stopped at the roundabout before Les Eyzies.

'Thank you, I enjoyed that,' he said, driving on when the road cleared. 'Normally I only sing for my dog. Or in the shower.'

'I usually have to sing alone these days so it's good to share it with someone. You carry a tune well.'

'Have you stopped performing?'

'Mostly,' she said, and shrugged. 'When I was at law school there wasn't time, except for parties, singing for friends. I'd love to keep it up, although I'm not sure it would do my career much good.'

'We do free concerts on the riverbank in St Denis during the tourist season, so if you ever want a holiday, all expenses paid, and a modest fee for singing in the evening, we can sign you up right away. I organize the concerts and do the bookings.'

'I'm flattered. It sounds like fun and it's something to add to my notes about your work as a policeman.'

He parked the car in the shadow of a huge cliff towering over the long main street of Les Eyzies. As they climbed out, he pointed upwards to where a giant statue of a man, done in primitive style, gazed out from a ledge in the cliff across the town and the river.

'That's our Cro-Magnon man, a symbol of all the prehistory we have within a hundred metres of where you're standing. I always salute him when I pass.'

Louise Varenne, the town policewoman, was waiting for them at the *mairie*. She showed no surprise at Amélie's presence; Bruno assumed Sergeant Jules must have phoned ahead to tip her off. Bruno had introduced Yveline, Jules and his wife to both of his police colleagues up the valley over a barbecue of fresh-caught trout in his garden. It was the first time that Louise had met the *gendarme commandante* socially and now they were on first-name terms, which did wonders for their cooperation. Food, Bruno believed, was a village policeman's secret weapon. The more people who came to eat at his table, the more he heard and learned and the more welcome he was in the twelve hundred households that made up the commune of St Denis.

'I made copies of your photo of the dead woman and took it around the campsites, shops and cafés,' Louise said after welcoming them, including Balzac. 'No success so far except for the guy at the petrol station who thinks the woman filled the tank of a silver Peugeot Traveller a couple of days ago. No credit card slip, she paid cash.'

Bruno related what the Count had told him about previous break-ins at Commarque. 'Do you know of any Templar enthusiasts around here?'

'Dozens, after that spate of bestselling novels came out about them,' Louise replied. 'I read some of them myself. But I don't think the craze lasted, except for people living off the tourist trade.'

Half the shops in the region offered toy swords, plastic helmets and child-size white surcoats emblazoned with a red cross. English tourists thought these items celebrated their warlike ancestors, while all the others knew it as the sign of the Templars.

'Do you know anywhere that sells blue-green nylon rope, or climbing ropes?' Bruno went on. 'Doctor Stern found some strands on the body.'

'No, but my brother's in the climbing club,' Louise said, reaching for her phone and calling him to explain her query. She listened a moment, thanked him and said she'd email him a photo of the dead woman in case she was known to any of the climbers.

'He says it doesn't sound like proper climbing rope, more like the cheap nylon stuff available in hardware stores. I'll let you know if anyone recognizes the woman.'

Bruno thanked her and led the way around the corner to the museum, where he embraced the two women on the ticket desk, introduced Amélie and asked if Clothilde was in her office. They knew he was to be *témoin* at Clothilde's wedding and he was told to go straight up. Climbing the stairs, he was explaining to Amélie that Clothilde was one of the leading prehistorians in France, when he heard footsteps above him and a voice saying,

'Stop it, Bruno, you'll make me blush. You'd better not put any of that flattery into your wedding speech.'

A small powerhouse of a woman appeared, with fiery red hair piled on her head and held in place with a pencil. She wore a man's shirt in green and white stripes over black leggings. Reading glasses dangled from a chain around her neck.

'I hope I'm not interrupting,' Bruno said, kissing her and introducing Amélie. 'I need to pick your brains about a woman found dead beneath the cliff at Commarque this morning.' He showed her the photo and explained that the Count thought she might have been a Templar fan, and about the pose that echoed the Venus of Laussel.

Clothilde shook her head at the photo. 'She's not known to me but I can scan it and put it on my Facebook page. A lot of us archaeologists stay in touch that way. But I can't see an archaeologist climbing up something. We usually dig down.'

'What about these letters?' He showed her his photo of the graffiti. 'We think she was writing them on the wall of the donjon when she fell. Do they mean anything to you, any language that springs to mind?'

'Sorry, no. But I can tell you it's not English.' Clothilde turned to Bruno. 'Oh Bruno, did you know that the ground-penetrating radar and seismic team are coming this very week? It's going to play hell with all my plans for the wedding. Horst and I will have to be there when they're working so we may have to call on you to tie up various loose ends.'

'I'd better check with the Police Nationale whether they're treating it as a crime scene, but whatever happens, I'll do my best to help out.' He grinned at her. 'You'll be pleased to hear that I've got my speech drafted. When does your *dame d'honneur* arrive?'

'Lydia Manners is flying in from London on Friday with her husband to be in time for the *dîner des témoins* at Laugerie Basse. They're opening the inside cave for us and we'll dine in there. Her husband is English, a former soldier, so you and he should get on. She's American but they live in Oxford where she works at the Ashmolean museum. And don't forget you're organizing the bachelor dinner with Horst and his male friends on Thursday and for God's sake don't let him drink too much.'

'Have you heard of some Templar scholar in Sarlat called Dumesnil?' Bruno asked. 'The Count mentioned him as an expert I might consult.'

'Dumesnil? You'll meet him at the wedding. Both Horst and I think the world of him. A brilliant man, written one of the few really good books on the subject of the Templars. He teaches history in Brive, but if you get a chance, visit him at home in Sarlat. It's like entering a medieval cloister and he's said to follow the Benedictine rule, although he's not a priest.'

'What's that?' asked Amélie.

'Monastic prayer discipline. Matins at midnight, Lauds at three in the morning, that kind of thing. If you ask me, he's slightly mad, but brilliant in his way, of course. He could waltz into a job at any university in Europe, but he says that being a school teacher is his version of the public service the monastic rule requires. He's a strange fellow but he's very engaging.'

'He follows the rule, but he's not a monk?' Bruno asked.

'No, nor is he a priest; Auguste claims to have no vocation, but if you ask me it's because they stopped holding services in Latin. He also helps with the choir at Sarlat Cathedral.'

After more coffee with Clothilde, Bruno and Amélie headed up the main road to Sarlat, Bruno pointing out the various prehistoric sites and chateaux along the way before turning off to Cap Blanc to ask the staff if they recognized the dead woman. When he'd checked the car park earlier that morning, the cave had not yet been opened to the public. The woman selling tickets looked carefully at the photo and said she remembered her buying some local guidebooks two or three days earlier.

'She spoke French like someone who hadn't lived here for a long time,' the woman added. 'It was perfect, but a bit old-fashioned, a bit stilted. And she had some American dollars in her purse along with the euros. I remember her because she asked if there was a path across the valley to Commarque and I pointed it out to her. It's not easy to find through the trees. And I noticed she was wearing walking shoes and carrying a rucksack. She took it off to put the books inside.'

Bruno made a note and thanked her before heading back to his van, telling Amélie he'd have to make sure all the hotels and campsites and holiday lettings agencies were shown the photo. 'If she's a foreigner or a visitor from another country, I'll have to get the Foreign Ministry to circulate her photo to the embassies. Tracking missing persons is about the most time-consuming job I know.'

'Can't you use facial recognition software?' she asked. 'I know there's a pilot scheme at the Interior Ministry trying to use the database of the photos on French ID cards, and you could try the

Americans. If she had dollars in her purse, she may well have been to the USA and they'll have her photo on file.'

Surprised to hear this, Bruno glanced sideways at her as he drove. 'In all the tons of paperwork I get sent by the various ministries, there's never been anything about identifying unknown persons from the photos on their ID cards. It could be very useful. I don't think J-J knows about it and he's the chief detective for the *département*.'

Amélie was already tapping at her phone, and Bruno noticed that she was doing so faster than he could type.

'Ever since the ISIS attack on Paris,' she said, 'there have been a lot of new projects to exploit the databases the state already controls, from ID cards to driving licences, passports and criminal records. It's a huge job and I don't know how far they've got with it, but I'm sending the photo to a friend from law school who's working at the Ministry of the Interior. Maybe she can run it through their database and also send the request to Interpol.'

'It's ridiculous that you haven't been informed of these new capabilities,' she said as she finished texting. 'That's exactly the kind of information I need to put in my report. How often do you see this J-J?'

'Quite a lot. He'll check in with me about anything that comes up in this part of the *département*. I saw him this morning at Commarque after I called him about the dead woman. A suspicious death is his business. We work well together and strictly speaking it's his job to identify her, but I'll always try to use our local contacts to help. Just because the Police Nationale and the gendarmes and I have three different employers, I don't think that stops us working together. We're all on the same side.'

Bruno's phone began to play the first notes of the 'Marseillaise', and he pulled in to the side of the road to answer. It was the man from the Templars' society, saying he did not recognize the woman and knew of no new reports about treasure at Commarque, but he'd circulate the photo around his members.

'Do the letters I-F-T-I mean anything to you, some sort of Templar lore perhaps? I ask because the woman seemed to be trying to paint a word with these letters on the chateau wall.'

'On the wall of Commarque? That's sacrilege, I wouldn't want to have anything to do with a member like that. But no, it means nothing to me. Again, I can ask around.'

'And you're pretty sure there was never any Templar treasure at Commarque?'

'Who knows? Commarque is one of three thousand sites in France with Templar connections but it was never a *commandérie*, or local administrative centre. There are five or six in the *département* of the Dordogne. But if they wanted to hide treasure from the King, they probably would not have used a *commandérie*.'

'So they might have used a lesser site, like Commarque?'

'Possibly, but the King's searches were pretty thorough. He put a lot of resources into crushing the Templars and he did it quickly. He sent out secret orders to all the bailiffs and seneschals across France for a single, devastating strike to be carried out a month later. More than five thousand Templars were arrested in a single night, Friday, October the thirteenth, 1307. No French state could mount that kind of operation again until World War Two. Even Napoleon couldn't have done it. Just imagine the numbers of troops or police required, the cells to hold them, keeping the secret while the orders were transmitted around the country on horseback.'

Bruno raised his eyebrows. He could imagine the scale of such an operation and would never have dreamed a medieval monarchy could have mounted something so efficient.

'Five thousand trained knights, all arrested at once. Did they go quietly?' he asked.

'No, the fighting knights were in Spain and Cyprus, facing the Saracens. In France, they were mainly old men, but even so, it was quite an operation. It shows the King's desperation to get their treasure.'

'But he didn't get it?'

'He got their land and their castles and manors, which was good enough. And he'd already forced the Templars to make him some huge loans. But he never found the treasure.'

'And you think it's still to be found?' Bruno asked.

'I think it was smuggled out across the sea, maybe to Scotland because of the masonic connections, perhaps even to Nova Scotia. There are various theories. I'm less interested in Commarque because there is so much archeological work being done. If there's anything to find, they'll find it, so the place has really dropped off our radar screen. But this woman who fell to her death: you say she was climbing the wall of the donjon? That seems unlikely to me. The donjon has been rebuilt, restored, thoroughly searched. If there's any treasure to be found, it will be in those caves underneath the rock.'

Bruno had his phone on speaker so Amélie could hear. When he ended the call, he said to her, 'Imagine, five thousand men all across France, all arrested on a single night. It wouldn't be easy to do that even today.'

'Just as well, when you think about it. Remember, it's the Justice Ministry I work for, not the Ministry of the Interior. I don't think I'd much like to work for a ministry that could do that.' She showed him the screen of her phone.

'While you were talking I was running a multi-language search for those letters, I-F-T-I. The only hits I got were in Arabic, mainly names, unless the T could have been an R and in that case it's *Ifriqiya*, the old name for North Africa. And if the final letter was unfinished and the extra stroke was making it into an A we could get *iftar*, the meal Muslims eat after the Ramadan fast. I don't think anyone would want to paint that on a castle wall. There's another one, *iftikhar*. It means proud.'

A very faint idea began to form and almost as quickly it went, too elusive to stay. He recognized these subterranean mental stirrings. Sometimes Bruno thought of them as hunches, and sometimes as an idea coming from a part of his brain that was not entirely his – a part formed of curiosity, experience and intuition, that kept churning, calculating and making hypotheses that would suddenly erupt into his forebrain. He knew the components of this latest puzzle: an ancient chateau and an Arabic name, Crusaders and Templars, a modern woman falling or perhaps being pushed to her death, and at some point and in some mysterious way they would fall into a pattern that made sense to him.

8

Bruno seldom paid much attention to the thirty-five hours per week that he was supposed to work, but wondered whether that might also be an item Amélie would be monitoring. He shrugged. The Ministry could hardly complain if he worked longer hours of his own free will. There was something he needed to check. But perhaps she was watching her own hours.

'Are you prepared for one more job today?'

She checked her watch. 'As long as I'm back at the hotel by seven. That gives us a couple of hours. I'm having dinner with some of the local socialists tonight. I want to see if I can get them to launch a youth group. It's depressing how few of the local parties have one.'

'Is that how you got interested in politics?'

'No, it began with my parents, who talked politics all the time. My mother's on the left and my dad's more of a green. Later when I was at school there were the riots in the cities when kids burned all the cars. Then came the recession and it all became more serious and now it's what I want to do.'

Bruno drove out of St Denis past Hubert's wine *cave* towards Le Buisson where he could take the road that led to the Dordogne valley. Making a mental note to introduce Amélie to the local wines, he turned off to the left to what he thought of as the suburb of St Denis, homes built in the fifties and sixties, now extended with new estates aimed at the growing numbers of retirees from northern and eastern France who preferred the kinder climate of the Périgord. Most of them were priced at around a hundred thousand euros, bungalows with two bedrooms, a single bathroom and a garden large enough for a lawn, a vegetable patch and a terrace to eat outdoors. They looked as though they belonged in Provence rather than the Périgord, with walls of white stucco and roofs of semi-circular tiles. Bruno stopped at one such structure on the corner of two roads. It was larger than the others, with more garden and a third bedroom in the upper storey of the small tower that anchored the two wings of the house.

When the door opened, he was embraced by Dilla, the wife of Momu, the maths teacher at the local college. They were good friends and he was fond of them both, and of Dilla's couscous and their annual *méchoui* feast, when they roasted a whole lamb for their friends. They were firmly irreligious, drank wine and spirits and always attended the town's rugby games to watch their son Karim, the team's star forward. His infant children helped to compensate for the loss of their adopted son Sami, an autistic boy whose death they blamed on jihadists. Bruno introduced Amélie, and then Dilla bent down to greet Balzac as Momu emerged from the sitting room to embrace him in turn. From behind Momu came the sound of baroque music.

After a brief exchange, Bruno showed them a printout of the photo he'd taken of the letters. 'The final letter could just be an accident, scrawled when the woman who painted it fell to her death. Mean anything to you?'

'Was this the unknown woman who died at Commarque?' Dilla asked. 'It was just on the radio news, but there was nothing about any writing. It's so sad, at such a lovely place. I'll never visit it again without thinking of her.'

'It was a fortress,' Amélie said flatly. 'A whole lot more people were probably killed there over the centuries.'

'Yes, of course,' Dilla replied, giving Amélie a sideways glance before leading them into the sitting room where Momu turned down the music and offered them a drink. Amélie asked for tea and Bruno said that would be fine for him. Beside Momu's armchair was a pile of his pupils' homework and a glass of what looked like scotch. The room bore not a single trace of his Algerian heritage and the bookcase seemed filled with books in French. A copy of the latest *Le Monde Diplomatique* lay on a coffee table.

'Why paint an Arabic word in Roman letters?' Momu asked, studying the photo. He read them aloud and shrugged. 'It could be *iftin*, which means light, or *iftinan* which means enchantment. It could be a name, Iftikhar, not very common in the Arab world, but you find it in Sudan and rather more in Pakistan and maybe Persia. There's a Pakistani poet, Iftikhar Arif.'

'Does the name mean anything?'

'That which creates pride or a sense of worthiness, so you could translate it as honour or glory. *Nichan Iftikhar* was the Order of Glory in the Ottoman Empire, a bit like our *Légion d'Honneur*.'

'Could it be any other word?'

'Not that I can think of offhand. But if you like, I'll call a friend who's more of a literary scholar than I am.'

Dilla came with a tray holding the tiny glasses for the tea and an old fat-bottomed silver teapot with a high neck and spout that she had inherited from her family. The room suddenly filled with the scent of mint and Momu stood up to pour the heavily sweetened tea into the glasses from a great height, evidently proud of his skill. Bruno knew that custom required that he drink three glasses. Balzac nibbled contentedly at the biscuit Dilla had brought for him.

'Is it always this sweet?' Amélie asked, after emptying her glass.

'Always,' said Dilla, solemnly. Amélie looked abashed.

Bruno thought he'd better change the subject. 'This is the woman who fell to her death.' He handed each of them a print-out of the photo he'd taken.

'The poor woman,' Momu murmured as he studied the face. Then he looked up. 'She doesn't look Arabic or Pakistani. I'd have said she's European.'

'She probably wasn't alone. Somebody took away the paint can and presumably also the rope that we think they were using for the climb. I can leave you the printouts. It may help your literary friend.'

Bruno finished his third glass of tea, thanked Dilla and rose to leave Momu to his marking. 'My love to the grandchildren,' he said as he left.

Bruno dropped his companion at the hotel, told her he'd be patrolling the town market by eight the following morning. She bid Balzac goodbye with a kiss on his head, shook Bruno's hand, wished him a good evening and thanked him for an interesting day. He picked up a bottle of Chateau Jaubertie white wine at the *cave* before heading for Pamela's riding school and the ritual of the weekly dinner with his friends. It was the turn of Fabiola and her partner Gilles to cook, so Bruno's responsibility was wine and getting some water from the spring on Pamela's land.

But first there were the horses to be exercised, and he looked forward to all of it, the perfect way to end a working day. There was the apple to be given to Hector, the struggle to pull on his riding boots and stamp them down to fit. There was the welcoming scent of horses and fresh straw, the heft of the saddle in his arms and the regular game of Hector blowing out his stomach as Bruno tried to secure the saddle girth. Bruno would knee him gently in the belly to remind his horse that he knew this trick and then tighten the strap.

The stables were empty when he arrived. He was a little late, but Hector was waiting for him and there was a note on Hector's door in Pamela's handwriting to say they had taken the ridge trail to Audrix. When he'd given Hector his treat he lingered, enjoying the warm breath on the palm of his hand, and leaned his head forward to rest it against Hector's neck. Bruno stepped back and saw Hector lean down to nuzzle the dog he'd known since Balzac was a puppy. Bruno wondered whether Hector thought of the basset hound as a miniature horse and Balzac thought of the horse as a gigantic dog. No matter, the two animals were friends, evidently happy to see one another.

When Bruno put on the bridle he noticed somebody had used saddle soap on the leather. That would have been Félix, transformed by Pamela's good sense and experience of horses from a sullen young delinquent into a helpful and enthusiastic stable lad and a promising horseman.

With no other horses to slow him down, Hector could barely restrain himself until they were out of the paddock, heading past the house and up the ridge. Miranda, Pamela's partner in running the riding school, gave him a wave from the kitchen window as he passed and then Hector was powering his way up the modest slope and onto the open ground ahead. Within moments he had gone from a canter to a steady run, not quite a gallop but a pace he could keep up for hours.

At the entrance to the bridle trail through the woods, Bruno slowed the horse and then turned him, waiting for Balzac to catch up and join them. They trotted on, the three of them together, past a place where Bruno remembered seeing a host of ceps the previous autumn. Then the trees thinned and he could see the small tower of Audrix church in the distance and a group of horses with their riders even farther off, maybe two kilometres ahead. He gave Hector his rein and with other horses in sight, Hector stretched into a gallop and Bruno narrowed his eyes against the wind.

'That looked like fun,' said Gilles as Bruno joined them. He was riding Victoria, Pamela's elderly mare. Fabiola was on a well-mannered Selle Français that had come with the riding school and Félix was riding the Andalusian. Pamela was on Primrose, the horse she had originally wanted to buy before deciding to make an offer for the whole riding school. Three more horses and a pony, all unsaddled, were on leading reins, just along for the exercise.

'It was glorious,' Bruno replied, beaming with the pleasure of seeing his friends and the thrill of the ride. They trotted on, past Audrix and back by the shorter route, Pamela leading and

Bruno bringing up the rear. It was a position Hector hated if his master was riding fast, but at this gentle pace he seemed content to enjoy the outing. They came over the top of the ridge and stopped, still stunned despite its familiarity by the magnificence of the view. The whole of the double valley opened up below them, the oxbow curves of the River Vézère flowing into the Dordogne. The houses of the village of Limeuil seemed almost to be clambering up the steep slope to the latest of the many fortresses that had squatted on this hilltop for centuries, watching over the confluence of the two rivers and the trade and revenues they had brought.

Pamela turned her horse's head and they rode on down the slope to come to the rear entrance of the riding school. Gilles and Fabiola left the horses still saddled and headed for the kitchen to start the food. Pamela gave Bruno a hug when they dismounted, holding him just a second too long as women seemed to do with former lovers, perhaps to remind him of what he was missing despite it being she who'd ended the affair.

Together with Félix they unsaddled the horses, brushed them down, hung the saddles and bridles in the tack room and then sluiced off in the stable sink. Balzac stood waiting for his dinner before curling up in the corner of Hector's stall. Félix filled his bowl from the sack of dog biscuits that Bruno had made at home. He'd brought a large stock to the riding school.

The others were already gathered in the vast kitchen of the old manor house, and Bruno felt a warm glow of affection for them all and a sense of comfort at the ritual they had established of riding and then dining together each Monday evening. The Baron was slicing cucumbers for the salad at the work surface by the sink. Gilles was cutting bread into cubes as Fabiola grated the cheese for her fondue. From upstairs came the sound of laughter and splashing as the children of Miranda and Florence, who taught science at the *collège*, enjoyed their bathtime together. Pamela began to prepare the cheese board. Miranda's father, Jack Crimson, was opening wine and Bruno added his bottle to the collection.

'Come on, we'll get the water,' Bruno told Félix, and the two of them set off up the hill with the big plastic *bidons* to the spring that burbled from a knot of rocks.

The trip to the spring had become another part of the Monday evening ritual. It had started when Pamela and Miranda first bought the riding school, moved into the big house and began to renovate the gîtes for rental. Bruno, the Baron, Gilles and Fabiola would bring casseroles and stewpots to help the two overworked women. Then Florence had joined them, bringing her infant twins to play with Miranda's children and help them learn French.

From the Baron in his seventies, Jack Crimson in his sixties down to the children and now the teenaged Félix, they covered most of the age groups. Bruno had one day been struck by the thought that this group of friends had become the nearest he had ever known to a family. He enjoyed the presence of the children, freshly scented from the bath, eating together at their end of the long kitchen table and then being carried sleepily to bed. The mix of languages the friends spoke together had done wonders for Bruno's English and for Miranda's French and the children seemed to have developed a Franglish patois of their own.

'Here's another new one for you to try,' said Jack, handing Bruno a glass of white wine when he returned with the water. 'Domaine de l'Ancienne Cure at Colombier. I went there today.'

Bruno grinned at the Englishman, retired after a career in British intelligence, who now spent one afternoon each week visiting a different vineyard of the Bergerac. With some nine hundred wine growers to call on, he claimed it was a useful incentive to live another twenty years. Bruno knew Christian Roche, the wine maker at l'Ancienne Cure, as well as his wines, but pretended he didn't since Jack so obviously enjoyed thinking he was educating Bruno.

'Very good,' he said, tasting it. 'How many did you buy?'

'A mixed case, half whites, half reds. We can try the red with the fondue.'

'By the way, did you spend much time in the Arab world?' Bruno asked. 'Something came up today, a woman fell to her death at Commarque while trying to paint some slogan on the wall.' He showed Jack the picture on his phone. 'A colleague who's good with computers could only find that combination of letters in Arabic.'

'Could be Arabic, but why write it in Roman letters? Email that photo to me and I'll send it to one of our old camels who might be able to help.'

'Camels?'

'It's what we call diplomats who specialized in the Arab world.'

Jack's voice rose in volume to compete with the thunder of children's feet rushing down the stairs from their bath before racing away to the stables in search of Balzac. Their mothers had evidently spent a few moments in front of a mirror before descending, renewing their lipstick and brushing their hair.

'I don't know how you both manage to look so good when you've just been playing sheriff to four little outlaws,' Bruno told them, kissing each in turn.

'Easy,' said Florence. 'We just told them if they weren't good, we'd turn them over to you. Now, where are our glasses of wine?'

Crimson poured out two glasses and Bruno handed them to Miranda and Florence. Both women were blonde, but there the similarity ended. Miranda was plump, with a complexion so fresh and clear that she could only have come from England's cool, damp climate. Florence was slim, and although she was roughly the same height as Miranda she looked taller with an erect posture and prominent cheekbones that gave her face a classic elegance.

Bruno remembered how he had first seen Florence, an over-worked and underpaid single mother after a difficult divorce, her hair uncared for and her clothes deliberately dowdy to fend off the unwanted advances of her employer. But now, widely respected as a teacher and in a job she loved, with a decent income and good friends, Florence was a different woman. She went shopping in Bordeaux with Pamela, which meant she dressed well. Pamela had also steered her to a good hairdresser, and Florence, Fabiola and Miranda all went to a Pilates class and played regular tennis together.

A generous woman, Pamela, thought Bruno, turning to offer her a glass and seeing that she was watching him quizzically, as though she had been reading his thoughts while he observed Florence and Miranda chatting together. He had not shared

Pamela's bed for many months, but he smiled at her with genuine affection. Along with Katarina, the Bosnian schoolteacher who had died in that vicious little war, and the enchanting Isabelle who had given him the most glorious summer of his life, Pamela was one of the three women who had claimed his heart and shaped his life.

She turned, suddenly conscious of his gaze on her, and did that trick of hers he knew so well, raising a single eyebrow in a way that was half-question, half-gentle mockery.

'Word has flashed around that you have a new escort in tow – from Haiti, I hear,' she said, amusement in her voice. Bruno knew his town well enough to work out the path the gossip had taken, from Doctor Gelletreau in the bistro to his medical colleague Fabiola and from Fabiola to Pamela. 'Might you bring her here to dine with us one evening?'

'You'd be in for a treat if I did. She sings like an angel, jazz or classical. I'm hoping to book her for one of our riverside concerts this summer.'

Pamela raised an eyebrow and gave a cool smile but said nothing. 'She's a magistrate, now working at the Justice Ministry,' Bruno went on, wondering why he felt the need to explain. 'She's here to research how the police and gendarmes might work better together. And she seems to know almost as much about computers as Florence.'

'You do have a way of surrounding yourself with interesting women, Bruno. It's one of your most attractive traits,' Pamela said, putting a hand on his arm and calling them all to the table.

They sat watching while Fabiola added the shredded gruyère and Emmenthal cheese to the simmering white wine and lemon juice, stirring steadily as the cheese melted. She sprinkled in some corn starch and then a spoonful of mustard powder and a pinch of nutmeg. On a separate burner, she was boiling some cubes of potato and slices of carrot. The children liked to try different vegetables on the ends of their forks before dipping them into the fondue. Bruno went to the door to call the children as Fabiola spooned their fondue into a smaller pot, then added two glasses of kirsch to the separate fondue for the adults.

'I heard from the forensics team in Bergerac,' Fabiola said in the brief moment of peace before the children returned. 'The dead woman had certainly been climbing with a cheap rope. They found more of the nylon strands in the flesh of her fingers but her hands were too damaged for fingerprints. What's more, she was about ten weeks pregnant.'

9

The weekly market of St Denis would soon be celebrating seven centuries since its foundation by royal charter, and as he gazed around the familiar stalls Bruno wondered how different today's wares might be from those of the early markets. Ducks and chickens, eggs and spices, fish, fruit and vegetables would have been sold just as they were today, he guessed, although there wouldn't have been either tomatoes or potatoes in the centuries before Christopher Columbus set off to find the New World.

Certainly people would have been selling knives and ploughs, spades and other tools, and leather goods from coats to harnesses for horses and oxen. The village square would have housed a separate market for livestock, trading or auctioning cattle, pigs and sheep. Visiting merchants would have sold cloth and occasionally silk for the nobility. Just like today, wine stalls would have offered the same free glass to taste. Anyone making a sale would have taken only gold or silver in exchange; in those days there was no paper money and no credit. Bruno was certain that the original markets would have been patrolled by somebody like him, a town watchman to keep order, settle disputes and ensure that tolls and taxes were duly paid.

The difference would have been the walls around the town, and the lookouts watching for marauding bands of soldiers. The attackers could have been English or French, it would depend which particular king was supposed to hold St Denis at the time. Flemish mercenaries and Genoese crossbowmen fought for both sides. There would be a call to arms, the closing of the town gates and an old soldier like Bruno to organize a hasty defence while someone on a fast horse was sent to seek help from the feudal lord, the Sieur de Limeuil, in his hilltop fortress downriver.

Today a bureaucrat from Paris was casting an eye over the market from the steps of the *mairie*. But in those days, the bureaucrat would not have been a young woman of Caribbean origin whose taste in clothes had half the town staring. Today she was in bright red capri pants with a royal-blue shirt and a vast white scarf that seemed to be wound a dozen times around her head and then tied in a generous loop around her neck. She looked more than ever like the French flag.

'*Bonjour*, Bruno. *Bonjour*, Balzac,' she greeted them, looking extremely pleased with herself. 'I think I tracked down your mystery woman.'

The Interior Ministry had heard back from the American State Department, whose facial recognition software had thrown up a score of possible candidates from its visa application photos. Bruno was impressed. But that was just the beginning, said Amélie. Her Facebook friends had done even better. She had a positive identification from a British friend in that country's 'Stop the War' movement who recognized the woman in the photo as a fellow activist in Israel's 'Peace Now' group. The

Israeli woman had spoken at a conference in Geneva, and Amélie had tracked down a name.

'Your unknown woman is an Israeli called Leah Ben-Ari,' Amélie declared, a note of triumph in her voice.

For a moment, Bruno was too surprised to respond. He shook his head. 'That's amazing, Amélie,' he said sincerely. 'Thank you indeed. I can't tell you how impressed I am.'

'All you have to do now is contact the Israeli consulate in Paris, send the photo and her name and ask them to follow up, check with next of kin and so on.'

'Yes, of course. Have you had breakfast?'

'Not yet, I was waiting for another of those excellent croissants.'

Because of market day, Fauquet's was more crowded than usual, but when Bruno held open the door Amélie sailed in as if assuming that everyone would make way for her, and so they did. She greeted Fauquet and said she had come for another of the best croissants she had ever eaten. This ensured instant service and a table by the window became miraculously free.

'You have to tell me what you think of my pain au chocolat and my brioche,' said Fauquet, placing a basket before her that was filled with his delicacies, along with two large coffees.

Amélie took a bite first of brioche, chewed thoughtfully and washed it down with coffee. Then she took a bite of a swirl of pastry stuffed with raisins, followed it with a taste of pain au chocolat and finally demolished her croissant. She finished the coffee, called for another cup, and applauded a blushing Fauquet as he came from behind the counter again to serve her.

'You're a master,' she said quietly, before polishing off the rest of the basket, leaving a few crumbs of brioche for Balzac. The café had fallen silent, watching her efficient dispatch of the pastries. Bruno suppressed a smile, knowing that she was doing it deliberately, to ensure that she would be known henceforth in St Denis not as that bureaucrat from Paris but as the person who polished off Fauquet's entire collection at a single sitting.

'What now?' she asked, licking crumbs from her fingers. 'Are you going to call the Israeli consulate first?'

'No, I'll inform J-J. That sort of liaison is his job. May I see the other photos from the Americans? Are they on your phone?'

She scrolled through them slowly, and they both focused on one image that looked uncannily like the dead woman in the photo. She was French, Leah Wolinsky, born in Paris, with a date of birth that made her age thirty-eight.

'Same first name,' said Amélie. 'That's interesting.'

'Could be a coincidence. Still, we'll let J-J sort it out. Send all that to my email and I'll forward it to him. I'd be grateful if you could put me in touch with this Facebook person who identified Leah. I need to put some questions to her. And I'll phone J-J from my office rather than broadcast it all over the café.'

They were about to leave when Bruno saw another of the regulars put the café's copy of *Sud Ouest* back on the counter. Reaching for it he saw the front-page headline, '*Mystery Woman Death at Templar Chateau*'. Beneath a colour photo of the daubs on the castle wall, the paper asked, '*Can You Identify this Mystery Graffiti?*' A smaller headline beside Bruno's photo of the dead woman's face asked, '*Was the Holy Grail Hidden in Commarque?*'

Inside, the Count was quoted on previous incursions by Templar enthusiasts and there was a sidebar on the history of the chateau, including some vague reference to a local legend of ghosts and another about the Templars. The only reference to Bruno was his request for any member of the public who recognized the dead woman to contact him. Bruno grinned and shook his head. Philippe had certainly gone to town on the story. It must have been a slow news day.

Beaming with satisfaction at the success of her researches, Amélie perched on the old-fashioned radiator beneath the window in Bruno's office while he called J-J.

'First time I've found a Paris bureaucrat doing something useful,' J-J grunted down the line. 'I've had detectives trying to trace those shreds of rope that you found. It was cheap nylon stuff you can buy in any supermarket, but no serious climber would use it. What we need is some lead to the person who was with her.'

'Still, it makes a nice change from all that Templar crap in the newspaper,' J-J went on. 'I had the Prefect calling this morning. It seems his wife read some novel about them and counts herself an expert. Perhaps I would be kind enough to keep her informed. Christ, I have enough trouble with her over that paedophilia case. She finds the whole idea of recovered memory to be fascinating. She's probably trying to remember why she ever married that pill of a husband. Anyway, thanks for this. Have you had any calls yet from anyone local who recognizes this woman Leah?'

'Not so far. I've circulated the two names, Ben-Ari and Wolinsky, around the hotels and holiday lettings agencies. Do you want to talk to Amélie? She's sitting right here.'

He handed over the phone, saw Amélie smile and then she said, 'You're very kind to say so, *Monsieur le Commissaire*. And yes,

Bruno is taking good care of me. He's even offered to cook me dinner this evening.'

She handed back the phone and Bruno asked if the archaeologists could start work at Commarque or was it still a crime scene? J-J said they had what they needed and the work could go ahead.

'Will you keep a watching brief on it, Bruno?'

'I'll drop by every day, but we might need some extra police presence if the Templar enthusiasts start turning up to watch.'

'Ask the gendarmes. We've got nobody to spare.'

J-J hung up and Amélie called her Facebook friend in London, put her phone on speaker and said the French police had some questions about the person Leah might have been climbing with.

'I don't know her that well,' came the reply. 'But she was living with a Palestinian guy, a historian she called Husayni. She posted some photos of the two of them together in Ramallah. But I had no idea she was in France or if she was with him.'

Bruno introduced himself in his primitive English and asked, 'Did she ever do alpinism?'

'He means mountain climbing,' Amélie interjected.

'I don't know about mountaineering as such, but she liked hill walking. We went hiking together for a day in Switzerland after the peace conference.'

'Did she ever talk about the Templars?'

'Not that I know. Why don't I just go through all the Facebook posts I got from her and share them with you, Amélie? Then you'll know as much as I do and you can ask to contact her other Facebook friends and her contacts on WhatsApp. She used that more for messages. I know she worked as an archaeologist and historian, but her passion was politics and the peace movement. She was born in France and her family moved to Israel when she was a kid. But that's all I know.'

'When you had the day in the mountains, were there other friends with you?' Bruno asked.

'Just one, an American girl, Jenny Shindler. She's in one of those Jewish liberal groups that supports Peace Now. She's always commenting on Leah's posts. That's really all I know and I have to go. Call me this evening, Amélie, and tell me how you get on. I'm really sorry to hear she's dead.'

Amélie closed the call and asked, 'I hope you don't expect me to start right away. I'll have to wait for her to share Leah's Facebook posts with me.'

'You've been very helpful and now you deserve a treat,' said Bruno. 'Let me just call J-J to tell him about this boyfriend of Leah's.'

Minutes later, Bruno was showing Amélie around the market and introducing her to his friends among the stallholders as he shopped for that evening's dinner. He bought some cod from Armand the fishmonger, and then fresh milk and some *aillou* cheese from Stéphane's cheese stall. He stopped to admire Marcel's premium fruits and vegetables, where Amélie swooped with a cry of delight on a small basket of multicoloured peppers.

'Scotch bonnet peppers,' she said, her eyes shining. 'I can make you an *épice*.' She added some spring onions and a fat lump of ginger.

'I've got the parsley, thyme and garlic you said you'd also need,' said Bruno. 'Is the ginger your mother's secret ingredient?'

'Not telling.'

After buying what he'd need for dinner, Bruno led her down the rue de Paris to Léopold's stall selling leather belts and sandals, wallets, T-shirts and bolts of African cloth from his native Senegal.

'Well, beautiful sister.' Léopold welcomed her just as Bruno's phone began to vibrate. 'Where might you be from?'

Bruno turned away to answer, and heard Horst's voice, with many more voices in the background, asking him to get to Commarque as soon as he could to deal with the crowds.

'That damn newspaper story has brought dozens of people and we've got to get them out of the way to place the sensors for the seismic survey,' Horst said. 'You'll need stakes, tape and a lot of gendarmes. Can you help, Bruno? Otherwise this whole project is going to be stalled.'

Bruno called his colleagues from Les Eyzies and Montignac to ask if they could rally round. Then he alerted Yveline, with a request for help from her gendarmes. Finally he deposited his food purchases in the refrigerator of the *mairie*. Ten minutes later, armed with rolls of crime scene tape and some temporary plastic fencing from the public works warehouse, he and Amélie headed for Commarque, followed by Sergeant Jules and three gendarmes in their van.

10

The scene at Commarque was chaotic. The track down from the car park was partly blocked by carelessly parked cars, and crowds of people were milling around at the base of the cliff. They were gazing up at the chateau and clambering over the large seismic machine, ignoring Horst and the Count who were pleading with them to get back. Bruno drove into the middle of the crowd, his siren blaring, and waited until Sergeant Jules and his men lined up. He told Amélie to stay inside, pulled a bullhorn from the back of his van, clambered onto the roof and announced that in exactly five minutes, he would put a parking ticket with the maximum fine of a hundred euros on every car that was not properly parked in the car park at the top of the hill.

At that, the crowd rushed back to their cars, and started a new round of chaos as they began sounding their horns and vying for space on the narrow track. But at least this chaos was away from the chateau and the gendarmes were able to close off the access road with the fencing and crime scene tape. Sergeant Jules and his gendarmes remained and Bruno's two colleagues were sent up through the chateau to watch the gate on the upper road. Amélie climbed out of Bruno's van, looking dubiously at the rugged, muddy ground and then at her white shoes. Bruno opened the rear of the van, allowing Balzac to jump out, took out the spare rubber boots and handed them to Amélie.

Three men climbed out of the cab of the sensor machine and various sensors were positioned. The motor was started and something that looked like a giant hammer slammed down hard onto the ground, sending out echoes through the earth that reverberated through the soles of Bruno's shoes and sent Balzac leaping nervously into his arms. The chief technician remained in his cab with a laptop, monitoring the geophone sensors and the seismic map they began to draw of the surrounding ground.

'Is that it?' Bruno asked Horst after introducing Amélie. 'A big slam on the ground and they record the echoes?'

'I'm no expert, but there's a lot more to it, which is why they'll be working here all week,' Horst said. 'This is just building up an initial picture.'

He explained that the technicians, on loan from the oil industry, also had something called a vibroseis, a big plate that could be laid on the ground and then set to vibrate at various frequencies to get a more detailed picture. The vibroseis was used in delicate areas where dynamite was too destructive. At the same time the technicians would be adjusting the location of the geophones. Then they would deploy the GPR system – ground penetrating radar. Depending on the nature of the earth and rock and the levels of ground water, its range could penetrate as far as fifteen metres down.

'What are you hoping to find?' Amélie asked.

'New caves, possibly graves or even hidden passages to get

94

in and out from the chateau. We also want to track the water courses.'

'What makes you think there are more caves to be found?'

'Informed instinct.' Horst smiled at her, an appreciative twinkle in his eye that went oddly with his white hair and beard. 'You have to remember that the ground level here is much higher these days, with all the silt that's been washed down by the river. It was four, maybe seven metres lower in medieval times. But in prehistoric times it would have been as much as twenty metres lower, so I suspect there are more cave openings that are simply below today's ground level. And given what we have already found here, this was evidently a major centre of prehistoric society, a real crossroads.'

'What did you find here already?' Amélie asked. 'I'm sorry, I don't know much about all this prehistory.'

Horst explained about the Venus of Laussel, the cave of Cap Blanc, the life-sized horse's head and various other engravings in the caves beneath the fortress. Prehistoric peoples had lived here at different times over thousands of years, he explained, so much that the habitation must have been almost constant.

'As well as being a natural crossroads for man, I suspect that this valley was a natural migration route for the reindeer on which they lived,' he added. 'That's why we think there's a lot more to be found.'

The chaos on the track to the car park having been sorted out, people were drifting back to the temporary fence. Sergeant Jules had moved it to allow access to the steps up to the chateau and the Count was smiling as Jean-Philippe sold entrance tickets and guidebooks to the crowds thronging to get in.

'What did you make of the graffiti on the castle wall?' Bruno asked.

Horst shrugged. 'The Middle Ages is not my period. I assume something to do with Crusaders or the Templars. You could always ask my medievalist friend Dumesnil who wrote a book on the Templars. In fact, he should be here by now since he's an authority on Commarque and wanted to see this new technology at work. But you saw the issue of *Archéologie* with my article on the Venus figurines? In the back, in the news round-up, there was a photo of some Crusader castle in Israel that had been treated the same way, the same neon-orange paint.'

'I'll look it up,' said Bruno, thinking that if the dead woman had indeed been Israeli, there could be a connection. 'Was it the same four letters or was it more?'

'I don't recall. I've got some copies at the museum so I can check it out when I get back.'

'Don't bother,' said Amélie, pulling out her phone. 'Did you say it was called *Archéologie*? And which month? It's bound to be online.'

Bruno and Horst looked at one another a little shamefaced, each realizing that they had not yet grown into this age of instant communication and instant research where Amélie was so evidently at home.

'What the hell . . .' Amélie's fingers were plucking fruitlessly at the screen of her phone. 'Don't say there's no signal. I can't believe it. What century is this? And how do you manage?'

This time the glance that Horst and Bruno exchanged was a little smug. For them, to be out of internet contact seemed quite normal.

'It's the same century, mademoiselle,' Horst said. 'But this is *la France profonde*, the very heart of the countryside. And I may be German but I've become very attached to this place and its ways.'

'And even more attached to the womenfolk,' said Bruno. 'Amélie met Clothilde at the museum yesterday.' He turned to Amélie. 'This is the man she's marrying after one of the longest courtships in history.'

'Not my fault,' said Horst. 'I'd have married Clothilde the first week I met her, given the chance.'

At that point, a fair-haired young man who had been descending the long track from the car park waved and approached them. He was dressed in what the French called the English style: heavy brogues, neatly pressed trousers of burgundy corduroy with a matching tie over a checked shirt and a beautifully cut jacket of heavy tweed. And he was smoking a pipe, which he removed to greet Horst and shake his hand. As Horst introduced him as Dumesnil, the medieval scholar, Bruno noticed the lines around the man's eyes. He was older than Bruno expected, perhaps in his fifties.

'Sorry to be late, Professor Vogelstern,' Dumesnil said. 'I was delayed by some confusion at the car park up the hill.'

'The confusion was all down here just a few minutes ago. Sightseers were brought out by the newspaper story on the Templars,' Horst said.

'Newspaper story?' Dumesnil replied, looking blank.

Horst explained and Dumesnil's face broke into a boyish grin. 'They may not be altogether wrong. I've long thought Commarque may still hold some secrets and frankly, my dear Horst, it's our turn. You archaeologists have unearthed some wonderful finds here, but not much for us medievalists.' He seemed to jump as the echo-sounder began pounding the ground again. 'Maybe they'll find something in my period this time.'

Dumesnil turned to greet the Count, who was walking across to join them, hand outstretched to be shaken, and announcing, 'I see you've met Bruno, our local policeman. He used to be a sergeant in the army and you can tell him what you told me about where the word comes from.'

'Sergeant was the name Richard Lionheart gave to his personal bodyguard of twenty men-at-arms in the twelfth century – sergeants-at-arms,' Dumesnil said. 'It comes originally from the Latin word for servant.'

Bruno nodded politely. 'Thank you, I didn't know that, but I'd really like to pick your brains a bit about the Templars. A woman fell to her death here yesterday in the early hours and the Count told us about earlier incursions by Templar enthusiasts looking for lost treasure. Is there anything in that?'

'Maybe, but I don't think anyone really knows. The Templars became a very wealthy order when they started doing more trading and banking than fighting. Whether they buried their gold, as many of these enthusiasts seem to believe, is a mystery. Being bankers, they probably preferred to have their money working and so they lent a great deal of it to the French Crown.'

'So what remains of the fabled treasure?'

'Some believe it is the Holy Grail and others say it is the Ark of the Covenant or the original tools of the masons who built Solomon's Temple. You should know that the Templars' full title was the "Order of the Poor Fellow Soldiers of Christ and of the Temple of Solomon". But most people assume it also includes the gold and jewels they managed to hide from the French King.'

'Do you believe this treasure exists?'

'No, I don't, but I'm prepared to admit that it's possible. The Templars invented modern banking, organizing financial trans-fers between Europe and the Holy Land. If you volunteered to go on Crusade, you could give money to the Templars in France or Germany, and be given a credit note that you could cash with the Templars in Jerusalem – but only after the Templars took their fee. They also ran a form of shipping insurance and financed trading caravans along the silk roads to China and the Indian Ocean. Over two centuries, they amassed a great fortune, but how much of it remains today is another question. They spent most of their money building castles that were then lost to the Saracens.'

'So even though you doubt whether the treasure exists, you think it possible that modern-day Templar enthusiasts might be looking for it here at Commarque?'

'Oh, we know they're looking, here in France, in Spain, in Scotland, even in Cyprus and the Middle East. And they certainly have been here. Over the years their metal detectors must have gone over every inch of ground. Not that it stops such people. As somebody once said, when people cease to believe in God, the problem is not that they believe in nothing, it's that they are prepared to believe in absolutely anything.'

The ground seemed to lurch beneath their feet as the great metal plate pounded again. Horst laughed as he staggered, just keeping his balance.

'If there is anything to be found, these seismic surveys and the ground penetration radar will find it.'

'What about you, Monsieur Dumesnil?' Bruno asked. 'Do you believe there is something to be found?'

'I certainly hope there's something. What is significant is what we have not found here so far. There are many prehistoric remains, which medieval people must have seen and pondered. But they left us no similar remains themselves, except for the chateau – only paper records of charters and endless lawsuits between families. Why should that be? I suspect that if anything new turns up, it's more likely to belong to my period than to Horst's cavemen.'

11

Bruno stopped at the *maison de la presse* to scan the back pages of *Archéologie* for the account of the graffiti daubed on the ruined Crusader fortress and to make a note of the details. Once in his office, he searched the internet for its name and found a news story in the English-language version of the Israeli newspaper *Ha'aretz*. A slogan had been painted in Hebrew a month earlier at a place in the Galilee called Beit She'an. The paper's translation was, 'The Testament of Iftikhar is a forgery.'

'Iftikhar – that fits with the letters at Commarque,' he said to Amélie, but her fingers were already flying over the keyboard of her phone.

'Iftikhar ad-Daula, the Muslim governor of Jerusalem in the year 1099 AD when he surrendered the citadel of the city to the First Crusade in return for free passage for himself, his family and his guards,' she said, reading aloud from a website she had found. 'There's some controversy about it, since the Crusaders slaughtered just about everybody else in the city, Arabs, Jews and even Christians. So why would they let him go?'

'Interesting question,' said Bruno. 'But what is this Testament?'

'Iftikhar supposedly wrote some statement as part of the deal to let him and his family go in peace, declaring that Jerusalem was of no religious significance to Islam and therefore he and his troops could abandon it with a clear conscience.'

'I thought the whole point about Jerusalem was that it was sacred to all three religions, to Jews, Christians and Muslims,' said Bruno.

'Me too. But now it seems there's a whole controversy with Islamic scholars claiming that the Jews had nothing to do with Jerusalem and that the place was always inhabited by Arabs called Jebusites or Canaanites and that Solomon's Temple was built elsewhere. Jewish scholars are countering that the Arabs fabricated the claim that Mohammed visited Jerusalem in a dream at the place where the Al-Aqsa Mosque now stands. And this Testament of Iftikhar is supposed to prove it.'

Bruno felt his head spinning. 'What has all this got to do with Commarque?'

'I have no idea, except that it now seems that the dead woman was Israeli. And we know Commarque had a Templar connection. This supposed Testament of Iftikhar, which had long since disappeared, had been in their keeping. The Templars' headquarters were on the Temple Mount, on which now stands the Al-Aqsa Mosque. That's the golden dome you always see on TV news reports about Jerusalem.'

'I think we'd better let J-J sort all this out,' Bruno said, and reached for his phone, which began ringing the moment before he touched it. A familiar voice was demanding, 'Have you heard the news about the Muslims?'

'*Bonjour*, Yacov,' said Bruno. 'No, I haven't. What news?'

Yacov Kaufman was a Paris-based lawyer, grandson of the elderly lady who was paying for the new Scout camp, as well as for a museum of the Périgord Resistance in World War Two and the sanctuary the region had provided for Jewish children. Bruno and Yacov had become friends when Bruno helped trace the family and the farm where Yacov's grandmother, Maya, had been sheltered.

'The Muslim Scouts have backed out, they're withdrawing from the opening ceremony,' Yacov said crossly. 'They won't send any of their Scouts for the opening week. They claim they just found out the camp is being financed by Israeli money.'

'Are the Protestants and Catholics still coming?'

'Yes, but the whole point was to make it a multi-faith camp,' Yacov said.

As they spoke, Bruno quickly scrolled through that day's accumulated emails on his desktop computer. Mostly they contained negative replies from hotels, campsites and *gîte* owners in response to his queries about any accommodation rented in the name of Leah Wolinsky or Leah Ben-Ari. Suddenly he paused, spotting the email from the Jewish Scouts that told him of the Muslim Scouts' decision.

Bruno shook his head in frustration, thinking that only in France did they have four separate Scout Associations, for the Catholic Scouts and the Protestants, for the Jewish Scouts and the Muslims. The formal opening was to be the following weekend, the spring holiday for schools.

'Why not invite some German Scouts instead? It makes for a good symbol of European reconciliation.'

'That's not a bad idea,' said Yacov. 'I'll make some calls. But I also want to know if it's convenient for me to come down this weekend, just so I can reassure Maya that everything is in order.

Then I'll come back to Paris, meet her at the airport when she flies in next week and bring her down for the opening.'

'I'm going to be a bit tied up with a wedding for some friends of mine on Saturday, but you're always welcome, Yacov, and so is your grandma. I can't put you up, I'm afraid. Several of the wedding guests are staying at my place.'

'That's no problem, I don't need babysitting. Who's getting married?'

'I don't know if you've met them: Clothilde Daumier from the museum in Les Eyzies is marrying Horst, the German archaeologist. They've been a couple for years and years but they're finally tying the knot.'

'I don't think I've met them. I'll try not to get in your way. Is Pamela still renting out her gîtes?'

'She is, but she's moved, taken over a nearby riding school. I'll ask if she has a place free, but I think she may be full with wedding guests. If so, I'll book you into a hotel. How many nights?'

Yacov said he'd stay just two nights, Friday and Saturday, offered to buy Bruno and the Mayor lunch on Friday and rang off.

'Who was that?' Amélie asked. 'It sounded rather official, but he has a lovely voice.'

'That was Yacov, a lawyer friend from Paris. You'll like him,' Bruno began. He was about to tell her of the Scouts project but almost immediately the desktop phone rang again.

'*Bonjour*, Bruno. Jack Crimson here. About that daubed slogan you showed me last night. One of my old colleagues rang me back to say he thinks it's connected to similar graffiti painted recently on a castle in Israel.'

'About the Testament of Iftikhar,' said Bruno.

'You know about that? I'm impressed. But it seems there are some tricky political and diplomatic issues attached to all this and I thought I should tip off our old friend the Brigadier that there may be more to this young woman than meets the eye. Unless, that is, you've already done so.'

'No, we've just come across this connection,' said Bruno. 'And it's all thanks to a colleague from the Justice Ministry with a smartphone that she plays like a maestro. She's even come up with a name, or rather two, for our dead woman. She's an Israeli called Leah Ben-Ari and she seems also to be a French woman called Leah Wolinsky. They may be one and the same and she has a Palestinian boyfriend called Husayni. J-J is working on it. If you want to call the Brigadier, go ahead. He'll probably take it more seriously from you.'

The Brigadier was a senior officer in the Interior Ministry. Bruno had come under his orders before, and turned down an offer to join the Brigadier's team in Paris. Jack Crimson and the Brigadier had worked together in the past, were on first-name terms and maintained friendly relations. Whenever both of them got involved in something, Bruno became aware that matters had reached far beyond his pay grade. The Brigadier always observed the courtesies, asking the Mayor of St Denis for Bruno to be temporarily assigned to his staff at the Ministry, but with a subtle threat to trigger Bruno's transfer from reserve status in the French army to active duty.

'Who is the Brigadier?' Amélie asked. Bruno gave a suitably cautious explanation.

'Sounds like intelligence,' she said, grinning at him. 'This is getting to be fun.'

'This is getting to the point where a country policeman like me bows out and lets the big boys take over.'

'That's not what I hear.'

Bruno gave her a stern look. 'What do you mean by that?'

Amélie shrugged. 'I already told you I wanted to follow you around on this job. There are some other intriguing stories told at the Ministry about some of the cases you've been involved in, some rich American you broke out of jail, a shoot-out in a cave, that mysterious business with the young jihadist who made bombs in Afghanistan, the autistic one . . .' She paused. 'Would he be something to do with that friend of yours we met yesterday, Momu?'

He ignored the question. 'Well, this is a straightforward case of identifying a woman who fell to her death and one that is best left in the hands of Commissaire Jalipeau and the Police Nationale. With any luck, our work on this is done.'

'Oh yes?' Amélie's voice was mocking. 'You have a Scout camp being opened next week financed by a wealthy Jewish woman and the Muslim Scouts have decided to boycott it. And at the same time you find an Israeli woman dead while painting something on the wall of your chateau that seems related to an Arab–Israeli dispute over Jerusalem. And you're telling me that all these things aren't linked?'

'I very much hope not. And it's not my chateau.'

'I know it's not your damn chateau, Bruno, but that's not the point,' she snapped at him. Then she sighed loudly and gazed at the ceiling as though willing herself to be calm. 'There must be a connection here. We just have to find it.'

'You may be right, but so far I don't see it,' he said evenly. Privately, Bruno had noted her use of the word 'we'. He accepted that Amélie was a gifted researcher who had saved him hours or even days of work. But she was not a policewoman, and he'd already bent some rules in letting her become so involved in the case.

'May I use your printer?' she asked.

'So long as it's official.'

'It's some material about this Jerusalem controversy and the Testament that I want to look at more carefully.'

She looked at the printer and the cable that linked it to Bruno's desk computer and shook her head. 'The first recommendation in my report will be to get all you municipal policemen up to date with technology. This printer must be ten years old. I'll have to email you the documents and let you print them out.'

To change the subject, he asked how her dinner with the local socialists had gone. She glared at him for a moment and then her face did not exactly relax, but it softened. Bruno had the impression that she was trying to focus on an object that was at the same time very close and yet far away.

'They were sweet and welcoming in a rather formal way but not what I think of as political comrades,' she said slowly, groping for the right words. 'They actually talked of "the workers", here in a town without factories. When I asked them what they did, they were pharmacists, teachers, insurance agents or employees of the *mairie*. None was under forty and most were older. I didn't have the heart to tell them they were classic members of the petite bourgeoisie.'

'I don't think they get many visitors from the national head-quarters, even from its youth wing. How did they react to your idea for a youth section of the party?'

'They said it was a great idea but wanted to know what the youth section was meant to do, supposing they could actually start one. I think they expected me to give them a detailed plan and hold their hands while they got started.'

Bruno nodded. He had not expected anything different. 'Well, let's go and see one of our local youth projects that might interest you, although it's not political. I've got to go check on this Scout camp that has to be ready by the end of this week. You'll need to change your shoes again.'

'You mean the one that you don't think could possibly be linked to this Arab–Israeli business?' she asked him, a mocking tilt to her eyebrow.

'You don't have to come,' he said.

'Yes I do,' she retorted, picking up her bag. 'It's my job.'

12

At the hilltop village of Audrix, Bruno paused to show Amélie the view over the valley before turning off onto the plateau where the springtime green was dazzling. He plunged down what had once been a hidden turning into a deeply rutted country lane flanked by bruised and broken vegetation that testified to the passing of many heavy trucks. He made a mental note to get some gravel laid here to fill the ruts before Yacov's inspection visit. He stopped the car as he came over a small rise. Below them unfolded the hollow containing the old farm and the restored barn, the roofs gleaming with new solar panels. A long stretch of pasture sloped down to the stream and a bathing place below the small waterfall. Beside the stream was a long stretch of flat ground, with a net rigged for volleyball and two goalposts installed to make a football pitch.

Two men were unloading army surplus tents from a truck. Bruno caught the sound of an electric drill coming from inside the farmhouse as he pulled up. The men with the tents stopped to stare as Amélie climbed out of the van, followed by Balzac. She waved at them and Bruno greeted them and went into the farmhouse. He found Arnaud, a local carpenter, fitting cupboards and bookshelves into the alcoves on either side of the fireplace in the room that was designed to be the office. The other room on the ground floor was a large kitchen and dining room, with a new bathroom installed in a lean-to at the rear. Upstairs was a bedroom for the caretaker and his wife and there was another across the landing for visitors.

'I'll be done before I leave this evening,' said Arnaud, putting down the drill and shaking hands with the visitors. 'The caretaker and his wife already moved in, they've just gone to do some shopping. Carlos said he'd come by later to check everything's ready. If you want to take a look around, I'll put some coffee on.'

Bruno went first to the old barn which had been fitted out with tables and benches. A double sink occupied the rear wall with waist-high cupboards topped with work surfaces to one side and a large wood-fired stove and cooking range on the other. A staircase and an upper floor had been installed with more bunk beds, enough for twenty or so people to sleep. Behind it stood a new barn for storage and a separate block for showers, rows of sinks and toilets. A long stretch of fresh-turned earth showed where the array of septic tanks had been buried. With eight Scouts to each of the big bell-shaped tents, the camp could house another hundred Scouts and a dozen or more Scoutmasters. There were stone fire pits for campfires, an old well that still functioned and a large terrace for outdoor eating that had a single basketball net at one end.

Amélie followed Bruno down to the stream and the swimming hole. She dabbled her hand in the waterfall, swiftly snatching it away, saying it was too cold for her. They strolled back, Balzac snuffling alongside them. Bruno pointed out the land that was intended to be turned into a vegetable garden by the first contingent of visiting Scouts, to help feed their successors later in the summer.

'It's idyllic,' said Amélie. 'A pity that the Muslim Scouts aren't coming, but that's their loss. Does the place have to be restricted to the Scout movement? Some of my youth groups in the party would love to have a place like this to visit.'

'I don't know. We'll have to ask Yacov when he comes. But Girl Guides will be coming, too. You saw the double facility in the shower block. I think the terms of the trust that was established to run this place limit it to Scouts. Maya, the woman who's funding all this, reckons the Scouts saved her and her brother's lives in the war.'

'Good for her,' said Amélie. 'I think this place is wonderful, a brilliant idea for a memorial. I just wish there was some way of making this available to all those kids in the high-rise ghettoes around Paris.'

'There is,' said Bruno. 'They simply have to volunteer to join the Scouts.'

'But I never see Scouts in the *banlieues*.'

'Now there's a project for your party's youth group. Don't you think it's better to get kids out in the fresh air of the countryside learning things than sitting in some hall talking politics?'

'Of course, but Scouts are mainly all white, middle-class.'

'Not so. There are thirty million kids in the Scout movement worldwide, and two-thirds of them are in the developing world. When this project got started I thought I'd better find out something more about it. And did you miss what I said about Scouts helping save Jewish kids in the war?'

'No, I got that. And now who's this?' She pointed to a car bumping along the rutted lane.

'That's Alain, the caretaker. He used to be a priest and left the Church to get married. He's been a Scoutmaster in Bergerac and he and his wife liked the idea of living here rent-free.'

'*Bonjour,* Alain. Madame,' Bruno said, and introduced Amélie. 'I gather you moved in already.'

'It's a lovely place, and much better than the cramped apartment we had in Bergerac,' Alain replied. 'We have the chance to make a garden, maybe start a small vineyard on that south-facing slope. And the Scouts will keep us busy once they start coming.'

Alain was a slim, wiry man of about fifty with grey hair and a ready smile. His wife, Anne-Louise, a kind-looking woman with an air of quiet competence, looked to be the same age. Bruno could never see them without thinking of the passion that must have brought them together and taken Alain from his vows in the priesthood. She had been working as a nurse when they met and then volunteered as a cleaner in Alain's church.

'Did you see Doctor Stern at the clinic in St Denis?' Bruno asked Anne-Louise. He'd suggested that Fabiola might find it useful to have a trained nurse available and Anne-Louise might appreciate some extra money in the winter when no Scouts were expected. And it was a bonus for the camp to have someone on hand with medical qualifications.

'Yes, thank you,' she replied, and gave Bruno a warm smile that lit up her eyes and helped explain why Alain had fallen for her. 'I'll be doing regular shifts at the clinic in winter and other times I'll be on call if needed.'

'Have you dealt with large numbers of teenage boys before?' Amélie asked. 'They can be quite a handful.'

'I'm accustomed to it, growing up in a Church orphanage,' she replied. 'Just like you, Bruno.'

'I was in Bergerac. Were you there?'

'No, at Mussidan, the place where all the fuss is.'

'So you'll have talked to Commissaire Jalipeau about the inquiry?'

'No, just to one of his detectives. I told him I never knew of any sexual abuse, but one of the nuns was very cruel. She used to beat us with a bamboo cane.' Anne-Louise raised her right arm and brought it down fast, saying, 'Swoosh.'

'You still get nightmares about it,' said her husband, taking her hand.

'Which nun would that have been?' Bruno asked.

'The one who's making the allegations, the alcoholic. Looking back, I'm sure she was drunk when she beat us. It was the priest, Father Francis, who finally stopped her and got her into a nunnery where they treated her for the drinking. He's the same priest she's making the allegations about. I said all this to the detective and I'm sure he didn't believe the dreadful stories she told about Father Francis. I can't believe this case is still going on.'

Bruno nodded. 'Another priest who knew him said he found the stories hard to believe. But Jalipeau is a good man, a fine policeman, you can count on him. He'll get to the bottom of it all.'

An hour later, Bruno dropped Amélie at her hotel and drove to the riding school, stopping only to pick up some veal for dinner from the Oudinots' farm. At the stables, he noticed Jack Crimson's elderly Jaguar parked by the main house. He greeted Pamela in the office, said he'd join her shortly and then strolled up to see Crimson who was sitting on the floor with his grand-children, reading to them from an English book.

'I'm making sure they don't lose their British culture,' he said as the kids broke away to pet Balzac. 'Do you know Winnie the Pooh?'

'Of course, he's very popular in France. We call him *Winnie l'Oursin*. Did you speak to the Brigadier?'

Crimson nodded. 'He said he'd check it out and asked me to give you his regards. His first question was whether you were involved. You'll be hearing from him, I think.'

'So he's taking it seriously? That's good.'

'He was checking with the French embassy in Israel how serious this business about the Testament of Iftikhar might be. I had to say I'd never heard of it until now, but the camel I talked with thought this argument about Jerusalem had surged beyond the historians into current politics. The Arab League and the Palestinians have put out statements questioning the Jewish origins of the city.'

'It's all a long way from the Périgord,' Bruno replied. 'Why on earth do we have to get involved?'

'First, because it's the Middle East. Second, because it's also the Holy Land. And third, because of the Sykes–Picot Agreement, named after a British and French diplomat who carved up the old Ottoman Empire in 1916. That was the year before Britain issued the Balfour Declaration promising to make Palestine a national homeland for the Jewish people. Between them, for better or worse, Balfour, Sykes and Picot created the map of the modern Middle East. We are now living with the consequences.'

Bruno sighed and headed back to the stables, checking his watch. His guests were coming at seven. He could ride for maybe forty minutes. Miranda was not back with her pony-trekkers and Pamela said she was still busy with paperwork and he should exercise Hector alone. That was no hardship, thought Bruno, as he saddled Hector and took him out through the paddock.

Bruno believed that he did his best thinking on horseback, his conscious mind on the route and the horse but some part of his brain ticking away at whatever bothered him. Right now it was this strange mixture of Templars, Crusaders, Jerusalem in history and Arab–Israeli politics, all focused on an Israeli peace activist and a medieval castle. The pieces did not fit together in a way that made any sense. If the woman had wanted to make a stir with her graffiti, there were far more prominent and better known castles with their own Templar or Crusader connections. There was the hilltop fortress town of Domme, where some of the Templars had been imprisoned and carved crosses on the walls of their dungeon. A message daubed on the town walls would have been seen by many more people and would not have involved a dangerous climb.

And the dead woman had been more than two months pregnant, so she might have known or at least suspected her condition. Would an amateur have embarked on a nighttime climb knowing that? Above all there was the missing partner, the person who took away the rope and the paint and also must have put that horn by her hand to echo the ancient pose of some prehistoric Venus figure. And what was the dead woman's motive? He chided himself for not calling her Leah; she was not just a body in the morgue, but a woman who had been alive, who had conceived a child. She deserved the respect of a name. But if Leah had been seeking publicity for some cause of Arab–Israeli peace, there were many better targets for her spray can.

Bruno knew no more of the intricacies of Arab–Israeli relations than anyone who read the papers and listened to the radio. He had heard of the Peace Now movement and knew it carried little political weight in Israel and that the supposed objective of a two-state solution for Israelis and Palestinians was further off now than it had been when Rabin and Arafat had shaken hands on the White House lawn. But that was about all he did know, except that there were various Palestinian factions but he was far from clear about the difference between Hamas and Hezbollah.

Suddenly he was aware that Hector was shaking his head with impatience. Bruno had been so lost in thought that he'd slowed to a walk and Hector wanted more than that. Bruno loosened the reins and gave Hector's sides a nudge with his heels. His horse almost bounded forward through the trees to the open country ahead, stretching out in that glorious, even stride that horse and rider enjoyed so much. All too soon, the ridge narrowed and a thick hedge squeezed him towards the trees until he was forced to dismount and lead Hector and Balzac back to the riding school.

13

Bruno took the cheese from his fridge and from his freezer removed the stock for the fish soup, which he'd made with the discarded shells and heads of shrimp from an earlier meal. He peeled half a kilo of shallots from his garden and put them in a saucepan with a little butter. He did the same with half a kilo of button mushrooms he'd bought in the market and cut the kilo of veal into cubes. He put the veal into his largest saucepan, covered the meat with water and put it on to boil before peeling a medium-sized onion and pushing into it four cloves. He then jumped into the shower and changed into jeans and a sweater. He fed Balzac, put the frozen fish stock into the microwave to thaw, and paused to consider. He planned fish soup, followed by blanquette de veau with rice, salad with cheese, and pears poached in spiced wine for dessert. They would be four since he'd invited Annette, the young magistrate based in Sarlat, to join them. She and Amélie would have a lot in common and her presence would stop it feeling too much like a working dinner.

He put one bottle of sparkling Bergerac rosé from Chateau Haut Garrigue and another of Pierre Desmartis' white Bergerac sec into the fridge and opened a bottle of Clos Montalbanie, a lighter red from Chateau Tiregand that he thought would go well with the veal. The veal was starting to boil so he turned down the heat, skimmed off the surface and then dropped in a chopped carrot, a rib of celery, the onion with its cloves and one of the bouquets garnis he made every few days. He adjusted the heat to let the meat simmer and then skimmed it again. Then he set the table, put out the champagne flutes, lit his wood stove and turned on the radio to hear how the local station was covering the events at Commarque. A reporter at the site was asking people what they knew about the place and every answer he got was about the Templars and their treasure.

His fish stock had almost defrosted so he cut the cod he'd bought into small cubes. He put two large spoons of duck fat into the bottom of his favourite flameproof casserole and put it on to heat. Then he peeled two potatoes and half a dozen cloves of garlic. He diced the potatoes and crushed the garlic with the back of his knife, mixed them together and tossed them into the casserole. He let that cook on a low heat while he went out to the garden to pick some salad, washed and chopped it and put it to one side while he added the cubes of cod, the fish stock and a tin of tomatoes to the casserole. He poured a large glass from the five-litre box of plain white Bergerac that he kept in the pantry, added it to the fish, stirred and tasted. A touch more salt was needed and he adjusted the heat to a very low simmer.

He checked his watch. Usually he would simmer the meat for as much as two hours to get it really tender, but this was Oudinot's veal, the best in the valley, from milk-fed calves raised with their mothers. The meat would be deliciously tender anyway and his guests would be arriving within the next fifteen minutes. He cleaned up the kitchen, tidied the books and papers in his sitting room and brushed away the ashes from the tiles below his stove. Then he filled his electric kettle with water and set it to boil so it would be ready for the rice and took a pot of double cream from the fridge.

Finally from the freezer he took the vacuum-packed bag with the last of the basil he'd picked the previous autumn. And when he saw Balzac's ears twitch and the dog move to the door, Bruno knew his guests were about to arrive. Balzac always heard the sound of an engine coming up the lane a good half-minute before his master. He opened the door so that Balzac could bound out and give the arrivals his usual noisy welcome. Before he followed Balzac, Bruno added another glass of white wine to the fish soup, tasted it and smiled to himself. It was good.

Sergeant Jules, in uniform, was driving his own car, with Yveline and Amélie in the rear and Annette in the front seat. Bruno shook Jules's hand, welcomed Annette and Yveline and helped Amélie extract herself from Balzac's obvious affections. This time she was wearing a bright yellow dress with a generous turban of some coarse cloth in blue and yellow stripes. Yveline wore black slacks, a cream silk blouse and fitted tweed jacket and Annette was in jeans, a white cotton sweater and a knee-length cardigan in black cashmere. They were three striking women, each in her different way.

'Will you stay for a *p'tit apéro*?' Bruno asked Jules.

'Better not,' Jules replied, with a glance at Yveline, his *commandante*. 'I'm on duty this evening. But give me a call at the station when you're ready and I'll come back to pick them up.'

'It made sense for us all to come together and go back together,' said Yveline. 'Annette is staying at my place tonight rather than driving back to Sarlat.' She handed Bruno a bottle of chilled Monthuys champagne. Annette waved a paper-wrapped bottle at him, saying it was his favourite Chateau Tiregand, and Amélie handed him a small glass jar of what looked like a greenish sauce.

'*Épice*, my mother's recipe,' she said. 'Ivan let me borrow his kitchen to make it. I gave him a jar and this one's for you.'

Once inside, the guests settled in his sitting room with glasses of champagne, Bruno excused himself a moment and went into the kitchen to check on the food. He added some lemon juice to the fish and wondered how to serve some of Amélie's gift. She'd certainly hope that he'd find a way for them all to try it. He opened a can of his own venison pâté. It should go well with Amélie's *épice*.

'I thought we should try it at once,' he said, returning to his guests.

'Not too much, it's pretty spicy until you're used to it,' warned Amélie, casting Bruno a grateful look. He gave her a grin in return, one cook to another as she spoke again. 'This is the heart of Creole cooking.'

It was hot, but not unpleasantly so, spicy rather than burning, and it went well with the venison. Bruno could imagine it working with chicken, but he recalled Amélie saying that rice and beans were a staple in Haiti, a dish of the poor, and the *épice* would add flavour to an otherwise bland but filling meal. Yveline fanned her mouth and asked for a glass of water, pleading that she wasn't accustomed to such fiery food. Annette, by contrast, added even more *épice* to her next slice, saying she had come to enjoy hot peppers when she'd worked for Médicins sans Fron-tières in Madagascar.

'Do you know anybody who works for them in Palestine?' Bruno asked suddenly, with a quick glance at Amélie. 'A friend you know well enough to call them and ask about that dead woman at the chateau? Amélie managed to identify her, an Israeli woman who lives with a Palestinian boyfriend.'

'Yes, a good friend who's a psychologist at the clinic in Hebron,' Annette replied. 'She works mainly with traumatized children. And I know another in east Jerusalem. Why?'

'Could you call them tomorrow and ask if they know anything about Leah Ben-Ari, or maybe Leah Wolinski and her guy, name of Husayni.'

'Saïd al-Husayni, a historian at the university. Sorry, Bruno, I meant to tell you, I heard back from the American woman, Jenny. She gave me his name.'

Annette pulled out her mobile and began typing a text mes-sage. 'Why wait till tomorrow? It's late there now but I should get a reply tomorrow.'

Bruno poured out the rest of the champagne, invited them to move to the table and went back to the kitchen to check the seasoning and toss some chopped parsley onto the fish soup. He opened the white wine and took it to the table, then brought in the tureen.

'If anyone wants to try adding some of Amélie's *épice* to the soup, that might be interesting,' he said, handing round the bread and then pouring the wine.

'I'll wait and try it when I'm close to the end,' said Annette. 'This is really good, Bruno, rich and hearty.'

'It's great,' said Amélie, stirring a spoonful of her sauce into her bowl. 'But since we're here to talk about policing, Yveline, what does a village cop like Bruno mean to you?'

'A lot more than I expected when I came here. A good local policeman is like a living archive of a community, a real resource of local history and knowledge. I'd be a fool to ignore it, which is why Bruno is now invited to my weekly planning meetings. In my future postings I'll do the same – but I might not find another village cop who can cook like this.'

'It's the same for me as a magistrate,' said Annette. She explained that when the *Procureur* assigned her to a case to see whether a prosecution was warranted, she'd learned always to talk first to the municipal policeman in order to understand the background. In juvenile cases the local cop could describe the parents before she went to see them, give her a sense of the local context and degree of family support she might expect.

'I didn't start out like that,' Annette added. 'In fact, I was very suspicious of Bruno as a hunter and rugby player. I thought of him as an old-fashioned male chauvinist, a rather sinister figure in a local green-hating mafia that would block and frustrate me at every turn.'

'It was hard for us locals to work out why they'd send a vegetarian feminist to be a magistrate in the Périgord,' said Bruno, smiling. 'That was before we learned you were a fearsome rally driver. Now I'm going to try this with the *épice*.' He stirred in some of the green sauce with the last spoonfuls of soup in his bowl and tasted the result.

'Not bad,' he said. 'But I prefer it without, since I don't think this would work with *chabrol*.'

'What's that?' asked Amélie.

'An old local tradition. Just watch,' he said. He served the remainder of the soup, then he ate the last pieces of fish until only liquid remained in his bowl and then added half a glass of red wine and stirred it together. Once this was done he put down the spoon, picked up the bowl with both hands, brought it to his lips and drank. He smacked his lips as he put it down and watched with satisfaction as Annette and Yveline followed suit.

Hesitantly, and with a doubtful glance at Bruno, Amélie did the same. 'Interesting,' she said, putting down the bowl. 'It's good, might be better if the wine was heated. What's the story about this *chabrol*?'

'There are different explanations,' said Bruno. 'The one I like says it comes from the English soldiers who were here in the Hundred Years War. There wasn't much meat around in winter when they were on garrison duty in the castles, so their staple food was pickled herrings, brought from the coast in barrels. The English term for a young herring is "shad" and their word for soup is "broth". Say them together a few times, and you'll see how the French could turn shad-broth into *chabrol*. And given the quality of the local wine the English could afford, it probably improved the wine as well as the herring.'

He gathered up the bowls and went to the kitchen, stacking them in the sink and turning on the hot water. Then he tasted the veal and nodded; it was time to make the blanquette. He drained the sauce from the meat over a measuring cup and put the meat aside, removing the bouquet garni and the carrot and celery. He poured the sauce into a separate large saucepan and left it over a low flame. He put the rice into a separate saucepan with a tablespoon of duck fat, stirring until all the grains were coated and then, added boiling water from his kettle, covered it and left the rice to cook.

Then he began to make his roux, using the saucepan in which the veal had cooked. He put three thick slices of butter into the pan and brought over his glass jar of plain flour. When the butter had melted, foamed and subsided, he reduced the heat a little and began sprinkling flour into it, stirring steadily with a whisk. Slowly, making sure the flour was fully absorbed, he added four tablespoons and then began to pour in the juice from the veal, continuing to whisk to ensure it was fully blended. He turned up the heat and brought it to a simmer, still stirring until it began to thicken. Then he added the veal, the shallots, the mushrooms and the pot of cream, stirring steadily until it returned to the boil. He turned the heat back down to a simmer, checked the rice, adding half a cup more water, piled the dirty dishes into the sink and opened the bottle of red wine.

Quickly, he peeled the fat pears he had bought, put them into a saucepan and poured in red wine until they were just covered. He added two cloves, some cinnamon and some grated nutmeg. Finally, he poured in half a glass of his own *vin de noix*, and left it simmering.

'Five minutes,' he said, returning to the table with the red wine and a bottle of mineral water. He shared out the last of the white wine and began to follow the conversation. It was clear that they had been talking about J-J's paedophilia investigation.

'But you only ever have the testimony of the victims to go on,' Amélie was insisting. 'The children hardly ever complain to other adults at the time so there's no chance of physical evidence or DNA. That thirty years have passed since the kids were molested is typical. And when you get three kids saying the same thing about the same abusers, that to me is corroboration.'

'But that's part of the problem,' said Yveline. 'When you get into detail, the kids are not saying the same thing.'

'The real problem is this psychologist and her use of so-called recovered memories,' said Annette. Both in Britain and in the USA, she noted, the medical authorities had treated such memories with great scepticism and warned against their being used as evidence without strong corroboration.

'There are several cases where these memories are now thought to have been suggested to the patient by the psychologist involved, often through the use of hypnosis. In this case that J-J is dealing with, hypnosis was used on all three,' Annette went on. 'As a magistrate, this is a case I would not want to take to court. The evidence is just too flimsy.'

Bruno excused himself to bring in the blanquette de veau and the rice, and was not surprised to find they were still arguing about the case when he returned.

'You can't seriously argue that the reputations of these adults are as important as the lives of the kids that were destroyed?' Amélie was saying fiercely. 'What about their rights?'

'*Mon Dieu*, this is rich. I'm going to gain at least a kilo from this meal,' Yveline interjected. Bruno threw her a grateful glance for changing the subject.

'This is a Pécharmant from one of my favourite vineyards,' said Bruno, pouring out the red. 'But it's light enough to go well with the veal. Still, if anyone would prefer to stay with white wine, I have some in the fridge.'

'Let me pay you a compliment, Bruno,' said Amélie. 'I would not want to add any *épice* to this dish. It's perfect just as it is. But I suspect Yveline is right about the extra kilos we'll be putting on.'

He offered second helpings of the veal, and despite her joke about gaining weight, Yveline was the first to proffer her plate. The others followed.

'There may be one more treat in store for us all this evening,' Bruno said, bringing in the dessert, adding a scoop of vanilla ice cream and a splash of cognac to his poached pears. 'We have a star among us, a singer who has recorded albums, and the moment I heard her I knew she was extraordinary.' He turned to smile at Amélie. 'I'm hoping that you'll grace our dinner table with a song. I promise not to join in.'

Annette clapped her hands and Yveline said, 'Now we know you're a singer we have to hear you – anything you like.'

Amélie beamed at them and remained seated. 'Well, now that I've got back into the habit since I've been driving around with Bruno, maybe you'd like a little Cole Porter, a favourite of mine that I learned off by heart.'

Tapping her finger gently on the table to keep time, she launched into 'Just One of Those Things', a song of a love affair that flared suddenly and magnificently but then died away as quickly, that then merged into 'Every Time We Say Goodbye'.

It was a song that hit Bruno like a fist, a lament of lovers parting that he had listened to again and again after Isabelle had left him. He felt tears prick his eyes. It was a song she had loved and she had written down the English words for him. He could never play it without wondering if Isabelle was alone in Paris, playing the same song and feeling the same regrets. Finally, sick of the melancholy it brought, he had put away the disc she had left him.

14

The next morning Bruno drove with Balzac to the stables to exercise his horse and then joined Amélie at Fauquet's café where she was enjoying her morning croissant. She raised her eyebrows at his dress, a tracksuit and running shoes rather than uniform, before thanking him for dinner. He accepted her offer of coffee and Balzac sat expectantly at her feet until she slipped him a corner of croissant and then a crust of baguette.

'Off duty today?' she asked.

'Depends what you mean by duty. Teaching the kids to play tennis is not part of my job, but I think it's good for them and I know it's good for my work.'

'How come?'

'They grow up knowing me as something other than a policeman. It helps once they're old enough to get into mischief that could turn into something worse.'

She pulled out her phone and began tapping in a note to herself. 'Sounds like you're a social worker as much as a cop. Anything else? Football or basketball?'

'Rugby in the autumn and winter, tennis in spring and summer, for boys and girls alike. Do you play any sports?'

She shook her head, which today was wrapped in a billowing yellow turban. She was wearing jeans with a yellow polo shirt, her leather jacket draped around her shoulders.

'I liked to play soccer but my brothers always wanted me to be in goal so I took up swimming. But you don't have a gym anywhere nearer than Bergerac.'

'There's a yoga and Pilates club that meets at the *collège*. Yveline's a member, so if you're interested you could ask her. I've done some work today already. Annette forwarded me the email she got from her friend in Hebron. Leah Wolinksy did some volunteer work for charities, but she was a historian and archaeologist, so not many useful skills. Mainly she was known as a critic of Israel's behaviour on the West Bank, got arrested a couple of times at demos. Her boyfriend is apolitical, but from a prominent family, landowners and politicians. I forwarded it to J-J.'

He checked his watch. 'The kids will be there by nine so we'd better go.'

The town tennis club boasted three open courts and one covered, all flanked by a modern clubhouse with a bar, changing rooms and a well-appointed kitchen, since it was a tradition that no communal activity could take place in St Denis without there being food and wine involved. The main room was filled with long tables which could seat forty for lunches and dinners during the annual club tournament. The kitchen was in use most days, when regular quartets of doubles players would end their session by cooking their own lunch. This morning a group of seven-year-olds was getting changed and several mothers sat on the courtside benches to watch them play.

Bruno had learned from experience that in each class, three or four children shone as natural tennis players, another dozen would show decent hand–eye coordination and the remainder would need a lot of practice. He put one of the natural players in each of the three open courts with a basket of balls and the others lined up in turn to hit balls back and forth until one went into the net and another player took their place. Eight of the better youngsters then went off to the covered court to play four-a-side under the critical gaze of Montsouris, a train driver who had taken advantage of the generous pension plan for his profession to retire at the age of fifty.

The only communist on the town council, Montsouris spent his time hunting, fishing and helping the various sports clubs, an endless round of activity that kept him from spending too much time with his relentlessly radical wife, who found his politics far too tame for her own convictions. He was also the master of the tennis club barbecue in summer. Bruno liked him and led Amélie across to the covered court where he introduced her to Montsouris and left them arguing happily about politics.

'Ça va, Bruno?' one of the mothers called from a bench as he passed. 'Who's the new girlfriend?'

He stopped to greet Giselle and her younger sister, Amandine, who had both been in his tennis classes only a few years earlier, and explained that Amélie was a colleague from Paris. Giselle was married to a local builder, had one child in the tennis class, two more in nursery school and another grinning toothlessly at Bruno from the buggy beside the bench. Amandine's official job was to spend four nights a week as a carer for old people in their homes, for which she earned the minimum wage, but she also worked unofficially as a cleaner, which allowed her to run a small car.

'That dead woman in the paper, have you found out who she is yet?' Amandine asked.

'No, have you seen her before?"

'Not sure. There was someone like her, about a week ago, came into one of the *gîtes* I was cleaning on changeover day. She was there early. I couldn't swear it was her, but there was something about the hair. Was she tanned, this woman, as if she was just back from a holiday in the sun?'

'Yes, she was, unusually so for this time of year. Which *gîte* was this?'

'Over towards Sarlat, just after Meyrals on that back road. It's called La Bergerie but I've never seen any sheep around there. You take the second left after that new art gallery and it's about two kilometres up there on the right. The last five hundred metres is a dirt road.'

'Who owns it?'

'A guy in Sarlat, that union guy who's in the papers. I forget his name.'

'Vaugier, is that the one?'

'Yes. That's him. Funny that he's always going on about the law on Sunday opening, but he pays me strictly cash. No receipts either.'

Bruno made a mental note to check whether Vaugier had registered his *gîte* with the local *mairie*. 'This woman, was there anything special about her? An accent, maybe?'

'She only spoke a few words, said hello and excused herself

and asked what time she should come back, but she sounded Parisian to me. Have you got any better photos of her than the one in the paper?'

Bruno took out his phone and showed Amandine the pictures he'd taken, along with the visa photo Amélie had sent him.

'It could be her. I couldn't swear to it but there's definitely a strong likeness.'

Bruno took from her a note of Vaugier's number and went off to supervise the rest of the tennis lesson until the next class arrived. This time it was the nine-year-olds, most of them by now able to make some sort of forehand and backhand drive and to place most of their serves into the right court. A new collection of mothers took their places on the benches.

When the tennis ended at noon, Bruno heated the soup he'd brought and Montsouris set out his own contribution, a big baguette with pâté and cheese. Amélie had learned from Montsouris that she could take red wine from the ten-litre box of cuvée Cyrano behind the bar, leaving a euro for each glass in the old biscuit tin that served as a cash box.

'Do you know this union guy Vaugier?' Bruno asked Montsouris as they began to eat.

'I've met him a couple of times, but can't say I know him. He's not what you'd call one of the boys, doesn't follow rugby or go hunting. Comes from the north, Lille or somewhere. He was in the Socialist Party but he moved to that new left-wing breakaway, the Parti de Gauche. He married a girl from Périgueux and moved down here when she inherited her parents' property. He's an ambitious guy, out to make a name for himself. Why do you ask?'

Bruno explained the court case in Sarlat, and Montsouris nodded, adding that his cousin's son worked in one of Hugues' bakeries, liked the job and thought Hugues was a good employer. The three of them made coffee and washed up the dishes together. Bruno took his uniform from his van, changed out of his tracksuit and set off with Amélie for Vaugier's *gîte*. There was no singing on this ride; the mood was too serious.

The place was deserted, with no car to be seen, and the key had been left in the door. Bruno put on a pair of evidence gloves, gave another pair to Amélie and let himself in. The place looked immaculate, as if it had been thoroughly cleaned. The pots and dishes had been washed and were stacked in the drainer. The refrigerator had been unplugged, the door open to reveal that it was empty and gleaming. There was no washing machine, but bedding for several people had been washed, probably in a launderette, and piled onto the dining table in the big room. A bucket and mop stood in the corner and there was a lingering scent of disinfectant.

'Whoever was here has made a very thorough job of cleaning up,' said Amélie. 'Not the way most tourists leave a holiday let.'

'It could be a way to get rid of fingerprints and DNA.' Bruno began taking photos with his phone, including a close-up of the cooking stove, fed by a bottle of calor gas.

'Why are you taking a photo of that?' she asked.

'It's an old dodge to avoid paying the *taxe d'habitation*,' he replied. 'It's easily removed, and if there's no working stove, you can say the place is not fit for residence and avoid the tax. But now we've got a date-stamped photo to say the place is liable for tax, and it will be interesting to see if he's registered it as a rental property.'

The barn was also left unlocked with the key in the door and newly laundered bedding piled onto each bed. The bathroom had been thoroughly cleaned, taps and porcelain shining. The waste bins in each kitchen had been emptied and so had the dustbins outside, all of them smelling of bleach. Bruno recalled seeing back at the road junction a collection of big bins where the locals were supposed to leave their rubbish in yellow sacks provided by the local council. They might not have been cleared yet.

Bruno called J-J to explain what he'd found. He was about to suggest a forensic team might find some trace of the inhabitants that had been overlooked in the cleaning, which was itself suspicious, when J-J interrupted.

'You'd better stay there until I arrive,' he said. 'I just had the Brigadier on. The Israelis are getting excited. Apparently this woman was high up on their watch list, Jewish but a pro-Palestinian militant, lives with an Israeli Arab who's also on their list. They've asked for her DNA and any information we have on her movements.'

'When you say "they", do you mean their embassy?' Bruno asked.

'Not any more. It began with the embassy, but now it's Israel direct. I'll let the Brigadier know about this *gîte* you've found and then come join you. Can you find out who owns this place? We'd better call them in.'

Bruno supplied Vaugier's name and number, suggesting they tell Vaugier only that there had been an anonymous tip-off of a sighting of the dead woman. 'It looks like this guy's main concern is to stay below the radar of the tax people,' he added. 'There's no sign of any internet connection round here, but there's a good mobile phone signal. You might want to get the phone records from the local tower.'

By the time J-J and his forensics team arrived, Bruno had established from the *mairie* at Meyrals that the owner of the house neither paid *taxe d'habitation* nor had registered it as a holiday let. He'd also called Amandine, who confirmed that she had regularly cleaned the place between tenants the previous summer. And he found two clear sets of what looked like recent tyre tracks on a patch of bare ground beside the pigeon tower.

J-J arrived in convoy, his own car followed by the forensics van which was in turn followed by a gendarmerie van from which a worried-looking Vaugier descended. The rear of the parade was brought up by a private car that contained the Mayor of Meyrals and his Town Treasurer.

Once the forensic crew had booted up and put on their 'snowman' paper overalls, J-J took Vaugier and Bruno aside.

'Don't bother lying, you're in enough trouble already,' he told Vaugier. 'Who's been renting this place most recently?'

'A woman, middle-aged, sounded like a Parisian,' Vaugier replied at once. 'She answered the ad I have on *Le Bon Coin*, the website. I met her here at the *gîte* just over a week ago. She rented it for two weeks and paid cash, five hundred euros in fifties. She was driving a silver Peugeot. I took the number, just a precaution.'

He took a notebook from his pocket and read out the number, adding that the *département* number was six zero. That signified the Oise, but to Bruno and J-J that meant almost certainly that the car had been rented, since the Oise was the cheapest *département* for registration and most of the hire companies had a base there. J-J called over one of his detectives, handed him the registration number and asked him to track it down.

'Not a bad start, but you're lying about the money,' said J-J, turning back to Vaugier. 'This is a four-bedroom place. Even out of season you wouldn't let this out for two fifty a week and you look to me like the kind of suspicious little bastard who'd want some security deposit against damages. So let's start again, shall we?'

'She gave me five hundred for the rental and then a deposit of five hundred, to be returned if she left early.'

'Did she come here alone?'

'Yes, alone in the silver Peugeot.'

'And you never dropped by to see how she was doing?'

Vaugier shook his head. 'Never.'

'Did she give you a name?'

'Marie Dubois. That's how she signed the letting agreement.'

J-J snorted, and Bruno could not repress a smile. That was so much the kind of common name an adulterous couple might use that it had become a cliché of TV comedies.

'It's not funny,' Vaugier protested. 'She even showed me an ID card with that name on it, and her photo.'

Vaugier handed J-J an envelope containing a single-page letting contract with an indecipherable signature at the bottom, the name hand-printed below in neat capital letters, along with an address on Avenue Leclerc in Paris, the Montparnasse district. Bruno took a note of the address and called the security number for France Télécom. He was not surprised to learn that the address did not exist.

'*Chef*,' called out the detective who had been checking the hire cars. 'It's a Europcar, a five-seater Peugeot Traveller rented at Gare de l'Est in Paris by a woman with the name of Marie Dubois. They took a photocopy of her licence and ID card. She paid with a BNP-Paribas credit card in the same name. I've got the account number and I'll check it out. The ID card was also issued in Paris, so I'll check on that, too.'

J-J and Bruno exchanged glances. Forgeries of ID cards and driving licences were not difficult to obtain, but indicated some familiarity with the criminal underworld, or links to serious intelligence networks. Establishing a fake bank account and credit card was rather more difficult in these days of routine identity checks against money-laundering.

'Did you see this woman again after that one time when she paid you?' J-J asked Vaugier.

'No, never.'

'Did you ever hear from her, by phone or email or note?'

'Again, no, I did not have contact with her by any method. The only time I heard from her was when she called about the ad on the website and then when she paid me.' He pulled out his phone and scrolled back through a week or so of calls to a number he read out. It began with 06, a mobile phone.

Bruno called France Télécom security again, gave the new phone number and the reply came quickly. It was a pay-as-you-go phone bought at a store at the Gare de l'Est in Paris, along with a prepaid phone card for forty euros. And under the new regulations requiring all such phones to be registered, it was one of two such phones that had been bought by one Marie Dubois, and a photocopy of her ID card was on file.

'Did you ever see anyone else here?' J-J went on. 'Maybe you drove past it once or twice, just to keep an eye on the place?'

'No, I never came by,' Vaugier insisted.

'So you were not at all concerned about your property?'

'It's not my property. It belongs to my wife.'

'Did she come by, just checking that all was well?'

'Not to my knowledge.'

'Right,' said J-J. 'You stay here and have a nice friendly chat with the Mayor and the Treasurer about your tax status until my forensic experts have checked the buildings and then we'll walk you round and you can tell me if anything is missing or out of place. Then we'll take you to my headquarters in Périgueux where you can look through a lot of photographs of suspected terrorists.'

'Terrorists?' Vaugier's voice went so high it was almost a shriek.

'Didn't I tell you?' J-J asked. 'It must have slipped my mind. We're holding you under the emergency regulations on suspicion of aiding terrorists. You must be aware of your duty to register tenants of your property at the *mairie*. You'll have some explaining to do about your taxes, and since this property is in your wife's name, we'll have to bring her in as well. What's her name and where do I find her?'

'Marie-France. At her clinic in Périgueux, she's a psychologist, uses her maiden name, Duteiller.'

J-J's eyebrows rose and Bruno's head snapped round as he heard the name. Marie-France Duteiller was the psychologist behind the allegations of paedophilia at the Mussidan Church orphanage, and the charge that J-J was dragging his feet in the inquiry.

'So that's your wife?' J-J said, a slow smile spreading over his face. 'That's interesting. I've had the pleasure of meeting her in another context.'

15

Vaugier had been driven away with J-J, and Bruno was just apologizing to Amélie for abandoning her when his phone rang. The special green light was glowing which meant that it was someone on the Brigadier's secure circuit.

'Bruno,' came the familiar voice. 'You seem to attract this sort of trouble.'

'Yes, sir,' Bruno replied, the safe and non-committal reply that all soldiers learn within weeks of joining an army.

'Do you know the difference between Mossad and Shin Bet?'

'No, sir.' That was not wholly accurate. He knew that Mossad was Israel's international intelligence service and Shin Bet dealt with domestic security, but that was all he recalled so a confession of ignorance seemed in order.

'We've got them both on our necks thanks to your chateau-climbing woman. Which means I have our Interior Ministry and our Foreign Ministry and the Élysée all pressing me for information. Any developments?'

Bruno explained about Leah Wolinsky being seen at the *gîte*, the van hired at the station in Paris, the phones and the false ID and driving licence. J-J's forensics team was still at work, trying to work out exactly how many people had been staying at the *gîte*.

'I've faxed the usual letter to your mayor so you'll be coming under my orders again, Bruno. What are your plans?'

'I'm going to start by searching the nearest rubbish depository. The bins here are empty so they must have dumped the contents. Then I was going to visit the launderettes in the area to see if I can find who washed all the bedding.'

'Good man. Let me know if you need more manpower and I'll get some gendarmes assigned to you.'

'If they could handle the rubbish, sir, I'll do the launderettes. They may need to liaise with J-J's forensics team.'

'Very well. I'll take care of that. Do you think this woman's associates are still in your area?'

'Hard to say, sir,' Bruno replied. He was thinking that forged ID papers seemed extreme for simply daubing some graffiti on a chateau wall. 'I think it would be safer to assume that whatever mission they came here to carry out might not yet be complete. The most obvious security concern will be the opening of Lascaux IV, but that's not expected until much later in the year.'

'Quite. It could have been a reconnaissance mission, but then why draw attention to themselves with this graffiti? When you can, draw me a timeline for this woman – when she first booked this *gîte*, when she hired the car, when she died and so on . . . whatever else you can scrape up. The Israelis have yet to tell me much about her. We don't even know when she left their country or who she was travelling with. You say there are four bedrooms at this *gîte*?'

'Yes, sir. They're all double bedrooms, but three of the beds only had one pillowcase, which suggests one couple and three singles. The car she hired was a five-seater and J-J already has it on the priority watch list. Forensics should be able to tell us more, but so far we have no idea who the others might be, although we do have the name of her Palestinian boyfriend, Husayni. Did you know she was pregnant?'

'Yes, J-J made sure I was aware of that detail, something that the Israelis did not know so we were able to surprise them. That name Husayni could be useful. Anything else about her or her companions you can find out, alert me at once.'

The Brigadier hung up in his usual brusque way, and Amélie looked up from the mobile phone to which she seemed umbilically attached.

'I'm going to need your printer again,' she said. 'I've found more material about this Wolinsky woman, stuff she wrote about the Palestinian issue, but mainly her historical work. She got her master's at Nice in international studies and a doctorate from the Sorbonne on Islamic settlements in eighth-century France. I've downloaded a copy. She was fluent in Arabic.'

'So she was a historian?'

'She wanted to be, but she had trouble getting a job in Israel. My friend from the Geneva peace conference said she was very bitter about it, claimed she was blacklisted because of her politics and could only make a living by working as an archaeologist. And Jenny, the American friend of Leah, has promised to send me some article Leah was writing.'

Bruno dropped Amélie at the *mairie* and told the Mayor's secretary that she would be using his office printer, and then began telephoning the region's launderettes, asking about people bringing in a large amount of towels and bedding on Monday. After calling the ones listed in the phone directory in Les Eyzies,

Le Bugue and Sarlat, he found a place in St Cyprien where the attendant recalled that a middle-aged Arab speaking what he called 'educated French' had taken over four big washing machines on Monday morning. A second man, also looking to be Arab, had helped him carry in the load. And yes, came the answer to Bruno's query, the launderette was open late so they'd had a security camera installed.

He drove there at once, calling J-J on the way, collected the tape and drove it directly to Périgueux. Within the hour, recognizable images of both men had been copied, digitalized and sent on to the Brigadier, who in turn forwarded them to the Israelis. But first, the Brigadier's team began running the images, along with Leah Wolinsky's photo, through the facial-recognition program in the surveillance tapes that had been collected from the Gare de l'Est. Since the first terrorist attacks in Paris, a crash programme had started installing surveillance cameras in public buildings, sensitive areas and transport hubs around France.

By the time Bruno and Amélie returned to his office in St Denis, Leah's arrival at the Paris station had been spotted on the tapes as she came up the stairs from the Métro. She had then spent an hour alone with a book at a café in the station until she was joined by the older man from the launderette tapes who arrived on a train from Cologne. Her greeting was affectionate and they held hands as they went to a different café in the big square outside the station where they were later joined by the second man from the launderette. He was much younger, and had arrived on another German train, this time from Frankfurt. Two more young men in hoodies then joined them.

Unknown to Bruno, a vast machine of international cooperation was then triggered into action as the images and travel dates of the targeted individuals were launched into a system of global databases that contained in total close to a million names. Many of them had no more connection to terrorism than a link through family, school or places of study, or through travel records that had been deemed interesting by the algorithms that had been programmed to track specific routes and patterns. The databases included Palestinians, Syrians, Iraqis, Kurds, Turks, Uighurs, Moroccans, Algerians, Colombians, Chechens, Afghans, Pakistanis, Irishmen, Sikhs, Bangladeshis, Indonesians, and now elderly Japanese, Germans and Italians from the various Red Army groups of the 1970s. The most recent additions to these expanding lists were an ever-increasing proportion of British, French, German and American citizens of Islamic origin.

The Brigadier first made contact with his counterparts in Germany's BND, the Bundesnachrichtendienst, and asked them to track the movements of the men Leah Wolinsky had met and any associates they may have encountered. As was routine, the photos were then forwarded by the Brigadier's staff to a series of organizations, beginning with the French joint anti-terrorism centre, and then to Europol, to the European Union's Intelligence Analysis Centre and to the office of the EU anti-terrorism coordinator in Brussels. In addition they were sent to the British National Counter-Terrorism Security Office, with whom the French worked closely, to the Global Counter-Terrorism Forum and to the National Counter-Terrorism Centre in the US. They also went to the Shin Bet liaison officer at the Israeli embassy in Paris.

There was too much data for any individual service to handle. The three thousand officers of Britain's MI5 and the thirty-five thousand staff of the FBI, let alone the handful of officials at the EU's various coordination centres, could not begin to trawl through the hundreds of thousands of data points that the computers logged each hour. Instead, the task was left to the algorithms to narrow down the mass to the significant, and from the significant to the seriously interesting. And at that point, a handful of extraordinary individuals took over.

One was a legendary woman in Paris, a veteran of the old Renseignements Généraux police intelligence service, who had a unique knack of recognizing a face from the shape of an ear and a hint of jawline. In Tel Aviv, an elderly Jewish man who had been born in Poland and taken to Israel from a Cyprus refugee camp while a babe in arms had a photographic memory for Arabs with terrorist connections. In London, a Chinese woman, formerly in the criminal intelligence section of the Hong Kong police, could even identify people from gestures and the way they walked. There were two brothers in Pullach in Germany, former members of the East German Stasi, who had an uncanny ability in facial and pattern recognition that allowed them to make connections between suspects. After years of coordination and meetings at conferences on counter-terrorism, experts like these had developed their own informal networks to communicate with one another.

It was the elderly Israeli who identified the older man who had met Leah at the Gare de l'Est station as Saïd al-Husayni, a member of an influential and well-established Jerusalem family who had studied in Spain and was part of the Islamic history faculty at Bir Zeit University just outside Ramallah on the West Bank. The university, which had been closed by the Israeli occupying authorities for four years before the signing of the Oslo Accords, was closely watched by the Israelis. They had no record of Husayni having any political or radical links, except that for the previous year, he and Leah had been living together in Ramallah. But Leah was on their watch list as a militant member of the Peace Now movement.

Yet despite all the computer algorithms and the surveillance powers of modern states, the real breakthrough came from Bruno's office in the St Denis *mairie*. Working on her own smart-phone, Amélie explained that she couldn't find anything in the usual databases about Marie Dubois using the date of birth on her ID card.

'What about health records, pharmacies?' Bruno asked when he returned from delivering the surveillance tape. 'If she's French, she should at least have a *carte vitale*.' Like every French citizen, he carried the small green card in his pocket that took care of most medical bills.

'I'll try it, but if she doesn't have an ID card . . .' Amélie sighed but began working her phone. After a few minutes she looked up.

'There's something interesting about this Marie Dubois woman. She's supposed to be in a psychiatric hospital in Paris, the Pitié-Salpêtrière.'

She had tried the Health Ministry database which was still under construction. But since Marie had been included in a Ministry survey into the costs and causes of long-term residential care, her name and details were on file. She had been a patient at the hospital, one of the largest in Europe, for the previous six years.

'And two years ago our own Leah Wolinksy was briefly a patient in the same hospital, under the same specialist, diagnosed with severe depression when she was finishing her doctorate,' Amélie added. 'Do you think she could somehow have stolen Marie's ID card? Maybe she claimed it had been lost and applied for a new one in Marie's name?'

Bruno called the Brigadier at once to pass on the information and then sat back to read the printouts Amélie had collated from her research into Leah's academic work. Her thesis was on the Arab occupation of southern France in the eighth century, after the Muslim invasion of Spain in AD 711. Within five years, the Visigoth kingdom of Spain had been pushed back to the Pyrenees and the Arab armies had then poured through the mountains to conquer the province of southern Gaul known as Septimania. Bruno sat up in surprise when he learned that for the next forty years they retained control of much of southern France from their base at the old Roman city of Narbonne.

'I had no idea they were in France for so long,' Bruno murmured, almost to himself.

'Nor did I,' said Amélie. 'Did you get to the bit about the Arabic words that stayed in the language? I never knew that our *chemise* came from their *qamisa*. Nor that the town of Le Bugue came from the Arabic *al-buca*. Apparently it means station, or military post.'

Bruno was skimming through the index, and then recalled that someone had once told him that in any academic publication it was important to read the acknowledgements. Leah

Wolinsky had mentioned 'two scholars to whom I am indebted for their support and their comments on an early draft of this thesis: the historian of al-Andaluz, Saïd al-Husayni, and the French medievalist Auguste Dumesnil'.

Dumesnil was the man who followed the Benedictine rule whom Bruno had met with Horst and who lived in nearby Sarlat. Bruno tried the number he found in the phone directory, reminded Dumesnil of their acquaintance and asked if it would be convenient to call round, to confirm the identity of a woman recently dead who was thought to be his former pupil, Leah Wolinksy.

'Leah, dead?' came the startled reply. 'But I saw her just last week and she looked in excellent health. And she wasn't my pupil, not in any formal sense.'

'What day was that?' Bruno asked.

'Let me see, Friday afternoon, a time when I had no classes. She came with Saïd Husayni, whom I was delighted to meet, although I only knew his work on the Moorish period in Spain, and of course his brilliant treatise on Avicenna. He spoke excellent French. But what happened to Leah? Was it some kind of accident?'

'She fell to her death from the wall of Commarque.'

'What? But when she came we talked of Commarque and of my hopes for the new excavations. And of course about this latest nonsense about Iftikhar's famous Testament. Leah was quite worked up about that and I must say I find it very hard to believe that it really exists. But are you sure this woman is Leah? You said the body was thought to be her. *Mon Dieu*, Commarque – I was just there, when I met you.'

'I know, I should have shown you the photo of the body then,' said Bruno. 'It was my mistake, I'm sorry. I should also have taken you beyond the chateau so you could see the letters we think Leah was painting on the wall when she fell. They were I-F-T-I which could be Iftikhar and I need to pick your brains about that. At the time I had no idea you knew her, not until I read the reference to you in her thesis. Since you are the only person in this area who knew her and might formally identify the body, perhaps I could come and show you the photo and then take you to the morgue in Bergerac?'

After a long moment of shocked silence, Dumesnil agreed to see him that evening at seven, when his choir practice should have finished. He was teaching the cathedral choir to sing Gregorian chant. Bruno ended the call and immediately phoned J-J, to say that he should be able to make a definitive identification of Leah from someone who had known her. Then Bruno turned to Amélie.

'It's after the workday ends, but if you're interested in this medieval scholar who knew Leah, I'm going to see him in Sarlat at seven,' he said. 'You remember, we met him at Commarque. It seems that his expertise does not stop at the Templars. He also teaches Gregorian chant.'

Amélie stared at him with an odd expression. He couldn't tell whether it was confusion or surprise.

'Gregorian chant? In Sarlat?' She paused, looking at him solemnly. 'Yes, I'll certainly come. Meanwhile, I have a phone number for Leah's American friend. It turns out that she's another historian and she's currently in Paris, doing some research at the National Archives. She's writing a book about Paris during the war.'

Bruno called and found Jenny Shindler having a sandwich lunch in a park just off the rue des Francs-Bourgeois. Her initital surprise at his call was complicated by the need to finish chewing. He explained in English that he was following up on the death of her friend Leah.

'I saw it on social media,' she replied in good French. 'Some kind of climbing accident at a medieval chateau, which doesn't sound like Leah. Why call me? We weren't that close and we parted on bad terms.'

'Her death looks suspicious. Certainly she was climbing with somebody who left her dead and took away the paint can and climbing rope,' he replied. 'I was hoping you might know something of her travelling companions.'

'I didn't even know she was in France. But she'd been living for some time with an Arab professor, Saïd Husayni, and I know they were hoping to have kids. I can't think who else she might have been with. Maybe someone from his family. Where was the chateau where she died?'

Bruno explained the location of Commarque and its Crusading and Templar connection, and the slogan she had apparently been daubing.

'Oh no,' the American girl exclaimed. 'Don't tell me she was still on that crazy trail. That's what we argued about just a few weeks ago. She wanted me to translate an article she'd written and get it into the American press, or at least circulated on social media, about the Testament of Iftikhar and Jerusalem. I told her it was just a distraction from the real issues of today. She sent me a very angry reply.'

'Do you still have the article she sent you?' Bruno asked, trying to keep the excitement out of his voice.

'I never got it. She sent me a letter and I skimmed it and told her to forget it. I wasn't interested and I doubt anyone else in the Peace Now movement would give a damn. We're focused on what's going down today, not what happened a thousand years ago. I should still have the letter in my emails.'

'Could you possibly forward it to me?' He gave her his email address at the *mairie*.

'The least I can do, I guess. We got on pretty well until this Jerusalem business blew up. I'll just boot up and launch the hotspot connection.'

Bruno heard the sound of laptop keys being tapped and then her voice, 'Coming through now.'

'Would you have any photos of Leah you could send, or of her friend Husayni?'

'Leah and me, yes, from when she visited me in the States, but that's all. I'll send them. You might find more on her Facebook page, she used that a lot. Do you really think her fall was no accident?'

'You might help us establish what really happened,' he said as his computer beeped with an incoming email. He looked to be sure it was the right one and sent it to his printer. 'I have it, thank you. I'll let you know what we conclude and thanks again for your help, mademoiselle. Good luck with your research.'

Dear Jenny, he read, the words written in French.

I'm really depressed and worried about the way things are going here. The Peace Now movement is on the ropes; so many of the old stalwarts seem to have given up or been intimidated and now the academic row over Jerusalem has entered a new phase. I told you about the way that Israeli and Arab scholars have been arguing like a bunch of schoolkids about who first built Jerusalem and whether it was really significant to the early Islamic faith. I can't prove it yet but I'm pretty sure that there's some dirty work around a long-lost document that we only know of at second and third hand. Some people tried to sound a warning by painting this graffiti, photo attached, on the walls of a castle here that was linked to the Crusaders and to the Templars, thinking with all the interest in the Templars it would be sure to make a stir. Photos have been sent to newspapers and history magazines around the world but so far it has been virtually ignored. Perhaps you could help get the word out in the US? I'm going to try again in France.

First, some background you'll need. Pro-Israeli scholars (and see the link I attach to to the article in **Middle East Quarterly**) suggest that Jerusalem only became an issue for Arabs when it had some special political status. After all, Jerusalem is never mentioned in the Qu'ran, but there are some seven hundred references to the city in the Jewish Bible, the one Christians call the Old Testament. The Dome of the Rock mosque on the Temple Mount was built by the Damascus-based Umayyad dynasty in the decade after AD 690 when they were faced with Zubayr's revolt in Mecca, the holiest centre of Islam. The Umayyads deliberately built up Jerusalem as a rival, pouring in money for new buildings in an attempt to give it equal standing with Mecca. In the Qu'ran 17.1 you will find the phrase referring to Mohammed's famous night journey, or dream:

Glory to He who took His servant by night from the Sacred Mosque to the furthest mosque.

There is really no proof that this 'al-Aqsa mosque' (the furthest mosque) refers to Jerusalem, where there was no mosque in Mohammed's lifetime. But the Umayyads built a mosque in Jerusalem and called it the Al-Aqsa

Mosque, in a transparent attempt to make the direct connection with the Prophet Mohammed. Once the Umayyad dynasty fell in AD 750 and the centre of the Caliphate moved to Baghdad under the Abassid dynasty, Jerusalem sank once more into obscurity – until it was brought back into prominence in 1099 when the city was first captured by the Crusaders.

Iftikhar al-Dawla was the governor of Jerusalem when the Crusaders took the city. Iftikhar retreated to the citadel and negotiated freedom for himself, his family and his personal guard – while the rest of the inhabitants were slaughtered, Jews, Muslims and local Christians alike. The brutality of the Crusaders was extraordinary; one of their monks reported that their horses were up to their fetlocks in blood. So it is all the more surprising that they agreed to let the enemy commander and his family and his picked troops all go free. Bribery alone can hardly explain it since the Crusaders could have taken whatever gold or jewels he had. He must have offered them something very special in return for his life.

The agreement Iftikhar reached with the Crusaders was written down, the celebrated Testament of Iftikhar, and entrusted by Baldwin, the first Christian king of Jerusalem, to the Templars. Iftikhar allegedly affirmed that the city was of no religious significance to Islam, and that its reputation had been an invention of the Umayyads to shore up their religious and political credentials. The Testament then disappeared, if it ever existed.

You can imagine the political impact today if this long-lost Testament were to surface, which I believe is about to happen. But I suspect it would be a very careful and professional forgery. That is why the graffiti was painted onto the castle and why honest historians have to do something similar in Europe and the US, where such a warning would not be ignored. Please feel free to show this to any medieval scholars you know.

You know my own views. I seek a two-state solution, for Israel and for

Palestine, with a shared capital of Jerusalem, and the old city itself under international control, open to all and shared between all faiths, Jews, Muslims and Christians – and Buddhists and Confucians as well, come to that. I know some Jewish extremists accuse the Peace Now movement of being traitors to Israel. This is untrue. I love Israel, and love it so much that I think the only way to ensure its future is to share it with our Palestinian neighbours. Otherwise I fear that we will disappear, just like the old Crusader kingdom. I'll do anything to prevent that from happening.

Yours in peace and love, Leah

Bruno reread the final paragraph and then looked across at Amélie who was reading the printout. 'Leah strikes me as an impressive woman and she could be right about the political impact of this Testament of Iftikhar emerging now.'

'I agree,' said Amélie. 'But what does this mean for these other men who were with her at the gîte? Were they trying to sound the same warning as Leah about this Testament? Or is something else going on?'

'We know Leah wasn't alone at Commarque when she fell,' Bruno replied. 'But who would want to stop her from painting that graffiti?' he paused. 'I'd better forward this to J-J and the Brigadier before we go to see this historian in Sarlat.'

'Dumesnil?' Her voice was clipped and Bruno glanced up, surprised.

'Do you know this guy?' he asked.

'I'm sorry. I didn't mean anything.' She turned away and began putting her papers together. 'What time should we leave?'

He ignored the question and decided to press her. 'Have you come across this Dumesnil before, perhaps in another context?'

'It's not that. I'm just upset because of that email from Leah,

154

a voice from the grave.' She snapped the catches of her bag shut and then looked at him, a challenge in her eyes.

Bruno was sure there was more to this than Amélie was prepared to admit. That reminded him to make the usual courtesy call to his colleagues in Sarlat to explain that he was coming onto their patch to see a possible witness. Then he forwarded Leah's email to J-J and the Brigadier, adding a brief note about its source.

16

Bruno was deeply attached to the old town of Sarlat, thinking of it as one of those magical places, like Notre-Dame de Paris or Mont St Michel or the battlefield of Verdun, where French history came immediately and thrillingly alive. It was not simply that the heart of the old town was virtually unchanged since the early seventeenth century. The narrow streets and crooked alleys, the ancient stone buildings with their Renaissance windows all made him think of d'Artagnan and his fellow Musketeers, plumed hats and rapiers. And passing the house of the de La Boétie family reminded him that Montaigne himself had strolled on these same ancient stones, cultivating the friendship that had inspired the immortal essays.

But a link that went back much further, to the abbey from Charlemagne's time and the medieval tombs built into the walls of the town, intrigued Bruno even more, along with the strange cone-shaped stone building known as the Lantern of the Dead. It had been built to mark the visit of Bernard de Clairvaux, the Cisterician monk who had written the rules of the Templars and whose preaching had launched the Second Crusade. He recalled a carving on the Lantern's wall of a horse and two iron crosses, a traditional sign of the Templars. Odd, Bruno thought, how the theme of the Templars kept recurring.

'I've seen it,' Amélie said curtly when Bruno offered to show her around in the ten minutes before his appointment. 'With my cousin, remember?'

Sorry you weren't more impressed, Bruno thought, without uttering the words but looking at her curiously. He'd grown accustomed to her usually sunny nature and had developed a sense of respect verging on awe for her research skills with a computer. If something was upsetting her, she would either reveal it or she wouldn't and her testy moment would then pass.

He took a roundabout path to Auguste Dumesnil's home on the rue des Consuls in order to pass by the cathedral, hoping that he'd still be rehearsing his choir. As they climbed the steps, the sound of a chant became audible, wholly fitting to the ambience of this ancient place. He and Amélie stood at the back, moved by sacred music that was centuries old yet seemed to embody the very spirit of holiness. Then Amélie craned forward, staring at the choir. A moment later she moved to one side for a clearer view, apparently looking for someone. She bit her lip, took her phone from her bag and slipped outside the church.

Bruno edged back to the slightly open door to hear her say, 'Is she there?' Then came a pause as Amélie listened to a reply. And then he heard her say, 'You're watching her play basketball? Is she winning? Give her my love.'

Bruno stepped back as the door opened and Amélie came back inside the church, her phone already disappearing into her handbag. They stood at the rear of the church as the music swelled around them, but Bruno was surprised to see the choir master was a woman. When the chant stopped and she thanked the singers before turning away, leaving the members of the choir to collect their bags and coats, Bruno followed her and asked where he might find Dumesnil. She simply shrugged and said he had failed to turn up.

Dumesnil lived in an old building whose doorway was open, leading to a wide spiral staircase of stone. Bruno knew Dumesnil lived on the second floor, found a light switch and began climbing the steps. The door to his apartment was closed and Bruno's knock brought no response. There was no sign of a bell. Amélie leaned across him and tried the door handle. It opened, and the now familiar sound of a Gregorian chant seeped out from within. He called out Dumesnil's name, but there was no reply. Looking through the doorway he could see tumbled books and an overturned chair in the corridor.

'Police,' he called out and went inside, telling Amélie to remain where she was. He located the light switch, but it wasn't working. He was instantly struck by the bitter scent of burnt cooking along with something else, perhaps hair or cloth.

He opened each door he came to, but every room was dark except for one whose double doors were open and from which a faint light leaked out. Inside, a guttering candelabra revealed more books scattered on the floor and furniture overturned, but that did not detract from Bruno's sudden sense of having stepped into another century. Walls that were not covered in bookshelves were draped in old tapestries, hanging in folds. The floor was bare wood, great planks almost a metre wide but smooth underfoot as if trodden by generations of feet.

Before one of the tapestries was a life-size wooden statue of a Madonna standing on a plinth, gazing down with one hand raised in blessing upon a prie-dieu which had an unlit candle at each corner. Bruno took the two long candles, lit them from the dying candelabra, left one in place and took the other to help him look around the room. The sound of chanting was coming from a stone archway whose iron-bound wooden door was just ajar. Now the smell of burning was stronger, but there was no flickering light that a fire might give. He pushed it open, calling out once more, 'Police.'

There he confronted a scene from hell, stepping into a room that captured the fire and torments of Satan. A gagged and naked figure, head sunk down on his chest and his arms bound behind him, was slumped and bent almost double on a wooden chair. It looked like an impossible pose with the man's knees almost as high as his head, until Bruno saw that his buttocks had fallen through what had been the woven cane seat of the chair. Then he saw the stub of burned-out candle overturned beneath the chair and realized what had caused the smell of burning and how terribly Dumesnil must have suffered.

He could detect no pulse in the neck but used his pocket knife to cut through the strip of cloth that gagged the man. His mouth was stuffed with something. Bruno pulled out a sodden sock. Then he put his wristwatch under the man's nostrils and saw the faintest misting. The poor devil was still breathing.

'Call an ambulance, now,' he shouted to Amélie, turning to see that she had followed him and was standing in the doorway, her hand to her mouth and her eyes wide in horror.

He strode forward and pushed her out of the room and used his own phone to call for the *urgences*, giving his name, rank and location and saying that the victim had very severe burns but was still alive. Then he called Fabiola's mobile and asked what he should do until they arrived.

'Third degree burns. It looks as if some flesh and muscle have been burned away,' he said when she asked how it looked. 'An ambulance is on its way.'

'Remove any constrictions like tight clothing, elevate the heart above the site of the burn and cover the burn with a cool, moist cloth,' she replied. 'If the victim's breathing is very faint, try mouth-to-mouth. Where's the burn?'

'Buttocks and genitals, mainly the backs of his thighs. I think he was tortured.'

'*Mon Dieu*. You have to keep him breathing. I'll call casualty now to let them know what to expect. They'll need to call in their burns expert.'

Bruno returned to the room, slammed his boot into the cross-bars of the chair and then pulled away the chair legs. It was the only way he could see to free the man. Only when the buttocks came free did the legs extend and Bruno could see the horrific extent of the burns.

'Find the kitchen or bathroom and bring me a clean, moist cloth,' he shouted at Amélie. This time she complied and by the time Bruno had the victim draped face down on a couch, his legs on the floor so the heart was elevated, she returned with the cloth and draped it over the burned area.

'Thanks, you're doing well,' Bruno said. 'Now can you help turn his head?'

She did so, saying, 'There's a pool of fresh vomit on the kitchen floor.' Bruno ignored her and began giving mouth-to-mouth resuscitation, rewarded after what seemed to be a long, long time with a faint groan and then a cough from the victim followed at once by the thunder of booted feet climbing the stairs and a call of '*Urgences.*'

'Keep his head up,' Bruno said, and went to the door to guide the ambulance men, explaining what he'd found and what he'd done.

'You did right,' said the first one. He took one look at the victim and pulled a portable oxygen mask from his kitbag and then a large torch that lit up the room. The second man unrolled the stretcher they had brought. They applied an oxygen mask and then checked Auguste's blood pressure before rolling him onto the stretcher, strapping him face down and taking him out and down the stairs. Bruno followed with the torch, helped them to load the stretcher into the ambulance and waved them off, but not before giving the driver his mobile number and asking to be kept informed of Dumesnil's condition.

He climbed back up the stairs and looked around the entrance hall for the fuse box, opened it and shone his torch onto the fuses. The orange master fuse had been turned off. So what was the source of the Gregorian chant he could hear? He turned on the fuse and a light came on in one of the side rooms. He tried the hall light switch and it worked.

'Amélie?' he called. 'Can you locate the source of the music?'

'In here,' she replied, and he followed her voice into a room that might have been a monk's cell. The outer wall was stone, the others whitewashed and a single iron bed stood in a corner, topped by the thinnest mattress Bruno had ever seen. Above it hung an icon that looked antique, of a stylized female head surrounded by a golden halo. At first Bruno thought there was some kind of white carpet until he realized that sheafs of paper had been scattered over the floor, apparently from the single waist-high bookcase, which had held manuscripts rather than books. Perched atop the bookcase was a small tape recorder of the kind Philippe Delaron carried for his interviews. That was the source of the music.

'Battery driven,' said Amélie, following his gaze. She was standing at a small table that seemed to be Dumesnil's desk. A fountain pen lay beside a thin pile of writing paper. It looked hand-made, the old-fashioned kind that was produced by one of the restored paper mills at St Couze.

'He was writing a letter to some professor at the Sorbonne about this Testament of Iftikhar,' she said, gesturing to a page that was half filled with neat handwriting. 'I haven't touched anything.'

Bruno nodded, looked into the kitchen and placed a chair over the vomit to preserve it from careless feet, thinking that the forensics team might be able to identify its owner's DNA. He pulled out his phone to tell J-J of Dumesnil's fate. He was told to remain in the apartment until J-J arrived.

'We're going to be stuck here for some time,' he told Amélie. 'It will be a late dinner. We have to stay here until J-J gets here, half an hour or more. And then I may have to wait until the forensics team arrives.'

'I couldn't eat, not after seeing that. What a terrible thing to do to someone, to anyone. I'd just like to stay here with you.'

He nodded, thinking she didn't have much choice. He pulled out his phone again and called the commissariat of police in Sarlat to explain what had happened, thankful that he'd made the courtesy call to them earlier. The duty officer took down the details and promised to send a town cop to guard the entrance to Dumesnil's building.

'Any chance of starting some door-to-door inquiries?' Bruno asked. And was told that would need authorization by the town's police chief, a morose man called Messager who was a year or two from retirement. Bruno had Messager's mobile phone number and found him at some mayoral reception where the background noise made it hard for Messager to hear what Bruno was saying. He waited until Messager had found somewhere quieter and then explained what had happened and that J-J would be taking over the case.

'Torture? Dumesnil? *Merde*, my wife's in his choir. She'll be distraught. It happened at his home, you say? I'll get the door-to-door inquiries started and then I'll be right there.'

Bruno closed his phone and looked at Amélie. 'Why not tell me what it is that was upsetting you about Dumesnil and why you went out from the church to phone when you realized he wasn't there?'

'Why do you want to know?' Her voice was irritated rather than hostile.

'Do you know something about Dumesnil that I don't?'

She shook her head. 'I was worried about something, but I think I was wrong. Let's leave it there.'

'Sorry, this is a crime scene. I don't want to have to tell J-J that I think you're hiding something that could be relevant.'

'*Merde*, Bruno. It's something personal, about my cousin's kid. She's fifteen and we're worried about her. She's had a sudden mood swing. Once she was always cheerful and bouncy, now she's silent and morose. Her mother is worried that she's a victim of something, maybe a paedophile. And since she's in Dumesnil's choir and he's such a weird guy . . .' She broke off and raised her hands in the air, an exaggerated shrug.

'Do you or her mother have any other reason to suspect him, other than that he's fixated on the Middle Ages and seems to live like some fourteenth-century monk?' Bruno kept his voice calm and matter-of-fact.

She shook her head. 'Not really.'

'Don't you think your cousin's daughter is going through what sounds like a fairly typical adolescence?'

'It's not typical,' she snapped. 'I wasn't like that, nor was her mother, nor are other kids. It's as though Jojo suddenly fell into this deep depression. That's her name, Joséphine.'

'Has your cousin asked Joséphine's teachers if her behaviour has changed at school? Have her marks suddenly got worse?'

'Look, I don't know. And I accept that her mother and I have probably been making two and two add up to five, and after seeing what's just happened to Dumesnil I feel terrible about it. I'm sorry, all right?'

'The town's chief of police is on his way here. Do you want me to ask him, very discreetly, if there's any gossip about Dumesnil? I doubt it since I've just learned that his wife is in Dumesnil's choir, which wouldn't happen if there was any whiff of suspicion about him.'

'No, let's drop it, okay?'

Amélie turned to leave, but Bruno said sharply, 'You can't leave until the place is secure and you have given your statement. You work for the Justice Ministry, remember? We have to do this by the book.'

She stopped, keeping her back turned to him, and let out a long, noisy sigh, as if her patience were being tried too far.

'Think about what just happened here,' Bruno said. 'You're missing the most important piece of evidence that might just support your suspicions. A man was tortured, but he was gagged so he couldn't speak. Why was that? Were his torturers not interested in what he might be able to tell them? So was the torture just a punishment, and an obviously sexual punishment, at that? Has some other relative of a young person jumped to conclusions and taken the law into their own hands?'

'The thought had crossed my mind.' She turned round to face him again.

'Well, it could also be that they were the same guys who met Leah in Paris. Perhaps they'd already questioned him, learned what they needed, and then gagged him before leaving him to burn. Maybe they left the tape deck on to silence his screams, although I'd have thought he'd have been loud enough to bring a lot of attention. Why did they turn off the main fuse and do everything by candlelight? It looks to me as if they were making some kind of search and I'd have thought that would be easier with the lights on. There are all sorts of odd things about this, as there often are at crime scenes. So we have a procedure. We try to build various scenarios that might explain what we find, and then we test those scenarios as we look for further evidence to see if they hold up. And one scenario is that you could be right, that Dumesnil was a pervert and someone was determined to make him pay for it.'

'The other scenario is that Leah was with some Middle Eastern terrorists who were desperate to learn something from him,' she said.

'Exactly,' said Bruno, as voices from the hallway below and footsteps on the stairs signalled the arrival of Messager.

'A waiter in the restaurant on the corner was opening up just before six when he saw four strangers leaving this building,' Messager began, slightly breathless from running up the stairs. 'Three were wearing hoodies and the bare-headed one looked like an Arab. Does that make any sense to you?'

'They could be the men we're looking for, connected to that woman who fell to her death at Commarque,' Bruno said, and explained that the Interior Ministry had already launched an anti-terrrorism inquiry. Messager's office must have received photos which should be shown to the waiter downstairs as soon as possible.

'I thought this was about an attack on Dumesnil? What's he got to with terrorism?'

'It's a long story,' said Bruno, and explaining it took up the time before J-J's arrival. Halfway through, Bruno had a call from the ambulance driver. Dumesnil was in intensive care but the doctor thought he'd live.

17

'The trail has gone cold in Germany, at least for the moment,' said the Brigadier, his face enormous on the video screen. 'We can't even track them from the stations where they boarded the trains. The Germans still have all sorts of legal limitations on security cameras and on storing the data. The good news is that we've identified one of the three unknown men. He's Mustaf al-Takriti, Iraqi, thirty-six years old and a serious threat. He's on the Americans' target list. Commissioner Perrault will explain.'

The Brigadier was in Paris and Bruno was one of four men attending the video conference in Périgueux. J-J was sitting at one side of a long table, flanked on his left by Prunier, the police commissioner for the *département*, and on his right by the regional general of the gendarmes. Bruno sat beside Prunier and he was feeling slightly dizzy, disconcerted by the way Brigadier Lannes' image kept jerking, slightly out of synch with his words coming over the speaker. The Brigadier adjusted something on the console before him and the camera backed away from the close-up and revealed the others in the Paris studio.

Beside the Brigadier was a saturnine man of middle age from France's joint anti-terrorism centre and an attractive and elegantly dressed young woman who made Bruno's heart turn over when he saw her on the screen. It was Isabelle, whom he still thought of as the love of his life though she had left him and the Périgord to pursue her career first at the Ministry of the Interior in Paris, then at Eurojust in The Hague. She was introduced as the Eurojust official attached to the European Union's anti-terrorism centre, which sounded like another promotion for her.

Bruno kept his face impassive but his eyes were hungry for this sight of her. She was still too thin, as she had been since being shot in the thigh during an ambush of a shipload of illegal immigrants. There were dark shadows under her eyes and her hair was longer, enough to be pulled back into a bun. Her outfit was plain, a black polo-neck sweater and a black leather jacket slung over the back of her chair. He wondered if she knew he was watching her, if the video screen at her end showed all four of them at the table.

'Mustaf al-Takriti comes from Takrit, home town of the late and unlamented Saddam Hussein, and is a member of his clan,' Isabelle said. 'He was a new recruit in the Mukhabarat, the Iraqi secret police, when Saddam was overthrown. His father, who was killed in the US invasion in 2003, was a Mukhabarat general and close to Saddam. Somehow Mustaf became attached to the Sunni resistance movement against the Shia-dominated government in Baghdad. He's now part of Daesh, the group we used to call ISIS.'

Isabelle paused, and gently tapped two of her fingers against her lips as if thinking. Bruno sat bolt upright and he felt his heart skip a beat. He knew that gesture. It had been her private signal to him when they were not alone that she wanted to be kissed. But was it for him? Did she even know he was there at the other end of the video link?

She went on to explain that ISIS was the English acronym for Islamic State of Iraq and Syria, but the jihadists called themselves Daesh. This was the Arabic acronym which asserted their claim to the whole of the Levant, which encompassed Lebanon, Jordan, Palestine, including the territory of Israel and North Africa, as well as Iraq and Syria. Daesh was committed to restoring the historic Caliphate and ruling all Muslims around the world under strict Islamic law.

'Mustaf has been identified as a senior figure in the Daesh force that occupied Mosul and then took part in some of the mass executions that followed. There is a reliable British report that he was seen in Raqqa, Syria, three months ago. The Americans have circulated a photo that shows he was also present in Derna when that became the first Libyan town to declare allegiance to Daesh,' Isabelle went on.

'The reason we have a good photo of Mustaf,' said the saturnine Frenchman, 'is that it comes from a mugshot taken by the Americans when they arrested him in Iraq in 2004. They put him in the Camp Bucca detention centre. That was where he got to know all the other Daesh leaders. The Americans ran the place almost as a holiday camp, with first-class healthcare, and the inmates were allowed to organize their own education and religious classes and even set up a football league, at which Mustaf was a star player.'

'And the Americans decided to let them all go, when Washington switched tactics and began to back the Sunni resistance against the Shia,' said the Brigadier, poker-faced. These video conferences were all recorded, Bruno knew, and the Brigadier was being careful of the diplomatic etiquette. The Americans could be touchy about European colleagues criticizing their policy shifts in the Middle East.

He waved to Isabelle to continue, and she nodded coolly and spoke again without consulting her notes.

'Mustaf, as a member of the country's elite under Saddam Hussein, went to an English-language school in Baghdad so he is fluent in that language. When he was a child, the family had a French-born nanny of Moroccan origin, who subsequently returned to France when Mustaf went to university. We have traced her and interviewed her and she reported that her job was to speak French to the children so that they would be familiar with our language. She added that Mustaf also studied Russian at school. His French, she told us, was very good indeed. He and his siblings regularly watched French-language programmes from the Lebanon, and he was a good football player.'

Isabelle looked up from her notes and gave that wry smile Bruno knew so well. It usually meant she was about to tease him. Then she spoke. 'The nanny recalls Mustaf avidly watching the 1998 World Cup games and being thrilled by Zidane's play when France won the final.'

There was a chorus of chuckles from the men on both ends of the video link and Bruno smiled to himself at the ease with which Isabelle had charmed them all.

'We know Mustaf has been with al-Husayni, the partner of the dead Israeli woman Leah Wolinsky, also known as Leah Ben-Ari. However, we are still trying to identify the other two members of the team,' Isabelle went on. 'The fact that the Israelis and the Americans don't have anything on these two may indicate that they are Europeans, either Muslim-born or converts. We are checking, but our files on European sympathizers, even French nationals who went to fight with Daesh, are far from complete. I suggest we have to assume that they will be able to blend easily into European and possibly even into French society. So far, we know more than fifteen hundred French nationals who have gone to Iraq or Syria to join Daesh.'

Isabelle stopped and turned to the Brigadier. He nodded and said, 'So Mustaf is a category one target for us. But he's a very skilled operator, fluent in our language and obviously dangerous. I'm sending down three teams of special forces, so you will have firepower on hand if you need it. We'll probably base them in Périgueux, Sarlat and Bergerac. Of course, we'd like to catch Mustaf alive. From now on we'll do these briefings daily, at eight in the morning, with another if required at six in the evening. Any comments?'

Prunier raised his hand and asked about possible reinforcements for his police and for the gendarmes to help search for the vehicle Leah had rented. 'Whatever you need,' the Brigadier replied.

'This has now been formally listed as an anti-terrorism inquiry,' he went on. 'My colleague from the specialist unit is drawing up a list of possible targets in your region, including nuclear power stations, chemical plants, dams and so on. I'll arrange for extra police from Bordeaux, Limoges and Toulouse. General, do you have space for them in your barracks?'

'Yes, sir. And Commissaire Jalipeau has just reminded me

to ask when can we expect the breakdown of calls from that mobile phone tower near the *gîte* where they stayed?'

'There's a team working on that and we should have something today,' Isabelle replied. 'I'll call J-J . . . I mean, Commissaire Jalipeau, as soon as it comes in. We also have a team going through all the other rail stations, ports, airports and entry points to see if we can find when and how those other two men in their hoodies came to France. Chef de Police Courrèges, I gather you will be coordinating the local search for whatever new base Mustaf has found. Will you need more staff?'

'Not immediately, commissaire,' Bruno replied, feeling slightly ridiculous at calling Isabelle by her rank when they had been lovers for a whole glorious summer. 'If we do, I'll let you know. But we might want sniffer dogs on hand to detect explosives so that they can patrol major tourist sites without arousing too much public concern. There is one further item, this Testament of Iftikhar. Can we track down some medieval scholar who may be able to tell us more about its significance? Perhaps the Israelis might help. They had similar graffiti scrawled on a wall of one of their castles. There's a professor at the Sorbonne called Philippeau. It looks as though our Dumesnil was writing to him when Mustaf and his team came in to torture him. I can call Philippeau but you'll have to liaise with the Israelis.'

'I'll do that,' said the Brigadier. 'What do I tell them?'

'This so-called Testament was obviously very important to Leah, and I can't think of any other reason why they would want to torture Dumesnil. Mustaf doesn't strike me as the scholarly type. And why else would Mustaf have this Palestinian history professor on a terrorist team? I hardly need to stress the political implications if this Testament were to be found.'

'Very well. Talk to the professor. We'll confer again tomorrow morning. By then, perhaps we can come up with some ideas of what these men are after. Thank you, messieurs.'

The screen went black and the four men in Périgueux sat back in their chairs. J-J stood up, stretched and then opened the door to ask a secretary to arrange some coffee. He came back and sat at the head of the table.

'We can't talk if we're all lined up in a row like schoolkids,' he said. 'Come round where we can see each other as we work out how to organize this.'

'My gendarmes can take care of the road traffic watch, the garages and petrol stations,' said the General.

'My guys can handle the rail stations, hotels, restaurants and *gîtes* outside Bruno's patch,' said Prunier with a grin as he glanced at Bruno. The two men had played on opposite sides of an army versus police rugby match over ten years earlier and had become friends. 'We all know Bruno has his own system in that valley of his. We'll also double-check all the internet cafés and other public access points, as well as security cameras in supermarkets and ones covering mosques. We also have the telephone monitors on standby for all calls in Arabic. I'm briefing the media after this so we'll have Mustaf's face on the front page of every newspaper and on TV. Am I missing anything?'

'Shops selling halal meat,' said Bruno. 'Motorbike and cycle hire. They probably won't want to use that VW of theirs, unless they've already found a new set of wheels. Camping shops; they may be living rough, so we'd better check places selling sleeping bags and portable stoves.'

'Is there any reason to believe they're still in the region?' asked J-J. 'They had an hour and a half to get away from Sarlat before we could even ask for some roadblocks to be set up. They could be anywhere by now.'

Prunier shook his head. 'They came here to the Périgord with this woman Leah for a reason. Maybe it was to do with the Iftikhar business, maybe not. But I think we can assume they went to see Dumesnil because they wanted to find out more about it from him. What I don't understand is why all four of them went and why they used torture. If al-Husayni had called on him alone, Dumesnil had reason to welcome him as a scholar and fellow historian.'

'Perhaps Mustaf doesn't trust al-Husayni out of his sight,' said Bruno. 'Al-Husayni doesn't seem to fit the usual profile of a Daesh militant.'

'That could be right,' said J-J. 'But what's here in the Périgord that would attract a senior Daesh figure? This region is about food, wine, tourism, farming and historic monuments. The big opening of Lascaux IV is months away. That would be a target, but right now it isn't even the tourist season.'

'To these guys, all monuments are targets,' said Prunier. 'Remember when the Taliban blew up those Buddha statues in Afghanistan, and then Daesh blew up the Roman temples in Palmyra and took pickaxes to the statues at Nineveh. They believe in destroying monuments and we've plenty of those.'

'Maybe they're here for more than one reason,' J-J suggested. 'There's something to do with the Iftikhar Testament, certainly, but maybe while they're here they want to take the chance to attack or destroy something important to French culture. To me that spells the ancient French treasure of Lascaux. Perhaps that's what the two unknown guys are for.'

'There could be another target: this Scout camp that we're opening outside St Denis next week,' said Bruno. 'Maya Halévy will be there, the Israeli woman who paid for the place as a memorial. She and her brother were sheltered there from the Nazis during the war. It was going to be opened with contingents from all the Scout groups – Catholic, Protestant, Jewish and Muslim – but the Muslims announced this week they were pulling out because of the Israeli connection. A hundred French youngsters and this Israeli philanthropist could be quite a target.'

'We hadn't been thinking of arranging any special security, but that could be a very bad mistake,' said Prunier. 'We can't leave them unguarded. Maybe we could use one of those special forces teams the Brigadier mentioned.'

'I can assign some of our *forces mobiles* with their own helicopters,' said the General of Gendarmes. 'They aren't special forces but they're very good, the ones we use to guard nuclear power stations. And I'll put in a request for GIGN.'

Bruno nodded his approval. GIGN was an elite unit, but he wondered how to steer the General away from the idea that all that was needed was firepower.

'I wonder whether just guarding the camp is the best approach,' said Bruno. 'These are kids. What are their parents going to say if anything goes wrong and we knew there was a threat? They could accuse us of using their children as bait to set a trap. Perhaps we should consider postponing the opening.'

He paused, and looked at Prunier and the General. 'If the politicians and the media start looking for scapegoats in the event of a disaster, they'll start with you two.'

'Point taken,' said Prunier.

The meeting broke up. Bruno pondered contacting Amélie. When Prunier had called him at dawn to attend the video conference, he'd left a note at her hotel desk explaining that he had to attend a security meeting to which she would not be admitted and he'd call her when he could. He'd turned his phone off during the meeting and when he turned it back on he saw an urgent text from Horst that said simply, 'Eureka. Join me at Commarque soonest.'

Bruno grimaced. He really should get back to his office and start going through the emails from his network of people in the local tourist business after he launched the search for the four suspects. And Commarque was out of his way. But Horst was a good friend, and about to get married. Bruno skimmed through the emails on his phone, saw nothing particularly urgent and set off for the chateau.

The crowds had gone, but the Count was there with Horst, Clothilde and two more of the archaeologists from the museum. Another truck was parked beside the seismic sensor Bruno had seen on his last visit.

'That's the ground-penetration radar,' said Horst who was shifting from one foot to the other in his excitement and clutching Clothilde's hand. 'They've found another cave, at least one. And there's something inside it. From the blurred shape which is all we can make out, it could be an altar or a tomb.'

'Congratulations,' said Bruno. He kissed Clothilde and shook hands with the Count and the other archaeologists before asking, 'Where is it?'

'The cave is quite deep, at least five metres below current ground level, at about the same depth as the cave where the equine engraving was found,' said Clothilde, her eyes bright. 'It seems to be quite close behind one of the troglodyte caves, one where we found animal bones, flints and pollen in the floor. They were dated between fifteen and eighteen thousand years old, Lascaux period.'

'When you say it's behind a known cave, is it sealed off or is there a way into it?' asked Bruno.

'The technicians are in there at the moment, trying to map the new cave and look for others,' Horst added. 'The seismic investigation showed the whole hill to be honeycombed with caves and what look like courses of underground streams. Heaven knows what passages between the caves we might find. Remember how much lower the ground was that long ago.'

There came a shout from the tower of the chateau, nearly a hundred metres above them. Looking up, Bruno saw three men, all waving down at them.

'You'll meet them this evening, the guests I told you about,' said Horst. 'Two colleagues from Germany and another from England, close friends of many years and very good archaeologists. One of the Germans is from Düsseldorf and although they are great rivals of my own Cologne, that is very significant for this region. Can you guess why?'

'I couldn't begin,' said Bruno, smiling.

'Here at Les Eyzies is where the first Cro-Magnon skeletons were found. But before that was the discovery in 1856 of

Neanderthal man, which everybody thinks must be in the valley of the River Neander. But there is no such river. The valley was named after a man. The river at Neanderthal is the Düssel, which flows into the city of Düsseldorf. So we shall have here archaeologists from the two great sites of prehistory.'

Horst threw up his hands with a flourish. 'What could be more suitable for a marriage of archaeologists? And I'm even more delighted that our wedding is coinciding with this latest discovery at Commarque. Clothilde and I couldn't have had a better wedding present.'

Bruno nodded, wished them luck, slapped Horst on the back and reminded him not to let the cave get in the way of his stag supper that evening. Bruno was in charge of the cooking, but the event was being hosted by the Baron at his chartreuse, since they assumed Horst's German friends would rather dine in a historic building than in Bruno's modest home. The Baron also had a much bigger oven than Bruno, which would be needed for the dish Bruno had in mind. Ivan at the bistro had ordered the whole wild salmon of three kilos from his supplier, to be delivered to him at the restaurant fresh that day. Bruno was providing the herbs and new potatoes from his garden and Fauquet was making the *Sachertorte* that was Horst's favourite dessert. Marcel, who ran the finest vegetable stall at the local markets, had promised Bruno two kilos of young green asparagus to begin and Stéphane from the *fromagérie* was preparing one of his special cheese boards.

Jack Crimson and Gilles were providing the wine, and considerable thought had gone into the selection. To begin, they had three bottles of rosé from Chateau Feely, which would be the aperitif and could also accompany the asparagus. The white wine for the salmon would be a cuvée Mirabelle from Chateau de la Jaubertie, but Hubert from the town's *cave des vins* had suggested they might like to try something unusual, a red wine that would go surprisingly well with the salmon, a Chateau Laulerie that was made entirely of Merlot. Since Horst preferred to drink red wines when he could, and Bruno and the Baron had tasted the wine and approved, they had three bottles, and two bottles of the honey-sweet Monbazillac from Chateau La Robertie for the dessert.

Bruno knew that his plans for the evening could be derailed by the hunt for Mustaf, but he hoped he could find some way to keep his commitments to Horst and Clothilde. He would need about an hour to cook the salmon and only a few minutes for the young asparagus, which he intended to serve only with butter. Young Edouard Lespinasse from the garage had agreed to collect them and drive them all home at midnight for twenty euros. The English archaeologist was staying with Gilles, the two Germans with Bruno and nobody lived more than four kilometres from the Baron's chartreuse.

18

As Bruno parked his van by the *mairie*, a woman called his name. He turned to see Amélie waving at him from a table on Fauquet's terrace. A copy of *Le Monde*, a notebook and her ever-present smartphone were before her, along with a cup of coffee. He went to join her, apologizing for abandoning her that morning.

'Where's Balzac?' she asked.

'At home. I couldn't take him to the security meeting. It was a video conference with Paris.' Even mentioning it brought Isabelle back into his head, a sudden memory of his undoing her hair from its bun and letting it trickle through his fingers. With an effort, he brought himself back to reality.

'Have you been here all morning?' he asked her.

'Fauquet has a good internet connection, perfect croissants and excellent coffee, and I've been enjoying the sun, reading the paper, going over my notes and being surprised that there's nothing on any of the newsfeeds about the attack on Dumesnil.' She gave a sudden shiver. 'I didn't sleep too well, remembering what they'd done to that poor man.'

'The hospital says he's in intensive care. There's nothing in the media because J-J wants to keep it quiet for the moment.'

'I presume this security meeting was about him?'

'Let's not talk about that here. Are you ready for some lunch?'

'Always. Are we going to Ivan's again?'

'No, to my place, so I can pick up Balzac and make you an omelette you'll never get in Paris. It will be a light lunch because I have a big dinner tonight for Horst, the bridegroom at Saturday's wedding. It's his stag supper.'

He picked up a baguette from Fauquet and they drove out on the familiar road home to find Balzac, who made a point of greeting every car he heard. As Bruno expected, the basset hound was waiting for them at the end of the lane and giving a tuneful welcoming howl. Now that he could sound like a grown-up basset hound, Balzac had become appreciative of his own voice.

'*Mon Dieu*, they could hear that back in town,' said Amélie, evidently impressed as she bent down to pat the dog.

'That's a sign of a good hunting dog, so I'll know where to find him in the woods when he's on a trail. He'll never be fast, but he can run all day. That's how bassets hunt wild boar, they run them down until the boar collapse with exhaustion. I think it's fine enough to eat outdoors.'

He left Amélie to set the table on the terrace while he went to his chicken coop and took out six new-laid eggs. He picked some rocket and parsley and used his pocket knife to collect the tiny green buds of *pisse-en-lit* that would eventually become the yellow dandelion flowers. But Bruno had a better use for them.

Once he'd collected about twenty of them, he went to the kitchen, opened a bottle of white wine and poured each of them a glass. Amélie leaned against the kitchen counter watching as he washed the salad and the buds, put a large knob of butter in his frying pan and broke the eggs into a bowl. Once the butter was half melted he added the buds of *pisse-en-lit* and began stirring them so they were well coated. He whisked the eggs together with half an eggshell of cold water, and some salt and pepper, and poured the eggs into the pan just as the melted butter began to foam. He left it cooking while he tossed walnut oil and a little cider vinegar with the rocket in his salad bowl, then returned to twirl the frying pan, folded the omelette and shredded the parsley on top before serving the food.

'I didn't know you could eat these,' she said. 'It's a very different taste, a little nutty, but it's wonderful to eat food so fresh.'

With a fork in one hand and a chunk of baguette in the other, Bruno grinned at her. Amélie picked up the wine bottle to read the label, looking surprised to see it came from St Denis' own vineyard. She sipped at it approvingly and then attacked her omelette again. They ate in silence, feeling wholly comfortable in one another's company, occasionally breaking off to hand Balzac a piece of bread that had been wiped on their plates. When they were finished, Bruno took the plates back to the kitchen and brought out some of his friend Stéphane's Tomme d'Audrix cheese, explaining that it was made just up the road.

'Eat locally, that's you,' she said, nodding in approval at the cheese. 'Now, what can you tell me about the security meeting?'

'Not very much, but one of the men who attacked Dumesnil seems to be from Daesh, a man with a very bad reputation. We don't know how he got into the country, nor what he's planning to do, but Paris is taking it all very seriously. Police reinforcements are on the way, along with special security teams. I have another video conference tomorrow morning, but it shouldn't take long. And this afternoon I have to work in my office, going through emails from my network.'

'You mean your other local policemen?'

'Not just them, but all the hotels and letting agencies, campsites, restaurants, car hire places, internet cafés, *mairies*, tourist offices and supermarkets from Lalinde to Montignac. I have a list set up so I can contact all of them with one email, and I've circulated the photos that we have of the four men and their car registration. With any luck, I might have some replies by now, maybe even a sighting.'

'You did that yourself?'

'Not a chance, that's way beyond my skills. The schoolkids did it for me as a club project. Do you want to drop in there and take a look as we go back to the office? We're very proud of our school's computer club.'

It was officially the spring holiday for schools, but since Florence was there to supervise, the computer room was half full when Bruno and Amélie arrived, her appearance exciting the usual stir. Florence seemed startled by their arrival, her hands fluttering to her hair and smoothing her dress before offering her cheeks to Bruno to be kissed. He introduced his companion to the others as a colleague from the Ministry in Paris. Two small children who had been playing quietly with a tablet on a couch in the corner suddenly realized Bruno had arrived and they scurried to him, to be lifted one in each of his arms.

'*Bonjour*, Dora. *Bonjour*, Daniel,' he said, kissing them both. 'These are Florence's children and they are much better on computers than I am.'

Amélie smiled at them and shook each small hand, although the pair looked not at all sure of this stranger. Amélie congratulated Florence on her children, but then her eyes widened as she looked around the room at the quality of the computers the youngsters were using.

'This is serious equipment.' She looked back at Florence. 'How did you afford these on a school budget?'

'The students can explain better than I can,' said Florence. 'It's their club.'

'We earned them,' said Maurice Cordet proudly. Son of a tree surgeon, he was in his final year at the *collège*. He explained that they had started with computers rescued from the town dump and then began building websites for local businesses. Later they developed a computer game and tried but failed to sell it. However, one of the games companies had liked their approach and donated their old computers to the *collège* when they upgraded.

'We do testing for them, telling them what we think about their new games, and they've invited two of us to their offices in Grenoble for an internship,' Maurice added.

'What are you working on now?' Amélie asked two girls sitting side by side before a big screen. 'And what are your names?'

'I'm Eglantine and this is Sylvie,' said the taller of the two. 'We're trying to build an interactive system to learn English, using songs and phrases and scenes from movies we all know. It starts with some fun, a karaoke session where you sing along and then the computer gets you to make new sentences using the words you know. It's fine with our voices because it knows them, but it takes ages to recognize new ones.'

'Impressive,' said Amélie. 'Which one of you set up Bruno's network for all his contacts up and down the valley?'

'We all did,' said Sylvie. 'It was just a data entry chore.' She glanced at Bruno. 'He's a dinosaur on computers, hasn't got a clue about social media.' It was said affectionately.

'I'm not extinct yet, and Amélie here has been showing me how it can help in my job, so I'll probably be back here for you lot to give me some more lessons,' said Bruno. 'We'd better get going. Thank you, Florence, everybody.'

Back in his office, Bruno called the hospital in Sarlat to ask about Dumesnil's condition. Stable, he was told, but still in intensive care. J-J had already asked to interview him when the doctors gave their approval. He forwarded to Amélie the photos of the two unknown young men from the Gare de l'Est, asking her to put them onto social media sites to see if anyone recognized them.

'No problem,' she said. 'Do you have Florence's number? I'd like to arrange to see her and ask how other schools might go about setting up similar clubs.'

He gave her the school number, Florence's mobile and her email. 'You need a live wire like Florence to get it started. She's a great teacher and a good friend and does an impressive job of bringing up those two kids on her own.'

Amélie gave him an enigmatic smile then turned back to her phone and murmured, 'She's an attractive woman. Great cheekbones. Is she one of those friends you dine with on Mondays?'

'Yes, and there's another young mother with children in the group. The other kids are English so they're all becoming very fluent in each other's tongue.'

'I suppose it makes up for not having children of your own,' she said, her eyes on her phone as her fingers darted over its virtual keyboard.

What did she mean by that? Bruno wondered, before rising and saying he'd better brief the Mayor about the security meeting. He was very fond of Dora and Daniel, but nothing really made up for not being a father. Nor could he say there was an important woman in his life. There was Martine, a businesswoman from the region who lived and worked in London and came to St Denis every couple of months to see her parents and develop the project for a new rally for electric cars. They had lusty reunions together on her visits, but Martine made no secret of her other love affairs in London.

'How are matters working out with Mademoiselle Plessis?' the Mayor asked as Bruno stood before his desk. He capped his fountain pen and pushed the letter he was writing aside.

'Better than expected. She's sensible, courteous and sings so well I'm hoping she'll perform at our concert evenings this summer. By the way, did you ever come across a medieval historian called Dumesnil who lives in Sarlat?'

'Yes, I knew something of his work. The staff around the coffee machine this morning were talking about this dreadful attack on him. Roberte has a sister who is a nurse at the hospital, so word has got around. I hear he's stable. Are you involved in that as well as this business at Commarque?'

Bruno explained the whole affair, stressing Amélie's role in identifying Leah and the way Leah had managed to establish for herself a new identity and bank account. 'I'm not sure that we'll be a target here in St Denis, but I think we have to postpone the opening of the Scout camp. Yacov Kaufman is coming down from Paris tomorrow to see the camp, and you and I are giving him lunch at Ivan's. It's in your diary. I think we have to be frank with him about the reasons for postponing.'

'Very well. Are we still going ahead with Horst's bridegroom supper this evening or has that been put off as well?

'No, we're going ahead. It's at the Baron's place, remember, and young Lespinasse will drive us all back afterwards. I'll get there about seven to start cooking and we'll serve drinks at eight. I think we'll be ten altogether.'

'I'm looking forward to it and to officiating at the marriage. I presume you saw Horst's latest piece in *Archéologie*?'

'Indeed, and I'll be quoting from it in my wedding speech, if I ever get time to sit down and write it.'

As he said this, a knock came at the door and Amélie poked her head inside, excusing herself but saying that Bruno had just received a new email that looked important. The Mayor waved him out.

The email had been sent from the Casino shop in Le Buisson. Best known in France for its giant hypermarkets, Casino also ran a chain of small, local supermarkets in rural villages that were otherwise ill served for basic foods and supplies.

He began calling the manager as soon as he read that one of the men in Bruno's photos had just spent over a hundred euros at the shop.

'Is he still there?' Bruno asked as he forwarded the email to J-J, Prunier, Yveline and the Brigadier.

'No, he left a couple of minutes ago in a white van, a Renault, no markings on the side. Somebody inside helped him load the bags and then they drove off on the Sarlat road. I took down the registration number and then emailed you.'

'Thanks. Give me the number and I'll be right there,' he said, sending second emails to the same addresses with the latest details. Then he went to his safe, opened it and took out his gun, a PAMAS 9 millimetre of the kind he'd used in the army. He checked it was empty, loaded a magazine, attached the belt holster with its pouch for a spare magazine and settled the gun at his side.

'Amélie, you'd better stay here until I get back. Please take care of Balzac.' He left, running down the *mairie* stairs and out to his car. As he got behind the wheel his phone rang. It was Yveline, asking if he wanted support, and indeed he did, asking her to call the Le Buisson gendarmerie and for her own team to join him at the shop. And could she arrange for roadblocks to be established at Siorac, Lalinde and outside Sarlat? No sooner had he closed his phone than it rang again, J-J this time.

'Have those special forces teams arrived yet?' asked Bruno.

'They just landed in Bordeaux, haven't been briefed yet.'

'If they have their 'copter, better get them moving and see if you can brief them in flight. I'm on my way to Le Buisson, with two squads of gendarmes on the way, and Yveline is asking for roadblocks.'

'That's what I want you to do,' said J-J. 'No point in going to the shop if they've left, but could you set up a roadblock outside St Denis?'

'A roadblock? What with? I only have a handgun.'

There was a pause before J-J replied, 'You'll just have to do your best. I've got motorbike cops heading your way. Where do you plan your roadblock?'

'I'll do it at the turn-off to Limeuil and try to get Yveline's gendarmes to join me.'

'I'll get her general to call her. Now get on with it.'

Driving one-handed as he tried to call the Baron, Bruno navigated the sharp S-bend at the railway crossing and then drove on cautiously, watching the oncoming traffic for a white van.

'Baron,' he said when the call was answered. 'Can you come to the Limeuil turn-off on the road to Le Buisson with your hunting guns? Please call other hunters from our club and ask them to do the same. We've got an emergency, suspects probably armed. I'm setting up a roadblock there with my van.'

'As soon as I can,' the Baron replied, a veteran who knew better than to waste time with questions. He'd been in the Algerian War and despite his age he still played tennis, hunted regularly and was a fine shot.

At the Limeuil turn-off, Bruno stopped and slewed his car across the centre of the road. Leaving his blue light flashing, he pulled out the accident hazard warning triangles from the back of his van and extended the block with them. He left only a narrow route through, part of it on a grass verge that bordered a ditch so any vehicle coming through would be forced to slow down. Then he put on the flak vest, left from a previous operation, over his uniform jacket.

The first vehicle that came was a tractor, driven by a farmer he knew, who stopped and eyed Bruno curiously.

'Emergency, Pierre,' said Bruno, his eyes on the road behind the tractor. 'There are some armed criminals on the loose. Sorry, but I have to commandeer your tractor. Use it to block the road where I've put the accident triangles. Then I'd like you to get in the ditch and stay there until reinforcements arrive.'

Pierre did as he was told, climbed down and asked, 'Have you got another gun? I did my national service in the infantry.'

'Thanks, but no, only my own weapon. Sorry, I'd use you if I could.'

A small blue Ford driven by a middle-aged woman stopped at the roadblock and Bruno waved her through. She was followed by an old Citroën he recognized, driven by Dr Gelletreau.

'What's this, Bruno? I'm due to be at the clinic.'

Bruno explained and asked the doctor to park his car behind the tractor, and then to stand by with his medical bag in case he was needed. Then from behind came the tooting of a horn and the Baron's stately Citröen DS cruised up to join them. From the back seat he took a shotgun and two Verney-Carron hunting rifles, each with a bolt action. He handed one to Bruno with a magazine already loaded, left the shotgun resting on the roof of Bruno's van and then loaded his own rifle.

'What's this roadblock for?' he asked.

'I'm not supposed to tell you, so keep it to yourself. There's an alert for a bunch of jihadist terrorists. Can Pierre borrow your shotgun?'

'Certainly. Jihadists, you say? I haven't hunted them since the Algerian War.'

At this point, Bruno heard a siren and turned to see the gendarmerie van coming from St Denis, Sergeant Jules at the wheel and Yveline in the passenger seat. Jules parked, leaving the siren blaring and his blue light flashing, and four more gendarmes piled out from the rear, each with a flak vest and a handgun at his belt.

'My general called,' said Yveline. She was carrying an MPF sub-machine gun, the only one stored at the St Denis gendarmerie. 'I'm under your orders until further notice.' She looked at the rifle at his side and gestured behind her to where Sergeant Jules was pulling something from the back of the van. 'Jules has brought his hunting rifle.'

'Good, I was feeling outgunned until the Baron arrived. Another rifle could be just what we need. Other hunting friends should be arriving with more, but we probably won't need them. If the white van hasn't shown now, I fear they're probably taking another route.'

His phone rang. It was J-J to say that the official registry recorded that the white van's number plate should have been attached to a black Renault on a forecourt for used cars at a garage in Bergerac. Local police were checking.

Five minutes later, J-J called again. The *urgences* at St Cyprien had been called to an incident. A motorcycle gendarme had been shot by the side of the road at Siorac, a crossroads about five kilometres beyond Le Buisson.

'The bastards could be anywhere,' he said.

19

Bruno drove over the bridge into the main square of St Denis. Amélie was standing on the balcony outside his office, looking out for his return. He waved once he'd parked, slung the Baron's rifle over his shoulder and broke open the shotgun he had borrowed. Entering the *mairie*, he heard the sound of her high heels clattering down the stairs to meet him.

Her eyes widened at the sight of the guns. 'Did you catch them? Was there a fight?'

'They took another route, shot a gendarme who tried to flag them down and disappeared.'

'Is he dead?'

'I don't know yet. He should be at the hospital by now.'

They mounted the stairs together and the Mayor was waiting for him along with Xavier, the *maire-adjoint*, some senior members of the town council and Fabiola from the medical centre. The Mayor led the way into the council chamber and asked Bruno to brief them all on the potential danger to the town.

'We have four armed terrorists on the loose,' he began, leaving the guns by the door. 'Two of them were stocking up on supplies at the supermarket in Le Buisson and we had little time to organize roadblocks. They shot a gendarme at Siorac and disappeared. He's been taken to hospital, but I don't know his condition. This is now a major anti-terrorist operation being run by the Ministry of the Interior. We'll be getting serious firepower. Three special forces teams including one from the elite GIGN group of the gendarmerie are being deployed with helicopters.

'We know the identities of two of the group and have photos of the remaining two. Their leader appears to be an important man from ISIS. We know they assaulted and tortured a man in Sarlat, but we don't know their mission. It could be Lascaux, since they like destroying monuments. It could be the planned opening of the new Scout camp here, but that is being postponed. It could be something or somewhere else altogether. We'll be coordinating a search from the gendarmerie here in town because it has good and secure communications.'

He was interrupted by a flurry of questions, but held up a hand until they were silent.

'That's all I know and probably more than I should tell you. Please do not speak of this outside this room and above all do not mention ISIS. We don't want people to panic. I know the Mayor and I can count on you. And now, excuse me, I have to get to the gendarmerie.'

He went to his office to say hello to Balzac and check his emails. Amélie followed him and he said she should stay; she would not be allowed into the command post being set up at the gendarmerie.

'I understand. I'll stay with Balzac,' she said. 'While you were away I was working on a couple of things. First, remember I used my phone to photograph that letter on Dumesnil's desk? Here's the number of the historian at the Sorbonne he was writing to.'

She handed him a piece of notepaper. 'And I was looking again at Leah's false ID. It was set up over a year ago, so how long has she been planning this? Was the bank account opened at the same time? I put the details on the paper with the name and phone number. And here's a copy of the printout from the till at Casino of the supplies they bought. The manager emailed it to you.'

He began to thank her but she interrupted.

'I'll stay here and answer your phone. This evening I'm having dinner with your friend Florence to talk about computer clubs. If you need me, just call my mobile. Now off you go, take care.' She gave him a quick hug as he thanked her and left.

The parking lot on the old parade ground in front of the gendarmerie had been closed to the public and was now occupied by three gendarme vans and a mobile communications unit. Bruno recognized J-J's car parked beside it. Three gendarmes with flak vests and sub-machine guns were standing by the roadblock formed by another van. Inside the building, J-J and the Gendarme General were already installed in Yveline's office, each of them talking on their phones, and Yveline was talking to a video link on her laptop. She was the first to finish.

'We're re-basing the helicopters at the Belvès airfield because it's closest,' she said. 'The Brigadier from Paris is on his way down here with some anti-terrorist staff and we've taken over the Royal Hotel to house people. They should arrive late tonight and we all meet here tomorrow morning at eight.'

'Talking of housing people, the bad guys are equipped to feed themselves for a week,' he said, giving her the copy of the Casino bill. 'Rice, eggs, bread, milk, noodles, olive oil, cheese, tomato paste, vegetables, fruit and fruit juice, a lot of coffee, sugar and jam, chocolate and nothing frozen. And no meat, presumably because they couldn't be sure it would be halal.'

'That sounds as though they have access to a kitchen with saucepans and crockery, which suggests to me that they've found a vacant house.'

'We have thousands of vacant holiday homes around here all closed up and waiting for the tourist season. It would take months to search them all.'

J-J finished his call and broke in. 'Isabelle sent me the breakdown from the mobile phone tower near Vaugier's place. We've got two numbers that we think must be theirs, with very heavy internet use. So France Télécom is now watching for those numbers on every mobile phone tower in the *département*. But they seem to know what they're doing, using a VPN and proxy servers along with TOR encryption.'

'What does that mean?' Bruno asked.

'A virtual private network using proxy servers is a way to hide your identity and location,' said Yveline. 'TOR stands for "the onion router", a way of encrypting data that's done in layers, like an onion. So while we might be able to track where they are, we can't read what they're up to.'

'And if they're that sophisticated, they won't be using their phones anywhere near where they're staying now that they know we're hunting them,' said J-J. 'They'll probably want new throw-away phones so we're checking on all smartphone thefts and all new sales. But maybe they brought extra phones with them.'

'Why should they have known we were hunting them?' asked Bruno. 'It's possible one of them just panicked when he saw a cop waving them down and shot him. So now they're panicking even more. They'll want to get new wheels, unless they already have them. Maybe they could do an amateur paint job on the van.'

'The problem is we can't block all the roads.' She turned to the large map of the *département* on the wall by the door. 'So we're doing the usual blocks, all autoroute access points and all national road intersections. Even with the extra manpower, we can't do much more than that.'

'We know when they were at Siorac, and presumably heading back to their base. We also know that at that time, we had motorbike cops at the obvious choke points – on the main road below Belvès, at Beynac, outside Sarlat, at Les Eyzies and your own block at the Limeuil turn-off. I think we have to work on the assumption that they're in this area – they'd have to know the back roads to get out of that net.'

'It's still four or five hundred square kilometres, and full of vacant *gîtes*,' J-J objected.

'Yes, but with all the major roads blocked and helicopters cruising the minor ones we'll at least have them pinned down,' Yveline replied.

Behind them, the General slammed the phone down. 'They say it can't be done, not with their current technology. Still, it was a good thought. Well done, Lieutenant.' He gave Yveline a quick smile and explained to Bruno that Yveline had wondered if the electricity network could pinpoint houses that had suddenly started using power after a week without.

Bruno excused himself to find a quiet space to make some calls, but the squad room was full of gendarmes being briefed and issued with local maps. He told Sergeant Jules that he'd be in the bar over the road. He ordered a coffee and called the number of Professor Philippeau in Paris. He explained himself, said that Dumesnil was in hospital without explaining why, but that he had been writing to the Professor about the Testament of Iftikhar. What could the Professor tell him about it?

'This is very odd. I hadn't heard of that supposed document for twenty years, but this is the fifth or sixth time it has come up in the last couple of months.'

He explained that it started at the annual meeting of the American Historical Association in January. He had given a lecture on Outremer, the Christian kingdom that was established around Jerusalem after the First Crusade. Afterwards, one of the American scholars came up to ask whether the Frenchman thought Iftikhar's Testament was genuine.

'A lot of historians are very dubious about it, me included. And then another one, who had been at some conference in Israel, said he'd heard a rumour there that it had been tracked down and some intensive tests were underway to establish whether it was genuine, the parchment and ink and so on. Of course I questioned him, but it seemed very vague, someone he didn't know talking about it in a group at a bar after a dinner but then shutting up when he realized he might have said too much. It's very political, you understand, this document. If it's genuine.'

'How did Dumesnil come into it?' Bruno asked.

'He was my pupil and I'm fond of him, a brilliant young man. So what's this about being in hospital? Nothing serious, I trust.'

'They say his condition is stable. When I spoke to him about it, he sounded very sceptical about this document, like you.'

'Yes, I rang him and we discussed the rumour, of which he had heard nothing. But it's possible because with all the chaos in the Arab world in recent years, museums and archives have been looted and destroyed.'

'Would that include documents?'

'Oh, certainly. There's a flood of Middle Eastern antiques and ancient books and documents on the world market, some price-less old Arabic calligraphy from the Baghdad museum. More has been reaching the market from Aleppo and more recently items from Nineveh and Mosul and Palmyra that Daesh has looted and sold. It's tragic that these collections have been broken up but I'm on a committee at the Institut du Monde Arabe here in Paris that advises on acquisitions. We're deluged with offers of material that a few years ago we'd have paid a fortune to have, but now they're being offered for a pittance.'

'So it's entirely possible that this long-lost Testament could suddenly have surfaced. But wouldn't the Arab museums have known what it was?'

'You wouldn't believe the state of some of these national museums, even before the Iraq War and the Arab Spring. They were underfunded, undermanned, too many jobs given as polit-ical patronage rather than to real scholars. The Arab curators were just as distressed, but even when the region was stable they had little influence.'

'So they might not have known what they had, what was there?'

'That's right. And we don't know what happened to the archives of King Baldwin other than that they were entrusted to the Templars. When Jerusalem fell to the Arabs in October 1187, Saladin was merciful. He allowed all the Christians to leave if they paid a ransom and there was a lot of haggling over the terms but finally the Templars and the Hospitallers agreed to pay the ransom of those without money, in return for being allowed to take with them their holy relics and ornaments. Heraclius, the Roman Christian patriarch of Jerusalem, left with wagons containing treasure and the relics from the Holy Sepulchre. The Templars led one of the refugee columns to Tyre, which was still in Christian hands, and they took their own treasure with them.'

'And that could have included the Testament?'

'Yes, it was supposedly shown to Richard Lionheart in Acre, when the Templars established themselves there. But after the rest of the Holy Land fell in 1291, except for a tiny offshore island that later fell to the Mamelukes, the Templars fled to Limassol in Cyprus and the trail goes cold. Whether it was lost in Acre, in Limassol or on the island of Arwad, we don't know. We do know that at this time the Templars had negotiated an alliance with the Mongols, who were ravaging the Muslims' lands from the east. And of course it could have been lost when Constantinople fell to the Ottomans in 1453.'

'So you think it's possible that the Testament was captured from the Templars, stored in some Muslim or Mameluke archive and has now reappeared in the chaos of the Arab world?'

'Yes, but it may be a fake. I joined one group in Baghdad a few years ago, with funds raised from charity to buy precious relics and bring them back to France for safekeeping. I was offered two Holy Shrouds, several pieces of the True Cross, nails from the Crucifixion and several swords of Saladin.'

'But only now are you hearing of the Testament of Iftikhar?'

'Yes, and I keep hearing about it, most recently from a British colleague, who said that somebody from the British Museum had been invited to Israel to help verify the document. And then two days ago I had a call about it from America, from a reporter on the *New York Times*, so word seems to be spreading. But until I see it and examine the original myself, I'm reserving judgement.'

'Do you have the name of this reporter and this British colleague?'

'The colleague is called Keenan, a medievalist at Merton College, Oxford, and the reporter was . . . let me check . . . yes, Jackson, Bill Jackson.'

Bruno thanked him, adding that he'd keep him informed about Dumesnil. Bruno then rang Amélie to relate what he'd learned and to say he needed her excellent research skills. He gave the names of the Professor's two contacts and asked if she could track down their phone numbers.

'No problem. I think my English is better than yours so do you want me to talk to them? I assume you're trying to track down the origin of these rumours about the Testament. And there are no new emails from your network – you left your email up on your screen. Do you want me to close it?'

'No, keep monitoring it. We're trying to organize a proper roadblock and search system. Thanks, Amélie.'

He sat back, reflecting on this remarkable young woman who'd entered his life. No, he wouldn't put it that way. Amélie was striking in her way, but not in any sense that stirred him. He respected her intelligence, her judgement and her readiness to help, and he admired her ambition. If he cultivated the relationship, they could become good friends, and he resolved to try to do so. As he was paying for his coffee, his phone rang. It was Philippe Delaron, asking about the shooting of a gendarme at Siorac and Bruno's sudden roadblock earlier that day.

'Call the police spokesman in Périgueux, Philippe. I'm not saying a word.'

'Nor is she, that's why I'm calling you. A cop shot, a teacher in Sarlat Hospital who's been tortured, gendarme helicopters and reinforcements and then you set up an impromptu roadblock outside Le Buisson. It's a manhunt for those guys whose photos you gave us. We can help, Bruno, if you could tell us a little more. I can put word out on the radio and in the paper.'

'I can put word out myself, Philippe, and when I can say more, I will.'

'Is it terrorists? Arabs? ISIS?'

'Sorry, Philippe.' He closed his phone and instantly it rang again.

'I just called the newsdesk at the *New York Times*,' said Amélie. 'They have no reporter by the name of Bill Jackson, and there is no freelance of that name on their books. But they told me that it wouldn't be the first time someone tried to impersonate one of their reporters. It may be significant that your Professor got a fake media call, almost as if somebody is trying to spread the news. Now I'll start looking for the guy at Oxford.'

'Wait, don't hang up. You mean that there is a deliberate attempt to spread a rumour about this Testament?'

'Absolutely. Something about this has triggered my suspicious little mind. After all, this all started with Leah's fall at Commarque and she was trying to paint something about it, and then that email of hers warning that somebody was trying to make a forgery. Why bother to make a forgery that could be disproved when you can make this document into a virtual reality by rumours.'

Bruno frowned, not sure he was following her meaning. 'Why would anyone want to do that?'

'There's one obvious suspect, and the strategy is smart: first the historians, some anonymous guy in a bar at a conference, then the newspapers start asking questions. Pretty soon I'll bet it's going to be on Twitter and then there'll be an internet meme. It doesn't have to exist in reality as long as people give it a kind of reality by talking and writing and arguing about it.'

Bruno understood. 'I get it. You and I had never heard any suggestion that Jerusalem was not really a holy site for Islam. But now we have. And as that word spreads, fed by rumour and hearsay, Israel's right to Jerusalem becomes stronger and the Arab claim weaker, even if this document never existed.'

'Exactly. You can't prove a negative. And that makes me wonder about what Leah was really up to.'

'On the face of it, she was sending a warning. But you're suggesting that she was trying to build this rumour, this myth of the existence of the Testament?'

'It fits, Bruno. Remember what you told me about trying to solve a crime – you start by building a hypothesis and then try to disprove it. This hypothesis of mine holds up. Assume for a moment that this is all some subtle Israeli intelligence ploy and that Leah, despite being known as a peace activist, was really working for Israeli intelligence. That might explain why she died. If the Arabs found out, they'd kill her for sure. It would also explain why she had set up a false French identity card and bank account over a year ago, long before all this had started.'

'You've been reading too many spy stories.'

'Maybe you haven't been reading enough. I'll ask the British Museum if they have really sent some expert scholar to Israel to examine a long-lost document from the Siege of Jerusalem. I'll bet they haven't.'

20

Bruno had learned in the army that there were few more point-less exercises than to hang around a headquarters getting in the way when nothing was happening. In those days he had taken such opportunities to catch up on his sleep, knowing that when something serious occurred sleep would be hard to come by.

So with the roadblocks in place, the helicopters cruising, and competent gendarmes manning the communications, there was nothing useful for Bruno to do. Rather than sleep, he needed the exercise and mental relaxation that he found on horseback. He collected Balzac and drove out, whistling, to Pamela's riding school with his dog, smelling faintly of Amélie's perfume, sitting alert beside him.

Breathing hard after a gallop with Hector along the ridge, Bruno looked down on his town as it nestled in the valley he knew so well. In the afternoon sun, the honey-coloured stone of the buildings and the arched bridge glowed the more richly. The stone and the red-tile roofs and the fresh green of springtime in the trees and gardens were all reflected in the river's smoothly flowing surface. He gazed, enjoying the scene, until he heard the familiar panting of Balzac finally catching up with his master and the great horse.

How strange and offensive that such a picturesque and peaceful scene should be under the threat of terrorists who had already destroyed towns and communities in their parts of the world. He had seen the newspaper photos and TV images of Aleppo and Homs. How could anyone seek deliberately to eradicate the monuments and the history of their own people? He felt sure they must fail. The past could never be wiped away with the arrogant sweep of a violent hand; the past always survived because memories remained and children grew up hearing them.

He knew that St Denis had known war within living memory; each day on the roads he passed small shrines to members of the Resistance who had been shot, *mort pour la France*. For centuries of the English occupation the Perigord had lived through war, and then suffered another century of France's own religious wars. And yet it had survived and prospered with its essence intact, the geography of the river and the rolling landscape shaping its character as a trading point, the fertile land and temperate climate making it a region that could feed far more than its inhabitants. But even as it attracted invaders and soldiers it could always hold out, endure, adapt and be rebuilt, if need be. Like their people, towns were resilient.

He nudged Hector with his knees, loosening the reins, and they set off down the trail through the woods at a gentle trot so that Balzac could keep up. When the woods thinned and the trail became a hunter's track, he increased the pace to the kind of canter that Hector could keep up for hours. Then, struck by an idea, he turned up another trail that led to the cabin used by the hunting club of St Cyprien, mostly formed of men he knew.

Two of them were skinning rabbits on the big tree stump outside the cabin when he arrived.

'You can't be going hunting with that,' said one of them, pointing at the gun on Bruno's belt. He was a man whose face Bruno knew but whose name he'd forgotten. Bruno shook his head, laughing.

'Seen any strangers in these parts?' he asked, after shaking hands and accepting a small glass of wine from an unlabelled bottle. He'd have preferred water, but wine was the custom. 'You may have heard, a gendarme got shot at Siorac by two guys in a white van and you'll see a lot of helicopters and roadblocks – but this time the cops won't be stopping you to check if you've been drinking. We think they've tried to hole up somewhere in the area. They're armed and dangerous, so if you see something suspicious don't get close, don't confront them, but let me know and we'll check it out.'

The two men shook their heads but said they'd pass on the word to let him know. Bruno shooed Balzac away from the pile of rabbit guts, mounted Hector once more and trotted back to the stables at the riding school. Once back at his office he greeted Amelie and then began calling all the hunting clubs in the area. Mostly, he had to leave a message, but usually he knew someone in each club and could track them down. He asked them all to let him know if any strangers were spotted, or a white van, or if any remote holiday home or *gîte* suddenly seemed to be inhabited.

'Networking the hunting clubs sounds like a good idea for other village policemen,' Amelie said, writing in her notebook. 'That's another recommendation for my report, like your email system to all the local hotels and campsites.'

'I'm afraid your report has been somewhat overtaken by events,' he said, smiling at her. 'You seem to have appointed yourself as my research partner, Leah being found dead on the same day you arrived.'

'I wouldn't have missed it for the world. It's been really interesting, giving me an insight into police work that I'd never usually get.' She bent down to stroke Balzac who was nuzzling at her knee. 'I hope I've been useful.'

'More than useful, you've been a godsend,' he said. 'You've got a gift for this, not routine police work but tackling this kind of emergency. I know you're planning on becoming a magistrate and building a political career, but I think you might find detective work more congenial.'

'How do you mean?'

'An English friend once told me of some statesman who said that all political careers were doomed to end in disappointment and usually in defeat. I imagine all politicians start off as idealists, hoping to achieve something, but politics is a rough game. I think you're impatient to achieve things, but you're likely to be endlessly frustrated. You must have thought about this.'

'Of course I have. But with a legal qualification, I'd have a second string to my bow if politics didn't work for me. And I think I have a talent for it.'

'No question, but you also have a talent for police work, for detection, or even for security, intelligence.

'That's not me,' she said firmly.

'Maybe not, but I'm sure you've realized that we in Europe are in for a long struggle. London, Madrid, Paris – they've all been attacked. This isn't going to stop and we're going to need a better, more subtle kind of security to defend ourselves against it, fresh minds, new thinking, people like you. It's your country, too.'

'Are you sure about that, Bruno? One reason why I think politics makes sense for me is that it's one career where the colour of my skin works in my favour. They need people like me because a lot of us have votes. Would I be as desirable to a police force? To an intelligence agency? To a bunch of detectives who find it hard enough to accept female colleagues, let alone a black one?'

'I can't challenge that, but have you felt the slightest whiff of racism here in St Denis?'

'No, but St Denis is unusual; you have a good mayor and it's a small town. Believe me, it's not like this in Paris or Marseilles.'

'But you accept the possibility that it could be if we do things right.'

'Yes, I do accept the possibility, but I think I can do more to bring that about through politics than I ever could in the security services.'

'You could be right, but it's their loss.'

'Thank you, I'll take that as a compliment. And don't forget I have another week to follow you around and watch you work.' She grinned. 'You may have changed your mind about me by then.'

He grinned back. 'We'll see. Now I'd better head off. I have to cook Horst's stag dinner and then be back at the gendarmerie at eight tomorrow morning for another security meeting. I'll see you here when I'm done.' He handed her a spare set of keys to the *mairie* and his office. 'And enjoy your dinner with Florence. Give her and the children my love.'

He collected the salmon from Ivan, who had kindly gutted it and removed the scales, picked up the young asparagus and lemons from Marcel and the *Sachertorte* from Fauquet. He drove home to feed the chickens and to collect his cooking knives, the new potatoes and some herbs from his greenhouse and *mâche* from the garden. Then he headed with Balzac for the Baron's house, where the red wines had been decanted and the table had been set for ten. Jack Crimson and the Baron were already drinking champagne in the kitchen, where Bruno unwrapped the fresh salmon and invited the two men to admire it.

'Do you want to use that for the salmon?' the Baron asked, pointing to the top of the wall cabinets where a metre-long copper poaching pan for fish had been gathering dust, unused for years.

'No, thanks. I'm planning to bake it.' He began to wipe the inside and the skin of the salmon dry with kitchen paper.

'I don't have a roasting pan big enough.'

'I'm going to do it on a rack, wrapped in foil. And I'll put more foil on the bottom of your oven to catch any drips.'

He chopped the tarragon and parsley and mixed the herbs with the zest of three lemons, a head of finely chopped garlic, a tablespoon of olive oil and salt and pepper. He used his favourite knife to score eight deep slashes into each side of the fish, stuffing a generous portion of his herb paste into each slash. He then sliced two of the lemons and used them along with half of the herb paste to stuff the salmon's stomach cavity. He spread a thin film of Dijon mustard over the top of the salmon and then added the remainder of the herb paste, and squeezed the juice of two lemons on top.

'Right, that's it,' he said, as he finished wrapping the fish in foil. 'When the guests arrive, I'll put it into a very hot oven for about fifteen minutes, then turn it down to medium heat while we eat our asparagus and cook the new potatoes. Now I just have to prepare the asparagus and the salad and make a vinaigrette.'

'The chef deserves a drink; champagne, scotch or wine?' Crimson asked.

'A glass of champagne, please,' Bruno replied. 'Do you know all the men who are coming?'

'All the locals, of course, and Horst, and I've also run across another of his guests, an English friend called Manners. He's a former soldier like you, retired as a colonel and now a bursar at one of the Oxford colleges.' Crimson poured out a glass of Monthuys for Bruno and refilled his own and the Baron's glass.

'I knew his father as well, also a soldier, who served around here with the Resistance during the war on one of the Jedburgh teams,' Crimson went on. 'They were dropped into France before D-Day to organize parachute drops of weapons and to train the Resistance fighters.'

'Was that when that second important cave was found?'

'I gather so. They also got caught up in some of the in-fighting between the communists and the Gaullists in the Resistance. It was a difficult time. But you'll like young Manners, and his American wife, Lydia, who was with him when they and Horst found the new cave. She's a stunner, now also at Oxford, a curator at the Ashmolean Museum.'

'So with you and me, Horst and the Baron, Gilles and the Mayor and Manners, that makes seven. Who are the other three?'

'One British and two German archaeologists,' the Baron

replied. 'I think the two Germans arrived today and they'll be staying at your place. The British one is staying with Crimson, a Professor Barrymore. He's upstairs changing. He got here about an hour ago, very excited about this new cave the seismic experts have found at Commarque. He said Horst was so enthusiastic about it he wasn't sure he'd get here in time for dinner.'

'He'd better,' came a voice from the kitchen door. It was Gilles, carrying a big cheese platter in both hands. He greeted his friends and accepted a glass of scotch.

'I like the look of that,' he said, admiring the salmon. Bruno set a kettle to boil and began washing the asparagus while the Baron trimmed them, bending the stem of each one until it snapped naturally. Gilles washed and chopped the salad, all of them working companionably side by side as they had done often before at hunting feasts and their own dinners.

By the time the Mayor arrived and the English archaeologist came down to join them, the salad and vinaigrette had been prepared along with the bowl of ice water that Bruno would use to blanch the asparagus once they had boiled for three minutes. Crimson was opening a bottle of sparkling rosé wine as young Lespinasse dropped off Horst, Manners and the two Germans. Bruno set the oven to 250 degrees for the fish, checked his watch and put the kettle on to boil for the asparagus.

Even without being told, Bruno would have known that Manners had been a professional soldier. He stood erect but relaxed, a half-smile playing on his face as he strove to be pleasant to a group composed mainly of strangers. He watched and listened carefully to the others and thought before he spoke. When he did say something it was short, to the point and in good French.

He also seemed comfortable speaking German to Horst's friends. In Bosnia, Bruno had come into contact with British officers forged in a similar mould, or perhaps a similar school. They were invariably polite to their men, attentive to their sergeants and usually ready to take responsibility. But then, he thought, the British had ended conscription and returned to the tradition of a small professional army before Bruno had been born. The French army by contrast still retained the heritage of the *levée en masse* that went back before Napoleon to the revolutionary wars.

The conversation ebbed and flowed as the meal unfolded – the fresh asparagus in melted butter, the salmon and new potatoes with the Jaubertie white wine. The Mayor, Horst and the Baron chose the Merlot from Chateau Laulerie instead. Horst had decreed that the language of the evening would be French, and the St Denis contingent were entertained by reminiscences of archaeological digs in Scotland, Germany, France and the Holy Land until Bruno cleared the plates and brought in the salad. The cheese board circulated as the Mayor asked about the impact of DNA upon their profession.

'I recall your lecture at the museum in Les Eyzies, on the way the DNA had proved there had been interbreeding between the Neanderthals and their Cro-Magnon successors,' the Mayor said to Horst. 'Have there been new developments?'

'Tell them of Professor Sykes, your Oxford colleague,' Horst said to the Englishman, Barrymore. He was small and dapper with curly red hair, brushed into order with hair oil. He had slipped into a pocket the tie he had been wearing on seeing that the others were all casually dressed.

Bryan Sykes was a genetics professor at Oxford, Barrymore explained, one of the world experts in the field who had worked on the five-thousand-year-old DNA of the so-called Iceman found frozen in the Alps, and had traced a direct descendant, a woman living in modern Britain. He had also used DNA to prove that the bodies found in Ekaterinburg in 1991 were indeed those of the Tsar of Russia and his family, slaughtered by the Bolsheviks. More recently, he had explored the mitochondrial DNA through the female line back to the original Eve.

'Not Adam's consort of the Bible,' Barrymore added. 'This Eve was an African woman who had lived between 100,000 and 200,000 years ago and was our most recent common ancestor, the woman from whom all known human beings are descended. Sykes explored the DNA further to establish seven subgroups from whom almost all modern Europeans are descended, and called them "the seven daughters of Eve". The most important, whom he called Helena and who had lived in this very region of south-western France, was the direct ancestor of around 45 per cent of modern Europeans.

'The next most important ancestress had been named Jasmine; she came from modern-day Syria or Israel and was ancestress to around 17 per cent of modern Europeans,' Barrymore added. He raised his eyebrows and looked around the table mischievously. 'I suppose I should write a letter to *The Times* suggesting that this could mean lots of those poor Syrian refugees are simply rejoining their family members long ensconced in Europe.'

Bruno was charmed by the idea that almost half of Europe's population came from a single woman who had lived in his part of France. But why name her Helena, he wondered? It sounded

Greek to him. Why not name her Francette or Marianne, or even Europa?

'Is there any map or graphic that could give some indication of where Helena's and Jasmine's descendants had spread?' Bruno asked. He had long considered the various wars of the twentieth and earlier centuries as so many civil wars between the various European tribes. Even more than that, he thought, the conflicts were family quarrels!

'You'll find various attempts on the internet,' said Barrymore. 'One of my postgraduate students is trying to do something more detailed. And I know our friend Horst, after his latest work on the Venus figurines, is wondering whether there is any connection between our great ancestress Helena and her sisters.'

'I've been looking in particular at two rare examples of Venus found near here,' Horst said. 'One comes from the cave of Laugerie Basse. She was dubbed by her finder *La Vénus Impudique*, or the Immodest Venus, since unlike most of the classic Greek Venus figures, she made no effort to conceal her breasts and vulva with her hands. She's slim and athletic, a striking contrast to the overblown matrons being carved in the same period. The other was also a slim young woman, whom I know to be a particular favourite of Bruno's, carved at a time about midway through her pregnancy. Known as the Venus of Abri Pataud, she came from the cliff behind Les Eyzies, where she was found in 1958, so named because Pataud had been the family that owned the land.'

'There's a recent book, very popular in Germany, *Why French-women Don't Get Fat*, which suggests to me that your ancestral Helena could have been one of these slim Venus figures,' said

Horst's friend from the valley of the Neanderthal, smiling broadly. 'She must have passed on the genetic gift of being slender to her French descendants.'

'What a wonderful wedding gift from Clio,' said Manners, 'to present you with this new cave at Commarque.'

Bruno was wondering who this Clio person might be, when Barrymore raised his glass and declared, 'A toast, to Clio, goddess of history, daughter of Zeus and muse of historians.'

'Clio, the cruel goddess, who rides her chariot over heaps of the dead,' intoned Manners, also raising his glass.

'Clio, she who has the power to make men famous,' added one of the Germans, and the others raised their glasses in turn. Bruno followed suit, smiling to himself that learned professors and academics could make just as much fools of themselves as anyone else when the wine had been flowing. A short buzz came from the phone at his waist to signal an incoming message. Discreetly, he checked it. Isabelle had texted him that the gendarme who had been shot at Siorac would live.

21

Thankful that the quality of the wine and his deliberate avoidance of Crimson's whisky had spared him a hangover, Bruno entered the gendarmerie shortly before eight the following morning. He had spent the previous thirty minutes in his office, checking emails and messages from his networks. At one point he had risen from his desk in excitement to study the map on his wall. On the way to the briefing he stopped at the *maison de la presse* to buy copies of the detailed local maps used by hikers, and marked each of them with his latest findings. Pleased that he had something significant to contribute, he greeted Prunier and J-J as their car pulled up. Despite the cardboard coffee cups each man carried, they looked tired and solemn. Bruno's bright mood did not last long after J-J looked at him grimly and asked, 'Heard the news?'

'Not yet. What's up?'

'That ex-nun in my paedo case, the alcoholic. She committed suicide yesterday, pills and a bottle of gin. The problem is, she phoned Madame Duteiller, the psychologist, who happened to be giving her statement at the commissariat at the time, on this tax evasion charge. So Duteiller didn't get the message and now she's saying that it was just a cry for help, and the ex-nun would still be alive if she'd been able to take the call. She says the nun told her she was going to end it all because there would be no justice for the innocent victims of Mussidan.'

'Did the nun leave a suicide note?'

'Yes, saying exactly the same thing and adding that she blamed me in particular and the police in general for not getting the evidence to sustain her story. Duteiller is now all over the radio saying the police are responsible for the nun's death. If it weren't for this case, I'd have been hauled up before the Prefect by now.'

'Is the radio also saying that Duteiller was in the police station because she was being charged with tax evasion?'

'We'll see whether the commune wants to press those charges after they listen to the local news. I'm not getting my hopes up. Right now, the nun is a victim of police neglect and Duteiller is the saintly angel of mercy seeking to bring justice to molested kids.'

Prunier shook his head. 'Don't worry, J-J. I'll give a statement to the radio as soon as this is over and put matters straight. And I'll make sure the commune files charges against Madame Duteiller.'

Sergeant Jules showed the three of them into Yveline's office and Bruno almost stopped in his tracks when he saw the Brigadier and Isabelle seated behind the desk, frowning at their laptops. She was the last person he'd expected to see back in St Denis. At least she hadn't seen his surprise, and probably would not detect the way his pulse was racing at the sight of her.

'*Bonjour*, messieurs,' the Brigadier greeted them, hastily adding, 'and you, mademoiselle,' when he noticed Yveline slipping into the room. 'I believe you all know the excellent

Commissaire Perrault, whose local knowledge and European connections I thought would be useful.'

Isabelle smiled politely and then rose to be heartily kissed by J-J, her former boss when she had been stationed in the Périgord. Prunier was greeted with a cool, 'Bonjour, monsieur,' while Bruno received only a courteous nod and a handshake that lingered just a moment too long. Half expecting this, he returned a beaming smile and she raised an eyebrow in return, an ironic facial gesture he recalled fondly, before asking after Balzac. She was looking well, a little tired but her eyes were bright. The thrill of the chase had always inspired her.

'I have to brief the Minister at nine before he goes to the Elysée to report to the President,' the Brigadier went on, 'and so far there's nothing new to tell him, except that the overtime bills will be going through the roof. I'm hoping you gentlemen can improve that.'

Nobody spoke. J-J made a gesture of deference to Prunier, who grimaced and said, 'Nothing new to report, sir, except that our roadblocks have all been manned throughout the night and minor roads patrolled by helicopters with searchlights. It looks as though these terrorists have found somewhere to hole up and eat the food they bought. Once they break cover, which we assume they will have to do, we should get them.'

'We're checking all known associates in France of this woman Leah and the scholar al-Husayni, but have found no such connection yet for Mustaf. The other two remain unknown to us or to our European neighbours,' said J-J. 'We're running their photos through various databases, but no hits yet. Sir, has the anti-terrorist team completed the list of possible targets?'

'We are adding to it all the time,' intervened Isabelle. She mentioned two possible human targets: a former French President and Prime Minister who lived in the region and a former Foreign Minister who lived near Sarlat. The Foreign Minister had been in office at the time of Iraq's invasion of Kuwait, when French troops had joined the Americans and British in liberating the oil-rich sheikhdom.

'There's also your neighbour Monsieur Crimson, former head of Britain's joint intelligence committee at the time of the Iraq War, the one we did not see fit to join,' the Brigadier added. 'He's authorized to keep a weapon for self-defence, but I've arranged for a guard to be assigned. Bruno, do you have anything for us?'

'Yes, sir, we may have something. As you know, my local network gave us the first sighting at the Casino store yesterday, and now a second network, of local hunting clubs, has come up with three rural houses which were certainly unoccupied a week ago but which now have signs of occupation. We're fortunate that the hunting season is not quite ended. The hunters noticed fresh tyre tracks, chimney smoke and, in one case, a crack of light showing where curtains had not been properly closed. I'm checking the records to see if we can identify the owners and plan to call each of them as soon as we're done here. Meanwhile, here's a copy of a detailed local map and I've marked each building, assuming you'll want to brief the helicopter teams.'

'Well, thank the Lord somebody seems to know what he's doing. Don't let us keep you,' the Brigadier said. He handed Bruno a small, square enamel badge, about the size of a thumbnail, formed of a blue and a white oblong inside a red border. Bruno saw that the Brigadier and Isabelle were wearing the same badges. 'Keep that on at all times. Everybody briefed for this operation will know that it means you're on my staff. And now back to your lair. Track down those owners as soon as you can and call me or Isabelle with the results.'

'Yes, sir,' said Bruno, before saluting and leaving. He had one owner's name already, of what looked like an old *fermette*, a small family farm in the sprawling rural commune of Urval. The owner of the second house, in the woods beyond St Cyprien, would have to be checked by the local policeman. The third house was in a commune too small to have its own local policeman, but the Mayor of St Denis was tracking down his colleague to open the tiny *mairie* early and check the map and tax records. As he approached the *mairie*, he spotted Amélie, who waved and called out a greeting from Fauquet's terrace. He tapped his watch in return, signalling that he had no time to talk.

'No, wait,' she called, jumping up from the café table and coming across to him at a perilous pace in her customary high heels. 'This is important. Those photos from Gare de l'Est. Did you notice they all smoked when they were on the terrace of the balcony on the square? Smokers need their fix. So I made a list for you of all the licensed *tabacs* in the area, emails and phone numbers and loaded it onto your computer yesterday.'

'Many thanks and *bonjour*,' he embraced her and darted up the steps of the *mairie* to send out the email to all the *tabacs* with photos of the four suspects attached.

Once he had collected the name of the property owners from the St Cyprien colleague and from the Mayor, he checked the *annuaire* for the three phone listings and began calling the houses his hunting contacts had identified. The first phone was answered sleepily by a voice speaking what sounded like Dutch. After Bruno repeated his question, the Dutchman said in halting French that he and his family had recently arrived from Rotterdam for a spring holiday. There was no reply from the house near Urval, and he could find no phone listing for the name of the owner in the tiny commune of Castels. It would have to be searched, and he emailed the details to Isabelle and the Brigadier. He then sent the email with photos attached to Amélie's list of tobacco shops and went back down the stairs for a coffee and croissant with Amélie.

'You really are very good at this,' he said. 'I wish you'd think again about what I said.'

'Forget it,' she said sharply. 'Any more thoughts about the target? I was looking through the local paper to see if there were any long-planned events that might attract them, like the big football match in Paris. I don't think local rugby games are what the jihadists have in mind. Nor this new cave at Commarque. Your friendly local reporter has used it to write about the Templars again.'

'I'm not surprised. He has to sell papers. How was your evening with Florence?'

'Great, I really liked her, once she stopped singing your praises. It was almost embarrassing, until she said she sang in the choir and then we started doing duets. She has a great voice. She said you'd got her the job at the *collége*.'

He shook his head. 'I just heard that the old science teacher was retiring, and she's a trained chemist with a university degree, which meant she was much better qualified than most of the science teachers we tend to get around here. She's getting her teaching qualification while working.'

'Yes, she told me that. And how she went about starting the computer club. And her kids are great.'

'I'm glad you got to know them. She's a wonderful woman, a real asset to the town. I expect she'll be elected to the council before long and become one of my bosses.' He paused, looking at his watch. 'I'd better get back to the gendarmerie to see if they have work for me. Meanwhile, I'd be grateful if you can track down these two property owners and see why their houses suddenly show signs of life.' He handed her the short list and said the first one had been checked, a Dutchman he'd woken up when he called him.

'If he's Dutch, why is his name de Villiers?'

'It's a fairly common Dutch name, from the Huguenot Protestants who fled there in our wars of religion.' He paused, reflecting. 'Maybe we should double-check.'

Leaving Balzac with Amélie, Bruno headed for the café to ask Fauquet if there'd been any Hollanders in today, but he shook his head. He began looking through his phone for the number of Willem, a Dutch friend from the tennis club, but as he returned to the terrace Amélie was already on her phone. She seemed to be asking someone to call the number to see if whoever answered was really Dutch and then call her back. She paused and laughed in response to something and closed her phone.

'What was the joke?'

'A friend in Amsterdam who's going to call them now. She said if there was any doubt she might ask them to say Scheveningen.' The word sounded as if Amélie had developed a persistent cough. 'It's the name of a town on the coast that only a Hollander can pronounce. Apparently it was how they identified Germans in the war.'

'First rule of policing,' said Bruno. 'Make sure you have friends everywhere.'

Amélie looked at her phone as if willing it to ring. But Bruno's phone rang first, the one he'd been given by the Brigadier during a previous case. Along with the special ringtone came a tell-tale green light that showed the caller was someone else connected to the special security network. It was Isabelle.

'Where are you?' she asked, her voice brisk as if to tell him that this was official. Bruno wondered why she bothered. Every call on this network was automatically recorded.

'Just leaving my office and heading back to the gendarmerie,' he said, in a tone as official as hers. Damn it, he thought to himself, we know each other too well for this. And allowing his voice to convey the affection he felt for her, he added, 'Shall I bring Balzac along? He'd love to see you.'

There was a pause and then he heard a non-verbal sound that seemed friendly; in a cat, it would have been a purr. 'I'd love to see him, but it's not a good idea. I'll try to see him later. We've got a helicopter on the way to the house near Castels and then it will check on St Cyprien—'

'Wait a moment,' Bruno interrupted, seeing Amélie answering her own phone and gesturing at him. 'Another report coming in.'

'No reply?' Amélie was saying into her phone. 'Are you sure? Somebody answered just a few minutes ago. Could you try it one more time? It's really important.'

Bruno spoke to Isabelle: 'We're checking on the house where

I spoke to someone, apparently a Dutchman. We're trying to confirm that with a native Dutch speaker and now the phone's not answering. I'll call you back.'

As soon as he closed his phone, it rang again and an unfamiliar male voice asked, 'Is that Chef de Police Courrèges?'

'Yes, speaking. Who is this?'

'My name is Laurier. I run the *tabac* on the main street in St Cyprien and got the email you sent. A man has just been in the shop who was the spitting image of the older man in your photos. I took a good look at him because he bought two cartons, that's four hundred cigarettes. Marlboros, and we don't often sell cartons here. A hundred and forty euros it was and he wanted a new lighter, some chocolate bars and mints. He gave me three new fifties and I let him have a lighter for free and a plastic bag to put it all in.'

'How long ago was this?'

'Five or ten minutes. I served him and afterwards I was looking at the news on my tablet. My wife gave it to me for my birthday. Anyway, after I'd looked at the headlines I checked the emails and saw your message.'

'What was he wearing?'

'I didn't really notice. Jeans, I think, and a roll-neck sweater and a leather jacket. I remember he was wearing a baseball cap.'

'Was he on foot or did he have a car?'

'I think he was on foot but I wasn't really looking, sorry. He might have had a car further down the street. Is this a criminal thing? Not forged banknotes, I hope.'

'No, it's just routine, not about forgery. But thank you,

Monsieur Laurier. Could you just take a look outside and see if he's still in sight?'

'No sign of him,' said Laurier after a brief pause and Bruno thanked him again, ended the call and turned to look at Amélie.

'No reply the second time my friend called.'

'Right, I have to go,' he said. 'That was one of your *tabac* men. He just sold two cartons of Marlboros to al-Husayni in St Cyprien. Thanks, Amélie, and well done. Could you keep trying that number where there was no reply? It strikes me as suspicious. I'll ring you from the gendarmerie.'

He called Isabelle as he trotted along the rue St Denis.

'We have a sighting,' he said. 'It happened minutes ago in the *tabac* in St Cyprien, within walking distance of that house with the suspect Dutchman. The shopkeeper identified Husayni.'

'But how—' she began.

Bruno interrupted her. 'I sent photos to all the *tabacs* and this one just called me. But you'd better warn the helicopter team that they may have a hot landing zone and see if you can arrange extra back-up.'

'Right, got it.' Before she closed the phone he heard her shout, 'Stop, everybody, emergency . . .'

Minutes later when he entered Yveline's office, he caught the mood of controlled urgency that he remembered from military operations rooms when a serious mission was underway. Isabelle smiled at him, put her hand over the mouthpiece of the phone she was holding and said, 'The GIGN helicopter is heading for St Cyprien, touching down in about fifteen minutes. Another one is on the way and we're rerouting all the motorbike cops to seal off the town.'

'There's more,' said Bruno, and the room fell silent, the Brigadier, Prunier and J-J all turning from the phones to look at him expectantly. Yveline stopped putting pins into the big map on the wall and turned to listen.

'About twenty minutes ago I called the house outside St Cyprien. A male voice answered claiming to be Dutch, just arrived at his holiday home. When I got a native Dutch speaker to call him, just ten minutes later, there was no reply. The house is marked on the map I gave you. Then I got the call from the *tabac* owner. He said that al-Husayni was carrying a plastic bag containing two cartons of cigarettes and chocolate bars,' Bruno said, and described the clothes he'd been wearing. 'This is the scholarly one, not a trained soldier.'

'Understood,' said the Brigadier and turned back to speak into his phone. 'We have a possible location. Please route gendarme helicopter call sign Angel Two to a house two kilometres northwest of St Cyprien, map reference seven-four-one-two-two-six. Land the combat team to observe only and then I want that helicopter circling overhead until we can get reinforcements there. I want the other helicopters to head for St Cyprien and await instructions.'

Prunier was barking out orders for police units to converge on St Cyprien and start door-to-door inquiries with the photographs, while J-J was telling his forensics team to head for the gendarmerie in the town and call him when they were about to arrive. And now we wait, thought Bruno, to learn the fate of the men we are sending into danger.

'Right,' said the Brigadier. 'Time for me to talk to Paris, so I'll be grateful if you'd let me have the room for a few minutes.

Carry on, everybody, and remember we want to get these men alive.'

J-J went out to the gendarmerie steps to have a cigarette. Yveline reloaded the coffee machine in the squad room and Isabelle asked for the ladies' room. Yveline gave her a key.

'Use my apartment. It's on the ground floor, to the right.' She pointed the way across the yard to the small apartment block, known inevitably as *la caserne*, the barracks where the gendarmes lived. 'The budget didn't run for providing a second bathroom for women in the gendarmerie. So we use my place.'

Prunier took Bruno's arm and said, 'Tell me about these networks of yours. How do they work, exactly?'

Bruno explained how he'd organized the first list as a way for far-flung members of the Police Municipale to keep in regular contact, then how he'd added the tourist offices, hotels and restaurants and recently the hunting clubs.

'The credit should go to this young woman from the Justice Ministry who's following me around to do a report on the future of the Police Municipale. Apparently her minister likes the idea of beefing up what she calls the Police de Proximité, closer to the public. She's a brilliant researcher, and she realized I hadn't taken advantage of the internet to bring together all my local contacts. It was she who had the idea of adding the *tabacs*. I'd never have thought of it, and she set up the list-serve system so I can reach all of them with one email. She's been extraordinary, using social media to identify Leah and then researching her background. We'd never have picked up on this Testament of Iftikhar without her.'

'What else do you know about her?'

'She's a rising star in the socialist party, on the executive of their youth wing, sits on their international committees and plans to go into politics. It's a shame. She'd be brilliant as a detective, or in intelligence.'

'What did she study?'

Bruno explained what he knew, adding, as Yveline joined them with a pot of fresh coffee, that Amélie had also graduated from magistrate's school.

'I had dinner with her at Bruno's place,' Yveline said. 'She's very smart, I liked her and she sings like an angel.'

Bruno wondered whether he should mention Amélie's concern about her cousin's daughter, but J-J returned, still talking on his phone. Isabelle came in through the rear door, and Prunier's phone then rang, followed instantly by Yveline's.

'They've got him? Brilliant,' Yveline said, and gave Bruno a thumbs-up as she replied to whoever was on the other end of her phone. Then her face fell as she put the phone down.

'*Merde*! He's been shot, but not by us. The Brigadier's on the phone with the Minister in Paris. I'd better go in and tell him. A gendarme van found al-Husayni. Apparently he was shot on the street while walking out of town, but he's alive,' she told Bruno, her hand knocking on the door of her own office. Before she slipped inside to tell the Brigadier she added, 'The gendarmes said they would bring him straight here to the clinic in St Denis.'

'Which direction was he walking?' Bruno asked her, looking at the map.

'The gendarmes van had come through Les Eyzies and Meyrals,' Yveline replied before disappearing.

'That's the direction of the Dutchman's house,' said Isabelle, wearing a single headphone and sitting by the main radio set. 'The GIGN helicopter is on the way.'

'It's no more than twenty minutes since I rang and spoke to the supposed Dutchman,' Bruno said. 'If they decided to flee at that point and abandon al-Husayni, they won't have got far.'

'The roadblocks are still in place. We should have them.'

The Brigadier came out of Yveline's office, closing his phone. 'One down, three to go. Do we have a holding charge we can use to arrest this al-Husayni? I'd rather not use the anti-terror legislation at this stage. We'd never keep that from the media.'

'Leaving the scene of an accident, Leah's fall,' said Bruno. 'Suspicion of being an accomplice to her murder and maybe breaking into the de Villiers' house, if that's where he was coming from.'

The Brigadier turned to Isabelle. 'Any word from the GIGN team?'

'Just that they're on the way; they have the new coordinates,' she said, the phone pressed tightly to her ear.

'Right, no point in sitting around waiting for news,' the Brigadier said. 'Who's going to interrogate al-Husayni when he gets here?'

'I'll do it with Bruno,' said J-J.

'Do we need an Arabic translator?'

'No,' said Bruno. 'Dumesnil met him with Leah and told me that al-Husayni speaks good French. And we might want to begin on the assumption that he may not be a hostile witness.'

The Brigadier gave Bruno a sceptical glance and then Yveline interrupted.

'The GIGN team has landed, taking positions and watching,

as ordered, sir. They report no signs of life at the house, front door open.'

'Send them in,' said the Brigadier. 'And make sure all the roadblocks are on top alert.'

22

Saïd al-Husayni was a bespectacled man in his forties, looking pale and exhausted as he lay in the St Denis clinic. His left arm and shoulder were swathed in bandages and his face was bruised and scraped.

'He's a lucky man,' said Fabiola, as Bruno and J-J came into the room. 'One bullet through the upper arm and another just below the shoulder that then glanced off a rib. He won't lose the arm but I don't know if he'll have much use of it for a while. We don't have an anaesthetist here so I had to use a local anaesthetic. You can have ten minutes, but if I tell you to stop the interview, you stop. Is that clear? He's lost quite a lot of blood.'

'Thank you for letting us see him,' said J-J. Like Bruno, he was now wearing one of the Brigadier's identifying badges. 'We'll do as you say.'

J-J greeted Husayni politely by name, preceding it with Monsieur, introduced himself and Bruno and asked if he would like some water or anything.

'Might I have some coffee, please,' came the reply. Al-Husayni looked bemused by the courtesy of his reception. 'And could I have a cigarette? They took my bag from me.'

J-J took out a pack of his own Royale filters, but Fabiola shook her head. 'You can have water, but we're out of coffee, and we don't allow cigarettes in this clinic.'

'How were you shot?' J-J asked.

'They all wanted cigarettes and I was told to go and buy some, but they didn't trust me alone so I was driven to the town by Sadiq, given money and told to buy two cartons. When I came out of the shop and walked back to the car, he'd turned the car around. He had the phone to his ear and when I opened the passenger door he shot me in cold blood, snap-snap, just like that.'

'Did he use a silencer?'

'I don't know, it was a very long barrel. Not very noisy, but I heard it clearly.'

'Were you with Mustaf of your own free will?' J-J asked in an affable way. He had taken a chair beside Husayni's bed. Bruno was in his shirtsleeves and leaning casually against the wall by the window after putting a tape recorder on the bedside cabinet and turning it on.

'The last time I was a free man was when I was studying in Spain,' said al-Husayni, taking a deep breath as if he were sucking on a cigarette. 'I have family in Ramallah and Mustaf told me they would be killed if I did not do what he ordered. You don't know what these men are capable of.'

'We know what they did to Dumesnil,' said Bruno.

'They are animals. They made me question him, a kindly, harmless man like that. It made me ill. Have you arrested them all?'

'Let's begin at the beginning,' said J-J. 'Were you there at Commarque when Leah died?'

'Died? She was killed.' Al-Husayni almost spat the world. 'Mustaf hated her. He despised women and she was a Jew. He only tolerated her as long as he did because of me. He liked me to tell him of the history of the Caliphate and the time of Arab rule in Spain. That was what he dreamed of, that such days would come again. He made me tell it again and again, that Arabs had once ruled here in this part of France.'

'How was Leah killed?'

'Mustaf cut her rope and pushed her off the wall when she insisted on painting her slogan. I was waiting below with the Belgian and saw her fall.'

Who might the Belgian be? Bruno wondered, exchanging glances with J-J.

'Ah, yes. The Belgian,' J-J said easily and opened a manila file on his knee, leafing through to a random page as though knowing what he was looking for and finding it significant. The file looked to Bruno like Yveline's duty rota for her gendarmes. J-J looked up from the file. 'And what name was he using with you?'

'Ahmed, but he spoke bad Arabic, very crude, with an Algerian accent. His French was better and he also spoke Dutch, or maybe it was Flemish. I think he came from Antwerp.'

J-J held up the photographs from the Gare de l'Est. 'You can see we've had you all under surveillance since you arrived.'

'Yes, that's Ahmed, and Mustaf and me with Leah,' Husayni said. 'And that's Sadiq, of course.' He pointed with his good arm at the remaining man. 'He's French, a convert originally from Normandy, never told me his original name. Ahmed and Sadiq had both been fighting in Syria and were very proud that Mustaf chose them for this mission.'

'How long ago was that, when they were chosen?' Bruno asked, thinking how long it had been since Leah set up her false ID and bank account.

Husayni tried to shrug but a spasm of pain crossed his face. 'They never said.'

'How about you? When did they force you to join them?'

'A month ago. I was smuggled out through Sinai, then from Cairo to Spain on a forged Spanish passport. They knew I spoke Spanish well. From Barcelona I was told to fly to Frankfurt and then go by train to Paris.'

'What about Leah? When did she leave?'

'The same time as me, but being Israeli, she could fly out to Cyprus and then to Paris. They told each of us the other would be killed if we did not do as we were told.'

'Did you know Leah had earlier set up a false identity?' J-J asked.

'Yes, of course. That was our plan. She told me that she'd done that so that she and I could be together in France as we felt we could never be in Palestine, or in Israel. We were waiting for a medieval history conference in Seville. We knew I'd receive a formal invitation there. That would allow me to get a visa to leave Israel.'

'Why would you need a false identity in France?' Bruno asked.

'Because I feared these people would look for me and demand that I work for them, once I was out.'

'It is not illegal for a Palestinian to marry an Israeli and live in Israel,' J-J said.

'Oh yes it is,' said al-Husayni, bridling. 'An amendment to the Nationality Act of 2003 barred a Palestinian from living with an

Israeli spouse inside Israel. And Israel's Supreme Court ruled in 2006 that this did not violate rights under the constitution, which they call the Basic Laws. Even if it did, the court said, this erosion of family unification was outweighed by security concerns.'

'I didn't know that,' J-J said.

'We wanted to be married, to start a family.' He took a sip of water. 'Leah was worried that time was running out for her.'

'I'm sorry to ask this, but did you know that Leah was over two months pregnant when she died?' J-J could sound very sympathetic when he chose, Bruno observed. He was more accustomed to seeing the big detective in bullying mode during interrogations.

The Palestinian rolled his head back to stare unseeing at the ceiling. J-J remained silent, waiting for Husayni to react. The seconds stretched out and then finally came the single word, 'Leah.' It was more like a sigh than a statement.

'She said she thought she might be. We hoped – we had dreamed – that she was.' He shook his head and raised his good hand to his eyes. Bruno glanced at J-J, willing him not to press Husayni too far. J-J maintained a sympathetic silence until Huysani was ready to continue.

'You must understand that once we were in France with Mustaf it was impossible to go to a doctor to confirm it. We would simply have given Mustaf even more of a hold over us,' he went on.

'When Leah died, do you remember seeing a cow's horn?' Bruno asked gently.

Husayni nodded. 'I tripped over it in the woods on our way

to the castle and when I saw Leah was dead, I left it by her side. Something about the way she lay, it reminded me of a piece of prehistoric art she loved. She had a postcard of it on the wall of our bedroom in Ramallah.'

'The Venus of Laussel,' said Bruno.

Husayni smiled at him. 'That's the one.'

'Why did Mustaf want you along?' Bruno asked, hoping to steer the talk towards Mustaf's mission. 'You're not a jihadi, not a fighting man.'

'Leah had been talking openly about this Testament of Iftikhar and the rumour that it was being verified and was about to emerge. She suspected it would be a very clever forgery and that this would have to be exposed by Western scholars whose criticisms would have far more weight than anything Arab scholars could muster. Some Islamic scholars took this very seriously and so did some influential imams. They alerted their contacts among the jihadists and we found ourselves conscripted.'

'Why would a jihadist operation in France compromise itself by bringing along two amateurs like you?'

'My younger brother is a jihadi,' said al-Husayni. 'He knew of our plans to get out of the country to live in France and knew that Leah had managed to set up an identity and bank account here. They thought that would be useful to them, and they would be able to keep a watch on us. I don't think Mustaf had much interest in the Testament. A clean bank account and French identity that he could use to rent cars and accommodation was much more important to him.'

'How did you find the second house?' Bruno asked.

'As soon as we got into the first place, Mustaf told the other two to look around for alternatives in case we had to leave in a hurry.'

'You mean Ahmed and Sadiq?'

'No, the other two, new ones, Frenchmen who joined us later. They had Arab origins, but were born and raised here. I only saw them once, when they took us to this place near St Cyprien. It's a pretty town.'

J-J scribbled a note, passed it to Bruno and asked him to give the news to the Brigadier. As he left, Bruno heard J-J ask, 'Did these two Frenchmen have names?'

Bruno called the gendarmerie, but the Brigadier was on his phone again so Bruno dictated J-J's note to Sergeant Jules and asked him to take it to the Brigadier and hold it up before his eyes. Within seconds, Bruno's phone rang.

'Two new ones, just what we need,' said the Brigadier. 'No names, no ID?'

'Not yet, but he's being very cooperative. We'll probably need an artist to do some sketches with him. What about the house?'

'The birds had flown and now we've lost them again. The coffee on the table was still hot. They left in a hurry, leaving some papers, a lot of prints. We're working on those now.'

'I'd better go back in,' said Bruno.

'Tell me about this car the other two guys were using,' J-J was saying.

Husayni shrugged. 'I don't know much about cars. It was smaller than the van we had, dark colour. It had a shiny badge on the front, like the Greek letter Omega. When I first saw them, the two men were very neatly dressed, jackets and ties, like businessmen. They could almost have been twins. Then last night when they came they were dressed casually, jeans and sweaters, khaki jackets like hunters.'

Fabiola called a halt, insisting that Husayni should rest until the police artist arrived to work on sketches of the new men.

'One moment,' Husayni said. 'Can I go and see Auguste Dumesnil? I must apologize for what was done to him.'

'You'll be better before he is,' said Fabiola. 'But now, this interview must end.'

'It was because Mustaf thought Dumesnil was the very image of a Crusader, a Christian militant,' Husayni went on urgently, ignoring her.

'That's enough,' Fabiola spoke sharply and Bruno and J-J left reluctantly, knowing there was more to be mined from Husayni's memory. Back in the squad room at the gendarmerie, the search and roadblock routine had been relaunched. Sergeant Jules was fielding calls from the media asking for a comment from J-J on the suicide of the ex-nun. Philippe Delaron, who had set up camp outside the gendarmerie, was brushed aside by J-J without a word. The place felt as if it were under siege. Bruno sensed the energy leaking away as the excitement of the chase gave way to frustration and routine.

This was a time, Bruno knew, when a team needed leadership, not the drive of a bully but something more refined, an ability to change and lift a mood. He was curious to see whether the Brigadier or Isabelle had such skills, running a complex operation that included police, gendarmes, elite mobile teams, traffic patrols and military units, all the while keeping the politicians happy. Bruno wondered what he would do in such circumstances to revive morale. It would need something different, a new focus for the search. Perhaps it was time to lift the search altogether, regroup and focus the armed units on a different mission, guarding the most obvious target points. It would be a risk to let the quarry run free but they might have a better chance of catching them if they did. And focus on the new dimension, the two strangers.

No sooner had he thought the words than Yveline turned from her phone and called, 'We have a match. Fingerprints from the house fit an ex-con called Abd el-Kader Demirci; he did two years in Fresnes for drug-trafficking.'

Where he was radicalized, thought Bruno, like so many other young men from immigrant families. Two-thirds of France's prison inmates were Muslim, and more and more of them were fervent jihadis by the time they came out.

Yveline darted across the room to the printer, where Demirci's prison mugshot was spooling from the roller, followed by his personal file and prison record. Yveline took the photo to the clinic, to see if Fabiola would allow her to show it to Husayni.

Bruno leafed through the other papers that came from the printer. Demirci came from a family who had been part of the Turkish minority in Algeria, descendants of the Turkish officials who ran North Africa in the era of Ottoman power. Mainly police, military and administrators, they had long been loyal to France during the Algerian War of Independence and many of them were persecuted after the French left and the war was won. Demirci had three brothers, and remembering what Husayni had said about the two men looking like twins, he asked Yveline to see if there were any files, photos or criminal records for the brothers. Then he began thinking about the implications of there being two terrorist combat teams in the area, able to hit two separate targets at the same time.

'Yves is at the scene,' said J-J, referring to the head of the forensics team. 'He's found the bullets that hit Husayni. It was a small gun, and he's sure it was fired from a Manurhin with a silencer fitted. It's a French copy of the Walther 5.56 millimetre, the calibre the English call a two-two.'

A small bullet and slowed by the silencer, thought Bruno. A bigger gun could have blown Husayni's arm off. But why would they want to kill him? Had he lost his usefulness? And the shooter had been talking on his phone, presumably back to his base. Perhaps Mustaf had panicked after Bruno's phone call, despite the way the Flemish-speaking Ahmed had sounded like a Dutchman. They must have called Husayni's driver and told him they were leaving and to get out fast and kill the now-useless Husayni. That call could be traced and the numbers monitored as they triggered each new mobile phone tower that came into range.

He called the familiar number at France Télécom and asked for an emergency review of the calls logged by the St Cyprien towers for the thirty minutes after the *tabac* owner's call to him. They should send the breakdown to Yveline's email address at the gendarmerie. Then he told J-J and Yveline that they might be getting some useful phone numbers before informing them that he had to leave for an appointment with the Mayor.

'Anything that you'd like me to say to Delaron about this ex-nun?' he asked J-J. 'He's camped outside, desperate for some comment from you. He probably also wants something on the helicopters, maybe the shooting.'

'There's nothing I can say,' J-J replied tiredly. 'I'm sorry the woman committed suicide, but we interviewed her several times, followed it all, up but found nobody to corroborate her allegations. Tell him to get some statement from the police spokesman. I'm not saying a word.'

'Can I tell him anything about this latest development with Husayni?' Bruno said. 'It might help. Every lead we've had has been because some member of the public has called us with information. And visible roadblocks, helicopters cruising over-head, a shooting in St Cyprien – we can't keep this secret.'

'We have to,' interrupted the Brigadier. 'The Minister wants this wrapped up quietly, no publicity, no panic. He's given us all the resources we need. It's now up to us to settle this.'

Bruno shrugged, picked up his képi and left, thinking to him-self that to live in a democracy was a wonderful thing, except for the politicians. Outside, Philippe was leaning against his car, camera at the ready.

'What's this about a shooting in St Cyprien?' he demanded.

'I'm not allowed to say a word to the press,' Bruno replied. 'And J-J says any comment on the ex-nun's suicide will have to come from the official police spokesman, sorry.'

'Can you tell me if this is linked to those photos you asked us to run, the woman who died at Commarque?'

Bruno raised an eyebrow, grinned and walked on.

'You know the psychologist, Duteiller, is saying that J-J was morally responsible for the suicide?'

'Don't tell me you believe that. Bye, Philippe.'

'Come on, Bruno. How about some give and take? I help you when I can.' Philippe tried to look appealing. It didn't suit him.

Bruno stopped and tapped him on the chest. 'You know the wonderful thing about living in a country with a free press?'

Philippe sighed. 'Okay, tell me.'

'It means I'm also free not to have to talk to you.'

'But you're a public employee. We pay your salary.'

'Quite true, Philippe, and I'm glad you brought that up. My salary has been frozen for two years, even with my promotion. May I have a raise this year, please?'

'Very funny.'

'I do have one lead for you, on this ex-nun who committed suicide. You know she was an alcoholic?'

Philippe nodded. 'That's old news.'

'Here's something new. If you go up to the Scout camp, you might talk to the couple who are the caretakers, Alain and Anne-Louise.'

'The priest who left the Church and got married to his cleaner?'

'She's a nurse. She was only cleaning the church as a volunteer. She's an orphan and she was at the Mussidan orphanage. Ask her about this ex-nun. She's talked to the police but nobody else has heard her version yet.'

23

Yacov and the Mayor were already installed in Ivan's bistro when Bruno arrived, to be greeted with a hug from Yacov and a wave from Ivan behind the counter, who called out, 'You're getting the *menu du jour* like everybody else.'

'It's been too long,' said Yacov.

'I don't see Bruno much these days, either,' said the Mayor drily. 'I presume you know something about all the helicopters and the armed camp that has sprung up around our gendarmerie.'

'And I'm under orders to say nothing about them,' Bruno replied. 'But since we have to inform Yacov here that security concerns require us to postpone the formal opening of the Scout camp, I'm sure he'll put two and two together.'

'That's what I just told him,' the Mayor said. 'I also told him what you told the council and swore him to secrecy.'

Bruno nodded as Ivan placed a tureen of vegetable soup on the table along with a bowl of bread. He returned with a bottle of the house white wine and a carafe of water.

'All sorts of rumours swirling around town,' said Ivan. 'Dead nuns, Arab terrorists, and now Fabiola performing some emergency operation in the clinic and a mysterious patient with a gendarme with a machine gun guarding his door.'

Ivan's eyes swivelled across the dining room to where Doctor Gelletreau was lunching with his wife, the pharmacist. The two of them studiously avoided Bruno's eye. He waved a greeting at them anyway. There was no way to keep secrets in a town like St Denis.

'I think I understand why the formal opening of the camp can't go ahead,' said Yacov. 'I even heard some rumours at the embassy in Paris.'

Bruno was not surprised. He knew that Yacov's law firm did a lot of work with the Israeli embassy, and Yacov, although a French citizen, had chosen to do military service in Israel and was still in the Israeli naval reserve.

'What were they saying?' he asked.

'Arab terrorists, something about a medieval document and the Arab claim to Jerusalem, plus a dead Israeli woman who was a Palestinian sympathizer.'

'Does Maya know about this yet?' Bruno asked.

'Yes, I called her, but she's coming to Paris anyway. There's a meeting of the family trust and I have to deliver a report on the camp's progress. And she wants to come down and see you and say hello to Pamela and the Mayor and all the schoolkids who did the design for the museum. She'll travel incognito, but she definitely wants to come and see the camp for herself.'

'We can probably arrange that,' said the Mayor. 'And we three can visit it this afternoon, if Bruno's other duties allow him an hour or so to join us.'

Bruno nodded and poured some wine into the last of his soup. 'I can do that.' He picked up the bowl and drank.

'*Chabrol*,' said Yacov, smiling. 'I remember that.' He put

a little more soup into his bowl, added wine and drank it down.

Ivan brought plates of pâté and pickles and said in a low voice to Yacov, 'The pâté is venison, is that okay for you? That green bowl with the pickles is our special new sauce, Caribbean *épice*. A friend of Bruno taught me how to make it and now it has become very popular – spicy, but I think you'll like it. Chicken chasseur to follow.'

'That's fine, thank you. I'm not wholly kosher. Venison is great and so is chicken. What's the dessert today?'

'Apple tart. You've eaten that here before, the last time you came. Red wine coming up. *Bon appetit.*'

'Ivan never forgets a face of anyone who's eaten here,' said the Mayor. 'I'd be delighted to welcome your grandmother here again, so long as the security question is resolved. When is she coming to France?'

'Monday. She'll rest for a day, hold the trust meeting Wednesday afternoon, and she was planning to come down here for the opening next weekend, but we can delay that until you're sure it's safe.'

The Mayor sighed and sipped his wine and they began to eat the pâté. After a while the Mayor spoke.

'I hate to say this, but after what happened in Paris I'm not sure we can say that anywhere is safe these days. Not even St Denis.'

'The question is whether we can ever bring over some Israeli Scouts to stay at this camp. As you'll understand, that is something that Maya very much wants to happen. And we'd also hope that Scouts from this region would come to camp in Israel as our guests.'

'We have no problem with that,' said the Mayor.

'When your Scouts come, I'm sure the Mayor would agree that I should move in and stay with them,' said Bruno. 'And we'll have every member of my hunting club patrolling the grounds while they stay. Round here, we take our obligations to guests very seriously. Your grandmother has done a lot for this town and we're prepared to do the same for her.'

Yacov raised his glass and Bruno and the Mayor clinked theirs against it.

'Celebrating?' asked Ivan as he cleared the plates.

'You could say that,' said the Mayor.

'If you're celebrating, where's the lovely Amélie?' Ivan asked, sending a stab of guilt through Bruno. He hadn't called to say he'd been held up. Despite all her help, he hadn't even thought about inviting her to lunch.

'She's tied up in the office working on the report she has to write,' he said smoothly, chiding himself for being so glib. 'But we're visiting the new camp after lunch and she'll be joining us for that.' He explained her role and presence to Yacov, adding how helpful she had been.

'I told you she'd be useful,' said the Mayor. 'I know you've been tied up with this security business, but I'm surprised you didn't invite her to join us for lunch.'

Feeling ashamed of himself, Bruno pulled out his phone. 'You're right, I should have done,' he said as he dialled.

'Sorry, Bruno,' Amélie answered. 'But I'm enjoying a perfect home-made quiche with Monsieur and Madame Fauquet in their apartment above the café. It's such a treat and they're very kind. Perhaps I could join you later for coffee.'

Bruno felt stunned, and the Mayor was equally surprised when Bruno explained. While the very soul of hospitality in their café, Fauquet and his wife guarded carefully the privacy of their home.

'I've never been invited up there for a quiche,' said Bruno.

'Nor me,' said the Mayor. 'And she's barely been here a week.'

'She sounds like quite a woman,' said Yacov.

Over the apple pie, they agreed that they would take the Mayor's car which could seat four in comfort, unlike Bruno's van. When the Mayor left to fetch it, Bruno took Yacov to Fauquet's for coffee and called to ask Amélie if she would like to join them. She should be ready to wear the rubber boots again, he warned her. He then called Alain at the camp to tell him they were coming.

Yacov stood, smiling appreciatively as Amélie approached their table. Bruno had grown accustomed to her colourful style of dress, but Yacov seemed captivated by the combination of her bright yellow jeans and matching turban, along with an even brighter red polo shirt. And Yacov's height with his slim, athletic build and dark good looks seemed to be having an equal effect on Amélie. She held out her hand to be kissed rather than shaken, and she treated Yacov to one of her beaming smiles as he brushed her fingers with his lips.

Bruno made the introductions and Yacov and Amélie quickly discovered that they had been to the same law school in Paris and began trading stories about professors they had known. When the Mayor rejoined them, he asked how was the quiche?

'Perfect,' Amélie replied, almost casually. 'The pastry was as light as a feather.' She turned to Yacov, resuming their reminiscences of law school.

It had become a perfect spring afternoon, bright sunshine with scattered clouds like white puffballs and a gentle breeze that set the young green leaves of the willows by the river quivering so that the trees seemed almost to dance on the water. Mother ducks paddled serenely, each with a row of tiny ducklings behind her like warships in line of battle. An angler standing in the shallows was casting his fly in a long, flickering curve that just kissed the surface of the river.

'I'm falling for this place,' Bruno heard Amélie say from the back seat. 'I've barely been here a week, but it's so green and the landscape so gentle. In Paris you forget that France is like this.'

The Mayor took a slightly roundabout route to pass Oudinot's farm, where half the hillside was filled with golden daffodils and the other half with grazing cattle. As the road climbed they saw ewes, their fleece grey after the winter, with their snowy-white young lambs. Picking their way along the skyline was a line of children riding ponies and it looked as if Pamela were leading them. Bruno rolled down a window to call and wave, but they were too far to hear him. Then to his delight came the unmistakable double note of a cuckoo, the first he'd heard that year.

'That's it,' he cried, turning to see Yacov and Amélie craning their necks and almost cheek to cheek as they stared out of her window to try to see the bird. 'The cuckoo makes it official. Spring is here.'

Bruno turned back to face ahead and saw the Mayor give him a wink; he'd obviously been watching Yacov and Amélie in his rear-view mirror. What an extraordinary gift it was, thought Bruno, this mystery of human attraction. What was it that made the current pass between two people? And why was it – he thought of Isabelle – that its power could endure so long?

There were women who were not conventionally pretty or striking, to whom he felt powerfully drawn, and there were stunningly beautiful women who left him cold. There were women he liked, and whom he acknowledged to be attractive and alluring, like Amélie, but who did not stir him that way. And yet Yacov and Amélie had responded to one another almost at once. He wondered what might come of it. And the miracle of human attraction had little to do with age. Horst and Clothilde were in their sixties, had enjoyed an on-again off-again affair for most of the last three decades and now they were marrying. Would that ever happen to him? A woman who he could commit his life to, with whom he could still have children, and grow happily old as they waited for the coming of grandchildren?

'We're here,' said the Mayor, bringing the car to a halt as it crested the last hill.

The rutted track was no more, filled in with freshly rolled gravel, and the sunlight warmed the honey-coloured stone of the farmhouse and gleamed from the solar panels on the barn roof. The bell-shaped tents reminded Bruno of the wigwams from American Western movies, or were they called teepees? Recent rains in the hills swelled the small waterfall into a tumbling foam. The bright new grass on the long slope down to the stream looked smoother than a carpet and the whole valley seemed blessed with an air of welcome and peace.

'It looks better than I could have dreamed,' said Yacov as the Mayor drove on and parked beside the farmhouse.

The small piles of builders' rubble had been cleared away and half a dozen chickens were clucking as they pecked at the earth and explored the territory of the coop that had been built since Bruno's last visit. Alain and his wife were waiting for them at a large wooden table on the terrace before the old farmhouse that was their home and office. Young geranium plants peeked through the potting soil in four big terracotta urns that flanked the terrace.

'*T'as fait chabrol*?' asked Anne-Louise as the Mayor shook Alain's hand. Have you had your *chabrol*? It was the old Périgord form of the traditional peasant greeting, inquiring whether the guest had yet eaten.

'We've eaten well and what a pleasure to see you settled in and the place looking so well,' the Mayor said, and introduced Yacov. Alain led the way to the barn, but Anne-Louise put her hand on Bruno's arm to keep him back and murmured that she had spoken to Philippe Delaron about the time at the children's home in Mussidan.

'If that old bitch could blacken the name of a good priest after his death, I thought it was only fair to do the same to her. She was a cruel woman, cruel and vicious. She enjoyed beating us, you could see it in her eyes. And as she hit us she would always tell us it was for our own good, that she was teaching us to avoid the flames of hell. Children are so helpless.'

Bruno nodded. 'You and Alain will make the youngsters who come here very happy. It looks homely.'

She looked fondly towards Alain who was pointing out to Yacov the places for the planned vegetable garden, the basket-ball court and sports pitch.

'He's happy here,' she said. 'He feels he has a purpose in life again. It was hard for him, leaving the priesthood, and I felt a lot of pressure on me, to make him feel that what we had together was worth the sacrifice he'd made.'

'Is he still a believer?'

'We both are, but not in a way the Church would recognize. I've never thought God had much to do with buildings, or with priests come to that. I think the God we believe in is closer to us here in this little valley. It's a place touched with grace.'

'I can understand that,' said Bruno. 'The shelter it gave to two Jewish children in the war makes it blessed. Did you know they were Protestants, the farmer and his wife who lived here?'

'Yes, Alain told me.' She paused, then looked him in the eye. 'I am glad you sent Philippe to see me. It's something I've long wanted to get off my chest but I thought the Church would just ignore it, sour grapes from a woman who lured a priest away from his vows. But it wasn't like that, Bruno. Alain was so unhappy, torn not between me and the Church but between himself and his own faith and what he felt the Church had become, a kind of obstacle between him and God.'

'It must have been a great trial for him.'

'He's found peace now. Let's go and join them.'

Alain and Yacov were upstairs in the barn and the Mayor and Amélie were exploring the kitchen area, Amélie using her phone to take photographs as the Mayor looked into the cupboards and then opened the fire door of the stove to see how much fuel it might take. Alain had already chopped a supply of firewood and kindling that was stacked neatly against the barn wall.

'It's great,' Yacov called down from upstairs. 'Better than I hoped for.'

'Have you got the package?' the Mayor asked Bruno. 'I put it in the boot of my car.'

Bruno went back to collect a parcel wrapped in brown paper and tied with string. It wasn't heavy, the thickness of a large book and about half a metre square. He handed the package to Yacov and suggested he open it. Two blue enamel plaques emerged, ordered by the Mayor from the same firm in Périgueux that made street signs for all the communes in the region. The first said, in capital letters, 'CAMP DAVID'. Beneath, in lower case, was written: *This camp is named in respectful memory of Professor David Halévy, who with his sister Maya found refuge here in 1943–44.*

The second sign said simply: *Here lived Michel and Sylvie Desbordes, who protected two Jewish children from the storms of war in their simple home, and who were killed by enemy fire in June 1944 while trying to return the children to their parents.*

Yacov stared at the plaques for a long moment, and then said a simple thank-you and shook the hands of the Mayor, Bruno and Alain. Amélie was weeping and trying to take photographs at the same time.

'We thought we'd put the Camp David sign above the barn doors,' said the Mayor. 'The other one for the Desbordes will go above the front door of the farmhouse.'

'That's great,' said Yacov. 'You've given me an idea. Maybe we could make a third sign, to put by the waterfall at that place where you and I went swimming, Bruno. We could call it "*Maya's Pool*".'

24

There ought to be a collective noun for a group of archaeologists, thought Bruno, as he entered the cave beneath the ruined chateau of Commarque. Before him was an excited throng of Horst's and Clothilde's friends, all jostling to see the image on the small laptop screen. Horst stood at one corner, perched perilously atop a rocking boulder. His arm was plunged into a gap in the cave wall and a long cable snaked beneath his arm and down to the laptop. Clothilde was trying to hold the boulder stable with one foot, while one arm was pressed supportively against Horst's back and her head was craned to catch a glimpse of whatever was on the screen.

Clothilde's call had come as they drove from the camp, asking Bruno to join them at Commarque at once. And with triumph in her voice she had added, 'Eureka!'

A 'dig' of archaeologists, he thought suddenly. That would fit. He could identify Barrymore from Oxford, Manners, the former soldier from England, and the German from the Neanderthal valley. There was one unknown woman in the scrum of scholars around the laptop, who Bruno realized must be Manners' wife Lydia. Conflicting orders were being shouted in German, French and English for Horst to move the lens this way or that and shine the lamp left or right, up or down.

'It's so exciting,' said the Count, extricating himself to greet the newcomers. 'They can look inside the cavity with that device and they've found what seems to be a tomb.'

'How does it work?' asked the Mayor.

'It's a much bigger version of the cameras doctors use to see inside the body. It lets us look into the cave behind the wall,' the Count explained. 'One of the Germans bought it as a wedding present for Horst, and once they realized this was a false wall they drilled through.'

'Wouldn't it be easier if you raised the laptop so that Horst could see which way he's pointing the cable with the camera lens?' asked Amélie, pulling out her smartphone and diving into her handbag for a small case that contained a selection of cables. 'Wait, I think I've got a solution.'

She burrowed her way through the throng of people, smartphone in hand, and re-emerged at the back of the laptop, examining the cables. A chorus of protests arose as the laptop screen went black, but then the ghostly grey image returned while a second image appeared on the screen of her phone. Amélie handed her phone to the Count.

'You're the tallest guy here,' she said. 'Hold the phone so Horst can see the screen and then he'll know where he's pointing the cable.'

'That's better,' said Horst, as the Count did as she suggested. The protests from the archaeologists gave way to murmurs of appreciation and a tumble of competing interjections, from which Bruno made out the words 'medieval' and 'tomb', followed by 'Crusader' and 'thirteenth century' and finally he heard Lydia's voice declare 'Templar'.

The Count handed Amélie's phone to Manners and left the archaeologists to it. Once out in the open air, the Count then explained that the seismic survey and the ground penetration radar had between them defined the dimensions of the cavity that lay hidden behind the one in which the archaeologists now stood. The cavity, which seemed to have no entrance or exit or connecting passage, was six metres deep and four metres wide and tapered from three metres in height down to a single metre the further it went back into the hill beneath the chateau. But this cavity appeared to be protected by an almost impenetrable wall, two metres thick, of solid stone.

Lydia Manners had then observed that she had never before seen anything quite like the strange geology of the cave they were standing in. She'd examined the face of solid rock that stood between them and the cavity. 'I've never seen limestone do that before,' she had said, pointing to the way the rock seemed to change in colour and texture, the chalky limestone running in almost geometrical streaks.

Then another of the archaeologists, the Count explained, had telephoned a geologist friend and emailed to him photographs taken with his phone of the rock, the surrounding limestone and the streaks of white calceous stone. The geologist had confirmed it looked like a schist boulder, possibly brought about by glacial action. By this time, Lydia Manners and her husband were scraping gently at the calceous stone and pronouncing it to be pure chalk. Clothilde commented that it reminded her of the hidden caves in Cappadocia, Turkey, where caves and passages had been concealed behind false walls formed of large boulders, mortared into place, the joins covered by moistened chalk dust which was left to dry.

'At that point there was no stopping them,' the Count continued. The archaeologists had begun to measure the outer cave and agreed that the boulder could have been rolled in to block access to the deeper part of the cave and thus form the hidden cavity. The boulder had then been sealed into place with smaller stones and chalk. At the top of the boulder, they found the chalk was only a thin layer. Scraping it away, they realized they could get a light and a mirror inside to get some sense of what the cavity contained. Horst's German friend from the Neanderthal valley then said he could do even better. The cable with its lens and light was brought, inserted through the thin gap in the chalk, and that was how they had been able to see the tomb. At which point Clothilde had called Bruno.

'So the cave was deliberately hidden by bringing in that boulder,' said Bruno. 'But it must weigh tons.'

'They could have brought it by rolling it over logs of wood as they did building the pyramids of Egypt,' the Count replied. 'And now they have found the tomb, which I imagine contains the remains of one of my ancestors, and who knows what else. Clothilde called the Ministry in Paris,' he went on. 'They'll have to authorize a full opening of the cave. It will be quite a job, drilling around the boulder. But now we know there's a tomb there, it should be just a formality. Usually when the Ministry gets such a request they consult the experts at the Musée Nationale, which is Clothilde. And I'm the landowner, and I suppose I'll have to agree.'

'You don't sound too happy about it,' said Yacov. 'Is there a problem?'

'It's certainly a medieval tomb. There's an effigy of a knight above the sepulchre with crossed feet, which is usually the sign of a Crusader, and a cross on his shield which looks like a Templar sign, which is interesting but a mixed blessing. It means we'll be overrun with Templar enthusiasts looking for lost treasure.'

Bruno nodded, remembering the crowd of cars and sightseers that had thronged this place after Philippe Delaron's story in *Sud Ouest*.

'Look over there,' the Count said, pointing across the valley to where a knot of people were staring at them with binoculars. 'I closed the chateau today, but we can't stop them walking through the valley, so they've set up camp to watch what we're doing. The moment we leave they'll be clambering all over this spot.'

'You could fence off the access to this cave,' said Amélie.

'That won't stop them,' the Count said glumly. 'We'd need a security guard round the clock and probably have to fence off the valley itself, which I'd hate to do, and it would cost money.'

'We might be able to help with that,' said the Mayor. 'I think we could find some money in the Conseil Régional budget.'

'And think of the publicity,' said Yacov. 'Commarque will become one of the hottest tourist attractions in the region.'

'And as you said, who knows what you might discover inside that tomb?' said Amélie. 'Maybe you'll even unearth this long-lost Testament of Iftikhar. You know the Templar legends – you could find the Holy Grail, the Ark of the Covenant . . . It's going to be huge.'

257

'Sorry to interrupt but I have to get back to St Denis,' said Bruno, looking at his watch. 'I just need a word with Clothilde before I leave.'

He headed back to the cave, and Amélie followed to exchange her phone for one belonging to Lydia Manners, checking that she had recorded the images of the tomb. The archaeologists were still clustered around the laptop.

'I'm heading off,' he said, addressing Clothilde's back as she peered at the screen. 'We'll see you at Laugerie Basse at seven-thirty. You can't miss your own pre-wedding dinner.'

'We might be late,' she said, not shifting her gaze from the screen. 'It looks like we could have some palaeolithic engravings on the wall inside this cave. I'm pretty sure that's a horse's head and there are some of those mysterious marks you see at Lascaux.'

'It's your wedding and they're opening the inner cave just for us so all your archaeologists can say they've dined in a cave that contains a prehistoric grave,' said Bruno. 'You can't be late.'

'Don't be silly, Bruno. All the guests are right here and the wedding itself isn't until tomorrow afternoon. That's the important bit.'

'For tonight, Clothilde, the food is the important bit and you know better than to mess around with a chef.'

She gave no reply. Bruno shrugged and headed back to the car, phoning J-J to say he was on his way back to St Denis.

'Sorry we can't take better care of you this evening,' he said to Yacov, turning round from the front passenger seat.

'You already told me about the wedding so I've invited Amélie to join me for dinner.' Yacov and Amélie exchanged the kind of glance that Pamela would have described as significant.

'He's taking me to the Vieux Logis,' she said. 'But I really like weddings. Would it be okay if we waited at the *mairie* tomorrow and threw rice and confetti?'

'You'd be very welcome,' he said. 'Clothilde couldn't be happier. It looks like they've found some prehistoric engravings as well as the tomb.'

Amélie was fiddling with her phone. 'I'm just emailing you some of the images from the tomb so you'll have them for your media friends.'

Back at the gendarmerie in St Denis, Bruno was greeted by the Brigadier with a testy, 'Where the hell have you been?'

Startled, since he'd already explained his plans to Isabelle that morning, Bruno reminded the Brigadier that he'd been with the Mayor and one of the trustees of the Scout camp to arrange the postponement of the formal opening. Evidently under intense pressure from Paris, the Brigadier grunted a reluctant assent.

Fortunately, J-J was waiting to haul Bruno across the road to the Bar des Amateurs for a beer, saying he couldn't stand the atmosphere of frustration around the gendarmerie for another moment. They took a seat on the small terrace with their drinks and J-J sank half of his glass before speaking.

'No news on the search for Mustaf,' he said. 'Isabelle thinks they'd already prepared some back-up accommodation, maybe even a camper van. The road patrols are now stopping all vans and trucks for proper searches, but we can't keep up the current level of manpower much longer. The overtime bill is going through the roof and there are no new leads, unless your hunters and hoteliers come up with something.'

Bruno shook his head. He'd already checked his phone for messages.

'And we've had to arrange a guard for some Professor Philippeau in Paris,' J-J added. 'The damn doctor forgot to pass on Dumesnil's message that he'd had to give them the man's name. Apparently it was the first thing Dumesnil said when he was able to speak. Thank heavens the nurse remembered. And it looks like they'll let us interview him at the hospital first thing tomorrow morning, so we'd better meet here at the gendarmerie at seven sharp. There's one bit of unrelated news which I personally found very welcome. We had a team searching through the records at the psychiatric hospital to find how Leah got the fake ID card from the patient, and an interesting name came up. Want to guess?'

'No idea.'

'Madame Duteiller, the psychologist who's been giving me such grief over the paedophile case. She used to work there, but they asked her to leave, citing professional differences. When pressed, one of her colleagues said they found her work – I quote – "less than reliable and not very helpful".'

'So she was sacked?'

'And walked right into a new job down here where we provincial dummies don't know any better. Anyway, it gives me a bit more ammunition when the magistrate and Prefect's wife start nagging at me again. In the meantime, we've asked the head of her clinic in Périgueux whether they checked her professional credentials with the Paris hospital.'

'You're playing rough,' Bruno said. 'Isn't there some proverb about never taking a sledgehammer to crack a nut?'

'I've barely started. One of my sergeants has a friend on the newsdesk at France Bleu Périgord and he's leaked what her Paris colleagues think of Duteiller.' He glanced briefly at Bruno. 'And I hear your friend Delaron from *Sud Ouest* has been making inquiries about this ex-nun beating the kids in her care. So if Duteiller thinks she can use the media to embarrass me, she's about to learn what it's like to be on the receiving end. You want to play with the big boys, you play by their rules.'

'Is she going to be charged on tax evasion on that *gîte* she was renting out?'

'Officially that's up to the *Procureur*, but he'll be reluctant go ahead unless he knows the Mayor of the commune wants a formal prosecution since it involves local taxes rather than national. But Prunier has been helping the Mayor understand the benefits of justice being seen to be done, particularly when it comes to renting to terrorists.'

J-J finished his beer, slammed his empty glass on the table between them and looked Bruno squarely in the eye.

'I worked that case as hard as we could, interviewed every-body, checked dates and times, ran cross-referencing on every single allegation and looked into the background of everyone who was said to have abused the kids. At the end of all that, we had no more real evidence than we did at the beginning – these recovered memories from hypnosis and the unsupported claims of the embittered ex-nun. What would you have done?'

'Laid it all out to the investigating magistrate and said if she wanted to bring in another investigative team, she was free to persuade Prunier to spend even more of his budget on a case that was going nowhere.'

'I knew Prunier would back me up, in spite of the Prefect's wife. But that wasn't the point. What I wanted to do was to come out and say the allegations were unfounded, that these people had been wrongly accused. And the magistrate wouldn't let me do that. She was content to let those allegations hang round the necks of those men, one dead, one senile and one too old to defend himself, rather than come out openly and say she'd been wrong. It makes me sick.'

Bruno turned down J-J's suggestion of a second beer, reminding him that he had a pre-wedding dinner to attend. He knew J-J, who had become friendly with Horst and Clothilde after meeting them during another case, had been invited to the wedding itself on the following day – if the manhunt gave him time to attend.

Bruno drove home, planning to feed his chickens and take Balzac for a brisk walk through the woods. And while he was not greatly surprised to find no sign of the two archaeologists who were staying with him, there was a strange car, a hire car, in his driveway. And there was no sign of his dog. He whistled and heard an answering bark from behind his house and a familiar voice called out, 'We're here.'

Isabelle, lit by the evening sun, was seated on the grass before the barn, Balzac looking ecstatic as he lay in her lap having his tummy scratched. There was a glass of white wine on a tray beside her and a bottle, nearly half empty, of Chateau des Eyssards, a dry Bergerac wine he liked. She knew where Bruno kept a spare key and felt sufficiently at home to help herself. The thought gave him a little thrill of pleasure.

'I thought you were going to the wedding dinner,' she said. 'But I really wanted to see him.'

'I just came back to walk him, feed the chickens and change before going out,' Bruno replied, noting wryly that it was Balzac she had wanted to see rather than him. Could he possibly be jealous of his own dog? 'It's good to see the two of you together. And congratulations on your new job.'

'It's mostly boring bureaucracy and politics so it's a relief when something real like this comes up,' she said. 'And every time I come back it always makes me wonder why I ever left the Périgord.'

A younger Bruno would have seized on that to suggest she stayed. But he'd been hurt too often by Isabelle on her occasional forays to the region. She always left again. Her career was her priority. Sometimes he thought that Balzac was the only chink in her armour. But Balzac loved her in return. It was only for Isabelle that his dog would not have come to welcome him.

'You change and go. I'll walk him and I'll feed your chickens and I'll lock up again when I leave. Have a good evening.' She blew him a kiss.

He went inside and checked his watch. He'd have time for a quick shower. But first he called Clothilde who was still at Commarque, full of apologies and saying she'd lost track of the time. He told her that Edouard Lespinasse would drop him at the restaurant and Edouard would then drive on to Commarque to collect them all. He'd see her and her other guests at the restaurant. Then he showered and listened to the local radio news while dressing in a clean shirt, khaki slacks and his blazer. Edouard had not yet arrived to pick him up. And Isabelle and Balzac had gone.

The first item on the local news was a report on what was

described as 'an anti-terrorist training exercise' involving helicopters and roadblocks, and Commissaire Prunier gave a brief
interview saying that any disruption was regretted, but he was
confident that the public would understand the need for such
training. The second item, which came just as Edouard drove
into his driveway, made Bruno pause to listen.

'The paedophile case in Mussidan has taken a new turn, with inquiries
now being made into the professional credentials of the psychologist
Marie-France Duteiller who treated the three people bringing the allegations that they had been abused at the orphanage. The director of the
clinic where she works announced today that she had been suspended
after he consulted her former colleagues at the mental hospital in Paris
on her qualifications. Madame Duteiller used the controversial technique
of hypnosis to recover the supposedly lost memories of the three accusers
who claimed to have been abused. One of them today told our reporter
that she was no longer sure of what she recalled.'

It was a thoughtful Bruno who climbed into Edouard's vehicle
for the short drive past St Cirq to Laugerie Basse. Madame
Duteiller was indeed learning what it was like to play by what
J-J had called big boys' rules.

For Bruno there were few sights more impressive in the
Périgord than the great sweep of the Grand Roc, a sheer
cliff over fifty metres high and nearly a kilometre in length,
sweeping down the flank of the River Vézère as it flowed
towards Les Eyzies. Almost halfway up this limestone wall
was a long horizontal slash in the rock, an overhang that
had created a *gisement*, or shelter, up to fifteen metres deep,
in which humans had lived for some fifteen thousand years.
They had left behind the richest and most impressive relics

of the culture of the prehistoric peoples: their arrowheads and spear points of flint; their tools and barbed harpoons; their marvellously carved spear-throwers engraved with animals and hunters; their needles and knives, stone saws and scrapers; the awls they made to pierce reindeer hides so they could use sinews to sew garments together.

He would always be grateful to Horst and Clothilde for the way they had encouraged him to probe a little deeper than the cave paintings of Lascaux and Font de Gaume and to see their creators as humans much like himself, responding with courage and invention to the harsh realities of their day. How would he have survived, Bruno often wondered, with only flint tools and a hunter's skill, to feed and clothe and warm himself and a family in such a desperately challenging environment?

But looking up at the Grand Roc with the eyes of a modern man, Bruno always smiled to himself at the readiness of the people of the Périgord to learn from their ancestors. Tucked into the long horizontal slice of rock where the cave people had found shelter was a cluster of more modern buildings, taking advantage of the way the rock spared them the need to build rear walls and complete roofs. There were dwellings, a small museum and a ticket office for access to the *gisement* and enough space for half a dozen cars to park. He climbed out at the foot of the steps and sent Edouard on to Commarque.

It was to one of these buildings built into the rock that he made his way, a local family-run restaurant that had become one of his favourites, serving plain but classic meals for reasonable sums. He and his fellow hunters lunched here weekly, enjoying the *menu du jour* of soup, pâté, confit de canard, salad and dessert for thirteen euros. In summer, he would eat on the terrace, the rock towering above him and the river flowing below. But this evening was a special occasion, arranged by Clothilde. The rear cave, containing the grave of a prehistoric man who had been buried in an upright crouch, clutching his knees, was very seldom opened to the public. The skeleton had long since been removed to a museum, but the damp chill of the cave and the sense of an ancient death made the place inviting only to archaeologists. Even the waiters crossed themselves before entering.

Tonight, for Clothilde's pre-wedding dinner, a long table had been laid inside and a special menu prepared by Madame Jugie. Bruno kissed her in greeting and left her to welcome the other guests who had arrived, Gilles and Fabiola, Pamela and the Baron, Jack Crimson and his daughter and Bruno's own guest for the evening, Florence from the *collège*. Clothilde and Horst and the other archaeologists had yet to arrive, but Manners and his wife Lydia were already enjoying a glass of champagne at the bar with the Count and his daughter.

Then Raquelle, one of the artists who had helped paint the copy of the Lascaux cave that the tourists now saw, arrived with Professor Barrymore and the German archaeologists. She explained that Clothilde had insisted on going home to change. Another bottle of champagne was opened and then almost finished when the bride-to-be arrived with her future husband. Clothilde looked stunning in a green silk dress that set off her red hair and had Lydia whispering 'Armani' to Florence. Horst looked as if he'd dressed in a hurry, his shirt buttons in the wrong buttonholes, and one of his shoelaces undone. But his guests were indulgent, warmed by the glow of pleasure on his face as he saw his friends assembled, and called for more champagne. Bruno felt that he'd been right to arrange once more for the taxi services of Edouard and two of his friends to drive everyone home.

They went through the special door at the back of the restaurant and down the steps into the inner cave, ducking slightly beneath the low roof to take their places at the long table, lit only by candlelight. Clothilde sat at the far end of the table and Horst stood at the place nearest the steps to give some formal words of welcome, and to tip a drop of champagne from his glass onto the place where the skeleton had been found.

'A libation to our ancestors,' he declared. 'And what better place for a marriage of archaeologists than this wondrous Grand Roc that has revealed to us so much of the life of early humankind. And what a day of discovery we have shared together at Commarque, which I take as a sign from the old gods of their approval of our wedding.'

The candles suddenly flickered and under the table Bruno crossed his fingers. He thought of himself as only occasionally superstitious, but to invoke the old gods and assume their benevolence in a cave such as this where the sense of the past was so palpable struck him as playing with fire. And looking around the table at the raised eyebrows and the nervous glances being exchanged, and then noticing the discreet gestures that Pamela, Florence and Fabiola were making to touch the wood of their chairs, he knew he was not the only one so alarmed.

'To Clothilde and Horst and the friendship that has brought us all here together,' Bruno exclaimed, raising his glass. And to his great relief, Madame Jugie chose that moment to descend the steps with a cheerful smile and a tureen of soup. Its scents of garlic and wholesome bouillon drove away his sudden sense of dread and replaced it with hunger and good fellowship.

25

Bruno had risen at six, drunk two glasses of water with aspirin and then forced himself into a brisk run through the woods with Balzac before taking a shower that he ran first hot and then cold. He fed his chickens, made coffee, boiled an egg and shared his toast with Balzac before driving down to meet J-J.

'I heard on the news about Madame Duteiller's suspension,' he began, as they set off in J-J's car for the hospital in Sarlat.

'Then you only know the half of it,' said J-J, jerking his thumb at the back seat where that morning's *Sud Ouest* had been opened to an inside page. Bruno reached to pick it up, and saw Philippe Delaron's story of his interview with Anne-Louise from the Scout camp, and her account of the beatings by the nun. Under a sub-headline that read '*I don't believe a word of it*', she said that in all her years at the orphanage she'd never heard a word about sexual abuse, just the endless physical punishments by the sadistic nun.

'Do you think this psychologist had any idea what a storm she was raising with this business?'

'I neither know nor care. What I do know is that with the news on the radio and in the paper, her mayor is going to have to file the tax charges against her and probably against her husband as accessory. He was the one who took the cash, and they file a joint tax return so he's liable.'

Bruno nodded, thinking that after what he'd done to Hugues, there was a rough kind of justice in Vaugier facing a stiff fine for tax evasion.

'So it looks as though the case will now go away?' he asked.

'Not until I can get some form of official statement that the inquiry is over and that the allegations were groundless. I want to repair what these fanciful tales did to those poor old men who spent years of their lives helping kids. If the magistrate doesn't have the guts to do it, I'll make my own statement, even if it costs me my job. I'm close enough to retirement as it is.'

'Have you talked to Prunier about this?' Bruno asked. As overall head of the police in the *département*, Prunier was J-J's boss.

'He always backs me up. The problem is the Prefect, or rather his wife. It turns out she's the daughter of a cabinet minister so her wish is our Prefect's command.' J-J levered his bulk out of the car and stomped into the hospital.

Auguste Dumesnil had been moved from intensive care into a room that usually contained two beds. He was alone, lying face down, reading a book that had been placed on a low table beside the bed. His legs were covered by a sheet and blanket that had been raised on some kind of cradle so the cloth did not touch his flesh.

The doctor had said he would be moved within the next two days to Bordeaux for a series of skin grafts on his thighs and buttocks. But he might have to undergo a further operation to ensure that he would be able to urinate normally. Bruno swallowed hard when he heard this, and then tried to make sure his face looked normal when he greeted the armed gendarme at the door and was shown into Dumesnil's room.

'The doctors tell me you're doing well, which is good news, and I may have something to help cheer you up even more,' said Bruno. 'I was at Commarque yesterday. They've found a hidden cave containing a medieval tomb. I've got some images on my phone.' He handed it to Dumesnil.

'Thank you.' He took it gingerly, careful not to move anything but his head and arms. 'It's not very clear, but that's a tomb of a Crusader, probably a Templar, late thirteenth or early four-teenth century, I'd say. And it looks like marble, which means somebody rich. I presume it hasn't been opened?'

'They can't even get into the cave yet. It was deliberately blocked with a big boulder and sealed. Those photos come from a remote camera that they were able to poke inside.'

'So with any luck, I might even be there when it's opened. That's something to look forward to.'

'Excuse my interruption but we only have limited time with you and I need to ask about your attackers,' said J-J.

'I expected that, so I made a tape-recording. The cassette is on the cabinet by the bed. I could identify only one of them, Saïd al-Husayni, obviously acting under compulsion. The big one, whose name I think was Mustaf, was twisting his arm to make Saïd translate their questions and my answers. Then Saïd collapsed and I heard him being ill and then another one took over the translation. He had an accent, maybe Dutch or Flemish. I told them everything I knew, which wasn't much, mainly what I'd already said to Saïd when he came to see me with Leah. Have you confirmed that hers was the body you found?'

'I'm afraid so. It seems both Leah and Husayni were being forced to work for these others.'

'I'm sorry about that. She was a very promising scholar and I liked her. Never did I dream that something as tame and remote as medieval studies would leave her dead and me hurt like this.'

'Are you still in great pain?'

'I wouldn't call it great, more a constant stinging. They gave me morphine, but I'm afraid of becoming addicted so I've asked them to stop. They say they're steadily reducing the dose and then they'll give me other painkillers. Since they told me I wasn't going to die, I've felt much better, but it's difficult to make sense of it all. I'm hoping you can help me there.'

'It seems to be Middle Eastern politics, with some Arabs determined for obvious reasons to suppress or destroy this Testament of Iftikhar,' said Bruno. 'If it exists.'

Dumesnil rolled his eyes. 'If it exists, indeed. I still have my doubts. And now it hardly seems to matter if the document is genuine or not. It would appear to have assumed a political life of its own.'

'Was that the only reason why they were torturing you?' J-J asked. 'Did they question you about anything else?'

'No, it was all about the Testament. I thought that by telling them everything I knew they wouldn't hurt me. But they kept wanting more, as if certain that I knew where the Testament was, maybe that I even had the original or at least a copy. Perhaps if I had lied, or not told them everything at first, it might have stopped them hurting me, but I think Mustaf took pleasure in it.'

'Did you hear any other names?' J-J asked.

'No, and I'm not sure about Mustaf. It was when the phone rang in the other room and the big one was hitting Saïd when he started to be sick. Someone shouted a question from another room and I'm sure he said, "Mustaf" . . . well, almost sure, as much as one can be at such a time.'

'Then what happened?'

'I'm not sure, I was passing out and then coming to. They threw water in my face a couple of times. But I think it was then or soon after that they left in a hurry. I remember trying to shift the chair so I could knock over the candle.'

'You succeeded,' said Bruno. 'It was what saved your life.'

'I was told that it was the policeman who first arrived who saved my life, with a black woman.'

'That was Bruno here,' said J-J. 'He gave you mouth-to-mouth until the ambulance came.'

'Thank you. I'm in your debt.'

'Not in the least. I'm just sorry I didn't get there sooner, except that men like that would probably have killed you as soon as they saw my uniform.'

'Have you caught them?'

'No, but we have Saïd Husayni. We'd tracked down where they were hiding and had helicopters looking for them, but they panicked, leaving Husayni behind. They shot him before they fled, probably thinking he'd outlived his usefulness. He's OK, in another hospital. And he's very worried about you and whether you're alive.'

'I am, as you can see, after a fashion. The doctor says I'll need three months in hospital and another three months to convalesce before I can walk again and get back to my normal life.'

'Could you identify any of the men from these photos?' J-J asked, showing Auguste the surveillance photos from the Gare de l'Est. He put them down, one by one, on top of the book Dumesnil had been reading.

Dumesnil studied them carefully in turn. 'This big one was the man I think they called Mustaf. He only took his scarf down from his face during the interrogation, but that nose and mouth are unmistakable. And I think the one standing while Leah is sitting at the café table is the one who spoke with the Dutch accent.'

'Did they begin torturing you at once?'

'No, they came in and hit me in the stomach and then slapped my face several times and Husayni and Mustaf began questioning me while the others searched the apartment. It was only when I said I had told them everything that they stripped me and bound me to the chair.'

'What did they ask you?'

'All about the Testament – what I knew, where it was, who else might have it, what the link was with Commarque. When I said I knew of no link with Commarque they became angry and started slapping me again. They seemed to think these new excavations with that seismic machine were searching for the Testament.'

'They knew about that?' Bruno asked.

'They thrust a copy of *Sud Ouest* into my face with a photo of Horst.'

'How long was it before they put you into the chair?' J-J interrupted.

'Ten, maybe fifteen minutes. I can't be sure. But I know when they arrived. It was shortly before five, I was about to leave for choir practice.'

'Did they talk among themselves?'

'Yes, but not in any way I could understand. My Arabic is classical, mainly for reading. Modern Arabic speech is very different. I could make out some words, some of them about whether I was lying, whether they should gag me and how would they hear what I had to say. That was all. There were some words about a Jewish farm and another group they called the "soldiers".'

A knock came on the door and a nurse entered, to tell them their time was up. When Dumesnil said he was fine and could continue, she took his pulse, checked the drip in his arm and then wrapped the black bandage around his arm to measure his blood pressure.

'Were you the nurse who remembered to tell us about warning the professor in Paris?' Bruno asked.

She nodded. 'I'm sorry I didn't check sooner that the doctor had passed on the message. Is he all right?'

'He's been under guard since about ten minutes after you spoke to us,' J-J said. 'And thank you for doing so.'

'The patient's pulse is fast and I'm not happy about his blood pressure,' she said. 'Just one or two more questions and then you'd better go.'

'No, we have enough,' said J-J. 'Did they say anything at all that might give an indication of where they were staying, any place name or road directions?'

'Not that I recall, except for the phrase about "the Jewish farm",' said Auguste. 'Please convey my profound regrets to

Horst and Clothilde that I cannot make the wedding and give them my best wishes.'

'Of course,' Bruno said. 'When they showed you the newspaper, did they seem to know who Horst was?'

'Well, yes. I'd talked about Horst and Clothilde and their dig at Commarque when Leah and Husayni had come to see me earlier. I even told them about the wedding because I said they might need to talk to them before they went off on honeymoon. Do you think I might have put them in danger?'

'That's enough,' said the nurse. 'He's getting upset.'

Outside the hospital, which perched on one of the hills that surrounded Sarlat, J-J paused to gaze around at the countryside. Bruno assumed that his friend was thinking of the vastness of this region and the thousands of empty farms and ruined barns, the great mass of holiday homes that would probably be vacant and the rental properties that were closed up waiting for the tourist season. It was a great place for terrorists to go to ground. And with much of the countryside thickly wooded, the helicopters would have trouble seeing through the spring foliage that grew thicker each day.

'During the war, the Germans brought in an entire division of troops who'd learned about fighting a guerrilla war in Yugoslavia, against Tito's partisans,' Bruno said. 'They were experts, but they still couldn't find the Resistance. It's an easy country to hide in.'

'What on earth are they doing here?' J-J said quietly, as if speaking to himself. 'Whatever can be their target? This is a big operation for them and I just can't see what makes it worthwhile. Not even in symbolic terms.'

'There was nothing symbolic about those cafés and restaurants, and the nightclub the jihadists shot up in Paris,' said Bruno.

'Yes, but it was the night of that big football match, France against Germany. There's nothing like that here, except maybe Lascaux and that's now well guarded. They even have sniffer dogs in the car park.'

'Just as well,' said Bruno. 'Horst and Clothilde have arranged a special visit there for their wedding guests this morning. Raquelle is going to be the guide and explain how they did the painting.'

'Come on, I need a coffee and a croissant,' said J-J, leading the way to his car. They drove down into Sarlat, parking on the Boulevard Eugène le Roy and strolling down to one of the cafés on the rue de la République. J-J ordered a double espresso, a croissant and a pain au chocolat. Bruno took a simple coffee.

'If it was me, I'd send suicide bombers or gunmen into Notre-Dame,' said J-J. 'Or into the queues of people waiting to go into the Louvre, or into Galleries Lafayette or the Place du Tertre in Montmartre, somewhere where they could be sure to hit lots of tourists. Or one of the big train stations or airports, or even the Métro. Remember they killed eight people that way in Paris back in '95 and look at what they did at the airport in Brussels. Those are what I'd call targets. I just can't make sense of their being down here, torturing harmless historians and asking about archaeology.'

Bruno's mobile rang. It had just gone eight-thirty. He answered and heard the Count's voice.

'Sorry to bother you, Bruno. I've just heard from the chateau.

I'm on my way there, my daughter's driving me. There's some-body standing on the battlements and threatening to throw themselves off. He says he wants to talk to the police officer in charge of the paedophile case, so I rang you to find out where I could reach him.'

'He's right here with me,' said Bruno, handing over the phone, gulping his coffee and putting down a five-euro note to pay the bill. J-J listened, rose, finished his coffee and stuffed the remainder of the pain au chocolat into his mouth, picked up the croissant with the other hand and began walking quickly back to the car, grunting occasionally into the phone.

Within fifteen minutes they were at the chateau, J-J risking the suspension of his car by driving too fast down the rutted lane, past the bridge over the stream that fed into the River Beune. He parked, and Jean-Pierre ran down the wooden steps from the big gate to the chateau, shouting, 'This way.'

From the main gate, Jean-Pierre led the way through the gatehouse, then left past the ruined chapel, up the slope to the Barbican, right to skirt the ditch and past the main living quarters into the stone tower of the donjon. As they raced, Bruno considered the military cunning of the medieval builders, forcing any attacker to turn, double back and then remain in a killing ground for archers before they could get to the defended core of the building.

The tower was now occupied by a single figure, a man dressed in a grey suit.

He stood on the highest possible point, a gap between two of the battlements, a hand resting on the stone to each side of him. He turned to see Bruno, the first arrival, panting his way up the stairs. J-J was some way behind, and Bruno could hear his friend's laboured breathing as J-J paused to rest before attacking the final steps.

'You might have to wait a bit. The Commissioner is not a young man any more,' he told the man on the tower. 'The poor guy is racing up here. He might have a heart attack.'

'I'm sorry,' said the man in the suit. He turned and Bruno could see he was wearing a white shirt and a wide dark tie that Bruno recognized as the fashion of the 1980s. The trouser legs were two or three centimetres too short and the jacket had been made for a much slimmer man.

'I see you've dressed up for this,' Bruno said. 'That's your best suit. You take care of your clothes.'

'I always have, the nuns taught us that,' said the man, in a local accent, before turning back to look across the valley. 'Put your trousers under the mattress to keep the crease and say your prayers before you sleep.'

'I remember,' said Bruno. 'I was brought up the same way. I still hang my clothes up before I go to bed.'

The man turned at that to examine him.

'You must be the policeman from St Denis, the one called Bruno. I suppose you're here because you think you can rescue me.'

'If you'd been a kid, maybe,' said Bruno, desperately trying to recall some item of paperwork he'd received, notes on dealing with suicide attempts. 'But you're a grown man. If you want to end it all, then as far as I'm concerned you have a right to do so. I'm just worried for the *pompiers*, the guys who'll have to scrape away what's left of you once you hit the ground below. They're volunteers, you know, not really trained for it. They won't be able to sleep for weeks.'

'I don't want be a bother, but I've already caused a great deal of trouble to people.'

'How do you mean?' Bruno used his question to climb two of the last steps, but the man wasn't even looking at him any more. He was staring across the valley again.

'I've brought shame and guilt to innocent people who never did me any harm,' he said.

'You mean the people at the orphanage?' Bruno took the last step onto the floor of the tower. The wind was strong up here, shifting direction and coming in sudden, unpredictable gusts, some of them fierce enough to blur the man's words, but not quite strong enough to make a full-grown adult lose his footing. He was in his forties with thinning brown hair and was freshly shaved.

'That's right. The Mussidan orphanage. I was at Mussidan until I was fifteen and then they found me a job in an office, wage bills and invoices. I was good at that. At least they taught me my letters and my sums, those nuns.'

'What's your name?' Bruno spoke the question loudly while waving at J-J to stay back. The brochure on dealing with would-be suicides said that only one person should establish contact and should then try to maintain the emotional link that might enable them to talk the person down.

'Francis. They named me after the saint. I was left in a basket outside the orphanage soon after I was born.'

'Just like me. I was left at a church,' said Bruno. Making sure that Francis was still looking away, Bruno pulled out his phone and turned on.

'I just stayed there, year after year, watching other children going away to foster families,' Francis said. 'I suppose I was an ugly child. Nobody ever wanted to take me.'

'Maybe the nuns thought you were too useful, Francis,' Bruno said, recalling that the brochure had recommended using the person's name to establish personal contact. 'You probably helped with the younger kids.'

'I don't know. I don't trust my memories any more. I don't trust any memories, not after I heard the radio this morning. And now I don't trust Madame Duteiller.'

'Are you still working at the office, Francis?' The brochure had said to change the subject whenever the victim began to focus on the reason for taking their own life.

'I was at Gaz de France before I fell ill. But they're very good, they kept me on for quite a while. Thanks to them I have the disability pension.'

'I didn't know you'd been ill, Francis. Was that recent?'

'Two or three years ago now. It was after I'd wanted to get married. I was a bit lonely, and somebody told me to try the internet and I found this nice woman – at least I thought she was nice. She was from Ukraine but she wrote very good French. We corresponded for a while and then I sent her money to come to France to join me, but then she had this problem with the father of her child. He wanted money before he'd sign the papers to let his daughter leave Ukraine.'

The poor, innocent bastard, thought Bruno, falling for that old trick.

'Then her mother fell ill and needed money for the operation, and I sent that, but that was my savings gone. And I never heard from her again. That was when I got my depression and they sent me to the clinic where I met Doctor Duteiller.'

'What happened then, Francis?' Bruno knew he had to keep repeating the man's name.

'She said the hypnosis would help in cases like mine, and she tape-recorded what happened when I went under, her questions about the orphanage and my replies. Then she brought me round, she played it all back and I was very surprised at the way my voice sounded.'

'How often did this happen, Francis?'

'Twice a week, sometimes more. She said we were really making progress. I remember thinking that I knew from her questions what she wanted me to say and I wanted to please her because she was very nice, like a friend. So I said all those things that I was supposed to remember but I didn't, not really.'

'You made it up to please her?'

'She was the first person who'd ever taken much interest in me. But now I know it was all pretending. Once I'd heard on the tape recorder the things I'd said, I couldn't back down. She said they were real memories, but they weren't. And then it all began, the police coming, the questions and the statements, the court case. Then she played me recordings of what the others had said and she brought in the terrible old woman who'd been a nun at the home, the one who used to beat me when I wet the bed.'

'It wasn't your fault, Francis,' said Bruno, advancing quietly towards the battlements. 'She wasn't a very good doctor and she did some bad things.'

'I know that now, but I said all these dreadful things about the priest and the director; she had them on tape. She played the tapes back to me and insisted that what I'd said was the truth and if I tried to deny them I'd be guilty of perjury and go to jail.'

'She was wrong, it wasn't your fault, Francis.' Bruno was almost close enough. Two more steps and he'd be able to grab the man.

'But it was my fault that those men were accused. I couldn't look at the old director when Madame Duteiller brought him in. It was so I could confront him with the truth, she said. But that awful old nun was there and I couldn't say a word. I wet my trousers when I saw her. I was so ashamed.'

He raised his hand to his eyes and Bruno leaped forward. He caught Francis above the knees, twisted so that his back and shoulder bounced off the stone battlement and then fell backwards to bring Francis tumbling down onto him, the wide tie flapping into Bruno's mouth. Then J-J was there and they were secure.

26

The Brigadier was in a better mood when J-J and Bruno returned from the hospital after entrusting Francis to the psychiatric wing. Despite the pain in his shoulder, Bruno drove so that J-J could dictate his notes of the interview with Dumesnil and his statement on the attempted suicide and email the sound file to Isabelle, with a copy to his secretary back in Périgueux to be typed up. They had then changed roles so Bruno could do the same. Once in the gendarmerie, they saw on the desk before the Brigadier a thick sheaf of printouts of photographs. Two of them had been extracted and were now being pinned by Isabelle to the corkboard on the wall.

'Isabelle's hunch paid off,' the Brigadier said by way of greeting. 'She thought the second of the two unknowns that Husayni mentioned might have done time in prison since that's where most of them seem to get radicalized these days. So she downloaded prison mugshots of all Muslims released over the past couple of years and persuaded Husayni to look through them. There they are.'

The first portrait posted on the wall was of Demirci, the man identified from his fingerprints. The caption to the second portrait listed his name as Idris Lounis, born in Paris, released

after serving three years of a five-year sentence for armed rob-
bery. He had been in Fleury-Mérogis, Europe's largest prison,
where two-thirds of the four thousand inmates were now reckoned to be Muslim. Most of France's terrorists had served time
and been radicalized there, including the Kouachi brothers,
who had been the attackers of the *Charlie Hebdo* magazine,
Amedy Coulibaly, who killed four hostages and a policewoman
in the siege at the Porte de Vincennes, and Djamel Beghal,
who served ten years for his part in an attempt to bomb the
US embassy in Paris.

'How in hell do we let this happen in our prisons?' J-J said
bitterly. 'They commit crimes, we arrest them, they go to jail and
they come out as terrorists. We're doing something wrong here.'

'We're working on it,' said the Brigadier, tiredly.

Isabelle rolled her eyes and then explained that all relatives
and known associates of the two men were now being questioned and their phones and credit card records were being
checked. Their photos were also being run through a new facial-
recognition search engine that was processing dozens of digital
surveillance cameras of the kind found increasingly in banks,
petrol stations and shopping malls. All that was routine but
they had one promising lead. One man Demirci had known in
prison, who now lived in Limoges and ran a used-car business,
was also being questioned and his inventory of vehicles and
bank accounts was being examined.

'Two cars that were logged into his books when he bought
them are no longer on his premises and there is no evidence of
any sale, so we are circulating their details,' she added.

'Have you checked for any robberies of *tabacs*?' Bruno asked.

'They wanted cigarettes and they didn't get the ones Husayni bought.'

'Good idea, I'll get onto it,' said J-J, opening his phone.

'I'm waiting for prison mugshots from the Belgian police,' Isabelle said. 'And Yveline is printing out French prison photos for men released the previous year and we'll show them to Husayni, as well.'

She then explained that they had some traces on phones from mobile phone tower analysis that might be theirs but Mustaf's team was highly disciplined, usually keeping their phones turned off and batteries removed. They only switched their phones on for brief periods and usually when they were moving between two or three mobile towers in dense areas so they had become hard to track.

'That means they are still mobile so we are concentrating on these new vehicles we think they got from this old prison contact in Limoges,' she added. 'But they could be using motorbikes or even mountain bikes. That's all we have at this moment.'

While listening to Isabelle, one part of Bruno's mind was thinking that she was skilled at this, keeping calm while co-ordinating a complex operation and bringing together different strands of information, never letting the routine stop her thinking of new ways to drive the process forward. She was good with people and with keeping up morale, brisk without being brusque, efficient without being cold. Curious, he thought, to have at once an impersonal admiration for a female colleague, while at the same time mourning the end of their affair and knowing that his love for her was not just dormant but eager at the slightest encouragement to blaze into flame again.

'Did you get anything out of Husayni about possible targets?' J-J asked, looking up from his phone. 'He told us Mustaf and the others didn't trust him or Leah and refused to discuss anything about their mission.'

'He said the same to me,' Isabelle replied. 'And I think he's genuinely trying to be helpful, as he was with the photos.'

'Getting shot by your supposed colleagues would tend to have that effect,' said the Brigadier, raising his eyes from a sheaf of mobile phone traffic reports.

'The big news was that he told us about their weapons. Demirici, the ex-bank robber, brought a cache of weapons with him, AK-47s, a box of what may be grenades and blocks of explosives. They also have gas masks, although we don't know what kind of gas they protect against,' Isabelle said, brushing her hand over her short hair in a way Bruno remembered. It meant she was tired. 'So now Paris is getting worried about the use of biological weapons or nerve gas.'

'Husayni also said that Mustaf was contemptuous of Leah and her focus on this Testament, even though her efforts had the backing of some influential imams,' Isabelle went on. 'Apparently Mustaf referred to Leah as a Jewish spy and accused Husayni of being a traitor to his people and his faith by living with her. Mustaf's only use for her was to get access to her bank account and her ability to rent cars and lodgings with a French ID. Husayni said he'd tried to persuade Mustaf of the importance of the Testament, but he's full of guilt about that because the only result was the torture session with Dumesnil. By the way, J-J, I got your notes of your interview with him, thank you.'

'You must have picked up on Dumesnil's reference to hearing

them talk about a Jewish farm,' J-J replied. 'Bruno and I assume that was a reference to the Scout camp. Maybe Mustaf and his boys don't know the event has been postponed, but I'll bet they know that the Muslim Scouts have backed out. Maybe they even had something to do with that.'

'It was going to be next weekend,' said Bruno.

'Maybe we could set a trap, see if Mustaf's killers turn up, even though they know we're looking for them.'

Bruno shrugged. If they were still searching for Mustaf's gang the following weekend, the Brigadier would probably be out of a job. Isabelle turned to look at him, but the Brigadier was on his phone to Paris again. 'I'll ask him later. It might be worth a try. I feel we have to do something.'

'You know I have to attend a wedding this afternoon and the dinner this evening,' Bruno told her. 'You remember Horst, the German archaeologist who got kidnapped by the Basques? He's getting married to another archaeologist. The guests are being given a special tour of Lascaux this morning.'

'Might they be eminent enough to be a target?' Isabelle asked. 'Husayni told me that to try and protect Leah, he'd stressed to Mustaf how important archaeologists were in France, and that Lascaux was like a national shrine.'

'Only if you're an archaeologist,' said the Brigadier, putting down his phone. 'And Lascaux is now well guarded by a gendarme mobile unit. What time are your archaeologists going there?'

'Their trip is booked for eleven-thirty,' said Bruno, looking at his watch. It was just past ten. 'I could join them, if you think it's worth it. Then they're having lunch in Montignac and getting back to St Denis at four for the wedding in the *mairie*.'

'Why not? I have nothing else for you to do except to keep on monitoring those networks of yours, and you can check for any holes in the security cordon the gendarmes have set up,' said the Brigadier. 'Make sure you're armed.'

Bruno called Amélie and found her still in her hotel room, and it did not sound as if she was alone. Yacov was supposed to be returning to Paris this morning, but maybe not. 'How was your dinner last night?' he asked.

'Sublime, that's the only word for it.' There was a joyous lilt in her voice that suggested the pleasures of the evening had not ended at the dinner table. 'Is there something you need me to do?'

'Not really. I need to keep an eye on the incoming messages, just in case the networks throw something up. But I can get those on my mobile and I'm calling to ask if you've ever seen the Lascaux cave? There's a special tour for the wedding party and all the gods of Périgord would curse me forever if I didn't make sure you saw the cave while you're here. I can pick you up in about fifteen minutes.'

'I'd love to see it. Is there room for Yacov to come, too? We'll wait for you outside my hotel. Do I need your rubber boots again?'

'Stout walking shoes will do. And certainly Yacov can join us. Make sure he brings his identity card.'

Bruno went to his office in the *mairie* but saw nothing urgent on his computer. He unlocked the safe to take out his personal weapon, his PAMAS 9 millimetre. Even unloaded, it was heavy, just over a kilo, but it fitted his grip like the handshake of an old friend. He cleaned it as he had so many times before, focusing on the task to dispel the sombre knowledge that he held the lives of as many as fifteen people in his hand. He loaded it, checked that the safety catch was on and donned his holster with its spare magazines. Then he picked up Amélie and Yacov and saw to his surprise that Yacov was wearing one of the Brigadier's special badges in his lapel. He pondered what that might imply about Yacov's status. It was not something he could raise in Amélie's presence, but he thought about Yacov as they drove out through Les Eyzies towards Montignac and the Lascaux cave.

It was a route he knew well, and on the way he tried to explain to his passengers why the cave was so important to him. Bruno now visited Lascaux at least once a year since his friendship with Horst had deepened his interest in the rich prehistory of the region. The whole valley had been designated by UNESCO as a World Heritage Site, with 147 separate zones of importance and twenty-five painted caves, Lascaux prime among them. Bruno had now visited sixteen of the caves, many of them with Horst and Clothilde. He'd collected a small library of books on the caves and the culture that produced them, and regularly attended lectures at Clothilde's museum and at SHAP, the Société Historique et Archéologique du Périgord.

Lascaux was special, Bruno explained, a great gushing torrent of art and colour that snatched his breath away each time he entered the dark cave and saw the tumult of painted life above. It was an effort to keep his eyes still, as his gaze was drawn in turn to the horses prancing around and the great and looming bulls with the raw power of their shoulders and menace of their horns. He had learned to look for the artists' special touches, the gap between leg and body that gave them movement, the suggestion of perspective that made the beasts seem about to wheel and charge. And then his eye would be caught by the sudden hints of other life, a bear, the twin horns of an ibex, the antlers of a red stag, a parade of ponies, some with the shaggy hair of their winter coat, so different from the plump brown horses with their dark manes.

It must have been a great leap, Bruno said, for hunter-gatherers struggling to stay alive and warm suddenly to blossom and explode into such artistry, such an act of creation and in so remarkable a communal effort to which they must have devoted years of their lives, perhaps whole lifetimes. It was not just the first flowering of human art but equally an unmistakable act of worship and of kinship with the painted animals they had made eternal.

Amélie was a good listener, leaning back against the passenger door so she could watch Bruno as he tried to convey his passion for Lascaux and all that it represented. Yacov was leaning forward from the rear seat, perhaps as much from a desire to stay close to her as to catch everything Bruno said.

What Bruno didn't tell them was his private thought that if his early life had been different, with better teachers in an upbringing that encouraged learning and kept books in the home, he might have passed his baccalaureate and gone to university and become a teacher or even an archaeologist. A decade or so earlier his regret had been that his schooling couldn't help him master the maths and science required to join the Air Force as a pilot. Maybe in a few years' time he'd have other regrets, not being a chef or a wine-maker, or not having children.

He crossed the old stone bridge in Montignac, and knowing

that Horst and Clothilde had made special arrangements for their group, he drove past the ticket office and out through town towards the hill that housed the caves. As he approached the vast building-site of the new Lascaux IV museum, he came to the first roadblock and two gendarmes wearing flak jackets and helmets waved him down, while two more stood, rifles ready, at each side of the road. Another twenty yards further a Berliet VXB armoured car was parked, engine running, and another gendarme was in the open turret with a machine gun.

He slowed his police van and waited for them to come to him and see his uniform and the Brigadier's special badge. When one of the gendarmes looked through the car window, casting an appreciative eye at the young woman beside him, Bruno said that he was armed and heading to join the archaeologists on the visit to Lascaux. Amélie showed her Justice Ministry pass, Yacov showed his ID card and they were waved through, the gendarme saying the archaeologists' van had passed less than five minutes earlier.

'I'll tell the guards further up to expect the three of you,' the gendarme said, keying the button on his lapel radio.

On the final curve of the road that climbed to the cave they came to another roadblock with the same complement of gendarmes and armoured car but with a sniffer dog attached to the unit. Bruno was waved through and parked under the trees, noting that there were fewer tourists than he'd have expected. He saw Clothilde and Horst and their friends standing under the shelter where groups waited to enter the cave in turn.

27

Raquelle was standing on a small stool, apparently giving the guests a lecture. Having been one of the painters who reproduced the exact copy of the cave paintings, she was a perfect guide. The guests kept darting nervous glances at the armoured car parked by the entrance to the bookshop, and at the watchful gendarme in flak jacket and helmet manning the car's machine gun.

There were usually about thirty visitors in each group, all the cave could hold, and the stewards tried to steer them through every fifteen minutes, rotating French, English and German-speaking guides. There was room for at most a few hundred people per day to pass through the main cave and narrow axial chamber. Since more than the two million tourists came to the region each year, mostly in summer, only a fraction of them could get tickets for Lascaux. That was why the new Lascaux IV museum was being built, to allow more people to appreciate the art and genius of their distant forebears.

Ahead of Clothilde's party were more armed gendarmes, each carrying a FAMAS assault rifle, known affectionately as *un clairon*, a bugle, from its modernistic design. Another sniffer dog was checking everyone in line. Bruno went up to the sergeant in charge to introduce himself and his guests. Amélie showed her official ID again with its red, white and blue stripes of *la République*, and Bruno asked where he could find the officer in command.

The sergeant saluted, evidently recognizing the badges Bruno and Yacov wore, and reported that the officer was moving back and forth between posts. There was another team covering the rear approach and patrolling the scrub and woodland.

'What about the original cave?' Bruno asked. 'You know this one's just a copy. '

'I don't know anything about that; we've just been flown in from Bordeaux. The only map we have is a tourist guide,' the sergeant said. He pointed to the microphone attached to his helmet. 'I'll ask the captain to join us.'

The captain arrived a few minutes later, a tall, rangy man of about thirty, carrying a Heckler & Koch UMP9, a sub-machine gun favoured by special forces, and wearing grenades on his chest webbing. Yacov seemed unconcerned with the high level of security and was looking around at the placement of guards and the weapons with what seemed to Bruno like a very professional eye. Bruno asked the captain if there was also security at the original cave. He pointed. 'It's in a fenced-off area about a hundred metres due east along that track with the signpost pointing to Le Regourdou.'

'What's that, a farm?'

'It used to be. It's now a tourist attraction, a site where the oldest Neanderthal skeleton was found. Have you not been briefed?'

'Yes, but very hastily. We were told Lascaux contained very

important cave art, attracted lots of tourists and we should start anti-terrorist patrols and check visitors but not stop the public visiting the cave. We're here until further notice, twelve hours on and twelve hours off.'

'You have one squadron, twenty troops?'

'Twenty-four, two armoured cars and a scout helicopter on call, and we're guarding the new museum, too.' He glanced down at Bruno's chest, noting the ribbon of the *Croix de Guerre* on his uniform jacket that the Mayor insisted he now wore. 'When were you in the military?'

'Over ten years ago, combat engineers, *sergeant-chef*.'

'And where did you win that?'

'Sarajevo. I was attached to the UN peacekeepers.'

'In that case, we're very glad to have you here. Have you heard anything new about the threat?'

'Just that their phone discipline seems remarkably good. At least three of them have been through ISIS training camps and they have AK-47s. These guys aren't amateurs; they'll watch for your patrols and they'll attack another way. Keep your eyes peeled on the woods to the south. Maybe you could get your chopper to do patrols from the air. Do you have access to dogs?'

'Only a sniffer dog for explosives,' the captain said, adding that he'd ask his commander about the helicopter.

'I'll see what I can do,' said Bruno, shaking his hand. 'Good luck.'

Bruno called Isabelle to pass on his concern about the lack of briefing and suggested she ask Commissioner Prunier if there was a police canine unit that could help search the woods. Then he joined Clothilde's group, where Amélie was already chatting with Florence and Pamela was asking Yacov if his grandmother was returning soon to St Denis. Pamela looked pointedly at Bruno's sidearm and said the so-called security exercise looked much more serious than she'd thought.

'Fabiola told me about the man she treated yesterday, the one who'd been shot,' Pamela added. 'Are we in any danger?'

'Not much more than anybody else in France these days,' he replied, aware that he was being evasive but determined not to cause alarm. 'Let's leave it there. I don't want to worry our guests.'

'Too late for that. Once they saw the armoured cars they've been discussing little else.'

In fact, Raquelle had been talking of Max Raphael when Bruno had arrived. He had heard her speak of him before. Raphael was a German-Jewish Marxist scholar who had taken refuge in France in the 1930s. She and Horst maintained that he had been the most significant art historian and theorist of his time. Raphael had said that the importance of the cave paintings, and the tumult of animal life depicted in them, was that it represented the first time humans had seen themselves as distinct from the animal world; the moment that we became conscious of ourselves as human beings.

Raquelle explained to the group how Raphael had taken detailed measurements and found to his astonishment that the prehistoric cave artists had used exactly the ratio that the Greeks of the classical age and the Old Masters of the Renaissance had defined as the Golden Mean: a ratio of 2.3 to 3.5. Euclid had studied it, Leonardo had sworn by it, the Renaissance scholar Pacioli had called it the Divine Proportion and modern mathematicians had related it to the Fibonacci sequence of numbers. Raphael's theory was that this sense of proportion was innate and emerged from the shape and proportions of the outspread human hand.

'I had no idea,' Florence murmured into Bruno's ear as they went into the cave. 'I must look into this and get the *collège* students to work on it. It seems like an imaginative way to teach mathematics.'

She stood close to him in the anteroom to the great chamber, where Clothilde explained the tools and pigments the artists had used. At one point Florence edged back to give the others more room and her hip brushed against Bruno's gun. She looked down, saw his holster and her eyes widened. He put his finger to his lips and stepped back slightly.

Then, one by one, they made their way into the almost dark Hall of the Bulls. Once they were inside, the last lights were extinguished and they found themselves in a darkness more complete than most of them had ever known. It lasted perhaps ten seconds, long enough to realize just how far they were below ground and how accustomed they were to the comfort of at least some gleam of light.

Then the lights blazed on, and a collective gasp of surprise, turning to enchantment, followed as the roof and walls above them exploded with life. As their eyes adjusted from darkness to light the great bulls seemed to quiver, almost to move, so confidently they had been depicted in their power. And then their vision shifted to the horses and smaller animals, their grace and delicacy balancing the size and the might of the bulls.

From somewhere, a hand reached out to grasp Bruno's right arm. It was Florence. He smiled to himself, understanding the reflexive need for human touch in a place so infused with animal strength. He felt her lean against him. Ahead he could see Horst and Clothilde, both of whom knew the cave well, standing entwined, their arms around each other, their faces lifted to the compelling display above them. In here, he thought, we all become infants again, feeling the innocent awe and delight of children at this moment of intense connection with the humans who made this sacred place some seventeen thousand years ago.

'The great historian Abbé Breuil, one of the first men of our own time to see this place, called it the Sistine Chapel of pre-historic man,' Raquelle said, and let the thought sink in. 'We don't know why they painted it, why they felt inspired to invest so much collective time and effort on this cave, whether it had a spiritual meaning or was something more prosaic, such as a display of wealth and grandeur to impress other tribes and clans. We do not know what kind of society had developed that could produce this great work of art. We know only that we people of modern times respond instantly to this ancient masterpiece and recognize that it came from people not unlike ourselves, with the same aesthetic sense, the same response to beauty.'

'Oh, Bruno,' murmured Florence, still leaning against him and her face turning towards his.

A burst of distant gunfire cut her off. It stopped for a few seconds, then started again in short but slower bursts of four or five rounds. It sounded to Bruno like two separate weapons.

'Stay here,' Bruno shouted and darted for the exit and up the stairs into the open air. The sergeant was on his radio, crouching behind the armoured car. The machine-gunner in the turret, his weapon now cocked, was looking nervously towards the woodlands to the south and a group of tourists waiting their turn to go into the cave was huddled in the shelter of the steps down to the cave entrance.

'Captain is on his way,' the sergeant shouted to Bruno as another long burst of gunfire provoked a chorus of wails from the tourists. 'Patrol in the woods saw something, then came under fire.'

'Where's that chopper of yours?' Bruno asked.

'Don't know, sir. They're not on this net.'

Bruno called Isabelle to report and asked if reinforcements were available, and if the roadblock outside Montignac could hold back any tourist groups heading for Lascaux until there was an all-clear. He heard her conferring, and then she came back to say tourists would be stopped and that a squad of army troops would be deployed by helicopter from Brive. Where should they land?

'On the access road, as near as they can get to the car park and the cave. Do you have an ETA?'

'At least thirty minutes. They have to be rounded up, briefed on the mission, issued ammunition and they reckon fifteen minutes' flight time.'

Bruno rang off as the captain arrived at a jog. 'At least two of them,' he panted. 'One fired at a patrol and now another one has started shooting at our chopper on the ground. I asked for orders and was told to stand by.'

'I've just been on to the command post,' said Bruno. 'A squad of army reinforcements is coming by chopper in about half an hour. Right now the priority is protecting these civilians. One group is already in the cave, the other is taking cover by the steps. I'll get them into the cave and your armoured car should stay here to protect them. Your men at the roadblock will be getting orders to stop all further tourists. Can your chopper fly?'

'I'm waiting for a report. We have one man down in the patrol.'

'You'd better stay here in command. Once we have these civilians under cover, may I take your sergeant to see what's happening with your helicopter? We can try to bring back the wounded man.'

'Good plan.'

The tourists, mainly Dutch and German, were only too happy to be steered into the shelter of the cave, crowding in with Raquelle's group. All except one, who shouldered his way to the steps to face Bruno. It was Horst's English friend, the former soldier called Manners.

'Let me know if I can help, Bruno. You seem a bit short of manpower.'

'Not yet, but thank you, monsieur. It would useful if you could keep them all in order down here. We don't want any panic. You may tell them that army reinforcements are on the way.'

'Leave it to me.'

The sergeant handed Bruno a FAMAS rifle from a rack in the rear of the armoured car and a belt with pouches containing extra magazines. Keeping a good ten metres apart, they set off leapfrogging through the trees, one moving and one remaining still. After a hundred metres or so, the sergeant called out, 'Fougières.'

From ahead, someone called back, 'Gaston.' Bruno recognized it as a standard password and response among gendarmes, a combination only they were likely to know. Gaston de Fougières had been the first known gendarme to die in battle and his remains were buried beneath the gendarme memorial in Versailles.

Bruno and the sergeant moved up, cautiously, to find one gendarme on watch from behind a tree, while close by another one was tying a tourniquet around the leg of a third. One field dressing, sodden with blood, lay beside the wounded man. Another had been applied to a thigh wound.

'He's all right, sarge, not an artery.'

In the small clearing ahead stood an unarmed and immobile Fennec helicopter with Air Force markings. There was a row of bullet holes across the bulbous glass nose and a large pool of oil or petrol spreading beneath it. From the position of the holes, the shooter had been to the east, somewhere to Bruno's left.

'How many are they?' Bruno asked the man on watch.

'Don't know. I heard only one gun that wasn't ours, but it came from different directions. Could be two shooters, could be one doing fire and movement.'

'Where's the crew of the chopper?'

'Don't know, they're Air Force, nothing to do with us.'

Frustrated, Bruno turned aside and opened his phone. He called his colleague, Louis, the municipal policeman of Montignac, to ask where he was and what was he doing. He replied glumly that the Mayor had told him to report to the gendarmes for orders and he'd be assigned to traffic duties.

'Are your Braques at home, Louis?' Bruno asked. The Braque de Gascogne was one of the best hunting dogs in France, able to deal with any type of game, 'from fur to feathers' as the hunters put it. They were excellent gun dogs, but also good in the chase. Bruno explained where he was, what he wanted the dogs to do, and assured Louis that by the time he reached Le Regourdou, Bruno would have arranged new orders from the Gendarme General.

He then called Isabelle, explained the position, and within the minute she came back on the line with the general's authorization. Bruno asked her to repeat that for the sergeant of gendarmes at his side. After a brisk 'Yes, sir – ma'am,' the phone came back to Bruno. The man on watch and the gendarme who had applied the tourniquet then carried the wounded man back to the armoured car. Bruno explained to the sergeant exactly what he expected to happen and what he intended to do.

Shortly thereafter came the sound of baying dogs in the woods over to Bruno's left, but it sounded like considerably more than the two Braques he had expected. Then the sound changed, from the bay of the hunt to the sharp bark that meant the game had been found. Bruno tucked the FAMAS into his shoulder.

A sudden burst of gunfire erupted, then a second, followed by the yelping of a dog in pain, then more barking. On the far left side of the clearing about two hundred metres away, a blurred shape emerged from the scrubland beneath the trees and began running, crouched low; branches that had been tucked into his jacket for camouflage were bouncing around the figure's head. Bracing his arm against a tree trunk, Bruno sighted carefully and fired two bursts of three shots into the man's hips and thighs. The sergeant beside him followed suit.

The man fell and then a large brown-and-white dog emerged from the trees, crept forward, low to the ground, and then pounced onto the fallen man's chest and began to growl with menace. The man raised his arm, a strange gesture, as if pulling at something rather than trying to fend off the hound. And with that came a sudden flare of brilliant white light, the boom and instant echo of an explosion and then a fountain of dark smoke from which clods of earth rose almost lazily before scattering around the clearing and spattering the shot-up helicopter. Of man and dog, there was not a single sign.

'*Mon Dieu*,' Bruno murmured to himself: a suicide bomber. Why didn't I think of that?

Some instinct made him look at his watch. '*Mon Dieu*,' he repeated. 'We all have to get to the wedding!'

28

Clothilde was looking marvellous as she descended gracefully from the hired Rolls Royce in a beautifully cut dress of heavy cream silk. It hung just below the knee and the flared sleeves came down almost to her wrists, just revealing a heavy bracelet of silver on one arm. She wore a necklace of the same metal in spirals that Horst had given her, a copy of a piece found in a Neolithic grave in Ireland. Her red hair was piled high on her head and she carried a springtime bouquet of white and yellow daffodils and lily of the valley, the leaves matching the bright green silk scarf at her throat. She smiled broadly as she saw the Mayor in his red, white and blue sash of office and Bruno waiting, hastily showered and dressed in his only civilian suit, to greet her. He forced his face into a welcoming smile, firmly repressing the memory of that blinding flash of the explosion and Louis' stricken features at the loss of his best hunting dog.

Lydia Manners, her matron of honour, had already climbed from the car and she was quickly joined by Pamela and Florence, her bridesmaids. Florence's two toddlers, Dora and Daniel, dressed in white, were staring wide-eyed at the bride. A small cheer arose from the gathering crowd of St Denis folk as the Mayor escorted Clothilde and Lydia to the lift. Bruno waited to

do the same for the bridesmaids and the children. Because of
the old custom that bride and groom should not be together
before the ceremony, Horst and his archaeologist friends had
already taken the stairs before the bride's arrival, discussing how
many centuries of feet had been required to carve such grooves
into the old stone steps. Bruno made polite conversation while
waiting, but spotted from the corner of his eye Yveline and
Isabelle, taking time off from their duties at the gendarmerie
to watch the show.

Ever alert to her surroundings, Pamela noted his quick glance
at the two women in the crowd and asked, 'Who's that woman
with the short, dark hair standing beside Yveline?'

'Commissaire Isabelle Perrault, from Eurojust in The Hague,'
he said, keeping his voice neutral. He was pretty sure that
Pamela had known who she was all along. He remembered her
being furious when she had been told by some local busybody
that Isabelle and Bruno had been spotted together at a hotel
in Bordeaux. It had been during an operation against a ring
smuggling illegal immigrants into France. They had each been
on duty and nothing had happened between them. Isabelle had
been shot in the thigh that day, leading the team arresting the
smugglers and their cargo of Chinese.

'*That* Isabelle? Your old flame?' Pamela drawled, ice chips in
her voice. Florence's eyes widened at her tone. Pamela turned
away so as not to be caught staring and looked at him fiercely.
'What brings her down here this time, more of your so-called
security exercises?'

'Indeed,' said Bruno coolly. 'It's her job. She's here with the
Brigadier, based at the gendarmerie.'

Isabelle and Pamela knew of each other, but to his knowledge had never met until now. He had loved each of them and a part of him always would. But why did Pamela seem to think she still had some claim on him after breaking off the affair for what she had insisted was his own good? He damped down the surge of irritation, knowing how he'd feel if he found himself confronting some new lover of Isabelle's, or a new beau for Pamela. Bruno remembered how shaken he'd been when he'd mistakenly thought Pamela had begun an affair with Jack Crimson.

Bruno shook his head to clear it of such thoughts. His role now was to officiate at a wedding and he was uncomfortably aware of the shoulder holster he was wearing beneath his suit. The jacket was sagging with the weight of two extra magazines in each side pocket. The Brigadier had insisted that he remain armed, despite the wedding. At least the jacket hung loosely enough to leave no obvious bulge. He'd have to tell Florence's children they were getting too big for his usual trick of picking them both up at the same time.

The lift came and Bruno led the way to the council chamber, from which the chairs had been removed and the ancient table pushed against the wall and covered with flowers. The Mayor's secretary steered Clothilde and Lydia to a nearby waiting room. Bruno turned as he always did in this chamber to the long window to enjoy one of the finest views of St Denis: the wide curve of the river and the old stone bridge, the quayside with its anglers and the gentle stirring of the willow branches as their tips kissed the surface of the water.

The room filled quickly behind him with the wedding guests.

The Baron and Raquelle stood to one side of Gilles and Fabiola, Jack Crimson and his daughter on the other. The visitors from Germany and Britain had somehow been steered by Pamela into the front row. He saw the tall figure of the Count towards the rear among the staff of Clothilde's museum, along with various well-wishers from St Denis and the surrounding communes. Wearing an enormous hat was Horst's neighbour, a plump and motherly type who did his cleaning. Beside her stood Sergeant Jules and Yveline, both in uniform.

Of Isabelle there was no sign. Philippe Delaron was crouched in a corner, two cameras around his neck. In the doorway Bruno spotted Yacov and Amélie holding hands as they made way for the Mayor, leading in the soon-to-be-married couple. Amélie winked at him. Bruno suspected that she, too, was looking forward to the little surprise they had arranged between them.

Bruno checked that he had the ring in his pocket and took his place behind the groom as Horst and Clothilde came in separately to stand in front of the Mayor to take their vows. There were no religious vows, though, in this civil ceremony, where the Mayor announced under the powers conferred upon him by la République française and according to Article 212 of the civil code that he was prepared to solemnize this union under the law.

First Clothilde and then Horst declared that they consented to take the other as spouse, the Mayor pronounced them to be united as one in marriage, and they signed the register. Bruno and Lydia Manners then signed as *témoins*, the witnesses the law required, followed by Barrymore and Raquelle. Bruno and Lydia brought out the rings for the couple to slide onto one another's fingers. Horst was formally handed the *livret de famille*, the Mayor took his usual bonus of being first to kiss the bride, and the deed was done.

And at that point, pure and high, Amélie's voice rang out in that most beloved of French songs of love, Edith Piaf's 'La Vie en Rose'. Clothilde turned to see, a wide smile spreading across her features, and Horst clapped his hands in delight until Clothilde took him in her arms and they began a slow, affectionate dance to the music of the song. It was, Bruno realized, their first act together as a married couple.

'*Mon Dieu*, that's delightful,' murmured the Mayor to Bruno as the song came to an end and the storm of applause died away. 'She has a marvellous voice and we must certainly have her at our concerts this summer. You see, Bruno, I know you hated the idea at first, but I was right to bring the two of you together. I presume you and she worked out this little musical interlude?'

Before Bruno could reply, Clothilde was at his side, clutching Amélie with one hand, and hugging him with her other and announcing what a lovely idea the song had been and that Amélie and her escort must come along to the museum for the reception. They would fit them in somehow.

Bruno knew that while only the wedding party would attend the dinner inside the museum's biggest room of exhibits, there was to be a much larger reception with drinks and cocktail snacks on the terrace where the huge statue of Cro-Magnon man stared out over the town. There would be plenty of room there.

On a ledge in the tall cliff that dominated Les Eyzies, the terrace was reached from the top floor of the new museum, along a cobbled path to the old ruined chateau that had occupied the ledge since the Middle Ages. The ruins had been bought by the state in 1913 and converted into the first museum of prehistory, a cramped, dark space now used as offices. The original stone archway to the old chateau led the way across cobblestones to the terrace and the statue. It was, Bruno knew, a splendid place for a party with room for a hundred or more people and Clothilde had invited all the museum staff as well as the wedding guests.

'Do you think we could ask you to sing again at the reception?' Clothilde asked Amélie, still clutching her hand.

'I couldn't refuse a bride and you look glorious, madame, and such a handsome husband,' Amélie replied. 'I'm glad you enjoyed our little surprise. It was Bruno's idea, but I was thrilled when you decided to dance.'

'Thank you. We'll talk at the reception but right now I have to circulate.' Impulsively Clothilde kissed her cheek and set off around the council chamber, being kissed by everyone. She stopped at Florence's children and cried, 'Our lovely little page and flower girl,' and bent to kiss them both.

'I'm glad it worked,' Amélie said to Bruno. 'I wasn't sure if it was quite the right song for a wedding.'

'It was perfect,' he replied. 'And you passed the audition. The Mayor tells me I have to get you for our summer concerts so tomorrow I'll introduce you to the guitarist who runs the local bookshop, the garage owner who plays drums and our choirmaster who plays piano and keyboard. They're pretty good, but I know they'll be delighted to accompany you.'

'Maybe I can get Florence to sing duets with me.'

'You're going to be adopted by St Denis at this rate.' He smiled and held out his hand to Yacov, who approached, kissed Amélie on the lips and then gripped Bruno's hand with both his own.

'A lovely wedding, Bruno, I'm glad to have been here for it. But I have to take you away for a moment. The Brigadier wants a word, urgently. Something serious has happened.'

As they pushed their way through the crowd, most of whose members wanted either to shake Bruno's hand or to kiss him in the general mood of celebration, Bruno was jostled against Yacov. He felt something hard and solid under Yacov's left armpit. The man was armed. He glanced at his friend sharply. Yacov put a finger to his lips and murmured, 'The Brigadier gave it to me.'

'What the hell is this?' Bruno asked, grabbing Yacov's arm when they were on the staircase. 'Since when does a Paris lawyer get given a gun by a senior official of the Interior Ministry?'

'You'd better ask him,' Yacov replied, gently removing Bruno's hand from his arm. 'He's waiting downstairs.'

A small crowd had gathered outside the *mairie* waiting for the wedding party to emerge, but the Brigadier and Isabelle were standing at the far side of the road and the Brigadier beckoned to him.

'So, you were right about Lascaux,' the Brigadier said when Bruno arrived. 'They found the remnants of the terrorist's gun, one of those AK-47s that flooded into Europe after the Balkan wars. The problem is that after a very thorough sweep by the army reinforcements, it turns out there was only one of them. The other four are still at large, and they may have joined up with others.'

Standing beside him, Yacov suddenly pulled out a phone and turned away, and after saying, 'Synch now,' he pressed a button on his keypad, which to Bruno meant that Yacov was using a scrambler. He began speaking in a language Bruno couldn't recognize. He assumed it must be Hebrew and wondered why he hadn't realized earlier that Yacov was something more than the patent lawyer he claimed to be. Firearms were not handed out by the Interior Ministry to just anyone. Could Yacov be the official Israeli contact that the Brigadier had mentioned in the video conference?

'We have to assume they are on the loose, still active and possibly with another target.' The Brigadier broke off to shake hands with Jack Crimson who had joined them, his daughter Miranda at his side. Bruno could see no bulge under Crimson's armpit, but remembered that the Brigadier had authorized him to be armed.

Bruno felt a shaft of outrage. St Denis was his town, its safety his responsibility, but suddenly people were being armed as if this were the Wild West. He hated it on those rare moments when he had to wear his own weapon, but now Yacov, Crimson and no doubt the Brigadier and Isabelle were all carrying sidearms.

'I gather you authorized a weapon for Maître Kaufman here, sir,' Bruno said. 'Have you some reason to believe a civilian, a Parisian lawyer, might be in any danger?'

'Yes, and don't ask. It's my decision.'

'I talked to Saïd Husayni again,' said Isabelle. 'That comment he made about the farm that we thought might refer to the Scout camp – it came in the context of a diatribe against Jews. So we concluded that the Scout camp was indeed a target and that makes Yacov Kaufman a potential victim. He's got military training, he knows his way around weapons.'

'Would he be this Israeli contact you referred to, sir?'

The Brigadier looked at him coldly. 'Again, Bruno, don't ask.'

At that point, the wedding party emerged from the *mairie*, Horst and Clothilde in the lead, the Mayor and Lydia behind them, and then the rest, all being showered with rice and confetti by the crowd. Philippe Delaron walked backwards before them, his camera to his eye, taking shot after shot. Horst caught Bruno's eye, waved, nudged Clothilde and they came across.

'I remember you,' said Clothilde to Isabelle. 'When Horst was kidnapped, you were part of the team that rescued him, so thank you for my new husband.'

'I'm glad to see you both happy,' said Isabelle. 'Please accept my congratulations and best wishes.' She gestured to the Brigadier beside her. 'My colleague here, General Lannes, led that particular inquiry so he's the one who deserves your thanks.'

Horst shook their hands. 'Perhaps you would do us the honour of joining us at Les Eyzies for a glass of champagne at our reception. It seems this wedding would not have taken place without the two of you and, of course, Bruno.'

'We're still involved in this exercise but if we can—' Isabelle began to say when Delaron came up, phone in hand.

'What's this about a shoot-out at Lascaux, Bruno? The newsdesk just called to ask if I can get there right away.'

'You can't leave. We booked you specially to take the photos at our reception and dinner,' Clothilde objected. 'And we've all just come from Lascaux. There was an explosion and some shooting, but it's all over. They evacuated us and gave us the all-clear.'

'Gunfire heard and an explosion, the place now sealed off and surrounded by troops and cops, that's all I know,' Philippe replied. 'Unless these types can tell me more.'

He held out his hand to Isabelle. 'I remember you from when you worked round here. I know you have some high-powered job in Paris. What do you know about this?'

'Even if I knew, I couldn't tell you,' Isabelle replied, without looking at the reporter. 'Sorry.'

'That's not good enough—' the Mayor began.

'The incident is over, none of our people was hurt and Lascaux is undamaged,' said the Brigadier, turning away. 'That's all I can say. Anything more will have to come from the police spokesman.'

By now, people were picking up the news on their mobile phones, clustering together and talking in hushed tones. Some began to gather around Bruno and Philippe, hungry for more information or some detail of the attack on a place that symbolized so much of their region and its long history.

Florence declared that she was taking the children home and added, without much conviction, that she might join them later if she could find a babysitter. Pamela demanded, politely but firmly, if Bruno had anything to add to the newsflash. Only that Lascaux was safe, he replied. She pressed him, asking whether they would all be safe at Les Eyzies. Bruno could only shrug and say that he was going there, when he saw a figure suddenly sinking down to sit on one of the stone bollards, her head in her hands. It was Raquelle, looking stunned, a handkerchief to her mouth. She had seemed fine in the cave and when they were escorted down to their bus. But she had given ten years of her life to reproducing the bulls and horses on the copy of the cave the tourists now saw. Shock must be setting in.

'Who is that senior-looking guy with Isabelle?' Philippe asked as Isabelle left with Yacov and the Brigadier. 'Is he down here for this?'

By now Gilles had joined them, notebook poised, Fabiola at his side but holding a phone to her ear, probably trying to check whether there had been an emergency call for doctors. They had seen the Lascaux cave before and so had not joined the visiting party. Gilles had taken early retirement from *Paris Match* but he still freelanced for them. The old newshound was back on the scent, Bruno thought.

Mon Dieu, how could he deal with all these people with their questions and their worries? They were giving him no time to think. He felt he was being pulled in different directions: the emotional needs of his friends, his duty to the Mayor and people of St Denis, his obligation to the orders and official status of the Brigadier, the threat to Lascaux, the unknown new danger of trained and violent men on the loose. With an effort, he resisted the temptation to reach into his shoulder holster and touch his gun to reassure himself.

'I thought all this was supposed be a training exercise,' Gilles said. 'It looks as though the guards at Lascaux were on alert, almost as if they suspected some sort of attack was coming. Is that so? And is this incident linked to that dead woman at Commarque and the gendarme who was shot at Siorac?'

'You can call him a senior official at the Interior Ministry,' Bruno replied to Philippe, ignoring Gilles' questions. 'You heard the man, there's no damage done to Lascaux and this is Clothilde's wedding day.'

Bruno left Philippe and Gilles and went to Raquelle to put an arm around her and whisper reassurance that all was well at Lascaux and that her cave had been untouched.

'What is it? Terrorists? Arabs?' she asked dumbly, her hair awry from the distracted way she had been running her hands through it. She gazed up at him. '*Mon Dieu*, will this ever stop?' He remembered that Raquelle's mother had been Israeli.

'We're not sure yet what happened,' he said as Amélie joined them, looking bemused and somewhat bereft at Yacov's departure.

'Come on,' he said, taking Raquelle by the hand. 'Let's all get to Les Eyzies, have a drink and celebrate with Clothilde and Horst.'

29

By the time Bruno and his carload arrived at the National Museum of Prehistory, extra glasses had been borrowed from the nearby café and Hubert had dashed back to his wine shop to bring two more cases of champagne. The sound of the party grew louder as they climbed the last spiral of the staircase and came out onto the flat roof and into sunlight and conviviality. They were on a deep and long ledge in the great rock wall that towered over Les Eyzies. Just one street wide, the town was tucked into the narrow strip of land between the rock and the river beyond. The guests had already overflowed from the roof of the museum to the wide terrace. Guests were drifting through the stone archway of the old chateau that was tucked into the vast rocky overhang and spreading out on the longer terrace beyond the giant stone statue of a prehistoric man.

The only access to these terraces was through the new museum, either by a small lift for the disabled or by climbing a wide spiral staircase whose walls featured two-metre-tall reconstructions of the layers of archaeological excavations. Climbing past the entrance to the lower gallery, visitors could see at the end of one alcove a reconstruction of a giant stag, its antlers ten metres wide.

Bruno often wondered at the courage of those ancestors, taking on such beasts armed only with spears and flint axes. In the upper gallery was a reconstruction of a hunter from around the time of Lascaux, seventeen thousand years earlier, aiming a slim spear with a point made from a reindeer's antler. But in neighbouring showcases were examples of the spear-throwers that could endow the spears with far greater force. He'd tried throwing one at a site upriver called Pech-Merle, where the family that owned the land had set up archery targets backed by thick straw. A good throw, Bruno had found, could penetrate through the straw from a range of thirty metres. No wonder humans had ended up on top of the food chain.

Raquelle had repaired her make-up in the car. She took a glass of champagne and went to join the archaeologists. Amélie was jolly as always, swigging half her champagne before being surrounded by a ring of people telling her how much they had enjoyed her singing. Bruno went to the bar and greeted the two barmen, one of them an old pupil from his rugby classes. He got a glass of champagne for Pamela, another for himself and escorted her through the tunnel of the stone gateway to raise a toast to the statue of prehistoric man. Horst and Clothilde were standing beneath it as their friends took snaps of them on their phones.

The terrace had been decorated with some of the spare life-size wax models of Neanderthal people from the museum's storage room. There was a seated man in furs talking to a naked child as he worked on a flint tool, two women scraping furs and a standing hunter, a spear poised in his hand.

'I think they'll be very happy,' said Pamela. 'It certainly took

them long enough before deciding to tie the knot. Clothilde
told me they first became lovers thirty years ago and they knew
all of the other's bad habits, but they'd grown so used to one
another there seemed little point in not marrying. You know
she's selling her house here in Les Eyzies? Apparently Horst's
place won because of that amazing new bathroom he installed.
I often wanted to try it, all those nozzles in the shower to spray
you all over.'

'I'm sure she'd be delighted to let you enjoy it.'

Bruno felt a little on edge. He had not spent much time alone
with Pamela since she had ended their affair. They had met often
enough, at the Monday dinners with their friends, at the stables,
in the market. But he'd been startled by the bitterness in her
tone when she finally saw Isabelle outside the *mairie*. He'd never
found Pamela easy to read, despite her almost perfect French.
She remained an English woman, or rather Scottish, not quite
familiar with all the unspoken assumptions about life and love
and *la République* that most French people unconsciously shared.
He had found it charming, the way she believed that a cup
of tea solved most problems or at least made them seem less
formidable, her passion for English crosswords and listening to
the BBC on her laptop as she did her household chores. He still
did, Bruno admitted to himself, and on impulse he took her
hand and squeezed it.

'Don't tell me you're letting this wedding carry you away,
Bruno,' she said, gently extracting her hand from his. 'I wonder
if anything will change for the happy couple? Whether Clothilde
will still want to come over for a girls' evening with Fabiola
and me?'

'Isn't Miranda also part of your girls' evenings?' he asked. 'You share a house with her.'

'She is once she's put the children to bed, like Florence. But there's a difference between women like Clothilde and me and those with small children, particularly when there's no man to share the upbringing. I must say, I rather enjoy having the little ones around – so long as they belong to somebody else.' She fished in her bag for her phone. 'I should call Florence and tell her she can leave the kids at our place. Félix the stable lad is there looking after Miranda's children.'

A cheer went up from the other terrace as Hubert arrived with more champagne and people rushed for refills. Jack Crimson and his daughter Miranda were among the first to emerge from the scrum and came through the tunnel to join them, each carrying two full glasses. As Crimson put the two extras on the ledge beside Bruno and Pamela, Bruno's phone vibrated.

'We've had patrols and choppers with infrared sensors beating those woods and they're empty,' Isabelle said. 'The guy who blew himself up at Lascaux was alone, which makes it look like a diversion while Mustaf's team are still going for their main target. That means him and three more on the loose.'

'Unless the diversion was to let Mustaf and his men get away from this area, maybe head for Paris. They must be feeling trapped.'

'Another person feeling trapped is the Brigadier,' she said. 'Can you imagine how much pressure he's under from Paris after all the resources they've plunged into this? And I can tell you he's made a lot of enemies in this job who are just waiting for it all to go badly wrong.'

'Have the *Mobiles* found any sign of the transport the bomber used to get to Lascaux? If not, that could mean he was dropped off.'

'They're scouring the area now. Got to go.'

'Wait,' he said. 'I presume this means you can't make the reception. Would that apply for J-J and Yacov?'

'Yacov left here some time ago and said he was joining you. J-J has gone to Lascaux. And I'll stay in touch. Sorry we can't make the reception.' She rang off.

Bruno noticed more and more people coming through the tunnel to this larger terrace, away from the crowd around the bar serving champagne. Hubert was among them, carrying a bottle of champagne and chatting with Amélie. Suddenly Yacov emerged from the tunnel and Amélie's face lit up when she saw him.

'How's my old friend Yossi?' Crimson asked Yacov jovially, holding out his glass for Hubert to refill it. 'Still running marathons?'

'No idea,' Yacov replied, looking uncomfortable and turning to Bruno to ask if there was any news. Bruno put down his glass and took Crimson's and Yacov's glasses and put them alongside his own on the ledge. Then he led Crimson and Yacov aside, towards the farther end of the terrace until they were well out of earshot.

'I know you've both been authorized to carry weapons, which makes three of us. So let's stop drinking, just in case anything goes wrong here.' He explained what he'd heard from Isabelle and that the four most dangerous men were still on the loose. 'I suggest we go through the tunnel to the smaller terrace, since that's the only way to get up here.'

'You don't think they could be coming here?' Crimson asked.

'I have no reason to think so, but let's not take any chances. And what was that crack of yours about Yossi? Who's he?'

'Yossi Cohen, head of Mossad, an old friend of mine,' Crimson said. 'We worked together when he was sabotaging Iran's nuclear programme. And he does run marathons as well.' He paused and looked at Yacov. 'Don't try to tell me you don't work for him.'

'I think Bruno just gave some good advice,' Yacov replied neutrally. 'Let's go through to the other terrace. We can talk about old friends later.'

'What are you carrying?' Bruno asked.

'Glock seventeen,' said Yacov and Crimson nodded.

'Same here.'

'Spare magazines?'

Yacov said one; Crimson shook his head.

'I'm carrying a PAMAS 9 millimetre, with two spare mags,' Bruno said. 'That's about ninety rounds between us. If trouble comes this way, I'll hold the head of the staircase, you two get everybody else through the tunnel and hold them off there.'

'You're serious about this?' Crimson asked, as Bruno led the way back.

'I'm serious about taking intelligent precautions.' At the bar, he asked for three glasses of mineral water, then installed himself at a corner where he could look down over the rooftops to the street and the entrance to the museum. He took out his phone to call Isabelle, but kept watching.

'Remember in J-J's notes of the interview with Dumesnil, he told us that he'd talked to Leah and Husayni about Horst and Clothilde and about their wedding?' he said.

'I don't recall that being in J-J's notes.'

'*Putain*, well, he certainly told us that, and that when he was being interrogated he even had a copy of the paper thrust at him with a picture of Horst and that seismic machine at Commarque.'

'Yes, I remember about the paper being pushed in his face, but I didn't make the connection. Do you think Horst is in danger?'

'I think it's possible this wedding reception could be a target. Can you get some reinforcements here urgently? We've got more than a hundred people at the museum here.'

'I'll get on it right away.' She rang off.

In the street below, he saw a figure in a police cap emerge from the museum entrance and start patrolling the street. It was Louise Varenne, the town policewoman. He called her number and saw her pull her phone from the case on her belt.

'Louise, it's me, Bruno. This is urgent. Make sure you're armed and come up to the roof terrace of the museum. We may have trouble brewing. And wear your flak vest.' As he spoke he recalled that the ones issued to the police were said to give protection against hand guns but would not stop a round from an AK-47.

'I'll have to go to the *mairie*. My weapon's in the safe there. What's up?'

'I'll tell you when you get here. Now move, as fast as you can, and bring all your spare magazines.'

They hung up and he saw her trot across the street to the small *mairie* and fish out a key to let herself in at the locked front door. He looked up and down the street, filled with the parked cars of the reception guests, but no other traffic was moving.

'You look very serious about this,' said Yacov, suddenly appearing at Bruno's side.

'All this seems to have begun with a sudden spate of rumours about the Testament of Iftikhar and the fall to her death of an Israeli woman called Leah Wolinsky,' said Bruno, his eyes on the street. 'You may know her as Leah Ben-Ari, supposed to be a Peace Now activist who was living with a Palestinian historian called Saïd al-Husayni,' he explained, his tone thoughtful rather than accusing. 'The two of them were blackmailed or threatened to join Mustaf and his group in France and somehow she believed that the Testament was connected to Commarque. She and Husayni went to interview her old teacher, a medieval scholar who was later tortured by Mustaf's gang, just as Horst was starting his excavations at Commarque. And there's a story in this morning's paper about the new cave and secret tomb Horst and his team have found there. I've been slow about putting all this together, but now I'm worried enough to have called Isabelle to send us some reinforcements. And I've been very slow about you, Yacov,' he went on. 'I should have realized when the Brigadier authorized you to carry a weapon. And now Jack Crimson has just confirmed that you're with Mossad.'

Yacov shrugged. 'If you're right about Mustaf's gang coming here, maybe we should move that table and glasses into the tunnel. We'll need everything we can to slow them down.'

'Good idea,' said Bruno, turning to the two barmen. He told them to start moving the bar under Yacov's direction before resuming his watch. Across the street, the *mairie* door opened and Louise reappeared wearing her flak vest, her holster now around her waist. Bruno and she had done the annual firearms refresher course at the Périgueux range together and he knew she was a competent shot. Louise paused, looking up the street where a white van had come into view and drove slowly down towards the museum. On the side of the van was the logo of one of the main local catering firms. Of course, he thought, they would be preparing the wedding dinner.

Louise stepped into the centre of the road and put up her hand, then pointed to the turn-off to the entrance to the museum. Then she seemed to start in surprise and began to reach for her gun but the man in the driving seat was faster, put a long-barrelled gun, out of the window and fired twice, two soft coughs that were lost in the sound of chatter and clinking glasses on the balcony.

30

Bruno craned over the railing and saw a face inside the van look up in his direction and at the crowd of people against the balcony railings. The van accelerated up the short lane and over the shallow steps that led to the glass frontage of the museum and then drove straight through it, the sound of breaking glass at last alerting the crowd on the terrace that something was wrong. As the van jerked and stalled, trying to push its way through the tangle of glass and metal, its rear doors opened. Two black-clad figures wearing headbands jumped out carrying what looked like Kalashnikovs and darted into the museum. They looked bulky, as if wearing flak vests, and they were carrying something else slung around their necks that he couldn't identify. Another two men, one at the wheel and the other who had shot Louise, had been in the driver's cabin.

The distance was too far for his handgun so Bruno shouted an alert to Yacov and Crimson, quickly phoned Isabelle and said, 'They're here and have already shot a cop. We need help now and an ambulance.'

'Emergency!' he shouted, closing his phone. 'Everybody back through the tunnel. Right now.'

Yacov and Crimson were trying to struggle back towards him through the crowd blocking the tunnel, the space even more cramped with the table and glasses. A tall figure emerged and began bringing order out of chaos, guiding people through the gap and pushing them forward, and then started examining the wooden doors folded back to the tunnel sides.

'I presume you'd want these closed,' he called to Bruno. It was Manners. Bruno took up a position, sheltered by the wall, from where he could fire at anyone coming up the final spiral of the staircase. Now Yacov was by his side.

'Empty champagne bottles,' he said. 'Toss them into the well of the stairs there, it could slow them, trip them up.'

'Go ahead,' said Bruno, keeping position as Yacov threw bottles. 'I think they're wearing flak vests. We might have to get them with head shots.'

'*Merde*,' grunted Yacov. 'This is a new gun for me.'

Then Crimson arrived, panting, his weapon drawn. 'Keep an eye on that lift doorway,' Bruno told him, pointing to the two metal doors. 'Put your ear to it and you'll hear if it starts working. Shoot anyone who comes out.'

'Everybody's on the rear terrace,' Manners called from the tunnel mouth, now almost closed by the wooden doors. 'Have you a spare gun for me?'

'Not unless someone else there has a weapon. Can you lock those tunnel doors?'

'Not that I can see. We'll try to barricade it with the bar table. Perhaps one of you three with guns could wait behind the doors. You'll need cover, Bruno, if you have to run back.'

'We'll try to stop them here,' Bruno shouted back. He turned to Yacov. 'We'll hit them from here with a volley and when I say go, you retreat to the tunnel doors and give me cover when I join you.'

'Any sound from the lift?' he called to Crimson, whose ear was pressed against its metal doors.

'Not yet. Maybe they don't know about it.'

Now Bruno could hear footsteps on the staircase and commands being shouted in Arabic.

'They're coming up the stairs,' he shouted to Crimson. 'Leave the lift, get back into the tunnel and as soon as Yacov and I come in, be ready to hold the doors. If we go down, seal the tunnel anyway and hold as long as you can. Help is on the way.'

Mon Dieu, he thought, as Crimson ran back, if they break through they'll have a hundred hostages under their guns. Then he heard voices again, much closer, the sound of a bottle being kicked aside and then a gun barrel was poked out from the side of the spiral stairs and sprayed three quick bursts of automatic gunfire, shockingly loud, but the shots went wild.

Another longer burst followed and two figures jumped out from cover and began climbing the stairs, firing as they came.

He fired two shots at the first figure, but too low, hitting only the chest, and then two more a little higher and the man went down, falling into the second figure who then lost his footing on an empty bottle and tumbled back down the stairs. An arm snaked out and pulled him to safety. Then the arm reappeared, tossing something up to the terrace.

'Grenade,' Bruno shouted, and ducked behind the wall. But there was no explosion, just a hissing and Bruno suddenly understood that what they had been wearing around their necks were gas masks.

'They've got gas,' he called to Yacov. 'Get back to the tunnel and give me cover.'

Bruno fired two more shots down into the well of the staircase, seeing the sprawled figure of the man he had shot. He was moving, sliding back down the steps, but he'd dropped his gun. Bruno, getting the first acrid taste of tear gas, fired twice more into the man's hips, beneath the protective flak vest. Then he fired twice again to keep the others' heads down, held his breath and ran back to slip through the gap in the double doors. Ten shots fired, he told himself, counting automatically.

Manners slammed them closed and Bruno and Yacov pushed the bar table onto its side as a barricade for the wooden doors. Bruno sniffed the air, which was clear, and took a deep breath.

'I've got people trying to topple that stone statue to help block the door, but it's too firmly fixed,' Manners said. He kicked a thick shard of glass from a broken bottle under the bottom of the door to help jam it in place.

'See if you can break into that storage house at the end of the terrace,' Bruno said, crouching low. As Manners left, Bruno shouted after him, 'Ask Clothilde if there's anything in there we can use for a barricade. Any furniture would be good, old chairs piled upside down, or if you find any flints, stuff them into any sacks or boxes you find.'

'Better keep down low, below the table,' said Yacov. 'Do you want to hold them here at the doors or from the far end of the tunnel?'

'The far end. The tunnel makes a natural killing ground and they won't see much for the glare.'

'But they can throw more tear gas down here and force us back, then rush us in the smoke,' Yacov said.

Bruno was about to reply that Yacov was right when a burst of gunfire hit the thick wooden doors above them, and half a dozen little holes began leaking sunshine into the tunnel. Soon there would be gas seeping through.

'Can you get us a couple of wet napkins to cover our faces against the tear gas?' Yacov called back to Crimson as Manners appeared with Gilles and the Baron and some other men, pushing and dragging something heavy along the ground.

'The warehouse had these boxes filled with flints, good protection,' Manners announced, ducking behind them and starting to push them up against the wooden door as two more bursts of gunfire opened more holes in the doors, much lower this time.

'No, leave them at the tunnel entrance,' Bruno called. 'These doors won't hold long.' Then to Yacov, 'Go back and help place those boxes, they'll give us good cover. Leave gaps for us to shoot through when we take shelter behind them. Then look for another position further back.'

Horst and one of his German friends appeared, and to Bruno's disbelief he saw they had lost their trousers and were carrying bone-tipped spears. 'It's a treasure trove in that storage house,' Horst said. 'We've got the rest of the men bringing more boxes of flints to build a barricade. We've got flint knives, axes.' Horst's eyes were bright and he looked almost cheerful.

'What about your trousers?' Bruno asked.

'Clothilde, Pamela and Amélie have the women tying trouser legs together and ripping up shirts to make a rope they can use to climb down onto the rooftops below and get away,' Horst replied. Despite the situation, Bruno grinned, knowing he should have thought of that.

At the far end of the tunnel, behind the boxes of flints, Bruno saw Barrymore manhandling into place the wax model of a Stone Age hunter with his spear poised to launch. Bruno approved. It would be the first thing Mustaf would see when he broke into the tunnel and would be the first target to attract his fire.

Something heavy slammed into the wooden doors above Bruno's head, some kind of battering ram Mustaf must have found in the museum. It slammed in again and a crack opened as the glass shard beneath the door shrieked against the cobblestones. Bruno fired three quick shots through the door at waist height. There was no cry of pain, but the battering stopped. Bruno knew it was time to go. He crawled back along the floor to join Yacov and Crimson behind the boxes of flints, ejected his old magazine and slipped in a new one.

'Where do those steps go?' Yacov asked, pointing to his left.

'Up to the next floor of the old chateau, where the rooms used to house exhibits for the old museum,' said Bruno, remembering that there were windows overlooking the terrace where Mustaf was now planning his next move. 'Thanks for reminding me. You hold on here, and I'll go up and try for a quick shot.'

The steps were guarded by a locked iron gate, but Bruno holstered his gun and climbed over it and up the steps. The door into the exhibit rooms was locked, but he leaned back and kicked hard at the lock. The wood beside the door lock cracked but didn't give. He tried again and it swung open, revealing an empty room, full of dust that caught the light from the mullioned windows.

Bruno crept forward, staying in cover behind the stone wall and then peeking out to see three figures at the wooden doors below. He pushed his gun through one of the tiny panes and fired twice. He saw one of the men go down, twisting and pointing his weapon to shoot back, but Bruno had already ducked away. By the time a burst of automatic fire came through the window Bruno had moved to the next window in line and fired again twice. The return fire stopped.

Four bullets gone, eleven remaining and one full magazine. In the silence Bruno heard the distant sound of a helicopter. Help must be on the way.

For the first time, Bruno began to think they might just survive this as he went back down the stairs to the barricade of boxes where Yacov waited alone, crouching behind a box of flints.

'Where's Crimson?'

Yacov jerked his thumb back. 'See that little stone turret, like a pulpit on the corner? He's in there. There's a small hole in the stone, just big enough to aim and shoot through. That's our last ditch. The women have started going down the rope.'

To Bruno's left, just behind the angle where the tunnel opened out, Manners was standing, a spear in his hand. He gave Bruno a grin.

'The seventh cavalry appears to be on their way,' he said, pointing down the valley where the clattering sound of a helicopter was growing louder, but it could not yet be seen, maybe hidden by the overhang.

'Whose idea was it to make the rope?' Bruno asked.

'Pamela, Clothilde, my wife, that black girl who sang – they just began to organize everybody back there. I thought at first it was simply something for them to do to fend off panic, but the rope line seems to be working.'

A helicopter swooped into sight about fifty yards away from the rock overhang, and hovered, a machine gun pointing menacingly from the open side door. Bruno stood to give a thumbs-up just as Mustaf fired again. Ducking hastily, Bruno pointed to the far side of the tunnel and the chopper backed away, rose and then moved gingerly forward and swooped again, its gun chattering.

That was when Mustaf came through the door, very low, two gas grenades preceding him, followed by a second man crouching and giving covering fire. Pushing the table before him for cover and firing short bursts the length of the tunnel, Mustaf kept coming despite Bruno's and Yacov's fire.

Bruno spun away with a yelp of pain as something hit his forehead. He clapped his hand to it and it came away bloody but he was still conscious. It couldn't have been a bullet, maybe a chip from one of the boxes of flints. Blood was flooding into his left eye and his right eye was watering so much from the tear gas that he couldn't see. He felt rather than saw the box of flints being pushed back into him, a volley of shots spraying just above the level of the box. He heard a cry and felt Yacov crumple against his legs. He lost his balance and fell to the floor.

He half rose, lifted his gun above the box and began firing blindly, hoping for a hit. The automatic fire stopped. Mustaf must be changing magazines. Bruno began to rise when he sensed a movement to his left where Manners had been standing. Dimly through his tears he saw the Englishman lunge forward. And then the menacing figure before him, one hand on his gun and the other on his fresh magazine, jerked and screamed in pain as the long bone point of the spear ripped into his neck.

Mustaf dropped his gun and put his hands to the spear to pull it out. Barely able to see, Bruno jammed the muzzle of his own weapon hard into Mustaf's gas mask and fired.

Epilogue

The bandage around Bruno's forehead had been replaced with a small plaster, just big enough to cover the stitches that would be removed later in the week. Horst and Clothilde stood before him, hand in hand, and Amélie had come down from Paris especially for the opening of the cave. The Count stood beside the American cameraman from the Discovery Channel as the engineers checked the tension of the hawsers. Finally they were ready and with a wave from the project director to the operator, the giant winch engaged, the steel hawsers tightened and the great boulder began to move.

They stopped the winch at once, checking the impact of the boulder's movement on the roof and side walls, and then one of the engineers signalled again to the winch operator. This time the boulder moved perhaps five centimetres before they stopped once more to use the camera on the end of the flexible cable to check the roof inside the cave. Again they checked the walls and the position of the rollers that would help the giant stone to be inched out from the cave it had sealed for centuries.

Engineers held Horst and Clothilde back as they tried to be the first in. The project director used the remote camera again and then sent in the workmen with the hydraulic props that would reinforce the roof. He then went in himself, tapping gently with a small hammer on the walls and roof before he pronounced it safe. The cameraman went in first to record the moment when Horst, Clothilde and the Count entered the cave and began looking around them in wonder.

'I can't wait,' Amélie squeaked, gripping the Count's hand. 'When are they going to open the tomb?'

She had come down from Paris for the opening, but she had also come each weekend to visit Yacov, still in hospital in Sarlat after taking two bullets in his chest and another in his shoulder. His arm had been saved, but he would not have much use of it in future. Bruno had been to see him three times, but only on the third had Yacov recovered sufficiently to talk and ask about the final moments of the attack after he was gunned down. Bruno explained that none of the wedding guests had been hurt. And by the time the French commandos had landed from the helicopter and reached them, all the women had escaped down the rope of clothes.

On the cupboards on each side of Yacov's hospital bed were two large bouquets of flowers. Bruno had looked at the cards. One was from Maya, Yacov's grandmother. The other was signed simply, 'Well done, Yossi.'

'Yossi Cohen?' Bruno had asked. 'I presume he's your boss.'

Yacov did not reply. Bruno continued. 'I've been wondering whether Mustaf had been right about Leah when he called her an Israeli spy. I can see why you'd want to have someone planted inside Peace Now, someone close enough to the Palestinians that a lot of them trusted her. And I can't work out why else she'd have wanted to set up fake identities and bank accounts. But it was a lovely operation that Leah ran, helping circulate that rumour about the Testament of Iftikhar, panicking the jihadists and running the scheme all the way to Commarque. I hope Yossi sent some flowers to Saïd al-Husayni.'

'Thanks for coming to see me, Bruno,' Yacov replied. 'We are friends, but I'm not talking about this.' He had then turned his face away and although Bruno waited, he said not another word.

'We're doing the opening of the Scout camp next month,' Bruno told him after a long silence. 'The doctors say you should be able to attend by then. And the Muslim Scouts are coming this time.'

'Good,' said Yacov, closing his eyes. 'I'll look forward to seeing you there, Bruno.'

Bruno had gone to the room next door where Louise, the policewoman of Les Eyzies, was recovering well from two shots in her right lung. She faced six months of rehabilitation, but the doctors had said she should then have a good prospect of returning to her job. Bruno suspected she'd retire, take her pension and then find a less perilous profession.

And now, standing under the great overhang of the cliff at Commarque, Bruno was giving a blow-by-blow account of the opening over the phone to Auguste Dumesnil. He was still convalescing but eager to learn what secrets the cave contained.

'Horst and Clothilde are looking at the walls and taking photos of the engravings, but I can't see them yet from where I am,' Bruno told him. 'I don't see any paintings. The Count is studying the tomb, just touching the lid with one finger, not trying to move it yet.'

The opening of the tomb would be the crucial moment for which the TV channel had agreed to finance the whole operation. But permission had come only after much haggling with the Ministry of Culture for their approval to open the cave, and a great deal of research. Much of it had been done by Dumesnil from his hospital bed, with legwork by Horst and Clothilde. Then in Paris some crucial political strings had been been pulled, first by Isabelle and the Brigadier and then by Amélie's friend the Minister of Justice, and the cultural bureaucracy had grumpily agreed.

Isabelle, back in Paris, had found the librarians who could track Leah's earlier research at the National Archives in Paris. Leah had been looking for any traces of a Crusader named Gérard de Commarque, an ancestor of the Count, and for another known only as Vélos. She had apparently found very little and expressed her frustration to the archivists. But she did establish that Gérard and Vélos had been French Crusaders who had been appointed constables of Beit She'an when it was briefly a royal domain. When it was later granted to Adam de Bessan of the powerful Béthune family, Gérard and Velos had joined the Templars.

Leah had also asked for directions to the Chapel of St Martin, built in the Vézère valley by King Henry II of England in penance for the murder of Archbishop Thomas à Becket in Canterbury Cathedral in AD 1170. Becket's assassins were four knights who interpreted the King's angry outburst, 'Who will rid me of this turbulent priest?' as an order for his execution. After murdering Beckett they travelled to Jerusalem and joined the Templar

Knights. Tradition says their tombs are located by the entrance to the Temple Mount in Jerusalem.

Intrigued by her research, Isabelle had taken the early morning flight to Bergerac to attend the opening. She stood apart from the others, on the small bridge that spanned the stream trickling down to the River Beune, gazing up at the soaring stones of the fortress tower. Bruno had not seen her since those last moments of the fight above the museum when she'd come up with the medics after the commando team had given the all-clear and she'd held his hand as his head wound had been dressed. After the medic had cleaned the blood from his face and flushed his eyes, her face had been the first thing Bruno had seen. Once assured by the medics that Bruno was in no danger, she had left to return to the command centre and begin drafting the after-action report. He would never forget that she had been there.

Leah's instincts had been sound in coming to Commarque. For when the top of the tomb with its sculpture of a recumbent Knight Templar was levered aside, it was not entirely empty. Inside lay a skeleton, crushed almost into dust by the weight of chainmail and rusted armour. Heaviest of all was the great iron sword whose handle contained a small ingot of gold, which almost entirely covered a sliver of ancient wood.

Engraved into the crosspiece of the sword were the Latin words *Ecce Vera et Sancta Cruz* – Behold the True and Holy Cross.

'A piece of the Holy Cross,' breathed the TV producer beside Bruno in what sounded like reverence. Bruno had learned from the Count that the Crusaders had bought from the cunning merchants of Jerusalem enough supposed pieces of the True

Cross of the Crucifixion to build a galleon, and enough of the nails supposedly hammered into it to build a modern ironclad.

From the intact skull, it was evident that the body had been bare-headed when it was buried. Behind the skull stood an ornate helmet, tall and topped with a dome and almost complete. Only the visor had fallen and crumbled away. Through the gap where the visor had been, something glinted.

'I can't get the camera in low enough,' said the cameraman, and the producer brought in the flexible lens that had been used to look inside the cave when it was still sealed.

'Jesus Christ,' said the cameraman. 'It's a bowl on a stand, maybe a cup. And I think it might be gold. A golden chalice.'

'Could this be the Holy Grail?' said the producer.

'*Mon Dieu*,' said Amélie, crossing herself.

'What? What?' cried Dumesnil over the phone.

'I can't see yet,' said Bruno, exchanging glances with the Count, who gave a massive shrug and rolled his eyes.

Bruno lifted his gaze to Horst and Clothilde, knowing they were even more aware than he of the large number of fake relics. They had turned their backs on the tomb and were staring in wonder and delight, hand in hand, at the prehistoric engraving of a giant mammoth with enormous tusks carved into the rock of the cave. Clothilde turned and beckoned her friends to join them. The Count led the way, Amélie still clinging to his arm. Bruno began to follow, and was suddenly aware of Isabelle at his side and taking his hand, her eyes on the great mammoth ahead.

'May I stay for lunch?' she asked. 'At your place.'

Acknowledgements

This is a work of fiction and all the characters and situations are inventions, except that some owe a little more to reality than others. My friend the Count, Hubert de Commarque, showed me round his wondrous ruined chateau of Commarque and sparked something in my imagination that led to this novel. The magnificent castle was built by the French upon the rock that contains the prehistoric caves and engravings. It was entrusted to the Templars when Gerard de Commarque went on Crusade and was briefly captured by the English in the Hundred Years War, embracing in one place and building much of the region's rich history. I hope that many readers will feel inspired to visit this amazing place, rich in tens of thousands of years of history, and share my admiration for the heroic efforts the Count has made to bring it back to life. If the Holy Grail were to exist, it could have few more imposing resting places. I warmly recommend the short films of this most noble of ruined castles that may be found on the website http://www.commarque.com/#!filmjp/c1qjf.

One of the indulgences an author can enjoy is to revive old characters from previous books. My first novel about the region, *The Caves of Périgord*, introduced two fictional archaeologists, the German Professor Horst Vogelstern and Clothilde Daumier, a

341

French curator from the National Museum of Prehistory in Les Eyzies. I have resuscitated them in previous books, but their two friends and colleagues in their first adventure, the American art historian Lydia Dean and the English officer Jack Manners, have lain dormant until now. It has been a pleasure to bring them back to literary life.

I have also enjoyed making the link between Les Eyzies, the home of the Cro-Magnon people, and the excellent museum by the River Düssel in Germany, where the first bones of Neanderthal man were identified after being unearthed in 1868. I am indebted to Sara Willwerth and friends at Buchhandlung Weber in Erkrath-Hochdahl who showed me around the museum and the historic valley named for a seventeenth-century German pastor, Joachim Neander.

Almost all that is written in this novel about the genetics of prehistoric people, about the Venus figurines and the marvellous cave of Lascaux is as true as modern research can establish. The Testament of Iftikhar from the fall of Jerusalem to the First Crusade in 1099 is an old and disputed legend, whose veracity may not match the explosive political potential of such a document in today's Middle East. Anyone interested in pursuing this vexed argument between Jewish and Arab scholars over the history of Jerusalem might start with Daniel Pipes' seminal essay, 'The Muslim Claim to Jerusalem', published in the *Middle East Quarterly*, September 2001.

I am grateful to the staff of the Musée Nationale de Préhistoire in Les Eyzies for the many interesting and informative hours spent attending their lectures and wandering among the exhibits, watching their videos of modern artisans making flint tools, bone harpoons and prehistoric paints and brushes. They deserve better than the carnage I have inflicted upon their terraces in this novel, but I suspect they might enjoy the image of a modern terrorist laid low by a Cro-Magnon spear.

As always, this novel owes a great deal to my friends and neighbours in the Périgord, to the warmth of their welcome, the quality of their food and wines and their generosity in introducing me and my family to the splendid way of life they have inherited from their ancestors and maintained to this day. It is a privilege to live among them, to eat and drink with them and hear their stories and to share something of their profound sense of the history they inhabit.

My wife Julia, coauthor of the Bruno cookbook, and our daughters Kate and Fanny are always the first readers of my drafts and my helpful and supportive critics, and Kate is the custodian of the website brunochiefofpolice.com. Jane and Caroline Wood in Britain, Jonathan Segal in New York and Anna von Planta in Zurich do wonders with my raw manuscripts and I am most grateful to them all. And our dear basset hound, Benson, is now very old and too lame for walks, but remains a great comfort and companion, sleeping beneath the desk and warming my feet as I write.

Martin Walker, Périgord